COLONIES OF THE HEART

This book is for Derek Hooper,
with love and gratitude

JEREMY SEABROOK

COLONIES OF THE HEART

THE GAY MEN'S PRESS

First published 1998 by GMP Publishers Ltd,
P O Box 247, Swaffham PE37 8PA, England

A CIP catalogue record for this book is available
from the British Library

ISBN 0 85449 267 4

Distributed in Europe by Central Books,
99 Wallis Rd, London E9 5LN

Distributed in North America by InBook/LPC Group,
1436 West Randolph, Chicago, IL 60607

Distributed in Australia by Bulldog Books,
P O Box 300, Beaconsfield, NSW 2014

Printed and bound in the EU by WSOY, Juva, Finland

DILRAJ: EMPIRE OF THE HEART

This story is a work of fiction. It draws upon elements from the lives of people I have known, especially in the portraits of the social and physical setting. The background psychology of the characters is also partly inspired by lived experience; but the whole represents no individuals, living or dead.

Jeremy Seabrook
New Delhi/London
June 1997

One

THE YOUNG man sat on a dented tin chair under the tamarind that shaded the hut where he lived. He was reading some sporting magazines, bought from the shop where the old man collected newspapers for recycling: battered and yellowing Western publications devoted to weightlifting, bodybuilding and cricket. He looked with a mixture of fascination and revulsion at the glistening bodies, the distended pectorals. How unlike the thin limbs of the people in the little North Indian town; another culture, another planet.

It was May, and the hot air simmered over the plains. In the distance the smoke of Dehra Dun shadowed the earth with its poisonous cloud. No wind disturbed leaves that hung limp and lifeless, covered with red dust, so that they looked as though sculpted in rusty metal. The only movement was a flash of saffron or violet, as some butterflies darted in the hedge. The sweet smell of dry cowdung; crickets in the grass. A weaver bird had made its nest in the tree behind his head: a few dry leaves, sewn up with cotton-like threads into a small perfect cylinder.

Suddenly the young man was aware of a vibration of the ground. Someone running. He sensed her agitated movement before his sister appeared. She ran barefoot, following the path around the field that had been planted for the first time this year with soya beans. He stood up, startled to see her use so much energy. It must be urgent; no one ran like that in the heat without good cause. Her hair was flattened by sweat, so that she appeared to have been running in rain, despite the cloudless day. The young man's first thought was that something must have happened to their mother. She had collapsed in the field cutting grass for the buffaloes; she had fallen into the well. Once, she had been bitten by a snake as she crouched in the field; normally so alert, her foot had touched the dry cold skin of a krait. She had come limping home, and ordered him to bite the wound. Terrified, he had done as she asked him, spitting the bitter mixture of blood and venom onto the earth. He had run to find the landowner's wife, who arranged for a doctor to come. His throat was dry, his heart hammered. What is it? he asked.

The young woman came to a halt, panting, and she took his hand. Prakash, she gasped, the schoolteacher is coming; and she dashed inside the hut to set the place in some kind of order before their unannounced visitor arrived.

The schoolteacher? How do you know? Disbelieving, he followed her into the single room where they lived. After the sunlight, the interior was dim, but he could see the cobwebs in the thatch, which his mother never touched, because they caught flies and mosquitoes. The teacher. Breathlessly, she told him the news, He came by cycle-rickshaw to the end of the road, and then asked the way. Some women in the fields ran to tell me. He's walking this way. He asked for our house.

The schoolteacher? No one knew where Prakash lived. He had never told them at school. He had never visited any of the houses of his friends, because he knew that he would be expected to invite them to his home in return. And that he could never do. He was ashamed of the hut, the cow-shed, as it was, in which he had been raised. He could never explain to those who lived in pakka* houses why his mother had been unable to provide a more solid shelter for them. Even worse, he could not begin to say what sacrifice and effort it had cost her to achieve even this shabby home. He had always carefully tended the distance he had created between school and his home. He remained aloof when other boys made arrangements to meet each other. If they insisted, he would say that his mother was sick; and no one ever questioned him. Now, it seemed, that space was about to be invaded, and not even by one of his school-friends, but by a teacher. Why would he want to come to the house? What could it mean? Prakash felt he must have done something wrong, although he couldn't recall any misbehaviour that would require a formal visit. The fear of doing something wrong, even without knowing what it was, had always been strong in him. He was afraid of being called to account, of punishment, of some obscurely deserved retribution, even though everyone in the village recognised his maturity, the devotion to his family, his blamelessness.

The sister was throwing a cloth – a bright shawl – over the old chairs. It floated for a moment, crimson and blue, and set the dust in movement that thickened the sunlight coming through the open door. He looked at the tin table, the wooden bench, the little cupboard, with the cracked glass with flowers etched on it, and the small china cups, chipped so that they cut the lips of those who drank from them. Shame, and the impossibility of explaining things, numbed him. He stood and watched Aruna, the sister, all activity and movement, exuding the faint

* See Glossary of Hindi Words on p.150.

smell of perspiration and of the cattle she tended. She fetched out the biscuit tin with its faded floral painting; looked inside, and broke open the single packet of Britannia milk biscuits. She lit the fire – a mesh of small twigs laid on the kitchen floor – under the saucepan, and threw a spoonful of tea-powder into the water. Before Prakash could figure out the meaning of such a strange – and unwelcome – intrusion, he was there; the teacher, a familiar figure, sweating and mopping his face with a big white handkerchief. It was obvious that he was unused to walking, and he seemed to have sprained his ankle on the rough land that led to their house.

The teacher was about forty-five; balding, stocky, with a bushy moustache and kind eyes. He was wearing a jacket, and carrying a cane, no doubt as a precaution against snakes or other unexpected encounters in the fields. He appeared ill at ease as his eyes met those of his pupil, and this, too, struck the young man as odd. It was he who should have been disturbed; but it was the older man who lowered his eyes first.

Prakash offered him the chair where he had been sitting. The teacher sank gratefully onto it, then rose again, aware that there was nowhere for Prakash to sit. The sister brought another chair from the house. She greeted him with the traditional Uttarakhand pailag, touching his feet in respect. He acknowledged her homage. His eyes lingered a fraction of a second on her bare feet, the soles of which were thick and blackened by the earth she trod each day, hard as the hooves of the beasts she tended. Then he turned to his pupil.

I wanted to talk to you. Now it was Prakash who looked down. In the faded grass, a few bright flowers that had survived the heat gleamed; some pale milkwort, tough orange karvi. He didn't know what to say. The schoolteacher, too, seemed uncomfortable; he who had terrified them with his authority and knowledge for so many years. I will come straight to the point. I want to tell you that if you wish it, I am prepared to give you some tuitions.

Prakash opened his mouth to say We have no money for tuitions; but the teacher anticipated him, and said I am not asking far money. I know how hard your mother has worked to provide you with a good education. I will give you some coaching freely, because you are, I believe, a good son and an able pupil.

He looked into the eyes of the teacher, which were suddenly soft and faintly moist; he didn't know whether from the heat or from the strange emotion with which the older man spoke. The teacher felt obliged to

11

explain himself. He spoke formally, a little pompously. I, too, am from a poor family. Without the efforts of my late father, who was a tailor, I would never have reached the position I enjoy today. You are a capable young man, and if I can help you on your way, I shall feel my duty has been accomplished. Although intelligent, you have somewhat wanted application. I'm afraid your dedication to sport has been at the expense of academic achievement, and this must be corrected. Something rang false in this rather stilted declaration, and the young man said nothing. He found it impossible to imagine the teacher, either as a young man, or being raised in the kind of poverty Prakash had known. If so, it must have been a long time ago; that was clear from the distaste with which, the young man imagined, he surveyed their home.

He could see his sister behind the door of the hut, listening. Irritated, he hoped the teacher would not notice her curiosity and rough manners. He called her: the imperious tone of a man talking to his inferiors, as though she were of a lower caste than he was. But when she came out with two glasses of tea, smiling, her black braided hair shining silver in the sun, he bitterly regretted the way he had spoken to her, and he felt a fierce pang of defensive love, and resentment of the teacher who had provoked this moment of betrayal. Aruna solemnly held out one glass to their guest, and the other she placed on the floor beside her brother's chair. She had prepared nothing for herself, and she did not sit down. Self-effacing, she said I must go back to work; then she was running off down the path towards the buffalo-sheds, the border of the dingy lime-green sari in her mouth. As he saw her go, the young man's heart was filled with a familiar mixture of helpless affection and anger; as though he and his sister were only distantly related, and not the same flesh and blood, divided by gender and sensibility. Certainly their social destiny could not have been more different.

The teacher took a biscuit from the coloured tin; he looked doubt-fully into the dark brown liquid on which a skin was already forming. Prakash could see ants in the glass, swirling around in the tea. Whenever any trace of sugar remained, the ants were sure to find it. He took the glass from the teacher, and offered him his own. The teacher hesitated and then accepted it. The young man gulped down the hot liquid, ants and all. He felt himself blush with pleasure. A good son and able pupil. He was un-used to receiving direct compliments. His mother never praised him; indeed, she constantly found fault with what she regarded as his extrava-gance, or the idleness, the distaste for labour, which she herself had cultivated in him. The feeling that bound him to her had no need of affirmation; it was as much part of him as the physical features they shared, the shape of the face, the gap between the front teeth, the honey-coloured eyes.

He didn't know how to respond to the older man whom he had always respected, and who had always been so patient with him, in spite of the fact that he was not really a good pupil at all. He was only really happy when he was running or playing hockey or football. Only in movement did he feel free. The truth was he hated studying. He persevered because he knew it was the return he owed his mother for her selflessness, for her obsessive desire to educate him, to lift the family out of the misfortune that had befallen them. The young man knew that his was a role of redemption. Everyone had been sacrificed as though in expectation of his triumphant work of expiation – his grandmother, his mother, his sister. Three generations of women had offered up their lives for him, a weight of human sacrifice which he had never sought, but to which he could not fail to respond. Until now, his awareness of all this had remained rather diffuse, a burden and obligation, the extent of which he had not yet measured. Now he was compelled to make some assessment of what was expected of him: for the first time he saw the shape of a future life; it was to be the existence of an educated man, whatever that might mean.

Gravely, he listened, looking up from time to time to see the eyes of the teacher on his face, insistent, as though searching for something in the young man's features. He became embarrassed, and passed his hand over his cheeks, as though to wipe away any blemish or stain that might be the cause of the teacher's obsessive attention.

Three evenings a week. You need mathematics, Hindi and English, don't you? The term will be starting within a month. If you wish it, we can start before then. Next Monday you will come to my house at six o'clock. You know where I live. It is only half a kilometre from the school on the road to Pathaknagar.

Yes sir. You don't need to call me sir outside of school. After all, said the teacher, you are eighteen, a young man. In school, of course, it is different. But I think we may consider ourselves friends, since what we have agreed is between ourselves. In spite of his smile, he spoke with an awkward formality. It was clear that he wanted to transcend the relationship between them, but could not find the idiom in which to express it.

Friends. It had never occurred to the young man that he might be the friend of a teacher. Teachers had always seemed so distant; he held them in high regard, for after all, they were the means whereby his mother's efforts on his behalf would be fulfilled. He felt suddenly elated. Perhaps this is what it meant – to be free from the cramping of home, to escape from the position of his mother and sister, their lowly acceptance of their status, their destiny of work and want, their habits of self-denial, their bowed backs in the long grass. It meant going into the homes of people who had two rooms, a whole house even – he had seen it – with a garden behind a high yellow wall, overflowed by dusty orange bougainvillea.

Yes, yes, was all he could say. I will come. Now he was eager for the teacher to be gone, so that he could savour his good fortune, and also, so that he would not be trapped into saying something foolish which would make the older man regret his decision. He felt he was not worthy of the effort the teacher had made, and would never be able to live up to it. But he said I will come. Of course. On Monday. At six o'clock.

Good. Good. The teacher stood up, and brushed some crumbs from his trousers. I'm sure we shall get along extremely well. Why don't you bring your English grammar on Monday so we can start with that. If you are going to college, you will have to be prepared for English medium of instruction. I'm afraid that much teaching of English in our country is not really of a sufficiently high standard. I once knew an Englishman who assured me that he had been unable to understand a single word that a so-called Indian teacher of English addressed to him. It will be difficult for you, but I'm sure you will not wish to disappoint the hopes your family no doubt place in you.

The teacher gave a vigorous handshake, and then turned to go. The young man watched him as he walked carefully on the dry rutted paths which had cracked under the sun; he seemed intent on preserving his dignity against a twisted ankle or an embarrassing fall.

Prakash sat back on the rusty tin chair, balancing backwards against the crumbling dry wall of the hut. The sun had gone behind the tamarind, but a breeze now moved the leaves slightly, so that the light seemed to be generated by the tree itself. He closed his eyes against the arrows of sunlight, and could see the colour of blood in his eyelids. He thought of the long journey he had already travelled. After all, Hindi was for him a foreign language. The familiar dialect he had grown up with had been abandoned long ago outside the family, the homely staccato speech of his mother and sister, which he had found so difficult to leave behind. His teachers demanded that the children speak Hindi in class, and for a long time, he had spoken little in school, afraid of being derided for using the language of home. This had earned him the reputation of being taciturn; but also, of being strong. He felt he was neither.

Sometimes, he longed to shout and sing the energy he felt within himself, his exuberance in the cold winter mornings, in the dense gold sunlight of the plains, his delight in the warm starry midnights when he slept on the charpoy outside the hut; but he always remained silent. He wanted to tell his friends of the love and sacrifice of the house of women. He would have loved to celebrate and show off the body he had cultivated in training for the athletics competitions, but he lacked the confidence to express the pride and power he felt. This suppressed feeling created a tense stillness, a powerful presence which others mistook for a self-reliant stolidity. He had the reputation for being dependable, reliable. Always there, to make up the team, to fit in, to oblige, to listen to others. He had begun to live in an appearance that was quite at odds with his capacity for passionate feeling; and this remained choked within him, just as the flames under the breakfast tea-kettle were extinguished by ashes from the previous day's fire.

He felt both honoured and confused. The future was suddenly clear as a September sky at the melting away of heavy monsoon cloud; full of the promise of privileges he had never asked for or expected. All he knew was that he was special; that he was destined to leave the fields and the little house; although he had never thought where this life might take him. He knew that he had been preserved from work on the farm of the landowner, because, his mother had suggested ambiguously, she had kept him from it by her own relentless labour, but also because he deserved something better.

He had led a solitary life. Although he had many friends, he always remained slightly apart from them, aware of the responsibility he bore to his mother, reluctant to follow the young boys in their wild meanderings through the countryside, stealing a mango from a tree here, a custard-apple there, teasing the children of the Untouchable families in the shacks which they shared with the buffaloes. Sometimes, the activities of his friends horrified him. When he was fourteen, an older boy had showed some of the younger ones how to get enjoyment by sticking his cock into the backside of a hen. Troubled and upset, the young man had run away; although he had been unable to chase the image from his mind; the docile bird held in the boy's hand, the adult spear of the erection.

He had always known that his destiny was different from theirs, and that he was to follow the separate pathway that his mother had constructed for him, although he had no idea where it might lead.

But this remained strong within him: it was as though the mother, unable to contain her feelings of humiliation and rejection, had flooded him with herself, just as the irrigation channel overspilled its banks in the rains and threatened to drown the chickens and goats in the field. All her life, she had held him so close to her that he had felt the beating of her bruised heart as if it were his own. He had grown up, not quite knowing where the limits of her unbounded suffering ceased and his duty to assuage it began. He felt himself part of a troubling fluidity, sometimes sad as the dead bird on the path, whose mysterious red innards were being eaten by worms, sometimes as joyful as the dance of bees around the vibrant blossoms of the frangipani. At times, he delighted in his own energy and exuberance, and at others was weighed down by a pain that was his and yet not his, oppressed by the fathomless grief, which, it sometimes seemed, was his mother herself; as though her identity had been devoured by this single feeling that had spread within her like an intangible untreatable cancer.

Two

HE WAITED impatiently for his mother to return. Each afternoon it took her exactly two hours to cut grass for the buffaloes. She would leave at two and come back at four for a glass of tea or, more often, a metal tumbler of water, before returning immediately to the landowner's house to prepare the evening meal. The landowner's family had grown accustomed to the food she made: her Rajput pride and cleanliness pleased her employers. She required no supervision and, as the years went by, no instruction. Her big countrywoman's hands turned over the chappatis so quickly that they fluttered like the wings of captive birds between her fingers. She had become indispensable to them.

Prakash walked the length of the field; the earth was dry where the wheat had been cut and the rice not yet sown. The pale stalks of the dry-season crop shone in the sunlight like bright slivers of glass. He looked to where his mother would appear, and saw the women and girls in the long dry grass, cutting fodder, weeding the field, hoeing and preparing the earth for the kharif crop that would be sown when the rains came. The colour of their sarees could be seen between the trembling grasses, and their braided hair gleamed, black as buffaloes. The women worked until dusk, and then, each day, along the raised pathways around the edge of the fields, they could be seen walking home, a frieze of exhaustion and submission. The young man knew that his privilege had been built on their curved backs.

Why was she so late this afternoon? The sun had gone behind the tamarind, behind the neem tree, and the shadow fell upon the shed where they lived. He loved the tree: it afforded some protection against the worst of the summer heat, and it provided its sour fruits for chutney. It sheltered a whole population of birds and insects, and some of its smaller twigs served as fuel for the cooking-fires. There was a little breeze now, and the sunlight came in dazzling, almost horizontal, spikes through the dark green. He wanted to see her face light up when he told her of the schoolmaster's offer. It was a tribute to her; a vindication of the years of sacrifice. He thought he would fall at her feet and thank her for all that she had done. A wave of love and gratitude swept over him.

Still she didn't come. The western sky grew orange and the two ripening mangoes on the tree in front of the hut glowed, globes of light that had captured the radiance of a dying sun. He walked to the edge of the field, towards the landowner's house. What was keeping her? He saw headloads of fodder moving through the tall bleached sedges; elegant burdens tied up with plaited grass that concealed the slight figures beneath of the women who bore them; so that from a distance it seemed that the loads were moving by themselves.

Suddenly, he recognised the headload of his mother: it oscillated more unevenly than the bundles carried by the other women. She walked slowly; her left knee had swelled up, and every day it took her longer to bring the twelve or fifteen kilos of grass which she carried back for her daughter to feed to the landowner's buffaloes. The young man saw her emerge from the tall grasses, and he went forward to meet her. Her eyes met his – or perhaps it was only the reflection of her own; which was why she didn't smile. She would not yield her burden to him, but silently continued along the path until she reached the hut. She set down the fodder, wiped the sweat from her forehead and the dark creases at the side of her bright brown eyes. The young man took his handkerchief and drew it gently across her face. She raised an arm to shield herself from his attention; the underarm of the dark blue blouse had been discoloured by sweat, and was in any case, full of holes. One day, he had promised her, he would take her to Delhi and buy a saree with a gold border. Then she smiled at him, his smile, the smile he owed her; the gap between the front teeth made her look mischievous, an incongruous transformation of her worn, sombre face. Now their eyes were transparent amber, mingled in sympathetic understanding of one another. He felt the wonder, mixture of delight and pain that flows between people who share the same physical features, but are divided by gender or generation.

Finally she heeded her son's excitement, and guessed he had something to tell her. She said Lakshmi Devi has walked into our house. No. The teacher came. He is giving me free tuitions. Immediately her mood changed. Why did you let him come here? He just came. I didn't ask him. You let him see how we live? He wasn't surprised or shocked. He told me his own family were poor, Poor. She spat, a blood-red jet of betel. They don't know what poverty is. Nobody knows what poverty is who hasn't worked eighteen hours a day on somebody else's land.

Why wasn't she pleased? He warmed the tea in the saucepan and poured it into the glass he had used. She sat on the tin chair, caressing the swollen knee, looking into the clouded liquid that made the glass almost too hot to hold. He crouched down on the grass beside the chair and put his head in her lap. She smoothed the dark lustrous hair almost automatically with her big hands; her hands which were his hands also, although he had never done any work in his life with them, as she never ceased to remind him. He felt the rough skin on his cheeks, and closed his eyes; a smell of earth, grass and animals.

It's because of you, he told her. The teacher knows what you've done for me. He wants to help. She stopped running her hands through his hair. How can he know? Nobody can know what I did. Nobody. I walked all the way from Chakrata in the rain, carrying two children. How can anyone know?

He recognised the familiar lament, the song of her life, the dispossession and the courage, the self-denial and the overwhelming, immeasureable love she had shown him. Every day she needed her sacrifice and her pain to be acknowledged, to be told it was the supreme gesture of self-abnegation, unequalled by any other mother in Uttarakhand, in India, in the world. It was a way also of telling him that he could never repay her. He had long ago become resigned to that; all he could do was his duty, and that he would do, no matter what it cost him.

His sister, too, had been part of the sacrifice, the terrible human sacrifice of women, which is part of India. The sister had never demanded recognition, although, if anything, she had greater claim to it. After all, if his mother had given herself, she had done so voluntarily, knowing what she was doing. The sister had had no choice. She had never been consulted. Her needs, her wishes had been of no account in the cruel calculus of survival. She had never been to school, but was in the fields when she was nine or ten, tending the buffaloes, hitting their sleek black behinds with a branch of acacia, helping with the weeding, the harvesting. It had not been thought necessary that she should read or write; and indeed, her irrepressible intelligence seemed to have no need of such accomplishments. She was sharp, with a ready tongue and a sense of humour that made the young man slightly awkward. And she knew so much! Her mind was a deep chamber of remembered things. She knew where to find medicinal herbs, edible fruits, nuts and tubers to supplement their diet, she was familiar with the lives of the numberless birds and insects of the foothills, she could read the coming storm in the serene skies, and could find water in the parched season. In the presence of her spontaneous banter, her brother would feel clumsy and tongue-tied. Perhaps her verbal agility was the equivalent of his physical prowess. He had inherited his mother's seriousness and anxiety too; or perhaps this was part of the tribute that she exacted from him in return for her measureless gifts to him.

In return for so much! For him, for the boy, for the male, symbol of continuity, pledge of future security, nothing was too good. He had never been allowed to work. Whenever he had offered to help in the fields, when the rice was being cut, and the moonlight enabled the women to work late into the night, he would take a scythe and go to join them; but his mother would remove it from his hands and lead him back to his bed to sleep. She herself had worked without pause; an emblem of tireless activity. There had been no limit to her labour, sixteen or eighteen hours a day; in the landowner's house, she prepared all the meals – and sometimes, when their friends came from Delhi, there would be twelve or fourteen people to provide for. Then she would work in the fields before returning to make the mid-day meal for her employers, who insisted that it be fresh each day. After that, she made tea for the afternoon and poured it into the silver vacuum flasks; and then went out again into the fierce desiccating afternoon heat to look for fodder and wood for the fire at home, so that if she had not returned before nightfall, the sister could make the meal for herself and her brother. At least the mother could eat in the house of the landowner, and sometimes she brought home good things for her son – who would never sleep before she reached the security of their broken-down shelter – and consoled him for the ache of unsought privilege in the acrid chamber of her tired arms.

Her employer was kind enough, although she looked upon her servant as a different kind of human being from herself, and that kindness did not extend to imposing any limit on her hours of labour. She expected the young man's mother to do everything, in spite of the fact that they were Rajputs: they must have been landowners themselves at one time, although not within the living memory of anyone in her family. Rajputs were the dominant caste in the region. The story the mother told was that they had fled Moghul rule in Rajasthan, and had retreated to the impenetrable forests of the Himalayan foothills, where they would never have to yield to the power of the invaders. This was how they had maintained their culture and their pride, although precious little else. They had retained also their warrior-caste prowess, and had provided soldiers for the British imperial army. Their fierce independence remained unimpaired, in spite of the fact that the fragile hills had been over-exploited, and the wealth of the region had benefited only the people of the plains. Now, more than half the adult men left Garhwal, to work in Delhi or the industrial cities of Uttar Pradesh. Women alone were left to defend the fragile hills, the forests which the men from the plains had tried to turn into timber, the waters that fed the sacred rivers of India. This had strengthened the women, and united them in the defence of their land and their trees. And in the protection of the next generation of men, on whose remittances whole villages now depended.

The mother had two obsessions – her boy's education and his marriage. She had been saving for both ever since she had come down to the plains with him as a two-year-old. Sometimes, it seemed to him, his life-story had been told even before he was born. Everything had been determined in advance. All that was left for him to do was to live once more through a known, antique pattern that could admit no alteration or change. And yet, to change everything for him had been her deepest purpose. What she wanted was an impossibility: a safe predictability, and yet, at the same time, a break with the servitude into which they had descended on the day she was turned out of her dead husband's family home, and she came down from the *terai* into the endless monotony of the plains.

He could not understand why was she so displeased that the schoolteacher had come. Why didn't she welcome his offer? Was it because she wanted to take the full credit for her son's success, that she couldn't bear to acknowledge help from anyone? In the same way, she had never wanted to share his affection with anyone else, even his sister. Whenever the two children had been laughing or playing together in the grass, the mother would appear between them, from nowhere, with an admonition to her daughter that there was work to be done, the buffalo sheds to be cleaned, some vegetables to be cut, a fence to be mended so that the goats should not eat the maize. And then she would cover him with caresses, sit him on her knee, whisper to him the secrets of her suffering and her plans for his deliverance, which would be hers also. His sister, who was four years older, had always carried him on her hip whenever they went out together, and a deep affection had grown between them. She bore the mark of her love for him in a slight deformity that had developed from where she had carried him: the stigma of her involuntary, poignant sacrifice. She had never offered him a word of reproach. Like all those destined to limitless subordination, she waited upon him as though her only pleasure were to be found in his satisfactions, and when he protested, it was she who became angry; and puzzled and chastened, he would desist.

Soon, he said to his mother, you won't have to work. I will have a degree, I'll get a job in government service, I'll send home all the money you need. What would I do without work? she asked. Indeed, it had been her life. Ever since he could remember, lying under the heavy quilt in the cold December mornings, he had heard her moving around in the darkness, the whisper of her coarse saree as she got ready to milk the buffaloes before five o'clock; carrying the kerosene lamp in her rough hands, and going to the well for the water for his wash; blowing on the scarlet net of twigs in the kitchen so the water should be warm for him. And he had drawn his knees up to his chin in the bed he shared with her and his sister, and enjoyed the warmth, and drifted back to sleep; until it was light, and she was shaking him and offering him warm milk and chappatis for breakfast, and telling him to hurry so that he would not be late for school.

Sometimes he would dream, or remember, he wasn't sure which. He saw rain and darkness, and felt himself being carried, now high by his mother, now closer to the path they followed, which, he thought, must mean he was in his sister's arms. He thought he could recall a long downward slope, the beating of a half-frozen rain on the hood of a shawl which protected him. They were running away; was it in disgrace, was it in fear? Were they being pursued? He never knew; only the running remained; and this he expressed in his greatest skill – his ability to win races.

On his way to school, he would sometimes pass his sister on the path, driving the goats or the cows to the grazing ground beside the broad slow-flowing nalla; and if he was with his friends, he simply waved to her distantly, as though they didn't know that the unschooled child with the torn dress and black bare feet was the same flesh and blood.

He had never been able to tell the sister how much he loved and respected her. Indeed, he had never spoken of his love for his mother either, but with her there was no need. She absorbed all his feeling, she drew it to herself, as the clothes in the washing-bucket sucked in all the water; and somehow there was nothing left over, nothing to share with the young woman who, in any case, had her own destiny of marriage and removal to the house of a husband; and that feeling – that her presence with them was only provisional – further inhibited him from expressing what he felt.

In fact, he had been only ten when she was married. She seemed to him grown up, extraordinarily adult at fourteen. He remembered his mother's excitement and relief. The husband had land; not much, but it was a beginning. She bade farewell to the slim child-like figure in the ornate dress, with her big country-girl's hands decorated with *mehendi*, and thanked Lakshmi in the litle shrine in the cowshed, that now she had only her son and herself to fend for. When she had gone, he felt lonely for the first time in his life; and he was able to measure how thin and depleted their family was, in the presence of the vast networks of kin in which most others lived. He became aware of the emptiness of a world in which there was no one to take responsibility for him and his mother; and knew that only his hands and body stood between her and absolute dereliction, should she fall ill or become incapable of work. This drew him closer to her, as though he could, out of the intensity of his love for her, weave an invisible fabric that would keep her from physical danger, from ageing and sickness, and above all, from what he dreaded most, death.

In the early years in the cowshed, it had been the grandmother who looked after him, who had slept with her stringy arm as pillow for his head. Sometimes, she would remain the whole night without moving so as not to disturb his sleep, no matter how uncomfortable she had been. It had been her rough hands that had swept the tears from his face, and had kissed his eyes with her milky breath. She had played with him, pretending to chase him as he ran through the high summer grass, or hiding in the darkness, from where she would emerge in a shower of fireflies, so that it seemed that her body itself had kindled the sparks. She had sung to him when he had fever, and enclosed him in the bony cage of her feeble protective arms.

His grandmother died when Prakash was sixteen. He had been practising in the stadium one cool evening when the stars hung low and the breath from his body, pulsing with energy, condensed in a white mushroom. The old woman had been ill, and Prakash was torn between the desire to dance away his energy in the cold evening, and the wish to stay beside his grandmother, to give back to her something of the comfort she had once so freely given him. Already, at sixteen, he knew what he owed her was incalculable. Long before he was adult, he had become like a poor farmer who had contracted debts long ago, debts which eventually would consume his fields, his house, his life itself.

His sister came into the stadium; an incongruous skinny figure, the only girl among the young men. She stood, waiting for the courage to ask someone where her brother was. When she saw him, she ran to him, and, in front of everyone, threw her arms around his shoulders; and he knew that the old woman was dead.

When he saw the body of his grandmother, long and unreachably remote, he could scarcely believe that she, who had sheltered him, and to whom he had run whenever he was frightened by the summer storms, should have departed so finally, and so suddenly. He hated the uninhabited husk, shrunken on the hard bed, and felt for the first time the cruelty of the desertions which, he now understood, life reserved for him. He wondered, would she return in another form; would he know her, would he then be able to say to her how much he owed her, or was it always part of the torment of living that you could never recognise the new incarnation of those who had loved you, and therefore never had the consolation of telling them all the unspoken things?

Next day, the family walked to the funeral pyre, a sombre small procession bearing her thin, almost weightless body. He realised how few people there were in his life. Others lived among crowds of relatives, thick and plentiful as forest trees. Now, there were just the three of them. As they passed through the familiar fields, the marigold and rose petals fell from the white-clad burden, and left a scattering of gold and crimson flakes on the earth. Then, at the burning-ground, the banyan wood, the orange flames, the body that was consumed as easily as if it, too, were part of the pile of dry branches. Soon nothing remained but some pale spent ashes; these stirred in the cool evening wind, restless as the spirits that left the burning ground each day to return to wherever they had come from. Perhaps, he thought, this is our only immortality – the return to the elements that sustain life; and the only continuity lay in the dust which would tomorrow be swept up in the making of some other life – that of a tree, a flower, a dog, a Brahmin, a beggar. It was scant comfort for our

poor existence, and he held the mother with one arm and the sister –
returned in shame from her unhappy marriage – with the other, and he
felt the sweet, fragile burden of their still living flesh pressed close to his
own.

Three

THE NEXT days passed for him in a dreamy indolence, and the most agreeable anticipation of a future unconfined by the rigours of landless labour.
Prakash was flattered to have captured the attention of the teacher. The
older man must have recognised something in him that set him apart. He
had always felt it himself, but could not say what it was. It seemed to
confirm his mother's obsessive concern, to strengthen the sense of destiny
which she had, not exactly cultivated but certainly communicated to him,
in everything she did.

Every evening, he went on his bicycle to the stadium to practise his
running. The bicycle was old, a black-painted frame, wheels with missing
spokes, handlebars that were out of alignment with the wheels; and it
jumped and buckled over the bumpy ground to the rough road that led
into town. He enjoyed the jolting ride, especially on the gentle slope towards the margin of the landowner's fields. He would take his feet off the
pedals and spread out his legs, so that he felt he was flying through the
scented evening air. His proudest possession was a pair of shiny green
shorts which the landowner's wife had bought as a reward for coming first
in the sports competition. They were imported, and all the boys in the
stadium admired them, wanted to touch the changing colours that the
light created on the fabric. One evening, at the stadium, he thought he
glimpsed the teacher on the crumbling concrete terraces; but imagined he
must be mistaken.

How he loved to run. It gave him the greatest pleasure to amble
round the stadium a couple of times, then break into a furious dash for
the last two hundred metres; afterwards, to sink onto the ground, breathless, looking up at the evening star and the darkening sky, elated, exulting
in the power and strength of his alert, palpitating body. This was when he
felt happiest; at such times, everything in him soared and sang.

Little by little, the trophies had accumulated in the metal cupboard
in the one-roomed hut: cups and medallions, inscribed with his name,
winner of the 200 metres, the relay, the 100 metres. They stood on the

cupboard, and, over the years, became tarnished from the corrosive breath of the monsoon. Sometimes he polished them; but they never regained their original brightness. They were an inferior alloy, as suited the rewards of a short-distance runner. His greatest regret was that he would never have the stamina for the marathon, the cross country, the 1500 metres. Sometimes he felt a sharp pang of envy for those who could sustain their strength for the longer races. He longed to become an international runner, and he dreamed of trips abroad, the green turf of the running tracks of the West, which he had seen in magazines.

He had always known that his distance from the other young men in the little town would take him away from them, but the exact nature of that separateness remained vague. It was an apartness of the sensibility; but it was represented for him, above all, by movement, by running, by a vague elsewhere towards which he felt he was perpetually running,

He enjoyed hockey also, and the games of kabbadi; the tugging and pulling and falling down together on the dusty floor with the other boys, so that at such moments, he felt not differentiated from them, but part of a single source of mysterious energy that animated them all; a common expression of their delight in living. He was nineteen. He was admired. He even admired himself a little in the clouded glass of the stadium dressing rooms. He was thickset, with broad powerful thighs, a sturdy chest, where the ribs held captive his dilating, yearning heart; and the slim powerful plinth of a neck on which his head with its blue-black curls rested with unselfconscious grace. He had the slightly elongated eyes of the hill people, clear amber skin and teeth so white that in the evening light, they shone like a gash of silver.

He was not a good student; or rather, he was a good student, but he didn't learn easily. He was good, in that he sat for hours under the lemon insect-flecked lozenge of light from the kerosene lamp, looking at the English verbs and the mathematical formulae. But his attention often wandered, and his mind followed his body in its leapings and racings through the countryside; he would find he remembered nothing of the pages he was supposed to learn. He liked Hindi poetry, but found it hard to commit to memory. Occasionally, some lines remained with him, he didn't know why: *'Jane kis ki bad donai thi, jidhar tha jirag mera wahin per hawai thi.'*

He sometimes identified the words with his destiny: a feeling that he was not really rooted in the dull, placid plains of northern Uttar Pradesh, but belonged somewhere else. One day, he dreamed, he would be carried off – by what, by whom? – to fulfil some glorious future that was already determined, inscribed, as it was, in the mysterious annals of the time to come.

On the Monday evening, solemn and dutiful, wearing his grey school trousers and white shirt, he travelled by bicycle to the teacher's house, carrying his books in the cheap plastic satchel on his back. The house was set back from the main road, which was busy with the buses and trucks speeding down the last slope that led from the foothills. It was a one-storeyed pakka building, surrounded by a crumbling wall and a screen of small Himalayan pines and bougainvillea. The crimson flowers trembled in the night breeze like butterflies that could not quite decide where to settle. To the young man, the house, lighted with electricity, appeared spacious and luxurious, an image he identified with his own future. He could see the inner room; a bulb in a metal shade shed a dazzling light on blue colour-washed walls.

He was nervous. Perhaps the teacher had forgotten his promise; perhaps he hadn't meant it. He might have been confused, mistaken him for someone else. At times like these he felt insignificant, insecure in the presence of those he recognised as his social superiors. When he was not running, he was often assailed by a sense of unworthiness, a feeling that he had no right to be where he was; an insecurity which passed for shyness. How would he make conversation to the teacher's wife, if he was left alone with her? Like his mother with her powerful communicative silences, he was sparing and suspicious of words; when he used them, they had to be full of meaning for him. He valued sincerity above everything, and was uncomfortable with polite conversation. He felt a constriction at the heart, something like panic. What about the teacher's children? He knew there was a boy about his age, and three younger daughters. One of them he knew was very pretty. He found it difficult to imagine that the teacher had known the kind of hardship his own family had grown up with. They seemed safe, serene, apart from the life of the little town. They were looked up to.

The teacher saw him from the window; he had evidently been watching for him. He came out to greet his pupil. He appeared happy to see him, and invited the young man to step inside the cool stone house. He said Monday is a good evening, because that is the day when my wife goes with the children to see her mother. She lives in Goregao. The young man knew this was a small village about 30 kilometres along the road that leads to Dehra Dun. The teacher showed him into a study; a simple room, but lined with shelves of books, a big desk, and a metal cupboard full of papers. On the wall were Western pictures, strange paintings of unfamiliar landscapes, trees he had never seen, but whose names he knew from English textbooks – elm and horse chestnut.

He sat at the desk in a swivel chair, and opened the English book. For half an hour the young man did not raise his eyes, but concentrated on the irregular verbs. Buy bought, bring brought. The teacher made him repeat them, and then asked him to make up sentences, using them. He drew up another chair, and looked over his shoulder at the same book. The young man soon became strongly aware of his proximity; a vague and troubling scent of maleness, tobacco and soap. He became distracted, enveloped by something he had never known, an emanation of the body that was very different from the familiar odours of his mother, grandmother and sister, that scent of buffaloes and sweet grass that made him ache with a dutiful and limitless love. The teacher exuded a different kind of warmth, disturbing, aromatic. He knew that he was blushing. His face burned. The alien presence and its musky masculinity drew him into itself like another kind of gravity. He felt stupid and confused. He made many mistakes.

Suddenly, he saw that the teacher's arm was lying along the back of the chair where he sat; he felt strangely protected. Part of him wanted to settle back against the angle formed by the elbow, which the thin khadi shirt-sleeve revealed. He could not concentrate on the verbs. He stammered and fell silent; he could feel he was sweating; hoped that his feet didn't smell through the cheap trainers, and that he would give no offence to the teacher. The arm dropped to his shoulder, and the leg of the teacher was close to his. He looked at the navy blue knee of the older man close to his own, grey-clad and slightly trembling. He drew away, rigid with apprehension. The teacher's arm followed him. Prakash began to shake. His throat was dry. The teacher said Look at me. He looked up briefly and then down again. The teacher's eyes bore the same look of tender concern he had seen on the day he had called at the house. What did it mean? The teacher got up and sat on the bed. He indicated to the boy that he should follow him. Obediently, the young man sat down beside him. His face was close. His lips touched the young man's cheek. He did not recoil. A hand closed upon his thigh. The teacher swept him into his arms and began to kiss his face, The young man squirmed and moved his head from side to side, so that the kisses should not touch his lips. He was aware of a strange sensation, a throbbing in the groin, a kind of ache he had never experienced. Gently, the teacher moved to cover the young man's body with his own. He no longer struggled, but closed his eyes and waited for what would happen.

It was dark in the room. The last violet strip of sky had turned black; the teacher had extinguished the light at the desk. Then his hand stroked the boy's face; his lips moved over his eyes, his cheeks.

He wanted to resist, but something stronger made him yield, and even as he intended to protest, his indignation was overcome by a more vigorous assertion by his own body of something he wanted. Prakash was suddenly shaken by a burst of pleasurable release, and became aware of a dampness in his pants; like when he had dreamed in the night and woken up, terrified that his mother would be able to see even the dreams in his head that had come out of his body and coagulated into the stain on his lunghi. He went to get up, ashamed and confused; but the teacher took his hand and placed it around his penis. The skin moved back over the taut shiny head with its small pink eye. Prakash had never seen another cock so close. The teacher tried to press his head downwards towards his erection, so that he would take it into his mouth. There was a stronger whiff of the same scent of a man, which now was repelling as well as exciting, and he resisted the older man's hand at the back of his head. The teacher placed the boy's hand around the quivering, straining cock that thrashed the air as though possessed of an independent life of its own; he moved Prakash's fingers under his own firm grasp until he, too, came, leaving loops of thick liquid around the young man's fingers.

His first instinct was to run away; but the teacher restrained him, and held him for a moment against his chest. His heart was beating, a different rhythm from that of running, a thump of apprehension and shame. The teacher told him to sit quietly for a few minutes. He left the room and returned with tea and biscuits. He was smiling. Prakash drank the tea. He was disturbed, confused, unable to separate the feelings of horror, curiosity, desire. The older man spoke to him gently, caressingly. He spoke of friendship, talked to him of the affection in which he had held him for some time, two years or more. Had Prakash not been aware of it? The teacher knew everything about his life; his mother's struggles, the sister's self-effacement, the boy's triumphs in the stadium. He shook his head dumbly. The teacher reassured his pupil that there was nothing to be afraid of. He really would give him tuitions; and as for what had happened, if Prakash didn't like it, he promised it would not happen again.

No, he said. I don't like it. He was angry and felt betrayed by the teacher. The teacher continued to smile, as though he knew what Prakash was going to say, and he made no effort to contradict him. He said that he understood the young man. He wanted the guidance of a father. The teacher would be happy to fulfil that purpose. Little by little, Prakash became calmer. He dared to look up at the teacher again, his eyes reproachful amber lights in their dazzling enamel. His tutor had a kind face; the smile accentuated creases at the edge of his eyes, and this reminded the young man of his mother. The teacher called him by his name, the name that means light. He felt an urge to cry; and his vision was blurred by tears that distorted the shape of everything in the room. The teacher held out a hand to him; his hands were strong. He smelt once more the faint aroma of tobacco and maleness. He was confused, but the anger had by now evaporated. He knew already that he would speak to no one of what had passed. He desperately wanted to leave, so that he could assess the conflicting feelings, take some measure of what had happened to him.

Before he left the house, he promised the teacher that he would come the following evening. He didn't dare go home immediately. He thought at first it would be obvious to everybody what had happened, that his whole body must be transparent to others from the violent experience that had shaken it. How could he not tell his mother? How could he possibly tell her? She would want to know everything. She did know everything. Sometimes she would look at him with her glittering eye, and tell him that there was nothing she didn't know about him; and because he had her face and her feelings, he could never be sure that she was wrong. He never told her lies.

It was still early. The whole encounter had not lasted an hour. He walked through the hot pre-monsoon dusk, wondering what he should do. Of course, he would say nothing; the sensation that had taken him by surprise was good. It was simply that the context was wrong; he had gone with the virtuous intention of studying; it had not been his doing that things had turned out against his expectations. He thought of the teacher's family, his children, his wife; the boy who was about his own age, who might have been his brother. It was true that sometimes he had felt an ache and an absence, but he had not been able to define them. He had longed for a brother, cousins, uncles, a father – the commonplace relationships that his peers took for granted remained for him inaccessible, beyond his experience. Yet his own life had been so dense with the affection of women, women both strong and yet submissive, that there had seemed no room for anything else.

But the women expected so much of him; it was sometimes hard to bear. Now, this evening, something had opened before him, which he had never suspected, a life so secret that it had remained hidden, even to himself. He was like a child who finds a piece of unvisited forest in a known landscape, and hesitates to enter for fear of what he might find there.

When he reached home, they were waiting for him beneath the kerosene lamp that swung and flickered in the evening breeze; welcoming, ceremonious, the mother and the sister. Well, how had it been? He said It is very hard work. He went to wash himself in the cool well-water beside the buffalo-shed. The water formed a silver sheath around him as it cascaded down his abdomen. He saw with shame the matted hair where the liquid from his body had congealed, and he scrubbed it vigorously with the harsh red soap. He went into the house; through the droplets of water on his eyelashes the light from the lamp was surrounded by rainbows.

They prepared the meal, gave him the best of the small brinjals that he liked; he bent his face over the fragrant breath of the rice, the black dal. His mother wanted to know what the house was like. Do they have a radio, a clock, a television? Were there cushions on the seats? Did they have china teacups? Were there brass vessels on the shelves? He disappointed them, for he could remember nothing but the books and the paintings of foreign landscapes.

That night, he lived every detail of the evening once more; he felt compelled to repeat over and again the scenes as they had occurred, as though he might have imagined it all. He often had these sensations of inauthenticity, as though what had happened had really happened not to him, but to someone else.

He was still convinced that what had taken place was repugnant to him, but the revulsion he had felt in the beginning had abated. By the morning, he was surprised to feel that it had disappeared completely. He even began to recall with a kind of reluctant pleasure how the hand and the arm of the teacher had moved closer. He imagined once more the hardness of the teacher's body, and his penis stiffened under the chadar. He placed his forearm between his legs, and comforted, slept, It was late in the morning before he awoke. The sun was already high. His mother came in and set the tin plate of chappatis, the metal tumbler of milk beside his bed. She asked what was troubling him. Nothing, he said. You had such a restless night, I could hear you. The teacher must have made you work hard. It won't do you any harm. It's not as if you've ever had to work before. I've made sure of that. Now it's your turn. My days of break-ing my back in the fields will be soon be over. She passed her broad hand over his face, rough with pieces of hard skin and the callous where the handle of the sickle had left its deep impression; and her touch effaced all other feelings in the young man. She had this power to obliterate him; as though he had no right to his own emotions, but must endlessly relive hers again and again.

He listened to the grieving voice. He wished she were less insistent; she had no need to reawaken constantly the sense of hopeless gratitude that never left him. He leapt to his feet, threw on his clothes, took the bicycle and pedalled in the hot wind to the stadium, not touching the breakfast she had set before him.

Four

WHENEVER HE visited the teacher's house, Prakash could not look his children in the eye, but passed them with face lowered and a mumbled good evening. The girls gazed at him curiously, but their brother appeared indifferent. The young man felt they held him in little regard, for they knew him as a poor boy who had become the object of their father's pity. He thought that even if the teacher really had been poor as a child, his own children were secure against want. He knew that nothing is forgotten so swiftly as poverty; although he resolved that his own children should know knew exactly what his mother had suffered. The young man re-sented his own insignificance in their eyes; and the knowledge he had of their father, which was denied to them, failed to bring him any comfort.

The teacher's wife was kind, and easy to talk to. She was warm and considerate, with a round face and spectacles, and whenever she was at home, she would bring tea and snacks into the room where they were studying; a dish of potato chips or some channa. She knew of the young man's mother, and always asked how she was. He was touched by her interest, and did not feel shy in her presence. He smiled with pleasure when she looked at him. Sometimes she even compared him favourably with her own son, who, she said, was spoiled and lazy. Her husband re-minded her that if that was true, it was she who had made him so. She sighed and said If only he would study as you do. I wish you could become friends, you would be such a good influence upon him. All he does now is waste time standing on the corner with his friends, talking about motorbikes and movies. A curious bond grew between the young man and the teacher's wife, and the teacher seemed relaxed when they were together, his eyes moving from one to the other, as though to encompass them both within a similar, privileged relationship; of which, however, the wife was, he well knew, quite unaware.

Although he was embarrassed at her attempts to create an impossible friendship between him and her son, the young man had moments, in that house, when he felt wildly happy and elated. If only he had been born into such a family! If only the woman with her softness and gentle grace had been his mother! As soon as such an idea had passed through his head, he thought with shame of the wasted limbs and tired angular body of his mother, and tried to chase the memory of his disloyalty to her. But these children would expect to go to college. The girls had never worked in the fields. He felt a pang of envy on behalf of his ragged, illiterate sister. They would marry well, and they would take a generous dowry. He thought of the scanty, skimped belongings his own sister had taken to her husband's home – some metal chairs, a wooden bed and a couple of brass pots – and how they had been despised by her mother-in-law. As for the boy, he would become a doctor or a lawyer, would live in Delhi or Mumbai in a high-rise apartment. His parents would continue to pay for his education as long as was necessary. There would be no haste for him to marry; he might enjoy his freedom until he was thirty if he chose. He might go abroad. They had cousins in England, in a place he had never heard of, but which sounded exotic and sophisticated; they kept a shop in a town called Hartlepool.

How the young man envied the son; not so much his good clothes and shoes, his new bicycle and walkman, but the sense of a crowded, family, with the chachas and mamas and kakas – a whole lexicon of kinship of which his own life was bare. As time went by, however, he felt a little bolder, as though he, too, had some right to be in the teacher's house: a right which he could not publicly acknowledge, but which gave him a growing confidence. As a result of this, it became his objective to coax a smile from the boy. He paused on the road in front of the house to admire his new red bicycle, and the two-coloured running shoes he wore. Little by little, the boy seemed to warm to him. One day he said I saw you win the inter-schools 100 metres. I'd give anything to run like that. The sincerity with which he spoke surprised and delighted Prakash. The boy was blushing; his eyes shone, the eyes of his father. The young man realised that the other's diffidence had come from shyness and not from a sense of his social standing. At the beginning, he had felt insignificant, unworthy in this safe, comfortable household. Yet here was this boy saying he envied him. He couldn't believe that such a khushnasib, favoured, youth could find anything wrong with his life. One evening, the boy was waiting at the gate for him. It was clear he wanted to say something. They spoke of the sports competition, the coming Divali holiday. Then, looking at him with his clear light brown eyes, the boy said My father likes you. He talks about you. I think he wishes you were his son. I think I am a disappointment to him. There was such sadness in his voice, the young man could make no reply. He stammered some denial of the boy's feeling and ran into the house.

The lessons continued. On Mondays, they were always alone. The same ritual that had occurred on the first evening was repeated. They sat over their books, and little by little, the teacher made the first move, tentatively, as though it had never happened before. The young man sometimes felt impatient, and wanted it to happen more quickly. One day, the teacher took him into the bedroom, removed all his clothes, and penetrated him. He had never shown his body to a stranger before. He had never slept naked. When he had taken off his underpants, he tried to shield his genitals with one hand, but his cock seemed to have a will of its own, and would not be concealed behind the ineffective defence of his splayed fingers. The older man pushed him gently onto the bed, the bed which, the young man realised with horror, he shared each night with his wife. He lay dumbly on his face, vulnerable, afraid; and when the older man tried to penetrate him, it seemed that his whole body was being opened, and he cried out. Little by little, the pain subsided, and rather than invaded, he felt comforted by the man's rhythmic movement inside him.

Afterwards, the shame always renewed itself, just as the anticipation of pleasure did beforehand. The revulsion he sometimes felt faded, and by the following week, his feelings had become more complicated, more ambiguous; he looked forward to the by now ritualised encounter. He walked to the teacher's house with an eagerness that made his steps awkward, his gestures, normally so fluid, jerky with suppressed desire. At last the sex became entirely natural. No longer an experience remote from his real life, but integrated, of a piece with it; as though being held by the man's arms folded tightly around him, and the strangely comforting hardness of his cock within were something he had been waiting for since... ever since he could remember. An inner emptiness was being filled; and the sex seemed a fitting enactment of that more abstract absence. Something was being restored, something which he had never even known was missing. Whenever the teacher wanted to fuck him, he said he wanted their friendship to become pakka.

Afterwards, the young man always put more energy into his running; and that year, he won the 100 metres and the 200 metres and his team won the relay race. The teacher told him how proud he was, and he spoke as if he had indeed been his father. The young man thought his heart would burst; he had no right to such happiness. Surely, he thought immediately afterwards, with a pang of apprehension, something must come to end it.

On Tuesdays and Thursdays they studied as if nothing had passed between them. The teacher never spoke about their Monday evenings, and sometimes the young man glanced up at him with a quiver of anxiety: perhaps it was all finished. He dreaded that the teacher would dismiss him, grow tired of him, find him a slow and inattentive pupil. But he was always considerate and tender; and a friendship grew between them that did not appear to depend on their Monday evenings. Each week, the young man was relieved when the teacher approached him, and he sat wrapped in the pleasurable exhalation of the older man's body, which consoled and reassured him for depths of inadequacy and failure which he had not imagined could ever be filled with such sweet companionability and protective tenderness. At night, he sometimes dreamed about him, thought of them alone together on a beach he had never seen, or in the mountains where the rose and blue glaciers of the Greater Himalaya were visible through the haze. Somewhere, at the back of his mind, there was a fear he was reluctant to define, a fear that he would go away to college, that the relationship was fragile, impermanent, and would one day cease. Then he felt sad; it was a foreshadowing of something that he had already known long ago, but he couldn't drive the idea from his mind.

Little by little, the resentment faded, and the young man accommodated the friendship within his increasingly flexible and tolerant view of the world. At the end of a year, he no longer felt shame, but accepted the relationship, and his role in it, as part of a wider reality that he acknowledged he would probably never understand. He observed from a growing distance, it seemed, his mother's daily puja before the little shrine which she had made in the cowshed; the ledge with the tiny red oil-lamp, the flakes of white coconut and marigolds, and the aromatic smoke of agarbatti. He himself did puja only when she chided him for his omissions. He had never defined precisely what he believed, but took his faith from his mother, as he had taken so much else. He accepted that Hanuman was his special deity, and always fasted on Tuesdays, but it was an indolent kind of acceptance, which he chose to shield from his own scrutiny, for fear that it might fall apart.

One Monday evening in winter, when the cold wind blew down from the hills whose tops were frosted with snow, the young man was surprised to find all the lights on in the teacher's house, and a sound of classical music coming through the open window. Outside, a new scooter was parked. The young man was introduced to a stranger who, it appeared, was the wife's brother. He had come home on leave all the way from Mumbai, where he was serving in the Indian Navy. He was staying at his mother's house in Pathaknagar, and had borrowed his cousin's new scooter to visit other members of the family in the neighbourhood. He asked the young man about his family; and he replied, concealing nothing about their circumstances. He felt liberated by no longer having to hide the truth about his family's poverty. After all, the teacher had said, the majority of the people in India are poor. The brother was interested, and when he learned that the young man was an athlete, he said We could do with some good athletes in the service. Had you thought about that? You are very well looked after. The athletes have a life of ease. They do no duty, but only have to win races. You should think about it as a career. They are very privileged young men, with nothing to do but keep themselves in good shape so that they carry off all the trophies in the competitions against the army, the police and the air force.

The teacher's son looked longingly at the new scooter. He said Let me take it for a spin. No, his father said. It is too dark and too cold. Go on, said his uncle, the boy has to learn to ride a scooter sooner or later. He gave him the crash helmet, and the boy, dancing with excitement, took the new vehicle out into the road. The engine revved up; the dust rose in a red cloud, and he was gone.

The young man stayed to drink some tea. The teacher apologised, and said we'll have extra lessons tomorrow. Everybody was in a fine good humour; the brother brought tales of life in Mumbai which enthralled the family. He spoke of the jewelled horseshoe of Marine Drive, where the buildings were as tall as those in New York, and the Taj Hotel, where it cost 10,000 rupees to spend a single night. After some time, the young man excused himself, saying he would use the unexpectedly free evening to do some extra practice at the stadium. He felt happy, pleased to have a Monday evening to himself. The lessons – or rather, on Mondays, what the teacher had come to call non-academic instruction – had already continued for over a year. The relationship with the older man had raised his confidence; he had also learned a great deal. His exams were due, and he no longer doubted that he would pass. Although he could now understand and read English, he was still too timid to speak in the presence of the teacher who articulated every word with such clarity.

That night, his practice was particularly good. He was invigorated by the cold air, and exhaled long white trails of vapour from his mouth. As he was coming out of the stadium some boys stopped him. They were chattering excitedly. There's been an accident. Where? On the road from Pathaknagar. Who? The teacher's son. No, I just saw him, an hour ago, it can't be. Yes, we just came from that place.

The boy had driven some way up the hill towards Pathaknagar, and was careering downward towards home, when a public carrier overtook him. He swerved and crashed into the vehicle. He was killed at once. The public carrier had then smashed into the wall. There was patch of dried blood on the highway. The road had been blocked off by a rough semicircle of stones. Splinters of glass glittered like frost on the highway; some tinsel and plastic garlands from the interior of the cabin were blowing in the cold January wind.

The young man rushed to the teacher's house. Outside were the remains of the scooter. From within, the sounds of weeping, shouting and recriminations. The woman was crying You should have stopped him. You should never have let him go. The young man crept round to the window. Nobody had seen him. He walked away, and was sick in the middle of the road. Next day he watched as the procession made its way to the cremation ground, the body of the boy wrapped in white cerements and carried on the shoulders of his father and his brothers. A crowd of people, so different from the thin group that had followed his grandmother to the funeral ground. The sky was grey and low, and people, huddled, with a shawl around their head against the cold, stopped at the side of the road to watch, and the traffic came to a standstill. The whole town seemed to be in mourning.

He didn't see the teacher for some days. He spent the week wondering whether he should call, write a letter, do something in an effort to console him for such a terrible loss; but he could think of nothing that would be adequate to the occasion. On the following Monday, he went to the house. The teacher was sitting alone, motionless, his eyes closed. The young man entered. He touched the teacher's arm. The older man shook off the trance, but his expression gave no hint of welcome. The young man sat down. He reached for the teacher's hand, which withdrew sharply from his touch. Slowly, the teacher raised his head and opened his eyes upon the young man's face. In them the young man saw something that chilled his blood; not only the deep grief he expected, but an angry and unloving interrogation he would remember all his life. The look said Why did my boy die, while you are still alive? Why couldn't it have been you? I have lost my son because of you. This is my punishment. And you are still here to reproach me. The accusation was as clear as if it had been written upon his face. Not a word was spoken, but the naked feeling looked boldly out of his eyes, like a stranger that has unexpectedly usurped the house of a friend; it seemed to be there independently of the teacher's will. Trembling, the young man ran from the house. He felt cold and alone. He knew that the friendship with the teacher had finished for ever.

But it wasn't, at least not quite. Two weeks later, the teacher asked him to call. Hope leapt within the young man. But instead of touching him, instead of studying, the teacher talked. He talked about his son. His brilliance. His beauty. The promise that would never now be fulfilled. He was barely coherent. The young man tried to comfort him; he held out his arms to him, but the teacher made no move towards him, offered no gesture of conciliation, no word of affection. Only remorse. He kept repeating the same words. It's a punishment, I should never have done it. Now he has been taken from me. The young man said I am not your punishment, I am your friend; but the teacher could not reach out to him. The rejection was complete, He could understand the association of the loss of his son with the act of betrayal he had committed with the boy who was his son's peer, should have been his son's friend; but he could not accept that his death was anything other than a tragic accident. Forlornly, he said goodbye. The teacher said You'll come tomorrow. The young man said No, I can't. The older man made no effort to persuade him to change his mind.

The teacher and what remained of his family left the town. The little house stayed empty. The door came off its hinge, and grass grew out of the roof. All around, the creepers sprang up in the rain; cobwebs appeared in the broken window, and the dust accumulated in reddish drifts around the unopened door. The insects made their home in the thatch; some wasps built their nest; termites made a rough architecture of their hills in the red earth; white ants ate the papers; blue mildew covered the inside walls.

Sometimes the young man paused to look inside, and to remember. He had a strange feeling of abandonment, which he recognised as having accompanied him all his life; only now it was made worse, because he had known and felt the presence of the teacher, a remedy, or at least a comfort for that old, deep feeling of nameless desertions that had happened beyond the reach of conscious memory. He tried to remember the aromatic spice and the tobacco, the flavour of his being, the emanation that had penetrated him, which he had breathed in and which had made him, briefly, whole. But feelings of past happiness cannot be remembered; they simply taunt and tantalise the time of loss. He banged his fist against the crumbling wall, and cried. Then he ran off to the stadium and ran and ran until he was exhausted.

He felt only grief at the loss of his friend; not guilt, but a terrible sadness. His mother circled around him, feeling the grief, but unable to touch it or to speak to him. She thought he was missing the companionship of the dead boy. She had always said to him that he needed friends of his own age, of his own sex; but she had never meant it. His attachment to her left him no room for anyone else. He sat on the tin chair inside the hut, while the rain splashed with its deafening roar on the metal roof of the hut. Memory stirred: the rain, darkness, walking; being carried by his mother and then by his sister. The grandmother. Was she walking behind, limping? Or had she followed later? Such a long walk. What were they leaving behind? This same feeling of abandonment, the desertion of death. His father. The flames. The sandalwood. The fire eating his body. After the cremation, the brother had told his mother You can't stay here. A widow, amputated of a husband, was an ill-omened thing, a living stump of a human being. Women had no right to live on after their men had departed. She, her children and aged mother were devourers of the pitiful household subsistence. They produced nothing. The brother was adamant. There is no place for you now he has gone. Our land is poor, it yields little. You must take the children and go. The same night, in the rain under inky clouds, in an act as determined as that which had driven widows in the past to throw themselves on their husbands' pyres, the mother had taken up her bundle, the two children, and walked defiantly onto the muddy crumbling road that led some 60 kilometres to the village in the foothills; close to where the lights of Dehra Dun turned the clouds a smoky orange, and until she came to the sodden little town that was Rangniwas. The boy had rested on the girl's hip, the young soft bone that he had deformed by the impress of his body, just as he sometimes felt, he had misshaped her whole life by his privilege, this unsought advantage, which was nevertheless such a burden, even an affliction.

Five

PRAKASH PASSED his exams, and took a degree in economics and business studies at the English-medium college. He could still barely speak a word of the language, but he wrote with tolerable precision; and he was comforted by the fact that many of his teachers were barely more fluent than he was. The memory of his friend's brutal rejection pained him; but at the same time, he was grateful for the strength and self-confidence he had gained from the relationship. He felt something incomplete within him had been finished at last, a sense of being settled within himself. He had been able to separate his own identity from that of his mother, and had detached himself a little from her pain, if not from her love; he was able to define limits beyond which he must not allow her existence to invade him.

Yet duty towards his mother was the strongest impulse in the tenacity with which he continued his studies. When he had taken his degree, the landowner's wife called him into her cool wood-panelled house, walls covered with faded sepia photographs of her husband in the company of Nehru, Ambedkar, and other historic luminaries of Independence. She asked him what he wanted to do, if he could choose. When he told her, she smiled at the modesty of his ambition, and promised to pay for him to go to a Physical Training College in a town a hundred kilometres from his home. Part of him disliked the patronage of the elderly elegant widow. He wanted to ask her why she had not extended her charity to a reduction in his mother's years of labour. Why was she showing him favours, when he had already received so many? Was it because her goodness would become known to all the world, whereas any abridgement of his mother's hours of labour would have passed unremarked by anyone but an insignificant old servant? But he lowered his eyes and thanked her; and then immediately regretted the lack of enthusiasm in his response. He was afraid she might see this as coolness and ingratitude, and withdraw her promise as arbitrarily as she had made it.

He ran across the muddy field of beans, trampling the edge of the crops. He could not contain his delight in the deliverance that had been offered him, but which nevertheless, in a way, perpetuated the family's bondage to their employer. He sat at his mother's feet, and thanked her for all she had done for the landowner's wife, which was only now being repaid, and not to her. He, the favoured, was to be the beneficiary of yet more of his mother's limitless capacity for self-sacrifice.

But what a relief it would be, after the cramping application to subjects that didn't interest him! To be free to do what he most enjoyed. His mother received the news cautiously. If he had expected her to throw up her hands in joy, he clearly didn't know her. You'll go away from home, she said. What will we do here, with no man to protect us?

He hated leaving Garhwal for the industrial town in the middle of Uttar Pradesh, with its chemical factories and leather workshops. The spirals of violet smoke rose into the sky from the tall chimneys. The factories disgorged their ragged workers to the music of a siren twice a day. The young man disliked the crumbling chawls in which the labourers lived. He hated the slums, with the green stagnant water that spread around the fragile huts, constructed of bamboo, polythene, cardboard, strips of corrugated metal. He went out of the college campus as rarely as possible. There, to use the homely dialect would have invited ridicule. He became another person: more austere, stiff, a Hindi speaker. Almost as foreign to him as being an English-medium student. Once every two weeks, he would wait for the rattling overcrowded bus that would take him home, home to where, it seemed, the women, not only of his family, but of a whole region, waited. They waited for remittances, for scribbled letters, for news from other returnees, and above all, for the loved, familiar figure that would suddenly appear, unnanounced, crossing the parched fields or climbing the dusty slopes, the exiled men of Uttarakhand, whose loved but fragile hills could not provide them with livelihood or security.

The accommodation at the college was poor: long dormitories with forty charpoys so close together that you could scarcely stand between them. There was only one shower for each dormitory. In winter, the breath condensed in clouds in the draughty wooden building; and in summer, the heat of the sun was intensified by the corrugated metal roof, and it was impossible to sleep at night. The day was structured in an impermeable programme of exhausting activity; and Prakash was glad of it. They were up at five o'clock in the morning, for running and gymnastics: the most rigorous programme of training – an archaic and undoubtedly colonial belief that unless young males were kept endlessly occupied, they would be up to no good. Many pre-Independence values had been absorbed into the new India; alien imperial traditions lingered, flourished even.

There he made one good friend who came from an Untouchable family in Muzaffarnagar; a quiet passionate man. He drew Prakash to himself precisely through his self-possessed stillness, his sparing use of words, which made them all the more intense when he spoke of his dedication to the work of the Dalit Panthers, those who would compel changes upon a somnolent and unchanging caste system. The young man's mother would never allow an Untouchable into her kitchen. Once an old woman had come from the hovels which the Untouchables shared with their cattle on the piece of flooded low ground beside the nalla. She was looking for work; and she had stepped over the threshold of the kitchen. Furious, his mother had driven her away, beating her with a broom. She had destroyed all the perishable food, even though they had gone hungry for two days afterwards. Poverty did not unite people; it only gave them a keener sense of their status, and made them thankful for the existence of those even lower in the unappealable hierarchy of caste.

The family of Hiralal, Prakash's friend, were landless; labourers in the fields of others. They were not allowed to use the village well, and their house was set apart from the main body of the community, so their paths rarely crossed those of the higher castes. This man's sister had been raped when she was thirteen by the son of a rich farmer. There was no recourse but for the family to leave the village. Justice, said Hiralal, is too expensive for the poor. They had used the opportunity to go to Delhi. A thikedar, who acted as recruiter for a construction company, had been gathering people for work on a new hotel complex in the city. His parents had decided to go. With trepidation and fear they abandoned the place where their ancestors had lived the same relentless and abject existence for generations; a life which, however wretched, was at least familiar. The known degradations were not to be lightly exchanged for others which might conceivably be worse. No one in the family had ever gone further than walking distance, none had ever travelled in a train or even a bus. And yet, they took their children to the city, to squat for two years within the compound of the building site. There, they lived in rough huts of straw and palm-thatch, freezing in winter, washed away in the monsoon. The whole family had worked on the site, the women carrying headloads of cement among the forest of wooden pillars that formed a scaffolding around the structure, exposed to the intolerable heat, the rain and the chill dry winds of winter that chapped the skin and made their hands bleed. Even the children carried bricks, the girls prepared meals and looked after the babies, the only ones who were spared the labour of construction. Prakash listened. He understood that his own family's uprooting was only part of the vast dislocation that was evicting people from settled ways of life all over India and sending them to labour in unfamiliar places for alien purposes.

Hiralal lived apart from his parents, with a kinsman who stayed in a slum colony adjacent to the building site, most of whom were sweepers, or Valmikis, as they preferred to be called. They had come from Rajasthan in British times, cheated of their land by moneylenders and higher-caste exploiters. Originally, they settled close to the Ajmeri Gate in Delhi, but had fled once more at the time of Partition, during the communal riots that broke out in the city. It was then they had settled on what was at that time a piece of wasteland.

Hiralal's relative had a tea-stall and shop that sold biscuits, soap and sweets. The boy went to school, and helped out in his uncle's business, sometimes sitting by the light of a kerosene lamp until late into the night. In the slum at that time, there had been a group of people belonging to the Dalit Panthers, a militant group struggling for the liberation of those outside the caste system. He had done well at school, and in his free time listened avidly to the passionate denunciations of privilege by the older men. Sometimes, he told his friend, the tears stood in his eyes at the stories of injustice and cruelty he had heard: young women whose breasts had been cut off, children drowned in the irrigation canal in retaliation for some infringement of the severe caste laws.

His uncle had encouraged him to study, so that he could take his degree. Something unheard of in that community – a boy from the caste of sweepers with a college degree. He would become a model and an inspiration to other young people in the future.

He spoke to Prakash about social justice, the ancient horror of the caste system, onto which new inequalities of class were now being imposed. He helped the young man see his mother's struggle in another context – not merely as an enormous sacrifice for himself (he had always known that) – but as part of a continuous impoverishment of the already wretched, the marginalisation and exclusion of the poor. Caste, said Hiralal, is the barrier which prevents the oppressed from perceiving the common source of their poverty. To Prakash it made sense.

For the poor, the family is always the only security. Prakash felt keenly his mother's rejection by her husband's family. Her expulsion had been like a sentence of death. For her to have survived alone, and without abandoning her children, made him feel afresh her power, her strength and love for him, Hiralal had seen many children abandoned in the city; they lived by selling braids of jasmine, by working in rusty workshops repairing cars, or in small metal units, beating molten metal from which the flying sparks burned their skin, damaged their eyes and left shiny scars all over their body. Some became labourers in factories at the age of nine or ten; others runners for drug-dealers, while some of the girls were prostitutes. He had seen them, eleven, twelve-year-olds, sitting behind metal grilles on plastic sofas, with flowers in their hair, their eyelids dark with kohl, their lips red as fire. Prakash thought of the fate that his mother had spared him and his sister. He listened to his friend, and went with him to the place where he lived.

It was a jhuggi-jopri settlement in South Delhi, close to the site of a hotel and some rich houses where his parents had worked. They were evicted from the construction site when the hotel was finished. Many had later helped build the pakka houses in the neighbourhood – three-storey mansions with marble terraces and wrought-iron balconies, guarded by men in sentry-boxes; but the workers themselves had no security. They had formed the slum community which faced the rich houses and the hotel where tourist buses with tinted windows came and went all the time; a reproach and a nuisance to the privilege whose amenities they had provided. There had been demonstrations against them in the area, in spite of the fact that the women from the slum worked as domestic servants in their houses. One night, somebody had set fire to the community; a bottle filled with petrol had been thrown into a crowded hut. A family of Muslims had died, and forty huts burned to the ground. Prakash saw the depths of suffering to which millions of Indians were condemned, and once more, he felt the enormous privilege which his mother's self-abnegation had provided for him.

The two young men would go the cinema in their free time, and watch escapist Hindi movies. The theatre was a vast concrete shell, packed with people who shouted and applauded the balletic violence, and sat entranced by the love songs. Afterwards, they ran, walked and practised together, wandered through the fields of sugarcane, and made plans for a future that remained agreeably, seductively, ill-defined. Prakash had had many friends, those who admired his athletic skill, his ability to win, but he had never been able to confide in them. Now he was to learn that attachments between members of the same sex can be powerful, though without any sexual content. He understood for the first time the meaning of a profound and peaceful companionship. When they strolled through the small town, sometimes they held hands, linking two or three fingers. To his friend he could tell everything, except the story of his relationship with the teacher, which he had confined to a distant place in his memory; in this, he was like a farmer who tethers a goat on wasteland in a corner of a field, so that it cannot damage the crops.

After a few months, they began to wonder what would happen when the year was up. Would there be work? They knew that India was full of graduates doomed to perpetual underemployment. What chance is there of getting a position as coach or physical education teacher? Neither had any influential contacts. They would not even have known to whom to pay the bribe necessary even to be considered for a post in a government school. There were, of course, private schools, but the wage paid by them was insignificant. Such schools opened and closed all the time, engaged and dismissed teachers casually; the employment they offered was even more temporary and unreliable than industrial labour.

Prakash remembered the conversation with the teacher's brother-in-law. The Navy, the Border Security Force, the Army – they all needed athletes for the prestige of the service. Both young men had good records. There was no reason why they should not join the military. In any case, Garhwal and the hill areas had always provided soldiers for the British. Today, they would be able to enjoy a decent life, without seeing any active service.

Nothing could have been more repugnant to the young man than going to fight. It was a paradox that there should be security in the armed forces – and security, his mother had always told him, was what she had most lacked, had done her best to create for him and his sister. The army seemed safe. At that time, there seemed little danger. They read in the papers of skirmishes with Naxalites, patrols in Kashmir, policing the insurgency in the north-east, but as athletes, they would be protected from such dangerous duties. It would guarantee them an income, they would be housed and fed, merely for doing what they liked doing best.

It was a great irony. No sooner had they joined, and been accepted for the year following their training college, than Operation Blue Star was mounted against the Golden Temple at Amritsar, and the long and bloody repression in Punjab began, a conflict that was to cause the deaths of thousands of people, both civil and military. Later, the situation in Kashmir deteriorated, and the north-east insurgency grew stronger. The army, which had seemed a guarantee of shelter and livelihood to them, was suddenly the principal agent of conserving what politicians called India's integrity. None of this, however, was to touch Prakash and Hiralal.

By that time, they were installed in camp in the cantonment area of Delhi – the most agreeable environment of the old imperial capital, where the jamun trees rained their purple plums onto the road, the gulmohars burst into orange flame in spring and the ratkirani filled the warm night air with its seductive jasmine scent. And although life in camp was austere, they led a pampered life by comparison with the other recruits who, within months of their training, were already in Punjab or Kashmir.

In the first two years, Prakash won all his races. He became captain of the camp athletics team. He never boasted of his ability, but remained accessible, sympathetic to others, encouraging and inspiring the team. He made many friends, but with none of them could he talk about things that lay close to his heart. They were joined together in a comradely solidarity, sweet enough in its way, and not without an erotic undertow that sometimes roused suppressed longings in the young man. The athletes were very modest, and never showed themselves naked. They cultivated their bodies, and constantly discussed their physical condition; but it was a strangely sexless life, a strict regimen of training and preparation for the competitions which took place among the different sections of the army and police several times a year. As long as they maintained their practice and won their races, they were free to come and go as they chose.

Whenever he had a holiday, the young man went back to Rangniwas. He had become well-known where he lived. When he went for training at the stadium, there would always be half a dozen young boys hanging around, and they would shyly ask if he would help train them, advise them how to follow a career like his. When he was home on leave for long periods – a month or more after a competition, or at Divali – he would practise with them in the stadium. He gave his advice and help freely, told them how they could improve their performance, sustain a high standard of fitness. He would run them round the track, give them gymnastics exercises until they fell from exhaustion. He had great patience and affection for them. The boys were artless and full of enthusiasm; they had not learned the disappointment, rejection and unemployment that would later take so many of them away from the region they loved. The young man could anticipate the slow erosion of their energy and enthusiasm, the cynicism and disillusion that would follow. He felt angry and sad for them, but could not speak of the apprehensiveness with which he viewed their – and India's – future. They worshipped him.

His mother lived only for his return home. Whenever he was expected, she fidgeted, restless and irritable. She stood at the edge of the field, waiting for his arrival. On those days, the daughter had to take a double share of the work, The young man always dragged his feet slightly as he walked, scuffing his heels on the ground. Long before he came into sight, his mother would cry out with relief Here he comes; and her daughter would look up from her work in astonishment, surveying the empty fields and wondering how she could possibly know he was near. She was never mistaken.

One day, coming over the fields from the main road, whistling, his bag over his shoulder, his eyes screwed up against the glare of the sun, he saw his mother sitting on the metal chair in front of their hut. He had not expected her to be there in the middle of the afternoon.

His heart leapt. Was she sick? Whenever he came home, he saw that time had bitten more deeply into her furrowed cheeks; the face had become thinner, the hair less plentiful and greyer; her scalp was clearly visible as she stooped in the sunlight. She always wore the same sarees until they became frayed and lost their colour, and the blouses were nothing but a lattice of holes. He had offered to buy her some new clothes with the money he earned from the army; but she said, obscurely, There will be time enough for new clothes when the day comes; as though anticipating some glorious festival, the date of which was known only to her.

But as he drew nearer, he could see she was smiling. She was sitting in a way that suggested triumph, satisfaction, almost – if the word were not such a denial of her sombre being – happiness. The sister came out of the hut with a glass of tea, as though they had anticipated the very moment of his arrival, the women who lived through him and in him. As soon as he came home, their presence invaded him, seemed to possess him, and would not be driven away, no matter how fast he ran, Sometimes, he was so oppressed by these existences which defined themselves only through him, that he longed to be free of them; only he felt such pain at what that freedom might mean, that these ideas were always followed by a rush of shame, and a desire to cancel the cruel thoughts. He touched his mother's feet.

The sister sat beside them. It was a ceremonious moment. In her lined, tired face, he could see jubilation, a sense of victory. What had she done? For a moment, she relished his curiosity and was silent.

Then she said Beta, this is the happiest day I have known since the day I first held you in my arms. Today, we are free. I am no longer dependent upon the landowner or his wife for our sustenance. I have bought five bighas of land from them. They have been good to us. They gave us shelter when we had nothing. They gave work to a woman on her own with two children. They have paid me enough so that, by living frugally, I could save. Everything I had I gave to my son. Now it is time to give him something more. The land I have bought will be enough to provide ourselves with a little rice, some wheat and vegetables. I shall buy some buffaloes, some goats. On our land – she gave a deep sigh and her eyes brimmed with tears of triumph – I shall build a house for my son and his wife. Today I can see the end of my labours, just as some days we can see the peaks of the mountains in the clear air. This is why I am not working. The landowner's wife has signed the necessary papers. The land is ours.

Land. Land that had torn her flesh and bent her back as she wrenched her livelihood from it, how it held her in its power. Land that had taken her energies and wasted her strength. Land, to her the source of subsistence and survival, represented the ultimate control of a human being over her destiny. Those who grow their own food and construct their own shelter, she always said, owe nothing to anyone, To have regained self-reliance was to her the greatest achievement of her life. To buy nothing in the market-place was to be free. Her eyes glittered with a strange passion, an ancient peasant avarice that is a hunger for freedom, a freedom which is all over the world being abandoned in favour of market-dependency.

He threw down his plastic satchel on the grass, and raised his mother up, his arms extended to support her. She threw herself against his chest. She could for the first time in a quarter of a century abandon the stoical endurance and relax the strength of her will that had sustained them all, and her body trembled, shaking in an intense, silent release that was close to grief. He comforted her, and touched her face with his, so that their tears formed a common stream. He stroked the greying hair, and the scaly scalp beneath. She scarcely reached his shoulder. He took her hands in his – those same hands, gnarled and scarred – but she continued to shake from the tension and effort that she had brought to her work of saving them from eternal landlessness and poverty. All the years of his idleness and study, she had been tirelessly building a bridge to the future with her bare hands; and at last she thought she could see the shape of the finished structure.

He had always known the fathomless obligation he had to her. Something immeasurable lay between them. She had made a vow that her boy would not suffer; and in this pact she had not even consulted her daughter. But now it was time for him to pay some of this enormous debt of which he had been the unconscious inheritor. Instead of the joy which she expected him to show, he felt a sombre apprehension, an oppression of the heart. He tried to smile at her, but his own tears only flowed faster. He wept, not only because of her frail exhausted body, but also because... because – he hardly dared express it, even to himself because... he hated land.

He loathed the earth that had destroyed his mother's strength, that had been made fertile by her sweat and energy. He saw her back, endlessly curved over the emerald blades of rice she was transplanting, he heard the swish of the sickle as it met the tough stalks of wheat, the metallic percussion of the hoe as it struck the stones in the fields. To her land was wealth; to him it was labour without end. And the tragic thing was, it was she who had made this transformation in him, she who had estranged him from it. Seeing his tears, she was touched and, not knowing their cause – which only made him feel even more wretched – she said You've nothing to weep for, I am the one whose life is finished.

But she was not a woman whose life was so easily finished. What she was saying was that it was his responsibility now to take over from her. Now he must marry, now he must help build the house. He was ashamed that he had been able to save so little of the 2,000 rupees that had been his salary. He must marry quickly, have children; two children, three, enough to ensure that there was someone to look after them when they grew older, someone to fulfil the prescribed destiny, the continuities of rebirth, with which they, in their bodily lives, mimicked the eternal cycles of reincarnation in the natual world. The duty of flesh to flesh; there is nothing else. All her life she had saved, saved for his education, saved for his marriage. Now, it was his turn. He would save for the education of his children, for their distant marriages. He felt overwhelmed as he saw the fulfilment of his mother's life, and felt his own unworthiness, his eternal incapacity to live up to her sacrifice. He wanted to tear himself away and cry No, no, I don't want it. I don't want to be another link in this unending cycle of work and sacrifice and poverty, I want to live for myself. But at the same time, he knew that the only thing that stood between himself and his own future dereliction and abandonment was the unborn children from the unknown wife; the children he would make who would take him to the funeral pyre, as he would one day surely accompany his mother on that last dutiful journey.

He touched her face with his hand. Her old skin was still soft. She took the palm of his hand to her mouth and kissed it. Then she beckoned to him and his sister to follow her across the field. They turned beside a row of eucalyptus trees, past the soya field, where the irrigation gurgled and sang in the rain. At the edge of the next field, she paused. There. Land bordered by the track leading to the metalled road, by the edge of the landowner's plot, and to the west, the hut of a sharecropper. Beside this man's hut was a soaring karanj tree, which marked the boundary on that side. The land had not been planted this year: it had been set aside by the landowner's wife for the young man's mother.

Five thousand rupees a bigha! How had she saved so much money? This was her gift to him, his security. The wild rice and creepers covered the land. So much work to be done, she said with enthusiasm; but this time, all for ourselves. For you, son,

The sister placed her arm through his. She looked at him from depths of gratitude and affection: their lives were intertwined, with each other and with the land; for her too, human lives were like the creepers that came up in the monsoon and covered the thatch of the buffalo sheds, shrivelled up in the heat and disappeared into the earth to await the next growing season. She had never thought with regret of her own unhappy experience. After less than one year of marriage, she had returned home, beaten, with two broken ribs. The mother had taken her into the house, and they had resumed their life as though she had never been married.

The sister had never expressed reproach for her lack of schooling, her long hours of labour in the fields that had made her look much older than her 27 years, the premature marriage that had finished so quickly in confusion and pain. The young man looked at her. Her eyes shone with a joy that derived entirely from the pleasure she anticipated for him, and which filled him with an unspeakable aching. She was an intelligent woman. She deserved something better. Her goodness was unbearable. The young man knew that because they had given him everything, he owed them everything; with his whole being, he dedicated himself to the sister with her laughter and her rough country sweetness that derived such fun from the events of the few people's lives which touched theirs. They had given their lives, and he now had to give his in return. Flesh for flesh. His mother sighed; an exhalation that, while it spoke of the end of her bondage, meant the beginning of his.

The women returned to the byre, where they made chappatis and cooked rice for the evening meal. They took some laukri, gourds, growing on the landowner's ground. They had always been free to cut vegetables for their own use, and that night, they ate as though it were a festival.

They sat late, watching the fireflies, talking about the future that was already predetermined for the young man. The moths and insects danced around the pale yellow light of the kerosene lamp, and their bodies threw shadows as big as birds on the verandah. The mother had not yet finished all she had to say. She still had some money, even after the purchase of so much land. She would start on the house after the monsoon. She would engage a mason to build a proper concrete structure. Then next year, it would be time for him to think of marriage. As she spoke, he shrank within himself. He spoke no word of contradiction to the picture she offered of his future life.

Six

PRAKASH WAS more fit than he had ever been. His timing for the 100 metres reached 10.7 seconds, only a second outside the record. He was aware that he would never better it, and would not make the national team. But he thought less of the races he wouldn't win than of the vast distance which, it seemed to him, he had travelled, from the cowshed in the northern plains, to captain of the athletics team. He was not by nature competitive; he simply took pleasure in what he had achieved. He enjoyed the slow build-up towards each championship, gradually improving his performance, almost indolently at first, becoming more and more intense as the competition came closer, until he was finally taut, clenched, waiting for the burst of energy that would take him effortlessly – or so it appeared – across the hundred metres of track. When he ran, he felt almost as though he were another creature, not quite human, a being of such swift and mobile elegance that he marvelled at his own power to transcend, not merely the limits of his social origin, but of his own body. Nothing else could equal this; it was more like a religious experience than anything he had known in rituals, temples or pujas. He continued to be sustained by the bitter-sweet symbiosis with his family, and burdened by the the weight of the precious, unasked-for gift of the effaced lives of the women he loved.

Since the schoolteacher had disappeared from his life, he had tried to forget what had passed between them; or at least, it no longer dominated his thoughts. Without such willed forgettings, it would be impossible for us to live our daily lives. And in any case, he was helped by the intense activity of his time in camp. The using up of his strength each day, the stretching of his physical powers, served as a repeated purge of more commonplace desires. He firmly believed, moreover – and this was part of the unspoken beliefs he had absorbed from a culture from which he thought himself emancipated – that sexual activity dissipates bodily strength; and he came to identify his success with abstinence. He was sure he could feel the vital force in his body concentrate itself at the core of his being; and he was proud of his ability to conserve it. Some of the athletes had been to prostitutes in Delhi. He listened to their stories when they came back late on Saturday night. They spoke of initiations and exaltations in which the bodies of the women who served them were mere instruments. They evoked the graceful contortions of young Nepalis, the vigorous limbs of tribal women, the secret places of virgins from Bhutan, kidnapped by middlemen and held captive in the brothels of Delhi. The young man was uncomfortable when he heard women talked about in this way, but he said nothing.

Sometimes at night in the long barrack room, where the athletes slept their profound and sometimes noisy sleep, dreams disturbed him. Occasionally, he dreamed of home, of running to reach his mother who was in some kind of distress; but the harder he ran, the further she receded. At other times, the dreams were of an amorphous and diffuse eroticism. From time to time, he would be wakened by a hot discharge, which cooled rapidly on the fabric of the lunghi in which he slept. He was afraid his companions would notice, but was surprised to find that it had dried by morning, leaving no visible stain. He wondered if any of them had the same experience; if so, they never spoke of it.

Some of the men, he knew, went to a park near the airport, an extensive area of scrubland where they had sex with other men in the jungle – the overgrown thornbushes and stunted forest trees that provided shelter for secret meetings and clumsy moments of release. They sometimes talked about it, expressing only contempt for the men who wanted to be fucked. They had a special name for them, the *kotis*, who prowled the bushes looking for sex for which they charged ten or twenty rupees – just enough to maintain their self-respect, so that they could convince themselves that they were doing it from necessity and not for pleasure; and indeed, most of them also had other work and the majority were married. The soldiers sometimes joked 'Something is better than nothing.' They did not feel that these encounters compromised their masculinity. 'A man gives, karta hai. A woman takes, karwati hai.' How could that damage their male self-esteem? In fact, some spoke as though it enhanced this; it demonstrated their power over the half-men who were so eager to drop their trousers for them. Prakash thought he was repelled by their conversation.

Sometimes, in the gaps in the time-table, through the interstices of structured time, he felt lonely. He was aware that the figures in his dreams were male, although they were not identifiable individuals. But he often woke up with a residue of an old sense of inadequacy, which he had thought he had overcome. He then recalled with poignant regret the complementary maleness with which the teacher had provided him during the months when they met. He missed him; and was surprised to find that his most powerful memory was not of touch or sight, but of smell, the pungent redolence of his flesh. The powerful male atmosphere of the barracks was no compensation. The energy was not sexual, or if it was, it was effectively stifled. He discovered that the army was not quite what he had expected; it was not a father. It offered neither affection nor guidance, only a discipline that sometimes consoled for the absence of both, but equally, at moments of vulnerability, weighed like a double denial.

He rarely went into the centre of Delhi, which was quite a distance from the cantonment area. After the midday meal, he and his friend usually slept for a couple of hours before evening practice. They would lie on the bed, sometimes leafing through sporting magazines, admiring this or that celebrity, sometimes chatting without enthusiasm about the daily trivia of the camp, wondering what the coach had meant by this critical remark, or that word of praise.

One day, in the middle of the afternoon, a heavy monsoon day in early August, when the sun had parted the violet thunderclouds and heated up the city almost to the pre-monsoon temperature, the young man could not rest. He got up, stood at the dusty grille that covered the window to prevent birds from flying into the room. He looked out onto the parade ground, the rows of barrack buildings, the rolls of barbed wire around the perimeter fence. He longed for the wide horizons of the plains and the gentle undulation of the foothills. Unable to bear the oppression of the camp any longer, he waited until his companion was sleeping, crept out of the room alone, and took the bus to Connaught Place, the centre of New Delhi.

He was filled with an unusual sense of excitement and freedom. This was the first time for many months he had been on his own. He had never been alone for long: the impermeable life of his childhood had left few spaces through which he could retreat into solitude, even though he was, by nature, solitary.

Today felt like a holiday. The bus hummed and vibrated on the potholed road, through the new apartments of Punjabi Bhag, with their terraces and protective metal grilles, where he imagined, the fat discontented wives of rich businessmen read Western magazines and planned trips to America; past the private schools and clinics of Patelnagar, where quack doctors offered remedies for kidneystone, cancer and AIDS, towards the bus station behind the well-tended arcades of Lutyens's imperial centrepiece.

There, the summer flowers were in bloom, the gaudy bells of hibiscus with their long red stamens, the blood-red plumage of canna lilies. Around the great grass rotunda roamed all the hustlers, the ear-cleaners, the shoeshine boys, the drug dealers, the sellers of Kashmiri handicrafts and Rajasthan blue pottery; the masseurs and the vegetable vendors; those desperate to make a livelihood from the tourists, not so many of them in this wet season, but a sprinkling of Russians, Americans, French. In the shade of the trees people slept, the effects of drugs or despair, thin, ragged men who lived on the streets, washed in the water from the hoses that watered the gardens, begged food from the back doors of the restaurants. Many of them, he observed, were migrants from Garhwal, and he was thankful he had not been driven by the same cruel necessity to the city that had broken even their tenacious and obdurate hill-people's spirit.

He went to a tailor in Mohan Singh Place, a vast eight-storey market, with fifty or more shops on every floor. Inside the building, the crowds shuffled in the stifling heat, He ordered a pair of new trousers, in a smart dark blue, with pleats, baggy at the knees, narrow at the ankles; he had seen the design in a sporting magazine. He was elated as he walked across the grassy space, where the people had left a litter of orange peel, peanut shells and banana skins. He liked Delhi in the monsoon. All the jamun plums had fallen from the broad trees that lined the long avenues, and left splashes of imperial purple on the road. Some women and children had gathered them, and offered them for sale in wicker baskets at the roadside. Here and there a vendor had placed a scarlet hibiscus flower in her basket, which glowed like an ember in the pile of dark fruit.

Prakash became aware of a small crowd gathered around a foreigner, a white man, talking to some masseurs and shoe-cleaners. He was speaking Hindi; not very well, but to hear a white man even trying to speak the language intrigued him. He lingered, obscurely attracted by the earnest charm with which he was talking to the group around him. After a few minutes, the foreigner became embarrassed by the growing number of people that surrounded him, and he extricated himself from the crowd which had now begun to ask him for money; a clamorous and competitive tale of hardship and need. He walked purposefully towards the main road. The young man followed him, not directly, but taking an oblique path that would meet with his. He did not know what impelled him; he was aware only of an urgent desire to be held, to be touched, to make a contact that went further than the comradely proximity of the men he was with every day, with their arms always around one another's neck, their heads in each other's lap, their constant closeness that expressed only their common maleness; not the violent longing for tenderness which now made him catch his breath, inescapable as though it were another aspect of the oppressive monsoon wind.

As they stood together on the edge of the pavement, waiting to cross the road, Prakash smiled. The foreigner did not respond at first. But they crossed the road at the same moment, and the young man took his hand to guide him between the jumble of taxis, autorickshaws, Marutis and scooters.

They looked at each other. The young man saw a tall foreigner, perhaps in his forties, with fair hair, blue eyes in a long thin face. The foreigner looked at the powerfully built Indian with clear brown eyes, corn-coloured skin and a smile broken by the gap between his teeth.

Prakash felt a rare recklessness that came from being alone in Delhi, from having evaded his companions. He had heard that Westerners are open about sex. He couldn't remember how he knew it, but the mysterious ways of Westerners were the object of so many newspaper and magazine articles; such things were universally, if vaguely, known. All the images, the appearance and bearing of Westerners suggested they were not offended if approached. The way they dressed, the way the women showed their legs and the contour of their breasts, the bare arms and shoulders, the style in which the men wore trousers that moulded their backside and genitals – everything indicated that, for them, sex was closer to the surface than it was in his own culture, where it lay buried, secret, fathomlessly mysterious. He stopped on the corner, and asked the man where he was from and what he was doing in India. The sun dazzled him; the fumes from the traffic swirled around them; the noise of the cars covered their conversation. The foreigner answered his questions with cool reserve. He said he was on a working holiday, with a non-government organisation, a charity devoted to the relief of leprosy. In turn, the stranger asked the young man whether he was working, and which was his native village. He asked how many people there were in his family, speaking a sweet fractured Hindi which delighted the young man.

Encouraged, he reached for the stranger's hand as they walked, but the foreigner withdrew it brusquely. Prakash asked if he would like a beer, He himself detested alcohol, but had learned, from the same mysterious source no doubt, that Westerners drink; after all, the villains in the Hindi movies were Christians, and they were always drunk.

The man hesitated; but looking at the eager, smiling face of his new acquaintance, agreed. They walked without speaking, The din of the early evening traffic and the crowds avoiding the heat under the colonnade made it impossible to walk side by side. The foreigner followed the young man into the Hotel Alka, through glass corridors and into a very dim interior. There, men on their way home from work sat on leatherette benches drinking Kingfisher beer or Peter Scot whisky, and ate masala peanuts, in an effort to prolong the time of male companionship, before they returned to their family, the wifely interrogations, the disorder of children, the vigilant scrutiny of old women. Prakash was not used to beer, and soon, the feeling of relaxation turned to slight confusion. His head swam, and the cigarette smoke made his eyes water. He had not remembered that Kingfisher was so strong. He told the sympathetic stranger something of his life in the army, about his home-place in the shadow of the Himalayan foothills, and of his ambition to win the 200 metres for his battalion. The foreigner, touched by his candour, smiled at his earnest manner, even though he could not understand everything he said in Hindi. Under the table, the young man sought the hand of the stranger again. This time, the foreigner did not retrieve it, but returned the pressure in the darkness with a firm grip, He told Prakash that his name was Frank. The young man's throat was constricted and dry in spite of the beer. He asked him, in a voice strangled by surprise at his own boldness, Your hotel? His companion shook his head. Why? I don't know you. Prakash was humiliated, and felt the blood rush to his face, which tinted with rose the tone of the skin. Although he did not know it, this enhanced his beauty; a beauty which the stranger distrusted, having learned in his country that beauty did not offer itself freely to middle-aged men, but was a counter in some emotional calculus which, more often than not, also involved money.

Prakash panicked; had he broken some unknown convention? His knowledge of the West was, after all, very sketchy, in spite of the intensive penetration by advertisement and propaganda. He was surprised, too. They had been talking together for two hours. He had told the truth. He said to his companion Don't you like me?

It isn't a question of liking you. How do I know you won't ask for money or rob me? You hear so many stories in Delhi. I was told about a young guy here who picked up foreigners and took them to a hotel. Then his father burst into the room where they were and threatened to expose the tourist to the police. Of course, it wasn't really the young man's father, but they had terrified the foreigner, and they made him give them all his money as the price of keeping quiet.

Prakash was shocked, hurt. I would never do that. Maybe not, but I don't know. Perhaps we should get to know each other better.

This apparently meant that he would have to answer more of the stranger's questions. He did so without concealment, but he found it impossible to speak his name. He maintained the polite form of the verb, *ap*, avoiding the more familiar *tum*, and certainly the intimate *tu*; layers of closeness wrapped in verbal formalities as voluminous as the mysterious folds of a woman's saree.

He told him about his mother; how she had come to the plains after the death of his father, and had found refuge in a tumbledown hut which the cattle had used; how his sister had worked in the fields with the mother 16 hours a day, so that he, the boy, might be spared the drudgery of the landless. Frank listened avidly to the young man's story, and seemed both moved and surprised, although to Prakash it was ordinary enough. He said it was nothing remarkable in India, where almost everyone can tell a tale of miraculous survival. Those who can't have already met their fate.

The stranger looked again at his companion: he saw the long goldflecked eyes of a hill-man, high cheekbones, a broad face, with a wide mouth and teeth that shone in the dark interior of the bar. He remained distrustful. He had met a number of young men in Connaught Place, who, after only the briefest conversations, had declared themselves his best friend, and had then immediately asked him, in that capacity, for money. He had looked at their sincere faces and listened to their inventive and circumstantial stories. He had no reason to believe that this young man was different. And yet, there was something in his demeanour that compelled trust. He had heard that the boys – as the men were called – from the hills are employed in the hotels and restaurants because of their integrity; their hill culture, which has been so damaged in the hills by deforestation, degradation of the land and the eternal flight of the men from the mountains, is nevertheless still useful to a tourist industry. This hill boy had never lived in the hills; but he seemed to express something of the same openness and honesty of those Frank had met who served in the hotels in the cities of the plains.

He was not, at first, particularly attracted to him. The young man had seemed a little too pressing; had taken it for granted that Frank would take him to his hotel. Did this indicate that picking up foreigners was something he did all the time? Many of the young men who haunted this part of Delhi were well practised. They would beg foreigners to find work for them in their own country; they expressed their willingness to do anything, drive a car, sweep the streets, work in a factory. A vast population had been conjured up by the presence of so many tourists and transients here, people for whom a passage from India had become an obsession. What was it, Frank wondered, a pervasive iconography of affluence and luxury, that made so many young men invest these rich foreigners with a magic and potency they could not possibly have? He told himself he had no wish to be part of this one-way traffic of mendacity and illusion; but he was, nevertheless, flattered by having been singled out by his new companion; he was drawn to his candour, and, he said to himself, his looks.

He said to Prakash I suppose you would like to get out of India, Why do you say that? I don't have the chance to leave India, even if I wanted to. In any case, my mother and sister depend on me. I have to stay and look after them. I couldn't go away. We have no other family here. Of course I know people who have gone out, to the Gulf, to Australia. They send money home. But how can that make up for their absence? People need their family, those they love. How can money make up for the touch of a loved one, the embrace of living flesh? Money you need, of course. But while I can earn enough here, I wouldn't think of going away.

He had spoken with deep feeling. Frank liked him. But he needed time to think about it. He asked Prakash if he was free the following day. The athlete smiled. I have no appointments, he said, no social engagements. They arranged to meet at about the same time, late afternoon. When they separated, he thought it unlikely the young man would turn up – his camp was an hour and a half away. He would have to practise in the afternoon, but promised to come into the city immediately afterwards. He could be in Delhi by six o'clock.

On the following evening, Frank sat on a stone bollard on Connaught Place. He had been approached already by two or three hustlers, who asked him what they could do for him. Change money. Smoke. Did he want a nice girl, a nice boy. Did he want to buy gold, jewellery. Did he want to visit the handicraft emporium, did he have something to sell? Did he want some ganja, some brown sugar, anything else? By contrast with this importunate commerce, Prakash seemed both restrained and honest. He had not asked for money – that was already a major point in his favour.

He watched the women from Russia and Uzbekistan with their enormous canvas bags, buying woollens, tea, silks. He had learned that they came on cheap tourist flights, bringing luxuries which were now available in their own country, selling them in Delhi, and stocking up on cheap products which they sold at considerable profit on the austere streets of Tashkent or Kiev.

He was thinking he would wait only five more minutes, when he saw Prakash, in blue jeans and striped shirt, bound across the road, his hands pumping away at his side in a caricature of running. He grinned, the gap between the front teeth a dark interval in the pale enamel. Frank responded spontaneously to the vital presence of the young man. I thought you wouldn't come. He said virtuously, I don't tell people I will come and then not do so. Frank remained suspicious; his new friend seemed a little too pious; almost too good to be true.

You must have a lot of foreign friends. Why? You seem to know your way around. I don't come here. Never. I only came yesterday because I had ordered some new trousers that I had to collect. But they weren't ready.

Prakash said he didn't want to drink beer. They remained for a moment in the warm darkness of Connaught Place, and sat on the ground that was dry and grassless in some places, while in others it was water-logged where gushing hosepipes had been abandoned for hours. The young man explained himself apparently without concealment. He spoke to the sympathetic stranger about his relationship with the teacher, and how it had ended. He told him how he had thought that abstaining from sex enabled him to improve his performance on the racetrack. Then he spoke of the nocturnal discharges; it was this need that had driven him to Delhi the previous afternoon and had impelled him to single out the stranger. He had had no sexual relationship with anyone since that time with the teacher. If I was too eager, it was because I don't know what to do. I've never done such a thing before. I only know how to say what I want. I'm sorry.

He looked miserable; Frank took his hand. They went to eat. The young man suggested a shabby Chinese restaurant, where flies made a dark mosaic on the torn plastic tablecloth. Frank was touched that he did not seem anxious to press him into a smart restaurant, where he would at least be sure of getting an expensive meal out of him. He said No, I haven't come to India to eat Chinese food, or to get cholera.

The young man protested he could not afford to eat anywhere more expensive. Frank said I have more money than you. His friend appeared genuinely distressed. Frank reassured him. It's all right; your country is getting screwed by the West; we get a handful of rupees for a dollar; the least I can do is pay for your meal. Prakash did not understand what he meant.

They sat for two hours in the restaurant, with its white tablecloths, its parties of rich Punjabi families; the children who ordered extravagant meals which they did not touch, and which were returned to the kitchens uneaten. The young man looked in astonishment at their wastefulness, and he thought of how he had been made by his mother to eat the last grain of rice that remained on his plate. Wasted food, she always admonished him, is nourishment for demons.

Frank soon noticed that Prakash was entirely without curiosity about him; he could ask the young man anything he liked, and always received answers of transparent sincerity. Frank was aware he had exceeded anything that two strangers in the West would be likely to ask each other at a second meeting. The young man scarcely looked him in the face. It seemed to the stranger that he wanted, not so much a relationship, as a symbolic figure, a role; was it sex or affection? was it a father? why a foreigner? Was the idea of a man in his life so strange, so inadmissible that it could be filled only by someone from elsewhere? Was this his way of keeping part of himself in the shadows of his life, which clearly revolved around the army camp, the athletic competitions, the family in the small town near Dehra Dun? Did he want someone who would go away and leave him, because he knew what being abandoned meant? Frank sensed an immense vulnerability in the young man, a naivety which anyone in the West would have done his best to conceal; and an apparent indifference to who he, the stranger, was. He didn't even know whether he was European or American; and he never asked. It suggested something Frank already well knew: that, to a certain extent, other people are always shadowy presences upon whom we project our own needs, desires and fantasies. Such a role was not disagreeable to him. He looked intently at the young man; and had a presentiment that he would play a significant role in his life.

Frank asked himself exactly what he was looking for. He wondered again why he had established no strong relationship at home, in his own society. He had had only one passionate friendship, with a man at university almost twenty years earlier. They had been deeply attached for many years, and although both were gay, there had never been any sexual relationship between them. Sex had become separated from the affections; he had reached a form of sexual emancipation – or at least self-expression – quite early, and this had hardened into an acceptance that sexual encounters should be without consequences. He had been at university at the time of gay liberation. The ideology that if it's sex it's good had not yet been darkened by the more sombre events of the eighties, the appearance of AIDS, the backlash. He now looked back upon it as a time of brief radiant freedom; but it had burned itself out, had left no residue. He had salvaged no enduring relationship from those years, and he felt himself increasingly alone.

In recent years, Frank had – deliberately, it seemed to him – kept his emotional life apart from sexual satisfactions. His friendships had always been without any overt sexual component, while his sexual contacts had been largely devoid of any feeling beyond the tenderness of the passing moment. He had, as he said to himself, learned to manage his life, and he knew this to be quite usual; and not only among gay men.

Although he told himself he was utterly at ease with his gay identity, he still felt there was something unsatisfactory about gay relationships. The reason, he thought, was obvious; people of the opposite sex had the advantage of constant renewal of their otherness; were, for each other, a reservoir of unknowable polarities. It was the sameness of the same sex that so swiftly dispelled mystery and led many gay people to multiple encounters. Was that why he now sought someone from another culture, of another race – as a supplement for the mystery which was absent from same-sex relationships within the same culture? Was he exploiting the fantasy of a young man about the West, by allowing him to project onto him who knows what wild fancyings and imaginings? Whatever his misgivings, however, Frank did not intend to let them interfere with what might take place between them.

He installed himself in anticipation in the role of teacher, father figure to the young man, which, he assumed, was what lay open to him. That he himself would be the one to receive instruction, such as he had never bargained for, could scarcely be expected to occur to him.

Seven

FRANK STILL harboured some suspicions – the yougn man's absence of curiosity about him made him fear that maybe he was planning some long-term act of treachery. On the other hand, his appearance of honesty and sincerity was maintained. His story was consistent and detailed. It seemed unlikely that he would go through so elaborate a procedure for the sake of the extremely modest gain he might make by robbing or cheating him. After all, Frank was not a tourist. He had been visiting aid projects which had as their aim the removal of the stigma of leprosy, promoting the idea that it is curable and easily preventable. He was doing this as a voluntary vacation task, and was on a restricted budget. But then, he reflected, the gradations of Western wealth are not evident to the poor; to them, all Westerners are rich.

He settled upon taking a room in a cheap hotel, where they could stay together. It was a government-run establishment, a shabby run-down building slightly away from the centre of the city. The adjacent area was a maze of ruinous one-storey houses, with washing stretched out on the bushes; stalls of vegetable vendors, and a fish-seller with stinking silver fish on a stone slab. The streets swarmed with cycle rickshaw drivers, men from Bihar and Madhya Pradesh, displaced from their land by poverty, drought, caste or communal oppression. As they walked through the streets, they called out to them, Connaught Place only 10 rupees. Prakash paused and spoke with some of them. He asked the kind of questions that Frank thought impertinent – where did they come from, did they have land, how much did they earn, how many children did they have – the sort of demand to which people in the West would say Mind your own business, or What do you want to know for. He was touched by the quiet dignity with which the young man spoke to them, and the truthful simplicity of their reply. He felt outraged on their behalf by the cruelty and indignity of their life in the villages; but whenever he expressed this, they invariably shrugged and said Kya karega, what to do? He asked his friend why people didn't get angry. He said Why waste energy on something you can do nothing about, when you need all your energy to survive a day's labour? One man, a lugubrious driver in his forties, when asked about his life, said he liked Delhi because here he could have two wives, one for cooking and one for fucking.

The cycle rickshaws were three-wheelers, with a horseshoe of a seat behind, covered in red leatherette. Some had a flimsy canopy that could be raised to protect the passengers against the sun or rain. The drivers worked incredibly hard; some wore a towel over their head to protect them against the sun. Most were thin; some appeared quite elderly, and Frank was shocked to learn that they were only 35 or 40. They had to pay the owners of the vehicles a rent of 20 or 22 rupees a day, according to the condition of the vehicle. There were too many of them in Delhi, Prakash explained, maybe two and a half lakhs. How many is that? A quarter of a million. Many of them slept on the side of the road, on their vehicle, with their body in the passenger seat, their legs on the crossbar and feet on the handlebars. Others lived, six or eight, in a small rented room.

Frank was moved. Although he had visited the country several times before, he had come to look upon the poor almost as part of the land-scape, an aspect of the street furniture; and he was ashamed of his own capacity for indifference. On the way to the hotel, they saw an old man pedalling up the slight incline of the street; the sweat covered his face and stringy torso as he strained every muscle to turn the wheels. In the back sat a young couple, a woman in a dark saree and a man in a white shirt, slacks and sandals. Their arms were around each other; and on their lap was the corpse of a child of about four, an inert bandaged shape, covered with a mosaic of gold and crimson flower petals, which they were taking to the burning ground.

Frank began to feel grateful to the young man, privileged because he was showing him what ought to have been obvious, and yet until then had remained unnamed and therefore unseen. As they walked, Prakash took his hand. His companion withdrew it quickly, looking around to see if anyone had witnessed this gesture of affection. He said primly, I'm sorry, but in the West, men don't walk hand in hand in the street. Why not? People will think that there is something bad between them. After that, Prakash never attempted to hold his hand in public again; and as Frank saw the young people in the city who touched one another, held hands, even walked with their arms around each other, he became aware that he had gratuitously denied himself an experience that he would have rel-ished, and which everyone here took for granted.

He had of course noticed that it was quite normal for men to walk with their hands lightly clasped in another's. At first, he thought this meant they were gay. The young man laughed. The laws against homosexuality had been enacted by the British, and never repealed. And although rarely enforced, it remains an offence punishable by life imprisonment.

Later, Frank came to recognise a sub-erotic component in many of the public relationships between men; maybe because of the segregation of the sexes, maybe because these were cities of lone migrant males, hundreds of kilometres from their home. But everywhere, he was aware of a tenderness, a sweetness between men that would never have been observable at home. He sometimes looked at men in the street, and instead of their gaze turning stony and hostile beneath his glance, they would smile at him, a dazzling look of complicity and sympathy.

They checked in at the hotel. The receptionist looked at them without suspicion. It's all right, Prakash explained, men share rooms all the time here. But what he had not perhaps realised is that foreigners and Indians do so more rarely, especially if the foreigner is older than his companion; and they became uncomfortably aware of the stares of some of the younger waiters and room-boys. Frank imagined he heard a snigger; and he gave an excessive tip by way of appeasement.

The room was a sad place, the carpet thin and full of dust, the curtains and the bedcovers shiny with use. It had at one time been colour-washed, but a mildewy stain covered the area beneath the window, and flakes of whitewash drifted down from the ceiling onto the beds. There was a fan, which squeaked and groaned as its metal blades rotated. It looked insecure, and Frank foresaw that one day it would fall and hack to pieces those in the beds beneath. There was a television, but the bare wires had been stuck into the socket for the plug; the light bulbs flickered. The showerhead sent jets of tepid water in all directions; the drain overflowed. Some red-coloured cockroaches scuttled away when the white strip light was turned on, a light that hummed and sang. The foreigner was amused by the pretentious restaurant, with its silver service and absence of diners. The waiters stood in formal poses, waiting for customers who never came, an imperial statuary of servitude.

The young man was nervous; the contrast with his earlier behaviour confirmed his friend's view that everything he had said was genuine. He took no initiative, but was compliant and passive; although once again, he appeared to show little curiosity about his companion. He didn't appraise his body, or look him up and down; he seemed too preoccupied with his own reactions, the inhibition which he had had to overcome in order to find himself in this place with this stranger. For the young man, even this dingy hotel room represented a level of luxury he had never seen. He seemed unwilling to take off his clothes, and wore singlet and dhoti which were his normal night-time wear. Frank was surprised and touched by his friend's lack of guile and a physical modesty that was close to shame. He tried to suppress a laugh, which came out as a grin, and the young man smiled back at him, a smile so artless and open that Frank felt the first surge of spontaneous affection.

Prakash was uncertain. He didn't know what to do, what conventions to observe. There was none of the ritualised preamble with which Frank was familiar from pick-ups at home. The boy clearly had little awareness of how attractive he was; and this induced a twinge of guilt in the older man. It made him feel like an exploiter. He had, of course, heard of Westerners who go to the Third World and buy young women and men; but then, he reflected, it had not been he who had initiated this encounter. The young man later explained his hesitancy by saying that the teacher – the only other sexual partner he'd had – had repeated the same actions each time they met. He had never taken the lead, but had simply waited for the teacher to determine the pace and pattern of their encounter. There had been only the ritualised approach, the sexual act had been brief and functional, and although the teacher had been kind, there had been little expression of tenderness or direct emotion.

Frank took off his clothes and looked at the young man. He admired the powerful muscular legs. A herring-bone of dark hair went from his chest to his groin, but apart from that his skin was smooth. He asked him to take off his dhoti and vest. He did so, but shielded his genitals with his hand. He said he thought his cock was small, and he always tried not to display himself in the shower at camp.

Frank touched him; he shivered and closed his eyes. As his arms closed around him, he felt that Prakash was trembling slightly. He caressed his head, which rested on the older man's chest. He kissed his face, his neck, his chest and nipples, and the young man's breath came faster. His eyes were closed, and his mouth relaxed in a dark crimson ellipse, so that the end of his tongue could be seen, a pale rose-coloured petal between silver teeth. On the tip of his cock a bead of liquid, a transparent crystal of desire. He turned his back towards Frank, the flexible ripple of the spine beneath the dark skin, the sturdy muscular buttocks. Frank made no effort to penetrate him; but held him close, and came between his legs. The young man appeared not to want to come. Immediately, he leapt from the bed, and rushed to the shower to clean himself.

Frank was disappointed, the more so when Prakash crept into bed, still half-wet, and curled up with his back to him. He thought it an anticlimax, deeply unsatisfactory. Taking his cue from his own experience, he assumed it would be without consequences. There seemed little reason to arrange any further meeting. He resigned himself to what was for him a familiar experience – a breakfast of constrained politeness, an exchange of addresses and then oblivion. With these chill thoughts, he drifted into sleep, wondering about the likelihood of fleas or bed-bugs. Yet during the night, he felt the young man's feet on his legs; he reached out and Prakash crept into his arms, foetal, yielding, and clung to him with an intensity that took the foreigner by surprise. He stroked the young man's hair in the darkness, held him close; and eventually, he fell into a deeper sleep, under the impression of something inexpressibly sweet and trusting.

Of course, thought Frank, he is gay. No question about it. A boy from a house dominated by women, with no significant male influence in his life; idolised by his mother, waited upon by his sister. A classic example.

Then he felt slightly ashamed at the stereotype he had described to himself. Such crude summaries could never account for another's reality, and he felt a movement of revulsion against his own reductive categories; or rather, the reductive categories of his culture which, in all other respects, he repudiated. He wondered at the courage it had required for Prakash to approach him in the street; what months and years of denial and pretence had gone into his efforts to forget the friendship with the teacher. What did the army mean to him, the company of young men – what had he sought from them that he had not found? What about the months of relentless practice, the endless running that always returned to the same spot, the denial of his sexuality. He must try not to interpret everything in the light of his own experience, a light that was turning out to be far less illuminating than he had assumed. And then he felt a second wave of repugnance against his own judgments: normally, gay men in the West judged whether someone was or wasn't 'good sex', a bleakly diminished assessment which usually determined whether a subsequent meeting would be 'profitable'. Why should he be governed by such unmerciful conventions, a kind of psychic market economics, by which people in the West had become accustomed to judge each other – what do I get out of it, what's in it for me, where's the pay-off, is it a worthwhile investment of my time and feelings, what is the bottom line?

The young man was up early. He showered, and Frank was alarmed to see him open the door before it was light. For a moment, he thought He's taking my belongings. He sat upright in bed and turned on the lamp. The young man said I'm going for my practice. I'm going to run to Nehru

Stadium and back. You sleep.

After an hour or so, he came back, filling the room with his warmth and energy. Frank looked at his alert and quickened body with admiration. Prakash fiddled with the television, and even sat and watched the singing of Vande Materam with the image of the sunrise on the screen. Frank wanted to touch him, but he held back; there was something unreachable, something intact and enclosed about his physical presence: a matutinal severity, which suggested a wish to cancel the vulnerability of night-time. He sat and watched the news in Hindi; then some tedious programme about traditional crafts in Rajasthan which his friend did not even attempt to follow.

The young man, he noticed, repeatedly glanced at himself in the glass; a look of appraisal, even self-admiration. But he could not be still; he walked to the window, he looked into Frank's bag, and took out his stick deodorant and after-shave; played with his razor, gazed in wonder at the stock of medicaments regarded by Westerners as indispensable for venturing into a diseased and impoverished India. Then he gazed out onto the courtyard below. The building was of concrete, crumbling, so that the rusty metal reinforcing rods of the structure were visible. One day it would surely collapse; he could imagine the paragraph in the newspaper, 100 killed in Delhi hotel disaster, another brief news item to confirm to the West that India was the site of endless tragedy and incompetence. No doubt, corruption had ensured so many rake-offs to the construction company that they had skimped on the materials of an already flimsy design.

They ate breakfast together in the restaurant, with its ornate wooden chairs and dark green carpet stained with ancient spillages of coffee and tea. A dingy gauze curtain separated the restaurant from the grounds outside, the oleanders that grew close to the building served as a shield against the busy road beyond, with its half-naked rickshaw pullers washing themselves under a public tap. Frank noticed a sleek rat that crept around the window. It faced up to a skinny ginger cat; the cat backed off and the rat went on its way.

Prakash had to go back to camp. He promised to return in the evening. Frank walked with him to the bus. Why do you have to go? I have to. He took his training very seriously. His friend was amused. It's not as if you're an Olympic champion, he said. The young man's face darkened. You don't understand, he replied coldly. Frank regretted his levity about something so important to his friend. He had not yet understood that the body which he so admired was the sole guarantee of security that his mother and sister would ever know. The young man looked at him; in his eyes a profound pain and hostility, a reproach to the older man's incomprehension of the jarring ambiguities which lay behind the cultivation of his body. After that, Frank never again made light of the earnestness with which Prakash pursued his career.

This abrupt departure characterised what was to become their relationship. The young man was always dashing off – to see his friend who lived on the premises of the railway stadium, to visit the landowner, who also had a house in Delhi, to meet friends, to buy something for his mother, to get some new running shoes, to do errands he had undertaken for others in camp; and especially to practice. He always came back late, but invariably affectionate, yielding and eager to please. Sometimes Frank offered to accompany the young man on his excursions into Delhi, but it was clear that he preferred to be alone. The relationship was for the night-time only, locked away, private, sequestered. It must not be allowed to invade the business of daily life, of real life. But at the end of each day, their friendship was renewed with great tenderness; and Frank was reluctant to break the pattern they had established. He spent much of the day arranging meetings with people to whom he had an introduction, but they seemed savourless in contrast to the time spent with his friend. He visited politicians in their extensive white bungalows, with their clerks and servants, and they spoke to him in infuriatingly polite clichés about India, as though he had never visited the country; while he felt what he had learned from his companion was worth far more than the courteous pleasantries which, under any other circumstances, he would have found both delightful and instructive.

He delayed his departure from Delhi. He was suppposed to be visiting some projects in other parts of India; he had some people to meet in Mumbai before the end of the month. But he surrendered to a kind of compelling indolence, which he had never known in himself, something that immobilised him, and installed him in the pleasurable yet irritating circumstances of perpetual waiting. He had previously prided himself that he always kept appointments punctually, and that when people failed to turn up, he gave them no more than fifteen or twenty minutes before making alternative arrangements for his night out, his visit to the theatre. And now here he was, on the sagging bed, its cover shiny with wear, looking out onto the orange dusk of Delhi, the subsiding violet thunderclouds and the faint blossoms of street lights overwhelmed by the inky warmth of the night. He telephoned his hosts to say he had been taken ill and would contact them later. Illness was always a plausible alibi in India, especially in the monsoon.

They fell into a habit of eating in the same restaurant, where they soon became known. The best table was reserved for them on the balcony, from where they could look down on the tourists all with their Lonely Planet guides to India. Frank was pleased with his relationship with the young man, and its public visibility; he felt it gave him privileged access to an India which few knew – poring over their tourist guides and obediently being directed to the ruins of earlier empires. It gave him a feeling of slight superiority, and although he was somewhat ashamed of this, it never left him altogether. Most visitors to Delhi stayed only two or three days, long enough to visit the Qutab Minor, the Red Fort, a day in Agra. But he remained; the rain ceased, the sky was serene; the nights become cooler. He came almost to savour the sweet indecisiveness which he felt he could end at any time, but which, he imagined, he was choosing not to.

A strong physical bond grew between them. It was not quite the same thing as sexual obsession; and this was the first thought to trouble Frank's understanding of his new relationship. It was something he had not reckoned with. Yet they were powerfully drawn together; and he derived from their tender companionability an elusive satisfaction which he could not define; was it, he wondered, thwarted paternal feeling, a brotherly complementarity, an undirected erotic longing? But then he blamed himself for trying to invent categories for the nameless but agreeable sentiment which flooded him in the young man's presence. When they were out together, however, in the street, on the overcrowded Delhi buses, Prakash became curiously detached. It was as though he was anxious to forestall any possibility that other people might read something too profound into their being together. He was capable of displaying great nonchalance, as though he had been thrown by chance into the company of his companion. Once or twice, a complicit rickshaw driver had invited Prakash to share with him the overcharged fare, and he was angry that his fellow-countryman could imagine nothing in their being together beyond the crudest kind of exploitative relationship.

Now it was Prakash who refused to take his friend's hand, as they walked in the street. Frank understood the interdict on being gay; the cruel statute that remained in the Indian penal code, the archaic puritanism that governed official relations between people, and was still embodied in legalistic regulations; old colonial administrative practice embalmed in the comfortable somnolence of bureaucratic behaviour. The only thing was that in every other particular – and probably in this one, too, if he had known India more deeply – everybody evaded the petty restrictions, even though it often required a great deal of ingenuity and time to do so, Even the sanction of the law did not deter people from coming up to him in the street and offering explicit invitations. 'I want to suck your cock' had been one opening remark from a man who had fallen in with him as he made his way across the railway bridge to the hotel. Another had followed him for half a day. Frank had begun to wonder if he was not being shadowed by the police. But in the end, the man approached him – a young man, not much over twenty – and said 'Is it true that people in your country like homosex'. Frank had, by this time, become too preoccupied with his friend's comings and goings to pursue anyone else, so he let pass the kind of opportunity that came all too rarely at home now, and would have afforded material for anecdote and speculation with his friends for days afterwards.

Yet in the end, there was also something unsatisfactory between them. For the foreigner, it had always been axiomatic that relationships were the central reality of life. It was irksome to him, this compulsion of Prakash to attend scrupulously to his occupation of athlete for some second-rate team. (He never said that now to his friend.) Frank, on the other hand, had simply abandoned his purpose in coming to India, and delayed his return to work at home. He knew, of course, that he himself was well off, there was little danger that he would be unemployed or without resource. To Prakash, the threat of destitution for himself and others overrode the pursuit of friendship, no matter how appealing. If he was concerned to win his races, this was only symbolic of a grimmer victory, because what he really had to win was a livelihood that would enable him to send money back home each month. Of the 2,000 rupees which the Army paid him, he sent half to his mother. It seemed to Frank that the young man's mind was always, in part, there, in the little town in the foothills of the Himalayas; and it came to irritate him, to cause him a kind of jealousy. An obstacle to access – but to what? He could never quite say.

One day, just before the end of the rainy season, the monsoon had redoubled its intensity; a day of lashing rain from great pendulous folds of grey nimbus that threatened to collapse on the city like the sagging fabric of an ill-erected tent. The streets ran with water, the motor rickshaw drivers placed plastic sheets beside their doors, but the rain still managed to penetrate everything. The cycle rickshaw men sat under their hoods, mournfully contemplating the rain. For the poor, nothing changed. The vendors waited for customers under their collapsing umbrellas, while the rain washed clean the piles of aubergines, cauliflowers, tomatoes, so these shone purple, cream and scarlet, and the rupee notes became soggy and stuck together. The people in the jhuggi-jopris could not keep the rain from their hovels, and the women were incessantly sweeping back the mud-coloured water that swirled around their ankles as they tried to light the stove and cook chappatis.

The young man arrived one evening, and announced that he had to go home immediately. He was uneasy and agitated. A letter had arrived at camp, written eight days earlier, to say that his sister was unwell. The mother did not know what the illness was. She had been to the hospital, but was losing weight rapidly. There had been some question of an operation. He asked Frank to go with him. They would not stay in his house, because, he said, it is too poor for you. There is no bathroom, no electricity. We will go to Kalgotri, a little further up the hills. That is a resort. We will go to a hotel there, and then next morning go down to where I live.

Frank protested that of course it was no problem to stay in the house. The young man shouldn't think that all people from the West had always been rich. He himself had grown up in a poor neighbourhood; his parents had been factory workers. He understood why people were ashamed of the poverty of their home, but with him, there was no need for such scruples. It really didn't matter. Yet the subtleties of the Western class system were incomprehensible to the young man. For him, his friend was scarcely a social being at all. Frank knew he was the beneficiary of a racism that inferiorised everything in India and exalted the West. Although he hated it, he could not quite bring himself to throw away the advantage this earned him. He tried to compensate by his enthusiasm for India, and by disparaging his own country. It didn't work.

Prakash insisted. He had to go. It might be a matter of life or death, They would get the early bus to Dehra Dun. It would mean leaving at five-thirty in the morning. Frank seemed doubtful. Please come, his friend entreated; and he placed his head on one side and smiled, displaying the gap in his silver teeth. Frank wanted to protest, I have my work, I'm late, I should be back home by now. But he said Of course I'll come.

Eight

DURING THE DAY while his friend returned to camp, Frank had time to reflect. Prakash evidently found it a great relief to talk about himself; and he continued to do so without reserve, with an openness that was very different from the candour with which Frank spoke about his life. In Frank's experience, the early phase of a new relationship was always a time for the exchange of confidences; it had happened so many times that Frank had a quite polished version of his life story at his finger-tips; none of the hesitancies and stumblings of his new friend. It was here no question of the over-rehearsed confessions which had become part of the preamble of most gay friendships Frank had known; and he soon realised that Prakash had revealed himself more completely to him, a foreigner, than to anyone he had known before. He was touched, and, he admitted, flattered.

Frank made no effort to match the disclosures of his friend. In any case, if he had tried, Prakash would certainly misunderstand the flippant references about how he and his brother had failed to grow up together, in ways so radically different that they had remained strangers to each other. And how could he speak of his mother, the need to extricate himself from her suffocating embrace, to the young man who unashamedly admitted that he loved his mother more than anyone else in the world. What would he have made of the story that Frank's mother had refused to acknowledge his gender for the first six months of his life, but had dressed him as a girl; so extreme was her desire for a daughter that it had blinded her to the physical reality of her child.

Yet as time went by, under the influence of the young man's ardent and touching sincerity, Frank, although he remained silent, began to experience his own life in a way quite different from the stylised presentation which had grown with repeated telling. It was as though something lay frozen within him, and the sweet ingenuousness of his new friend was beginning to thaw the numbness beneath the surface. He felt it as pain once more. He thought of his mother with a new, forgotten tenderness; and his separation from her no longer seemed quite the triumph of self-determination it had once appeared. He remembered afresh, and with an old distress from which he had thought himself finally free, even the cruel, ugly moments fixed in his memory, tableaux of horror that he had later learned to describe with verbally adroit incisiveness. He had always claimed to have had an absent father, even though he lived under the same roof.

He drove a truck, and used the vehicle for other kinds of freight than that which he was paid for. One night, he remembered, his father had come home, late, and Frank had heard his mother screaming at him. 'You stink of whores,' she was crying; and the child had not understood, thinking she was talking of horses; and he wondered that his father should be chided in this way for his association with creatures so sleek and splendid. Terrified, he had watched from the top of the stairs; they had not even noticed his presence, so caught up in their own drama. Frank had forlornly gone back to bed rather than disturb their intense, excluding quarrel. Next day, he had said to his mother 'Why is it wrong to smell of horses?' This story had entertained all his friends at university. It had ceased to be a searing memory, but had become a piece of the social coinage in which people paid for their right to the company of others.

One day, Frank's father did not return. To the child's persistent questions – he was eight – Frank's mother refused to reply. Later, he asked his aunt, a woman of similar sombre and taciturn sensibility, and she said to him that Daddy had gone to live with the angels. He had taken this piece of information to his mother who had laughed, a bitter, cold mockery of laughter, and said that there weren't many angels in Runcorn, as far as she knew, but of course, she might have been misinformed. After a few weeks, he reappeared, contrite, and begging to be taken back. His mother had agreed, but from that day, until Frank went to university ten years later, she did not speak to him. Not a single word passed between them. Sometimes, they communicated through the children; and Frank referred to this as his early training as a medium. Dumbness descended on their relationship.

But the silence was powerful, intensified by the feelings of resentment, anger and betrayal which found, as it were, their home in a muteness that was turbulent, unquiet, profoundly expressive. Later, Frank realised they had kept up a significant dialogue through the years of silence, a communication which had been curiously satisfying to both of them, even though it had been a torment to the children.

He realised that she was a deeply unhappy woman, with a temperament of Victorian melancholy which she expressed in the sombre imagery of a decayed religious tradition. For her, life was a burden. She used words like woe and grief and sorrow, and spoke of her trials; even though she did not believe she would be judged at the end of them. During her lifetime, Frank said, she forefeited her belief in the life to come, but this occurred too late for her to be able to enjoy this one.

She turned to Frank for consolation. He thought bitterly that she demanded from him what she ought to have provided him with – security and protection. Instead, she wanted him to comfort her, to reassure her, even to give her life a meaning. She wanted company in her misery, like an imperious noblewoman demanding that a companion travel with her into a distant and dangerous country from which she might not return.

She was explicit about her disappointment with her husband, what she saw as his betrayal. She did not conceal the rapid decay of their sexual relationship, in spite of his inability to stay away from women. She spoke to her son as though he were an adult, and a female at that, a sister or confidante. He later realised he had resumed the role she had ascribed to him at birth. This was his punishment for being male. He had listened to her long anguished monologue of the strange, mysterious desires of men, their inconstancy and incontinence. Her own inability to contain herself was wholly emotional; and her fierce feelings broke their banks frequently, and flooded her son until he almost drowned in them. She urged him to grow up, to become anything, as long as it wasn't a man.

One of the consequences of the relentless pent-up secrets which she poured into his scarcely comprehending ear was that it drove Frank increasingly out of the home. Unhappily, in the small industrial town, there was nowhere to go. He walked the streets until he knew every feature of the bleak, stony landscape; the abandoned mill-buildings with their broken windows and nailed-up doors, still black with decades-old grime; the red-brick funnels of streets where ancient cobblestones appeared through layers of tar; the area designated for slum clearance, the intimate bedroom wallpaper flapping in the wind, black grates where fires had once blazed, the winter sunlight streaming through the rafters of a roofless house. He walked around the new industrial estates, designed to provide employment in place on the declining textile industry, light engineering works and factories that produced food – cans of acid-green peas and slices of pink cold meat in plastic packets. He looked at the old people in the streets – men in mufflers and bent whiskery women who had been made stone deaf by the clatter of looms, and who had learned to lip-read, redundant now, an embarrassment, as they haunted the sites of demolished mills and vanished workplaces.

The park, with its statue of Queen Victoria still holding the sceptre and orb, but her features effaced by the weather and industrial smoke, was his favourite destination. In it, there was a pavilion modelled on the Crystal Palace, but with most of the glass lying broken on the floor; whenever you walked on it, it had the satisfying crunch of walking on bones. Here teenagers took shelter from the winter storms, and had their first experience of sex.

There was an aviary, a short alley with green-painted metal cages containing peacocks and pheasants, canaries and flamingoes, and a small museum which exhibited a model of St Paul's Cathedral constructed from matchsticks. There were two or three paintings of the Dolby family, to whose house this park had originally been attached, and a re-creation of a mill, circa 1840, with dusty papier-maché models of operatives at their looms. Around these, schoolteachers tried in vain to inculcate into groups of incurious children some sense of their own past, a past from which they had been severed.

But the real fascination for him was the public lavatory close to the road, a secluded place of laurels and privet, with crazy paving that led to a cavernous urinal, He would sit and watch the comings and goings of men – few women seemed to use the facility. He noted that some people remained inside for half an hour, an hour or more. Men leaned their cycles in the bushes; occasionally a car or lorry remained parked on the road for hours at a time. He was frightened, yet drawn to the place. Once or twice, he had entered, but there was no one there; the doors of the cubicles were locked.

It was there, in this desolate, exciting place, that he acknowledged he was attracted to men. One day he had gone into the urinal: a white ceramic slab with rusty pipes dripping into the slate trough below. As he stood there, a middle-aged man came and stood next to him. Instead of pissing, he moved his hand to and fro over his penis. Frank peered round the cracked white wing of the stall. The man seized Frank and pushed him roughly into one of the cubicles, locking the door. Terrified, the boy had made no move to escape; and the man had forced the penis into his mouth and was moving it so fiercely that he thought he would choke. A few seconds it seemed, and he withdrew, discharging a salty liquid which dribbled down his chin and onto his nice Fair Isle jumper. The man threw his still swollen and dripping cock into his trousers as though he were locking an escaped beast into its cage. Furiously he did up the buttons of his trousers, slammed the door and left Frank trembling, shivering with cold and shame.

Frank walked around the town, and saw it as one whose life has been radically changed always sees things; with a new consciousness, a more intense clarity, which was in fact the external aspect of the transformation of his own inner life. The sooty parish church, the dingy secondhand shops, with their imitation-coal electric fires and rustic-cottage teapots, that gave way to the grander emporia of the chain stores, the Home and Colonial, where women shaped pats of butter with wooden spatulas and cut cheese with wire, the gentlemen's outfitters with their tweeds and twill. It was not the brusque horror of the experience that frightened him; it was rather that he now knew something about himself that could not be unlearned or forgotten, the irreversibility of consciousness.

After two or three weeks, the remembered violence faded. After that, it seemed to him that sex was everywhere in the dingy, repressed little town. If he went to the cinema, he would notice which men changed their seats, whether they sat next to a young woman alone or sought out a boy. At the bus station, he observed the older men at the bus-stands who struck up conversations with schoolboys, and who saw with indifference the buses they were apparently waiting for come and go. It was as though he had been given a vital clue to the mysterious behaviour of adults, which, despite her explicit confidings, his mother had never provided.

There was one cinema, not far from the industrial area where they lived, half-tiled, with round windows ornamented with stone laurel wreaths. There, he could wait in the dingy foyer with its fly-blown pictures of stars on the walls, and ask to be taken in by an adult. He always chose a man on his own, who would sometimes buy him an ice cream or sweets, and press his thigh close to him in the darkness. In the winter evenings, even in the grimy urinal which smelled of beer and emptied directly into the dingy canal beneath, there would sometimes be workmen furtively masturbating in the fog, while the homegoing buses and cycles clanged and shrilled around them. He did not know how he found his way to these places; he simply knew they were there, guided by an instinct unlocked by the rusty bolt on the door of the cubicle in the park.

None of this secret life appeared at home or at school. His mother would sit and look at him, until he could no longer bear her eyes upon him; a devouring tenderness which he neither deserved nor wanted. Frank was also clever; and he became the vessel for all her thwarted ambitions and the education that had been denied her. She never tired of telling him how she had passed the exam for the Grammar School, but her mother had said it was not for people like them to fill their head with fancy ideas; the next day she took her to start work as a dressmaker's apprentice in one of the big shops in the town centre. To his role as provider of meaning was also added that of social redemption.

Frank did not work hard at school, but relied on an intuitive intelligence to help him through. He had friends, but was separated from them by the knowledge he had of sex, and which found no counterpart in their sniggers and jokes and drawings of what they imagined women's genitalia looked like. He fell in love with boys in his class, and could not understand why the intensity of his own feelings failed to draw forth a similar response from the object of his infatuation. Once or twice, he went to stand outside the house of one of these boys; in the numbing cold, he watched the semi-detached house with the stained-glass image of a yacht in the front door and the dead rustling heads of hydrangeas in the front garden; he strained for a glimpse of the bedroom as a woman closed the curtains, a room in which only the plywood back of the dressing table was visible from the road.

No one from his family had been to university before. His father expressed the view that he ought to roll up his sleeves and do a proper job, but his mother organised a tearful ceremonious farewell; appropriately valedictory, as it turned out, because he never went back to live there again. He amused his friends with what they regarded as exaggerated stories of the deprivation with which he had grown up – the frost flowers on the windowpane of his bedroom, where it was so cold that even the piss in the bucket was covered with ice; the father who had taken to sleeping in the cab of his truck rather than return to the violent conjugal silences which were more debilitating than any argument could have been.

Frank was at university at the time of Gay Liberation; and this was for him a moment of revelation. He had until then known only the word homosexual to describe himself, an idea that had been reinforced by the reference books he had consulted in the Public Library. It was a recognised condition, a pathological one at that; and it had a precise significance. It meant what men did together. It designated sexual activity only. Frank believed in words, and he assumed that those to whom the word referred were doomed to act forever within its cold prescriptive meaning. He had felt a profound attraction to boys at school; but sex was something brief and secretive, associated with toilets in the park and the darkness of the cinema. He had deduced from this experience that such men were destined to seek each other out for sexual contact only, but could never find love, fulfilment or other kinds of satisfaction together. In fact, he had set out to meet halfway a tragic destiny of permanent exclusion, when he discovered that the people in the Gay Society at university were talking about something else: not merely claiming sexual freedom, but also proclaiming real, loving relationships between gay men and women.

There had followed a number of friendships, some of them briefly passionate; that none lasted more than a year or so did not trouble him. If he found it impossible to restrict himself to a single partner, this became a virtue under the influence of the new ideology of liberation. He still experienced romantic attachments, as he deprecatingly called them, but generally, the split between sex and friendship, sex and love, remained: a wound that refused to heal. Frank attributed this to the influence of his family. 'Not a broken home,' he would say, 'but an internal fracture, which went untreated.'

He stayed in the city where he had studied, and became a teacher in a Comprehensive School. It wasn't that he chose a career; rather that teaching at that time seemed a reasonable option: secure employment, with long holidays. He wasn't entirely cynical, however. Although he didn't quite express it like this, he did entertain some hope that he might lessen for the next generation the joyless rigours of learning to which he had been subjected. His mother's sentimentality about teachers had been in sharp contrast to the aloof and pretentious academics who supervised his intellectual and mental development at the Grammar School. In reaction against this, he thought he could also make himself more accessible to his pupils. He had had no teacher in whom he would have dreamed of confiding, teachers were there to cultivate the mind only; another split, another fissure in the multiple fragmentings of his upbringing.

He brought a certain crusading zeal to his first job; identified himself with the young people he taught. At twenty-three, he was on their side, as he told himself (and his pupils too), a fact which they failed to recognise. Tolerant, libertarian, easy-going; he soon discovered that such qualities were not admired. It rapidly appeared to him that those he was supposed to educate had been educated already, formed by different values, another culture. The boys would tell him jokes. Sir, what's the difference between a lorry-load of gravel and a lorry-load of dead babies? You can't unload gravel with a pitch-fork. Have you heard about the new German microwave oven? It seats six. Why do Pakis carry shit in their wallets? For identification. He was shocked.

He spent so much energy explaining to them why these jokes were cruel and illiberal, what they meant, and the horrors to which they would lead. He dwelt at length on the Holocaust and how it had convulsed Europe, and tried to show them that they were the beneficiaries of the better world that had been achieved. He decided he would get them out into the community, doing things for other people. He organised visits to elderly people on the estate, to do errands, dig gardens, clean houses. He discovered one group of his pupils had been exacting payment from an old lady for their weekly trip to Tesco's; an old man's cat lost half its tail. One boy sold to a market stallholder a number of little treasures belonging to an old couple, and Frank had to go and buy them back one Saturday morning.

Nothing seemed to dent their sensibility. He could not understand it. His mother had spoken of her teachers with tears in her eyes. He, it seemed, figured only on the margins of the lives of those nominally in his charge. The peer-group, the mass media, the parents – all of these he saw as malignant obstacles to the message of liberation which he thought he was delivering.

But the greatest shock lay, as usual, not in the realm of intellectual revelation. There was a boy in his class, solitary, aloof from the others; a fifteen-year-old, the son of a single mother who worked in a baker's shop close to the school. He had sad blue eyes and ash-blond hair. Sometimes, he would linger after school, as though he wanted to talk to Frank. Frank found himself drawn to the boy, and saw, or thought he saw, something of himself in the fate of the unhappy youth. One day, towards the end of the summer term, the boy was waiting for him at the bus-stop. When the bus came, he sat beside him, and said with suppressed and irresistible urgency that he needed to talk to him.

Frank arranged to meet him in a city centre cafe early in the first week of the holidays. Before the appointment, he was unusually nervous and strangely exalted. He looked at himself in the glass; still in his twenties, his hair was already thinning, but he still appeared youthful, and had always dressed fashionably, a self-conscious presentation, role-model and object of obscure hero-worshippings; or so he believed, although he had never articulated this to himself.

The boy seemed eager – over-eager – to tell him that he liked men, that he didn't know what to do about it. Will it go away? Is it just a phrase I'm going through. Phase, Frank corrected him. But he responded to his apparent confusion, and reassured him. I'm gay, Frank said, so it's not such a terrible thing. The boy expressed incredulity. It is always a struggle, Frank told him solemnly, because in spite of the formal decriminalisation of homosexuality, nothing could be done to alter the attitudes of intolerant people. But things were changing; at that time, Frank still believed in social progress. He was deeply touched by the boy's sincerity; he thanked him politely and said Frank had been a great help to him. He made no mention of any further meeting, and Frank was disappointed when he left him abruptly at the cafe entrance, saying I wouldn't want anybody to see us. Frank watched him; he skipped down the road, knocked over a litter bin and kicked a dented tin Coke can into the windscreen of an approaching car. It was not until the first day of the following term, when he found graffiti all over the school building, telling the world that he was a pouf and a queer, that Frank realised his error.

He resigned, and the following spring moved to London, where he taught sociology in an adult education college. Afterwards, he took great care to separate his personal life from his place of work; a split which he had believed, in the moment of liberation, would no longer be necessary.

None of this could he tell his new friend; nor how, at home, he felt increasingly at odds with the spirit of the times; how the people who were running the country were strangers to all the values he had grown up to cherish; how they had devalued compassion; how being a do-gooder had become a terrible term of abuse, as though to do evil were both more natural and more desirable; how inequality had become, not a social wrong to be mitigated, but an instrument of policy, indispensable to the mysteries of wealth-creation.

He could speak, neither of his personal experience, nor of the social context in which it had all taken place. Normally, this would have seemed to him an intolerable privation, and a barrier to understanding his companion; but with Prakash, he wonderingly acknowledged, it did not matter. As he held him close, the consoling presence was enough. It did not need words. The young man's lack of curiosity about him gradually ceased to be an irritant; and he sank into the silences between them – so different from the punitive silences of his parents – as a tired traveller might fall into bed after a long arduous journey.

But that was not all; under the influence of his friend's admission that he loved his mother more than anyone in the world, Frank began to feel within himself, like the movement of ancient rusty machinery, the stirring of sentiments he had long suppressed. He had learned to be dismissive of his parents; even of his father's death he had said 'Oh he forgot to wake up one morning; but then he was never really alive, so no one really noticed it.' And he became aware of the pain he had stifled, the pathos of lives which had marked him so deeply, the scars of broken kinship which he had thought hardened by time. And he buried his face in his friend's arms and wept; tears which Prakash could not understand. But he stroked Frank's balding head tenderly, as though he, and not the older man, were the protector and the comforter. As they set out for the Prakash's home, Frank felt for the first time that, despite the young man's deference to him, and his superior status, he might not be, after all, in control.

Nine

ON THE day they went to Dehra Dun, they checked out of the hotel before dawn. They found an autorickshaw with some difficulty. The driver wore a grey shawl over his shoulder in the early morning, as though he were still clinging to the sleep from which his work had called him; for the temperature was high and the air sultry. The young man directed him to the Inter-State Bus Terminal. Frank was surprised by the number of people on the street before 5.30. He reflected that if wealth were the reward of hard work, then the people of this blighted, sulphurous, choking city ought to be among the richest people on earth. Along Shaheed Bhagat Singh Road the headloaders were already buying their vegetables for the day, stooped over the baskets of tomatoes, cauliflower and peas. Hamals ran, pushing long carts, already loaded with metal rods for construction, bricks, vanaspati cans, plastic toys, spare parts for motor scooters. At public taps, men were washing, a towel round their waist, their bodies glistening with water in the tepid dawn. On the threshold of jhuggis, women were washing children; with no more than an old soup tin full of water, they scrubbed them clean and dressed them in a neat school uniform, so that when they went out, with the outsize satchel strapped to their back, the girls with hair looped in shining braids and tied with red ribbons, they were transformed; no one would ever know from what wretchedness they had stepped.

The Red Fort stood against the early morning, its rose sandstone crenellations a border of lace in the light from a wasting moon. The Great Mosque spread the pale onions of its domes against fading stars. Already, a line of beggars and mutilated people were in place; a man whose truncated torso rested upon a rubber pad, a deformed boy with chappals on his hands, the blind guided by small children. Elsewhere, some people still slept on the sidewalk; in the half-light, bodies wrapped in a chadar lay still, elongated like corpses, victims of some natural disaster. Food-stalls were already serving breakfast: a blackened teakettle boiling on the gas-ring, the tea ladled into glasses, a ribbon of ochre liquid; a shallow metal pan where vegetable cakes burned in transparent blue smoke. In the jhuggis themselves, the light from a kerosene lamp gleamed through the thin hessian; young women emerged, shaking their head vigorously, and stretching after the cramped night in the single room shared with six or seven others. Here and there, in the gutters, men were shitting, with their backs to the road, the dark excreta that would soon be biodegraded by the sun. Frank reflected that he was more disgusted by the pollution that came from the backsides of the traffic, the trucks and buses that spat out a private smog wherever they passed, a sour choking exhalation that uncoiled itself along the closed road; with nowhere to go, it thinned into streaks of blue fumes that simmered above the surface of the road. On a tiny traffic island, a rectangle of crumbling concrete, a family was living; naked children with runny noses sat chewing an ancient chappati, silently absorbing the waste from the traffic that would numb their brain and corrode their lungs. Frank closed his eyes; but the teeming after-images of human sacrifice would not be shut out.

Inside the Bus Terminal, ancient battered buses came and went, setting up an even greater concentration of gases in the enclosed space. Haryana Roadways vehicles, scratched and dented where they had collided with trucks or cars foolish enough to contest their right of way as they lumbered along the narrow highways. Every two or three minutes another bus departed: to Jaipur, Agra, Madras. Madras? Frank looked again. The journey would take maybe 48 hours or more. He marvelled at the patience of people who would sit in the crowded vehicles uncomplaining in the heat, who could sleep in the most uncomfortable positions, and take up the life they had gone to meet at the other end – a wedding, a visit to a sick brother, a business meeting – as though the long journey had never happened.

The trip to Dehra Dun was relatively short – a mere eight hours, although even this seemed to Frank interminable. All around, the bus station was besieged by crowds, filling up the interior with tin boxes and brown paper packets tied up with rope, dingy suitcases, the precious, pitiful belongings of migrants. When the buses were full, people sat on the roof, hoping that the vehicle would not pass under low bridges. That same day, there had been a mishap near Delhi, when some workers being taken to the brick-fields by bus had simply been swept off the roof by a bridge. Several had been killed.

The suburbs of Delhi passed slowly; Frank was depressed by the extent of the strangely rambling buildings, the ruinous courtyards, inhabited equally by people, goats, buffaloes and fowls. Living here appeared austere, improvised: women washing in a dark smudge of stagnant water, green with algae or dark blue with the pollution from a chemical works. They passed the Indraprasthra Extension, where soaring apartment blocks set in a sea of mud and rubble rose like a separate city; expensive flats at 7½ lakhs of rupees for two rooms, where the newly emerging middle class would live, with their private English-medium schools, their polyclinics and security guards at the gate cocking their rifles at the approach of any visitor; the new middle class, the pride of India's modernisation, the great market coveted by the invading West. In these places, new dependants of the global market were being created; people who would stop at nothing to feed the lifestyle they had gained, who would be prepared to accept any rigours that might be visited upon the poorest, if these were required in order to maintain their small privilege. This alien version of wealth made Frank sad, in a way that indigenous poverty no longer did.

Prakash showed no interest in the scenery which he had, anyway, passed so many times before. He slept, and his head rolled onto his friend's shoulder. Frank was pleased, but he looked round the bus furtively, to see if anyone had noticed that Prakash slept so close against him. No one paid the slightest attention. He enjoyed the jolting intimacy, and in spite of the discomfort, did not disturb the young man who leaned against him with complete abandon. A blurred orange sun was rising through the ubiquitous eucalyptus trees. The foreigner was aware of a rare, growing sensation of well-being, which he was compelled to recognise as happiness.

The bus seemed to have been designed for the penance of travellers. The green plastic seats were upright, devoid of padding and with almost no leg-room. Frank kicked off his shoes and sat cross-legged, his knees in the lap of his sleeping companion, whose head struck gently against him with every movement the bus made. There was an altercation at some checkpoint, when the driver refused to pay a bribe to the soldiers who were posted on all the main roads leading to Delhi.

Later, when he looked back on his time with his friend, the foreigner thought that this day had provided him with the moment of greatest peace and contentment with his companion; even though at the time, it was excruciating to be in the overcrowded bus, with the migrants and a group of Rajasthani pilgrims on their way to one of the holy cities, Rishikesh or Haridwar, with their blankets smelling of goats, and taking it in turns to be sick out of the windows.

Delhi merged into Ghaziabad, forty kilometres away: the trucks, public carriers, brightly painted with flowers and images of gods, festooned with garlands of tinsel, and carrying builders, labourers, the cheapest form of public transport. As the bus emerged into the countryside, it picked up speed. The drive then became terrifying. It seemed to be the objective of all drivers in India to overtake the vehicle in front of them, independently of oncoming traffic, and whether they could see this or not. There were many near misses, calculated by the driver to the last second, before he swerved in front of a bullock cart loaded with fodder in the face of an approaching public carrier, which did not reduce its speed even for a moment. Here and there was evidence of frightful road accidents; trucks overturned, buses and lorries an interlocking tangle of metal and broken glass; some vehicles gutted by fire. In one place, the accident had been recent: the bloodstained bodies of two men were lying on the side of the road, uncovered. The traffic did not pause. If Prakash thought of the day when his friend's son had been killed, he said nothing to his new companion.

Frank had spoken to his friend of the absurdity of dependency upon the growth of road transport, when it was impossible for a Third World country to build the highways it required. He was angry that Western patterns should be transplanted in this way: he thought that it merely caricatures Western development, and reflects how damaging and destructive it is. Somewhere Frank had read that 60,000 people die on the roads of India each year; over 2,000 in Delhi alone. Prakash showed no sign of sharing his concern. His friend fell silent and watched, the panorama of mal-development unrolled. But his disapproval was soon overtaken by the more basic emotion of fear. He became more tense and unhappy, and began to wonder whether his trip to India had not perhaps been a fateful summons to an appointment with violent death. He became momentarily irritated by the serene slumber of the young man, and tried to wake him. His head merely fell forward onto his chest. He slept on. Frank placed an arm around his shoulder, and he stirred in his sleep, nestled closer and relaxed in the protective chamber created by his friend's body.

The journey through the plains of Uttar Pradesh was like a voyage through every form of misguided development it was possible to conceive. Not only the roads that could not bear the traffic expected of them, but the brickfields, where farmers had sold their topsoil and made the rich land unsuitable for agriculture. The red fingers of brick chimneys pointed upwards, while ragged women and children carried headloads of bricks from the kilns to dry in the sun. There were acres of sugar-cane, pale green cockades of stalks and leaves which required the most intensive use of scarce water, much of which was channelled from the foothills into the plains. Everywhere, the deforested lands were bordered by eucalyptus trees, which also need prodigious quantities of water. Many of them had died and their trunks snapped, spectral as bone in the bare earth beneath them, stark as desecrated graveyards.

From time to time the bus stopped, and around the parked vehicle a throng of vendors appeared, even, it seemed, in the middle of nowhere – bananas, sweet limes, channa, peanuts, bags of Uncle Chipps crisps, Cadbury's chocolate, bottles of Pepsi and Mangola. Men pissed unself-consciously at the roadside, an arc of silver, and then shook their uncircumcised cock as though it were a living thing they wanted to punish. The floor of the bus was strewn with paper, orange peel and nutshells. Frank marvelled at the ability of Indians to transcend the filth of their environment and keep themselves scrupulously clean; but this, it seemed, was at the expense of their surroundings, the wanton disregard of which only made the task of keeping clean more arduous. He found it exasperating and incomprehensible.

When they reached Dehra Dun, it was dark. The Doon Valley was a star-specked cavity in the darkness. They changed buses, a smaller vehicle which could manoeuvre the mountain road that led to Kalgotri. By this time, the rain had started again. Visibility was poor, the air cool; but they could still make out the degraded hills, the landslips, the deforested flank of the wounded mountains, the symmetrical replantings of chir or teak. The last 40 kilometres took an hour and a half; the hairpin bends in the mist, the slippery roads, the gorges below; here and there you could see where traffic had left the road and plunged into a ravine. It proved even more frightening than the journey through the plain. The drizzle decorated all growing things with beads of silver.

When the bus arrived in the little hill town, it was surrounded by Nepali labourers and hotel employees, waiting to carry luggage, to offer passengers the competitive comforts of their establishments. They carried huge headloads on their back, secured by a strap around their forehead. The little square became the scene of intense animation and excitement; as though the arrival of the bus were the only important occurrence in a day of eventless monotony. The bus station was sodden, misty and dirty. Ignoring the entreaties of the coolies, they walked beside a polluted stretch of water, which was supposed to be the pride of the little resort. Kalgotri had been selected by the British as the summer capital of the Northern Provinces in the 1840s. It was easy to imagine the women in their sedan chairs shouting their orders to bearers and servants, the imperious sahibs carrying their mildewed papers in chests, hoping that these precious records of imperial transactions would be proof against the destructive power of damp and white ants. The railway had come to the foot of the hill only in the 1890s; the first motorised vehicle reached the uplands in the twenties.

The town was cool and wet; breath condensed in the humid air. The few tourists – not foreigners, but mostly Bengalis, who for some reason travelled all the way from Calcutta to this small and dispiritingly shabby resort – wore raincoats and boots, with quilts around their shoulders against that same rain which must have gladdened the hearts and assuaged the homesickness of generations of administrators of empire.

They saw a rickety colonial hotel perched on the cliffside; terraces and turrets in red slate, with worm-eaten woodwork painted yellow and green. Frank was delighted with its archaic aspect, and begged his friend that they might stay there. They climbed the long stone staircase carved in the cliff, and entered a kind of Victorian conservatory that was used as the reception area. The hotel charged only 200 rupees a night in this off-season time. From the window, they could look down upon the pines, the lime-trees and other familiar species brought by the British in their efforts to recreate the world in their own image. Around the lake were vestiges of rundown colonial architecture – stone churches and schools, bungalows and mouldering administrative buildings; an embalmed and run-down Malvern, was how Frank described it to himself.

The suite where they stayed was cavernous and smelled of mould. There was a kind of outer room, once doubtless used as a sitting or reception room – who did the British exiles receive, wondered Frank, apart from each other, offering decorous and ceremonious example to the unbiddable hill-people? There were decayed wicker chairs and glass-topped bamboo tables; a bedroom with a vast damp bed and moist quilts. An efflorescence of mildew covered the ceiling, and the damp caused the thin filament in the electric light bulb to flicker like a living orange flame. In the bedroom there was a great carved Victorian wardrobe, a chest with a specked and tarnished mirror from which the ghost of a reflection returned. Tea was served in thick cracked cups by lugubrious elderly Nepalis, who lingered, plaintively asking for backsheesh to supplement their earnings, to send back to the even more impoverished homeplace they had fled.

The rain didn't let up; the misty indigo dusk enveloped everything in its wet blanket. They walked round the water under a small umbrella with a floral pattern. The iron machinery of the funicular railway that led to the Himalayan view was still – you couldn't even see the top of the funicular, let alone the distant peaks of the fragile Himalaya. They ate a meal of greasy tomato soup, sticky rice and stringy chicken, but they were light-hearted and good-humoured in the sodden gloom. Prakash said he loved the cool and the mist. His companion said tartly he would feel differently if he had to live with it for more than half the year. That would depend, said his companion. If I was with you I wouldn't mind. They played rummy with a pack of cards the young man found in his bag. Frank always lost; and he was faintly amused by his companion's obvious desire to win at so trivial an occupation. His face was intent, his forehead creased as he inspected the cards in his hand. Afterwards they held each other tight under the damp quilt; the unfamiliarity of the environment, the unreality of the frozen archaism it represented made them laugh. The shortcomings of linguistic understanding were never less evident. It was, perhaps, the happiest night Frank could ever remember; he even said so to his friend, who, however, made no reply.

Ten

THE NEXT morning they went down from Kalgotri to Rangniwas, the little market town where Prakash's family lived. Kalgotri was full of Maruti vans which stood in a row at the bus station. These were taxis, each carrying five or six people, which set off as soon as the drivers had attracted enough passengers to make the journey worthwhile. They took less than half the time of the buses. As they sped around the bends, the passengers were thrown against each other. Frank held on to the plastic handle at the top of the window, and allowed himself to be jolted into agreeably close contact with his friend; he could smell the sweet breath and slightly musty exhalations of his clothing which had been gathering the damp in the cold bedroom all night.

Rangniwas was the frontier of the quite different world of the plains. In the town at the base of the hill it was a great deal warmer. As they walked through the streets, Frank appraised his friend's home place. He loved the villages of India, but as soon as these grew into a town, they became congested, ugly and dirty. There were a couple of smart hotels, for travellers intending to rest before they proceeded to the hills on the following day. There was a green painted temple, with effigies of Hanuman and Ganesh; a white mosque, in front of which a few beggars crouched. Most of the buildings had become discoloured with damp; ornamental carved balconies had crumbled, ironwork rusted. The traffic in the narrow streets suggested strange historical overlappings. The road was shared by pedestrians, women under spreading headloads greater than their bodyweight, oxcarts of green fodder, upon which elderly men sat, ruminating imperturbably while cars designed for Japanese motorways tried to overtake them. Nothing disputed their right to bring the street to a standstill: the same vehicles had followed these roads for a thousand years. There were tangles of bicycles, black and silver, which sometimes got caught up in a single inextricable entity; then the riders had to dismount before they could disengage themselves and continue. Scooters and motorcycles, three-wheelers; then Maruti and Padmini cars, an old Ambassador, vans, trucks and Ashok Leyland snub-nosed goods carriers; always the snorting, honking buses which filled the funnels of the streets with their poisonous smoke. Often, the traffic came to a complete halt. Drivers leaned furiously on their horns. Nothing moved. Most people still travelled by foot, and they easily overtook the dense mass of impeded traffic. On every piece of waste ground, some boys played cricket with improvised stumps – an old tin, a wooden plank. A cow placidly consumed a discarded garland on a rubbish tip, a loop of faded marigolds hanging from her mouth, while a solitary black crow perched on her back.

Prakash stopped at a sweet-shop: a smudged glass stand with some greasy scales, displays of green, tawny and yellow sweets covered with silver paper. Some of the flies which had landed on them could not escape the sugary stickiness, and they had perished, captive, in the deadly sweetness. The stallholder cheerfully filled a cardboard box with this confectionery, leaving an occasional thumb or fingerprint on the surface of each piece. Frank prepared his excuses for not eating them when they were passed round.

They took a cycle rickshaw to where the road petered out. Actually it ceased long before they dismounted from the vehicle, a grassy rutted track across which the cycle lurched, almost ejecting the occupants, who clung to each other and laughed, as they sought to avoid being thrown onto the grass. When they stopped, Frank wanted to offer the driver – a man in his early 20s, with an angry-looking face and very dark skin –

twenty rupees. The young man snatched the note from him, and gave the driver five. Frank protested. He said It's horrible work. I don't like sitting there and being drawn along by someone little more than an adolescent. It makes me feel uncomfortable, like some imperial sahib. Prakash said It's their job. They make an honest living out of it. This isn't Delhi, where foreign money makes them greedy. Frank was abashed by his friend's criticism. It was true. He did offer money over the odds, a compulsive Western guilt at taking advantage of any of the services on offer, because of the unfair exchange rate, because of too keen an awareness of a colonial past. Sometimes, astonished rick-drivers would look at the 100-rupee note he had given them for a journey which should not have cost a third as much; and then Prakash would castigate him, saying You can't make up for all the wrongs that were done by the British. It wasn't that rick-driver who was punished or shot or thrown in jail. They don't understand. Treat people fairly, that's all. It was the same when he gave to beggars, the women miming their hunger outside the restaurant. Prakash would make impatient noises and say They're all controlled by some dada. Then Frank would become angry and say There's nothing wrong with charity. You benefit from it. His friend said with dignity I don't ask you for anything. But you never refuse. That was as close as they came to quarrelling; not very close, but they drew back, having glimpsed gulfs of possible cultural misunderstanding and personal disagreement. When mutual incomprehension finally did come, it was not to be in the realm of social theory.

They walked through a metal gate, beside fields of soya beans. A large house, double-storeyed, with a garden of fruit trees and the sweet smell of frangipani. The hedgerows were full of creepers that grew almost visibly in the warm rain – scarlet bells with long yellow stamens and lilac-coloured flowers that opened their brimming cups to the sky. Bulbuls and shintolas darted among the greenery. Dragonflies and wasps filled the air with the shimmering hum of their wings. For the first time, Frank heard the true sound of India – the infinite rustlings and stirrings of the countryside, the eager palpitations of life, its almost audible flowering, extinction and renewal. He took a deep draught of the humid air and smiled in appreciation at his companion.

The young man paused beside the house of the landowner's family, and pointed out the now derelict cowshed where he had lived. Still shaded by the tamarind tree, the door hung loose on its decayed wooden hinge. Frank was shocked when he learned that it was now home to an old man, who was mentally unbalanced. The landowner gave him shelter and food, and he was supposed to work in the fields; but in fact, his infirmity was such that he could do little. He should be looked after properly, said Frank, thinking of his mother in the nursing home, the converted house of a former mill-owner on the edge of his home town. Who should look after him? His wife is dead and his son has gone to the Gulf. You have to understand, Prakash said, there is no bottom line in India. There is no level below which people are not allowed to fall. Frank was about to say But this is not a poor country. Look at the house of these people, look at the land they have; but he checked himself, because without the charity of the landowner, the man he was with would now be a landless labourer. He looked at the young man, and found it not difficult to imagine him bent over the earth with his broad coarse hands pulling at recalcitrant weeds, standing in the padi-field in ragged shorts, with water up to his knees, knowing nothing of a world beyond the horizon of a ferocious climate of cauterising sun and lashing rain... How close he had come to such a fate, a fate that would certainly have precluded any meeting with him, the visitor from the West. He felt keenly how precarious the young man's security was; and began to understand why he took such pains with his athlete's body – it was either that, or the fields, which would have to yield him a living.

There it is. They still had to cross two more fields, by a zigzag path that followed the boundary of the landowner's property. Then a row of eucalyptus, an irrigation ditch, a shed for the two buffaloes, thatch with stone floor; and, twenty metres beyond, the house that the young man's mother had begun to construct for him. It was, as yet, simply a concrete cube. It stood on a raised platform with a verandah in front, the roof supported by two concrete pillars. There was a second room at the side, where the young man slept. The floor of the verandah was painted red and black, and swept clean of dust. Stacked against a wooden table on the verandah were a number of metal-framed folding chairs with green and white plastic strings. On the left of the building, a small room, which was used as kitchen; a gobargas cooker, some cupboards and shelves stood open to the air. Outside, on a flat stone to keep it cool, stood a round red earthenware pitcher for drinking water. Over the cattle-shed a creeper with swelling pumpkins. A papaya tree with the breast-shaped fruit, a bright unripe green. White starry flowers of chilli pepper. A lemon tree bearing small green globes; mint for making chutney; herbs and sweet orange karvi flowers. Frank was struck by the simplicity of the structure and the enclosure of greenery which sheltered it. He said It's very beautiful. His friend, to whom it was commonplace, nothing like the elaborate structures of the well-to-do in the town, with their ornamental grilles and coloured marble, looked at him quickly to see whether he was mocking him. Frank placed an arm on his shoulder, and squeezed vigorously. His eyes were suddenly, inexplicably, full of tears.

The pale spikes of rice seem to float in their flooded field. There was a patch of broad leaf vegetables; on a blade of one of these a tiny bird sat, so light it scarcely inclined the leaf. Pale grey butterflies rose up from the wet grass, each stalk of which held a row of perfectly formed beads from the previous night's rain.

The mother and daughter greet the stranger, who recites his textbook Hindi. They laugh with embarrassment and pleasure. No foreigner has visited them before. They do not wonder at the man who is a friend of their son, for they know nothing of Delhi, and even less of the nature of the attachments that may sometimes be formed there. Frank experiences a moment of compunction and sadness for what he knows about the son and brother, and they do not; he feels compassion for their inviolate unknowing. Nevertheless he responds to the evident warmth of their welcome. Prakash falls with relief into his native Garhwali, voluble, laughing, at ease. Frank looks with amazement, as his friend is transformed by the language, becomes another person, someone the foreigner does not recognise. His diffidence gone, his speech is rapid and fluent. The shyness which Frank had found one of his most engaging features has vanished. He is suddenly confident, assertive. What is more, he falls into what is easily recognisable as a familiar male role: when he wants something, he asks for it unceremoniously, and it appears.

The women are anxious to serve him. Their visitor is disconcerted, and resolves to tell his friend sharply about talking to women in that tone; but once again he holds back. What right does he have to interfere with the twenty-five years of their relationship? Even so, it makes him uncomfortable. He decides at least that he will ask him about it. There is no need to challenge him, he tells himself. I am their guest, I must not judge them by the values of what is, after all, a minority, even in the West, the values of liberal privilege.

It is obvious that the sister has been ill. She has lost weight, and her eyes eat into her thin face. She has been given some medicine, which is only a tonic, some antibiotics and painkillers. She is in constant pain. They pass the medicines to the young man, so that he may tell them what is wrong with her. He looks gravely at the drugs made by transnationals, and says something that evidently reassures them. He looks at his sister. How skinny you have become. He pinches her face between his thumb and finger, and she playfully pulls his hair; but almost immediately, her bony hand flies to her lower stomach, and she pulls a face as the pain pierces her. Sometimes she gasps for breath and tears drown her long hillwoman's eyes, A deep sigh escapes her as the pain subsides for a moment and she can relax her tensed body. The two women look at the young man's face, with a searching intensity Frank has never seen: their look says Tell us what we must do, make it all right for us, give us hope. Frank feels himself excluded from something that both repels and intrigues him. It is the absolute dependency of flesh upon flesh. He thinks again of his own mother, in the nursing-home where she has lived for the past year, the building well-tended, with carpeted corridors, floral curtains, and a patio where baskets of geraniums blaze in the summer sunshine; and he, in turn, is assailed by a pang of love and loss. His mother has already been passed over to private caring agencies, paid for by the state, so that he can be here, in India, observing these ties of kinship that knot hearts together in an inextricable tangle of duty and dependence. For a moment he has the impression of visiting his own, vanished past. His eyes fill with tears again. This, he discovers, is happening frequently, a sudden melting, thawing, dissolving sensation. He feels ashamed; not of the emotion, but of his own weakness in the presence of the dry-eyed stoicism of those who have plenty to weep about, but who conserve their tears, as they conserve everything else in their frugal, wanting lives.

Prakash says with authority – a tone his friend has never heard, Tomorrow we will go to the doctor again. I shall come with you. We must ask him to do the operation at once. She cannot continue like this. He will do it, and she'll soon be herself again.

Their relief is tangible. His words have made her feel better, his presence has restored something. Again the foreigner senses something akin to jealousy: envy for relationships that can express themselves with this directness, that are not mediated by a dense and obfuscating thicket of symbols. He feels strangely humbled by a love that causes those encompassed by it to be so visibly lifted up, as the two women respond to the presence of cherished flesh and blood, separation from which is as hard to bear as an amputation. Even when Prakash is away, Frank can imagine them, wondering what he is doing, whether he is eating enough, when he will come home. He feels it is wrong to live through others; and yet he wants to belong like this, he wants someone to care for him in just this way.

Their mood lightens. The sister keeps saying Thank God you've come. She takes his hand in hers, and lays it against her cheek in a healing gesture; and she smiles, a radiant new moon of a smile that lifts her whole face. Oh, she says, how long we've been waiting for you. The young man had written to them, warning that he would bring his friend. Every day they have been preparing curd, which, Prakash had told them, was his friend's favourite food. The mother says nothing, but from time to time, she looks at the foreigner with shrewd, creased eyes, in which he is disturbed to imagine he can detect a mixture of cupidity and distrust; but then he thinks of his own earlier suspicions about her son, and he is ashamed.

In spite of her illness, Aruna goes to prepare the food. She shakes the rice in a woven bamboo vessel to sort out the tiny stones and specks of dirt. She throws it into the air, and it cascades, a creamy wall of dusty grain, and then, one by one, she picks out the impurities. The mother takes a curved knife, goes to cut some vegetables from the landowner's field. Frank says Surely she shouldn't be working. She's sick. Prakash indicates to his friend that he should not interfere. Frank is ill at ease. He watches the young woman, bent double; she is wearing a dingy white sari with pink and yellow rings; from time to time she looks up at her brother and his friend, and smiles the transforming smile which makes Frank's heart ache at her guileless faith in her brother. The flies hover around the food. The foreigner watches anxiously, and thinks about the time he had amoebic dysentery; he does not speak.

The day is hot, the sun just visible behind swollen silver-grey clouds. The hills in the distance are grey-blue through the rain, although on the plain it is now almost dry; only a few big splashes that fall and fade instantly on the hot concrete. A flight of steps beside the house leads to the roof; there, the mother stores fuel, sticks and dead branches which she has found on her visits to the forest. Some vegetables have been left to ripen, chillies and gourds. The young man follows Frank onto the roof. One day, he says, I'll build another storey. But before that I have to make a bathroom and a lavatory. We don't have electricity yet. Water comes from the well, and drinking water has to be fetched from the landowner's house every morning.

When the mother returns from the field, she is carrying a green gourd and a cauliflower. She passes them to her daughter, and comes to sit close to her son. The presence of the stranger does not inhibit her; she lapses into her habitual monologue of gentle complaint. Her own health is not good. She must still be up at five every morning to milk the buffaloes. Now that her daughter is ill, she has more than ever to do. She had thought that buying their own land would mean a lessening of the burden of labour; instead, it just brings more responsibilities. The sharecropper's goats stray into the maize-field. There was a strange pest in the stems of the rice. The rainwater poured into the kitchen last week. Working in the fields, fetching fodder, taking water from the piped supply in the yard of the landowner, there is no rest. She sighs. Beside the little house lie her tools – a scythe, a hoe, a mattock. Frank can understand little of the Garhwali language, but he knows she is saying to her son that she has worked so long, for so many years, now it is time for him to come home. The house is nearly ready. He must marry. A young woman in the house, children. Even Aruna, now over thirty, has worn herself out; she is sick. Will she recover? What if she doesn't, what will I do? I can't live here alone.

Prakash does his best to stem the flow of the old woman's lament. The old woman – Frank realises with a shock that she is not many years older then he is. The first thing, says her son, is to get help for Aruna. He promises that he will stay the night, and take her to the doctor tomorrow morning. Frank will go back to the hotel, and Prakash will join him there the following day, after they have taken advice as to what should be done about his sister. After that, there will be time to talk about marriage. She says to him Why have you bought new trousers? Is that a new shirt you're wearing? No wonder you never have any money. The young man said My friend gave it to me. Again, Frank thought he noticed the same gleam in her eye.

They eat in the young man's room, the metal chairs are placed beside a small table. The food is served on metal plates. The rice and vegetables are steaming, the chappatis hot from the stove. Frank forgets his reservations and eats with relish. The spices have been freshly prepared and a cardamom pod bursts on his tongue. He says How good it tastes. They say It is nothing, we eat simply because this is all we have. He eats a spoonful of the strong smoky-flavoured buffalo-milk curd.

The room is a kind of temple to the male child. There is a litle shrine to Hanuman, with some fresh marigolds in front of the effigy of the god. His athletics trophies are on shelves that have been put up for that purpose; fragile cups and medallions, the cheap metal long clouded by the damp. On the shelf is a tin of Old Spice talcum powder which he was given as a prize for winning his last race. These tangible emblems of his achievement are no longer enough for the mother; she wants him to present her with children, another generation, the only safeguard against destitution. She has been so close to it that the fear haunts her. Only her body and its labour shielded the children from hunger, sickness, death. And now look at it, she says, holding up a withered arm; rubbing the swollen arthritic knee. It is all used up. Make another generation that will take from us this burden of labour. Frank is struck by what he sees as the sombre, epic dignity of their lives: their existence has not been banalised by junk culture. They know what matters. For all that is wrong with their society, they have not been estranged from their own lives. However strong the pull of Westernisation upon the young man, their humanity has not been damaged.

It is already evening. The foreigner thanks them for their hospitality. They ask him to stay; but he has left his things in the hotel, he must go back. The young man takes him to find a taxi that will return him to Kalgotri.

As Frank returns to the rain-soaked mountain resort, he feels lonely and abandoned, although he is secretly very concerned about the sister. He thinks she may be terminally ill. Their security is so fragile. Flesh and blood, he reflects, are in many ways a far less dependable form of security than a guaranteed income. Buying-in has its advantages.

He walks around the misty lake, its placid olive water disturbed by a flotsam of plastic bags and leaves torn by the wind from the planes and limes. He eats a solitary meal of soup, rice and dal, and when the rain starts again, he sits in the cavernous room and tries to read. Alone, he cannot settle. He walks around, listening to the rainwater, the drip, drip from the roof, and the streams as they make their way down the mountainside.

In the vast bed, he rolls himself up in the damp quilt. He misses the warmth of Prakash and cannot sleep. He has learned more from his friend than he has been able to offer him in return, in spite of the fact that the relationship appears very unequal, with himself the dominant force, the controlling partner. He doesn't feel it like that at all. For one thing he thinks, watching the glassy reflection from the lake on the bedroom ceiling, I have until now overvalued sexual competence in relation to the comfort of physical closeness. It is never comfortable to have to re-assess things that have always been taken for granted; and that sets up ambiguous feelings about the man from whom he has already learned much.

Another involuntary perception comes to him as he drifts in and out of sleep. Why would a vigorous and attractive young man like his friend be drawn to him, a stringy red-faced foreigner with thinning hair? It would certainly be unlikely at home. It is because of the colour of his skin, the long inferiorisation of India by its conquerors. He is the beneficiary of a racism internalised by his friend, which sees nothing beyond the skin colour. And yet, he thinks of the beauty of his friend, the cinnamon-coloured flesh and the silver teeth; however uncomfortable the thought of his own exploitation makes him, he is not going to throw away the advantages it brings. How can the affection he feels be racist? He would defend the young man with his life; surely, he says to himself, such sentiments transcend the burdensome colonial inheritance. At last, confused and troubled, he sleeps, with the sound of the rain on the lake, and the patches of glaucous light moving on the mildewy ceiling.

Eleven

THE NEXT morning, Frank walked in the rain around the stretch of water at the centre of Kalgotri; it was badly polluted, and there seemed to be no visible source of renewal. It looked, he thought distastefuly, as though it had been unchanged since British times. The hills rose steeply all around; creepers, ferns and moss grew in the rocks, and water cascaded through gorges, across grey boulders, falling in crooked tributaries through the hillsides. In the misty distance, the colonial churches and schools still looked resplendent; only as he drew closer did it become obvious that they had fallen into musty decrepitude. In places, steep zig-zag paths climbed the hills, on which precariously placed houses were built, up to a height of several hundred metres; higher than that the slopes were too fragile for construction. The houses were colour-washed, pale blue, yellow or white, reached by steep steps or paths overgrown with grass and blotted by the blooms of white daisies and blue gentian. He was amused to see so many of the flowers that adorned an English summer – dahlias, salvias, ageratum. He could imagine the British bringing the distant progenitors of these blooms in the mid-nineteenth century, in their efforts to transplant their northern ecosystem, just as they had tried to replicate their social administration in India.

He stood by the rail overlooking the lake, where a few hardy Bengalis were boating in the tepid drizzle. He fell into conversation with a youngish man and his wife who were walking in the rain. Where are you coming from, they asked in Indian English, which he reflected, would have meant something quite different in Britain or America. They spoke to him of the long-term out-migration from Garhwal, the tradition of supplying the British army, later government service, and domestic workers for the middle class of Delhi. The man said that now even the army has difficulty in recruiting young men from the region; too many have been weakened by alcohol, drugs or malnutrition. Look at the degradation of the hills – how can you expect the people to remain untouched by the ruin of their resources and their habitat? He said there are 60 lakh people in Uttarakhand – the wider region of which Garhwal was a part – with about half as many again outside; and it is only their remittances that keep the hills from even more total ruin and economic collapse. People dream of coming back from their exile in the plains, but the truth is they can't; the pressure of population on the spoiled landscapes leaves no place for any large-scale return. He said it is better they live with their dreams rather than damage reality yet further by putting them into practice.

Frank told the stranger about his friend, and how he longed to come home. The man said that he would probably do more good by staying outside, but sending money home regularly. He himself had returned, and he now edited a magazine devoted to the preservation of the mountains and their people. In his relatively short lifetime, he had seen the wounds inflicted on the hills, and had been drawn to the ecological movement. Deep ecology, he said, is attractive philosophically, but economically and socially impossible. That is the dilemma for the hills, as indeed for the wider world. Development is vital, but of what kind? That is the question which no one can answer. The deep greens see preservation of the environment independently from human survival; and those who insist on economics as the source of salvation have no answer to the ruin of the resource-base. He smiled sadly: here you have in a nutshell the fundamental problem facing the whole world. But as long as the world won't face the problem, it can only become more intractable.

He said that Uttarakhand had been exploited since colonial times, and this did not change in Independent India. There is a growing movement for separate statehood for the hill region. Ours is a different sensibility, quite apart from the plains of Uttar Pradesh. Even Nehru had said in 1938 that the foothills should form a separate state. The stranger insisted that they were not seeking the break-up of India, but justice for people whose loyalty to India had been taken for granted. He added that what had been done to the hills and its people was violence; and the reaction was likely to come sooner or later.

Frank thanked him for this courteous but melancholy view of the hills. He went back to the hotel. How he would love to ask the young man to come with him to Europe. Perhaps he could find work there, send money back to his family. If he didn't find work, thought Frank, I could probably keep him and spare enough to send to India each month. The idea comforted him. But he could not imagine Prakash in the British indoors, in the darkness of winter. Although he hated land, he had been formed by the plains and the closeness to the hills. And then it occurred to Frank how his friend would change if he were to go abroad, how his personality would be reshaped by Western habits and customs, and he knew that the outcome would be less attractive than it was now. These thoughts disturbed him: did he want to maintain his friend in a state of innocence of the gay world in order to preserve him for himself? In the West, he would swiftly become an object of attraction, and soon learn to adapt to the values of the commercial gay scene. Frank knew he would slip away from him. He would become another person, just as he became someone else when he returned to his family in Garhwal. Was it exploitative and controlling, he wondered, wanting to keep him as he was, in the atmosphere of obsessive concealment in India, which ensured that he remained attached to him, almost, he said to himself, in his power? A prisoner of a frozen morality. Was this a reflection of yet another aspect of Western domination – this time, a monopoly of knowledge that enabled him to keep his sweet friend chained in grateful subordination?

He went to collect the key at the reception desk of the hotel, but was told his companion had already returned. Prakash was sitting in the wicker chair under one of the big quilts, shivering. When Frank entered the room, he stood up and, as he always did, walked over to him without a word and placed his head on his chest, a curious gesture that suggested both trust and submission. He had a fever, and was shaking violently. Frank helped him off with his clothes, and he let himself be put to bed, as, doubtless, his mother had put him to bed many times before. Frank felt at the same time sad and tender; but of the depth of his feeling for the young man he could no longer have the slightest doubt; and this, he thought, cancelled all the misgivings that came to him whenever he had the time to think, whenever he was separated from Prakash.

When the young man was lying down and had warmed up, he looked up at his friend and smiled. He said My sister is very ill. She must have an operation. The doctor said it was urgent. But there is no surgeon in the government hospital who can do it for many weeks. If it is not done soon, she will die. They told us she will have to be operated on in a private clinic. How much will that cost? About 8,000 rupees. How much do you have?

Prakash had saved about 3,000 rupees. He said his mother was going to sell one of the buffaloes the next day. Without hesitating Frank said I can give you the money. The young man turned his head away. It's only about 200 dollars. I can afford it. The young man shook his head, and his eyes filled with tears. Of course I will. How could you imagine I would do anything else?

Prakash held him tight, and clung to him with an intense, pitiable dependency. Neither slept very much. He could smell fever on the young man's breath, and his sweat drenched them both. Frank was moved and disturbed; he felt obscurely that he was taking advantage of his friend, his naivety, his openness, his difference. He was ashamed that he had been the one to distrust the young man; it was Prakash who ought to have been more wary of him. He hated himself for what passed through his head, the irreversibility of a consciousness that saw life as something to be exploited for what could be got from it, the psychic and emotional calculus that interrogated all relationships, all associations and bondings, in order to draw up a balance-sheet of profit and loss of the feelings; an economics of the soul.

Although Frank had offered the money spontaneously, it didn't make him feel good. He thought his friend emerged from the transaction more honourably, more nobly, even though his was the act of charity. He could not make sense of it; yet making sense of everything had always been his greatest competence. He had a strange impression that all his values and assumptions were being relativised.

By the morning, the young man was better, cheerful and energetic once more. Then Frank felt weary; not for the first time, he felt that the young man had taken something from him, leaving him with a strange and intangible sense of depletion and emptiness, and his own generosity, which had the day before seemed to him entirely to his advantage, now appeared somewhat more ambiguous.

In the early morning, they took a taxi to the foot of the hill. The rain had not let up, and drizzle silvered the oaks and Himalayan rhododendrons. They could see nothing of the landscape. Inside the taxi, condensation blurred the windows. No sooner had Frank cleaned it with his sleeve than it misted over again.

They waited for the bank to open, and Frank changed some money. It was a long bureaucratic process. The numerous tellers behind the glass partition looked at his travellers' cheques with a kind of bewildered wonderment, as though nothing like them had ever passed through their hands before. The young man recognised it as a means of appearing busy while doing very little; the art of make-work which, after all, in a society that has so many unoccupied hands, was perhaps preferable to a more rigorous efficiency.

They returned to the house. All around, the rain was dripping – from the roof, the trees, the flowers, a gentle music of water on leaves and blossoms, in puddles, on metal. Aruna was sitting at the table, her face the colour of the wood-ash which she used to scour the plates. Prakash told his mother that they had the money. They would take her to the hospital immediately. The mother and sister expressed no surprise that the money had been found, although, thought Frank, they must have known where it had come from. He imagined he saw the same flash of avarice in the old woman's eye; as though she wanted to ask how much, but cannily knew when to be silent. Prakash told them he would stay for a few days while his friend returned to Delhi. But first, they would make breakfast.

Again Frank's suspicions were roused. He hated himself for his inability to trust others, this odious habit which he had brought with him of expecting the worst of people. The ideology of his own society asserted that everybody was out for number one, that it was dog eat dog, the law of the jungle – though the true jungle was a product of wonderful cooperation and symbiosis. Reality had to be falsified to feed the ugly myths of domination. Why, he asked himself, was his own culture so dedicated to the revelation of ever greater depths of depravity, venality and cruelty, a cumulative disgracing of humanity; and why could he not be free of the same compulsion?

He even wondered whether the young man's interest in him had been part of an elaborate ruse to obtain money in this way. He tried to dismiss the idea. He had known him a month, the letter from the sister had not arrived when they first met. But perhaps Prakash had known about her illness beforehand. It could have all been preconcerted. Perhaps he had singled him out, befriended him deliberately and coldbloodedly, as part of a plan to find the money required for her health care. Perhaps, after all, Prakash was in fact a very smooth operator, a sophisticated manipulator. What was he doing that day, hanging around Connaught Place, where so many foreign visitors were? Frank remembered their time together; the tenderness, the hesitations and the growth of their friendship. No, surely not. Nobody would go to such lengths. But he felt uncomfortable.

He didn't know whether to be reassured by the transformation in their attitude towards him. For the first time, they all looked at him at once. The mother asked him about his family. He felt strangely shy under their collective gaze. How many brothers and sisters do you have? One sister. Where is she? I don't know. What do you mean, you don't know? She is in Canada. When do you see her? I don't. But you write to her? No, we've lost touch. There was a silence while they assimilated this idea. They couldn't. You only lose touch with your own flesh and blood when it dies; and not even then, for the caresses of loving hands make marks in the flesh deeper than time, said the old woman. He almost gasped in astonishment at her perspicacity. But then, he reflected, her experience of life has not been less valid than his own; on the contrary, her poverty has given her insights which have, perhaps, been masked for us by affluence, by welfare, by habit, by whatever it is that divides us from one another.

But the interrogation was not yet finished. What about your wife and children? I'm not married. This startled them even more. Why not? It isn't necessary in our country. It is always necessary to have children. They are the future. No. I don't want children. I don't want to bring them into such a cruel, hard world. The world may be cruel, said the mother, but there is no other world to bring them to; to soften its unkindness is the purpose of children. Frank heard himself give all the plausible justifications which he had absorbed at home; but now, what had appeared as unanswerable logic and common sense had become, quite simply, the wrong answers. Their eyes were more puzzled and more penetrating, until at last, his was the gaze that was cast down.

Do you have a Mummy and Daddy? My father is dead, but my mother is living. Is she waiting for you at home? I don't live with her. Who looks after her then? She is in a nursing home. What is that? She is very old and ill, and she is looked after in a kind of hospital. She needs to be nursed all the time. She is tended by professionals, he said; and then his voice faltered. He thought of his mother's last entreating look before he had left for India. Oh, suppose she died while I was away. His eyes filled with tears.

He felt vulnerable and exposed under their gentle but insistent inquiry. The directness of their questions frightened him. At home, other people always colluded in the account you gave of the impossibility of looking after those you loved, they went halfway to make excuses for the breakdown of ties of kinship; the dissolution of family relationships was no longer a tragedy, even though it had perhaps ceased to be the liberation it had once appeared. He felt strangely orphaned, alone, excluded. He tried to say that in his country all this was quite normal, but he couldn't find the words. He felt it wasn't normal. It wasn't even quite human. They looked incredulous. Who looks after you? I look after myself. Nobody can look after themselves. Explanations about the welfare system of his country froze; what was the point? Prakash came to his rescue. He said with a sweet spontaneous smile, You have a family now. What you are doing for us will never be forgotten. Apse wada karta hun. I promise you.

Frank saw pity in their eyes; and he felt a moment of revulsion. How can these people whom he has just rescued from the probable death of their daughter, possibly pity him? The young man walked over and put his arm around him, protective, incongruously paternal. Another strange sensation: he was behaving towards Frank as Frank had treated him. Even the gesture he had learned from him. He said When you are old, you will come and live here. I will build another storey on the house and that will be for you. You will stay here, and I shall remove the staircase and make a ladder so that you cannot leave. Only I will be able to climb up to see you. He spoke with such warmth that Frank felt a flush of guilt and shame at his earlier suspicions. He felt sorry for himself, and a rush of affection and gratitude for the young man and his family. He meant what he said. He put his arm round the young man's neck and hugged him. A tear splashed from his cheek onto the red and black pattern of the verandah. The mother looked down. Then her eyes returned to his. He had to lower them before she did; her shrewd mixture of fierce love and possessiveness intimidated him. Then they were speaking Garhwali again, making the arrangements for the day, and the questions ceased. Frank could feel them return to the security of their culture. The brief, uncomprehending excursion into his life had been like a journey into an unknown forest, from which they had prudently turned back before being engulfed by the trackless dark.

Prakash cooked breakfast; an omelette, salt, chappati and tea. They watched him eat, as though half-expecting even so basic a need to be accompanied by rituals as bizarre as those which appeared to them to attend the simplicities of kinship. He felt acutely uncomfortable, pitiable, inferior. Inferior: that was his country's bequest to India, and here they were, turning the tables on him. He was thankful when the time came for him to go.

In the dripping morning Prakash accompanied him over the wet field. The mother and sister came to the edge of the little piece of land, beside the buffalo shed, under the deodar tree that marked the boundary on the south side. He turned and waved to them; they stood and waved back. Frank continued to turn and wave. They returned his signal. They would not be the first to move. Every few steps he turned again. He could no longer make out the smile on their faces. Soon, all he could see were the arms raised in farewell; not until they had disappeared behind the landowner's farmhouse did the two women move. Frank tried to imagine their conversation, but then thought he would rather not know.

Prakash waited with him for the bus. But he was impatient, he walked up and down, swinging his arms. Frank wanted to tell him For God's sake be still for two minutes. The bus didn't come. They had nothing more to say to each other. Then, just as the tinny old receptacle which the young man referred to as 'the de-luxe coach' came snorting and vibrating round the corner, he smiled at his friend and said with a grin, My mother and sister like you. My mother says she now has two sons.

In the bus, he looked at his crumpled reflection in the grimy glass of the window and wept.

Twelve

PRAKASH REMAINED with his family for a week. The operation, for a burst appendix, was sucessful. He visited Aruna each day, taking food from home in a stainless steel tiffin can; and he sat with her through the afternoon and into the evening, while the rain beat so hard upon the roof of the hospital that they couldn't hear each other speak. She asked him about his friend, but all he would say was that he was a good man. She used her role as invalid to insist. How had they met? The young man and his friend were well aware of the anomalous couple they made. Accordingly, they had devised a plausible story. Frank had been an athlete when he was younger, and they had met at Nehru Stadium one day while the young man was practising. Prakash was ill at ease with the lie, and he felt an enormous pity for the unsuspecting sister who accepted it so trustingly. It was the beginning, for him, of a self-conscious secrecy and concealment which were not in his nature.

He began to feel a different kind of distance from his sister and mother, his friends in the little town, even his fellow-athletes; his separation from them became deeper and less bridgeable. For the first time in his life, he knew what it was to be lonely – the pain of a sharpening differentiation between people who had never seen themselves divided by individual needs and desires, but had bathed, as it were, in a common pool of humanity, whose joys and griefs were all shared, and more or less the same. Of course, people had always been set apart by character or sensibility, by varying attributes jealousy, anger, kindness, tolerance – but this had never interfered with the social patterning of birth, marriage, the bonding of the affections. Roles remained more important than relationships; but once the distinction has been glimpsed, the consciousness to which it gives rise cannot easily be reversed. And this Prakash was now discovering.

He reappeared one day at his friend's hotel in Delhi. He greeted him as usual. Without a word, he placed his head on the older man's chest, closed his eyes and waited for his arms to encircle him in the protective shelter which, Frank was beginning to understand (although he thought he knew it already) is the only security we shall ever know, the only barrier between ourselves and utter dereliction.

Frank feared that the young man's fresh demonstrativeness might have arisen out of a sense of obligation to him. You have helped us so much, he said. I don't want gratitude, I want affection, he said. Yet Prakash obdurately – or so it appeared – refused to detach his sentiments from what Frank interpreted as a mere pretence, that he was only responding to his friend's generosity towards his family.

But in spite of the young man's devotion – and he travelled to and from camp each day, always coming back in the evening so they could be together, despite growing fatigue and exhaustion – Frank began to feel acutely the long hours he was compelled to spend alone. That period of his life appeared, in retrospect, to have been one of constant waiting for the friend whose duties claimed him elsewhere. Sometimes the bus was late, or the traffic at a standstill in the monsoon floods. One night, the young man failed to arrive. The older man ate a lonely and lugubrious meal, and he anticipated how he might feel when their relationship ended. He was sad; then angry. It had been a day of torrential rain and flooded roads that had become impassable. He would not permit even this natural phenomenon to interfere with his indignation against his friend.

Early the next morning, Prakash was at the door. Frank looked at him coldly and said Ap kya chahta hain? What have you come for? He blamed the young man, called him unreliable and a false friend. The athlete sat and looked at the floor, his face flushed, his fingers working nervously. He could not understand why his friend could find fault with an absence caused by something so uncontrollable as the monsoon; and he said nothing. His companion prolonged what had become only a pretence of anger; it afforded him a new, unfamiliar pleasure, of which he was later ashamed. But it made the inevitable reconciliation all the sweeter.

Frank knew that he had outstayed the time he intended to be in India. He had done none of the work he had promised to do. The visits to the leprosy hospitals had been deferred; the report remained unwritten. Sometimes, at the railway station, in front of a mosque, he saw the outstretched stumps of the leprosy patients, and he felt guilty that he had neglected his work in pursuit of his own needs. He said to himself, It was voluntary, I'm not being paid for it; and then was ashamed to find himself making judgments in accordance with a calculus whose cruelty he hated. It was already mid September, and soon he would have be back at work. But he delayed by a few more days, and then a few more. He felt trapped in a sweet indolence, a dawdling inertia that he had always imagined quite foreign to himself. But then he had learned so much, so quickly in the brief months of a relationship that had shaken him as powerfully as a tree bending to the monsoon gales.

Somehow, Prakash could never completely let himself go. He always avoided being kissed on the mouth; it took some effort for the older man to persuade him not to wear his singlet and dhoti in bed. A traditional prudery – or was it modesty? Frank was no longer really sure – still governed his responses. In the morning, accustomed to rising at five o'clock, he would be up and out before his friend was awake, returning in such a glow of energy and health that he was never disposed to return to bed, nor even to touch his friend. It seemed at first that the preoccupation with his training claimed him afresh each day; but it came to appear to Frank that the rigour of the training was designed to efface the memory of the night before, to start each day detached from what he regarded as a weakness, the aberration of the preceding night. He felt that Prakash saw his relationship with him as something apart, clandestine and inauthentic in his life; or rather, Frank could not perceive how his friend made sense of it, how he integrated into the wider pattern of his existence. His time with Frank was limited, controlled; it was relegated to one period of the day, or rather, night, the time of concealment and darkness. When he came back in the morning, the young man, in order to distract himself, compulsively turned the buttons on the tv set, although there were only two channels;

he spent hours looking out of the fourth floor window at the building site below; he became absorbed in the sports news in the *Times of India*. Frank was irritated and felt excluded by what began to appear to him as an ostentatious display of indifference.

At night it was different. Prakash was affectionate, passionate even. The strength of the physical attachment grew, although sexually, it remained undeveloped, crude. This surprised Frank who, like many people without long-term attachments, had become dependent – or so he thought – on technique, expertise, in securing for himself the enjoyment he wanted. Now it began to appear to him in a changed light. He saw that he had grown accustomed to using other people instrumentally; a mutual no-strings casualness, relationships that would be abruptly broken off if they became difficult, 'heavy', if either party made demands that were burdensome to the other. He had with him his diary, strings of first names and telephone numbers which had become detached from even the memory of faces, let alone identities; an accumulation of waste from relationships, used up like any other item of consumption.

Something had transformed him. The warmth and the comforts of predictable proximity exercised a power over him which he had never known. But then the young man slept so soundly, and in the morning he smiled, stretched and yawned, and appeared to remember nothing. It seemed that the pleasure and the playfulness of the previous evening had been effaced by sleep. Each day meant starting the relationship anew. Frank found it exhausting.

Sometimes, he tried to get Prakash to talk about his feelings, but he became – or pretended to become – puzzled. Occasionally, he would groan and pound the bed with his fists; which his friend took to mean that he wished his life could be otherwise; but that was as close as he came to articulating any dissatisfactions he might have felt at his fate. When his friend insisted, and sought to make him give voice to his emotions, he simply turned away. This made Frank resentful; he, who had been used to talking about how he felt all the time, encountered what seemed to him a wilful refusal to articulate, a stony incomprehension. They looked at each other blankly, and neither budged. Frank thought Prakash was only pretending not to understand. The young man merely wondered at the strange preoccupations of his friend; surely, he thought, actions are more eloquent than words, especially words in English, in which I am doubly removed from my mother tongue. Why does he want me to say things so self-evident that words will only break against them? Frank was left with an obscure sense that he had, after all, been cheated, abused, although not at all in the way he anticipated when they first met.

They went to the Purana Qila. From the hill that looked down over Delhi Zoo they could see the monkeys and the pelicans which spread their wings over the tops of the trees to form a canopy of white, and their white shit whitened the ground. The day was cloudy, but the heat of the sun could be felt through the flocculent cloud. They sat on some warm stones; the huge ants worked, clearing boulders in the form of grains of sand from the entrance to their hills; butterflies flashed by, ghost-grey and crimson, black and saffron. It was quiet. The young man drew pictures in the dust with a twig. He said Next year I shall marry.

Frank was scornful. What for? Prakash said Because it is time. Do you want to? The young man answered softly I want to. Don't you like me then? was his friend's reaction. Prakash looked at him to see if he was joking, and when he saw that he was serious, he smiled. What has that to do with it? I have to marry. My mother talks about it every time I go home. She is old. Look what she has done for me. Now I have to give something back. She needs a strong pair of arms to help her at home. She needs grandchildren to give her mind rest. There is no one at our home but the children I shall bring to it.

This was one of the longest speeches the laconic young man had ever made. But Frank now felt he had a legitimate reason to express an anger which until then had remained diffuse and wanting a sufficient motive to declare itself. You don't marry for the sake of other people. Other people? My mother is not other people, I am part of her, she is my mother. You have a choice, said the foreigner. Look, I'm not married. I don't miss it. I've had relationships with women, but I don't want to marry them. The young man said It's not relationships with women; it's a wife. You are what your family is. That is it, that is how you measure yourself. That is how you know who you are. You don't have a choice.

Superstition, convention. Hypocrisy. Anyway, you're gay. The young man smiled, and said he didn't understand. He didn't know the word. You like men. I like women also. How do you know? I want to be married. I have to have a wife. I want to. I want children.

Frank saw that his animosity only strengthened what he saw as the young man's obduracy. He thought to himself, Oh yes, let's see. I know how you respond to me. You are gay. You'll just make yourself unhappy. Sexually, you are attracted to men. All this social orthodoxy, this worship of the family, how awful, worse than the worship of cows. Yet he could not possibly say this to the young man and felt partly ashamed of his own reaction. He knew he was being aggressive, intolerant, transferring values from his own experience, from his own cultural tradition, onto that of his friend; the friend from whom he thought he had learned so much. There was, it appeared, a deeper learning, one of which he had not yet been capable. He fell silent.

Yet when Frank remembered the struggle he had had, the painful war of liberation from his mother, the wreckage of whose body had remained unvisited in the nursing home for the three months he had been in India, he could not bear to think that his friend's experience was different from his own. He wanted him to share, by force if necessary, the same pain and the identical sense of desolation. He wanted to feel less alone, and was prepared to use violence to achieve it. This made him project even more fiercely his own feelings onto the normally placid and compliant young man.

Yet Prakash had forcefully rebutted Frank's suggestion that he didn't want women. The question didn't, couldn't, arise for him. Getting married was part of an inescapable social duty. He had never felt the need to account for his affection for Frank. It existed so clearly in everything he expressed towards him that, for him, it had no need of being discussed or questioned. For him, the life of feelings was given, like the life of flowers or insects or birds. His relationship with this man had been, after that with the teacher, the most significant event in his adult life. Surely that was obvious. Yet it wasn't enough: the foreigner wanted avowals, commitments, which the young man could neither give nor even comprehend. Frank had helped him. He had saved his sister's life. He said to him simply, You are my heart's friend. Frank was disarmed by this touching designation; he said, There you are then; as though the remark confirmed what he had been saying from the start.

Now it was the young man's turn to fall into an obstinate silence. Later, he returned to the discussion, but only in order to repudiate the idea that he was gay. There seemed to be something too categorical, too final in the word. He had never before heard the term. Nor queer, not even homosexual. Gandhu was the only word he had heard; backside-fucker, a term of abuse, and even of endearment, among young men when they are larking together; but actually, a very ugly expression. No wonder he wouldn't identify with it. Frank thought he would educate the young man. Teach him the significance of coming out, the importance of knowing who one is; the politics of identity. He knew that he was falling into the mode of Western tutelage; but he felt keenly, fiercely, what he was saying, and could not help himself. You have to discover who you are in order to express yourself.

But, said Prakash, I know who I am. I am a Hindu. I am a Rajput. I am a man from the hills. I am an athlete. I am a son and a brother. I am a man who has a kind friend from the West, the person who knows me as no one else does. What more do I need?

No, said Frank firmly, what you are most profoundly, that is your identity. It is something fundamental, the key element in who we are. I am a gay man. Everything else is peripheral. Everything else is secondary.

Now it was the young man's turn to be mystified. He put his finger over the mouth of his friend. Don't say that. You are more, much more than that. No, said the foreigner. That is who I am, because that is who I choose to be. We don't choose to be who we are, said the young man.

Later, Frank asked him, Do you think you had another life before this one? Prakash hesitated; his friend had made it clear that he thought religion, all religion, mumbo-jumbo, superstition. He said I'm not sure. If you did, persisted his companion, do you think that in this life you are being punished or rewarded for your deeds in the previous one? Prakash considered the question seriously. Then he said I think I must have done good in my past life, because I have you for a friend. But you like sex with men. No, with you. But I'm a man. Yes, but you are my dear friend. You mean, if I were not your friend, you wouldn't want to make love with me? But you are my friend. I would do anything for you. There you are then. What? You must be gay. It doesn't follow, said Prakash; I love you because you are part of my life. You are part of my family. How can I be part of your family, asked his companion scornfully. You had your own father. Anyway, I am the wrong colour. The young man lapsed into silence again. Now you are sulking.

Their conversation went round and round inconclusively. Frank was affronted; when he thought of his own effort to come out at home, the tear-stained silences in the kitchen when he had told his mother, the attempt to exact recognition of who he was, he couldn't bear this dismissal, this removal to the margins of what he regarded as most central in his life. Did the young man really believe it? It was impossible. It was an elaborate pretence, to avoid facing up to himself. Then he thought, maybe that is what a different culture means. He tried to contemplate the possibility that he had come to this country with the same colonising assumptions, the same universalising tendency that Westerners took with them everywhere, even those who came ostensibly seeking truth or enlightenment, even those who came in the earnest desire to repudiate their colonial and imperial antecedents. He was well aware that the government of India was at that time meekly accepting the economic prescriptions, the conditionalities of the Western financial institutions, which were certainly to the long-term detriment of the people of India, especially the poor, especially people like his dear friend Prakash. He was disturbed, and thrust the thought from his mind; that he might conceivably be an agent of similar violence, the same violence, in his personal, deepest friendships, was a possibility that appalled and repelled him. He could not bear to think about it, and fell back upon his sense of virtuous indignation.

Something had passed between them that would not be wished away. Prakash remained distant over their meal. He refused the beer which Frank always pressed upon him, because it made him relax a little, and Frank could feel the tautness, the tension in him dissolve. Prakash said I don't like alcohol. Frank was troubled. He felt forlorn and rejected. That night, Prakash turned his back to him, and was soon asleep. Frank lay awake in the darkness, while the fan turned on its squeaking motor, and the mosquitoes failed to be blown away by its rotating blades. For him, it had always been axiomatic that being gay overrode all other distinctions; for the first time he glimpsed the possibility that there might be other determinants that would prevail over what he had come to see as fundamental. Why was it that people from the West had all other cultural characteristics stripped away, so that they were reduced to their most basic instincts and impulses, their most irreducible features – they were black or white, male or female, gay or straight, young or old? Was this perhaps an impoverishment rather than a reaching through to the essence of what being human meant? He thought of his own childhood – the cultural heritage that had been stripped away by the years: the religion, with its little golden, rosy Jesus, the hymns, from Greenland's icy mountains to Afric's coral strand, there had been no difficulty in discarding all that. The working-class culture, the regimented clatter of boots on the pavement at eight o'clock in the morning as the men walked to the mill, the brass band in the park on long chill Sunday evenings, the labour which took his father away from the house for so much of the time – all that had gone anyway, there had been no need for renunciation. The neighbourhood where he had lived – that had all crashed to extinction in a cloud of red brick-dust when it was demolished. Most painful, the tissue of kinship that had filled the streets adjacent to where he lived with aunts and uncles and cousins he would not even recognise them now, didn't know whether they were dead or living. He began to see his life from another perspective; and he wondered whether all that he had accepted as being part of the order of things, the removal of layer after layer of cultural accretion like importunate and heavy garments, had not actually been stripping layers of skin; and that to be left naked, shivering and dressed only in the most irreducible element of one's being were not, after all, to have forfeited what all other cultures, through all other times, regard as a heritage. He didn't sleep. He resented the young man, the soft untroubled breathing; and thought of him waking each morning, the white smile in the smooth honey-coloured skin, as he reconstituted the elements of his being; Hindu, Rajput, Garhwali, hill-boy, son, brother, athlete... lover; and this last of all.

Thirteen

FRANK DECIDED that in order to resolve these troubling questions, and perhaps to get closer to his friend, he would take him away from Delhi for a few days. Out of town, he would have no pretext to disappear for hours at a time. They would go somewhere where the young man could not possibly have any mysterious appointments or urgent errands that could take him away for the greater part of the day. In order to make the trip more appealing, he resolved to go to Agra, which, although only a few hours by bus, could also be reached by air. The young man had never been in a plane, and he showed his excitement with unfeigned exuberance. Frank was faintly perturbed by a feeling that he was manipulating his friend. Everything they did was on his terms. It depended upon his money. It was what he wanted, although he presented the trip to his friend as if it were a gift to him. Yet at the same time, Frank felt that, in important ways, none of it was in his control; and this gesture was partly an effort to re-assert a dominance he was no longer sure of.

Prakash could scarcely sit still in the Indian Airlines Boeing. The cabin crew distributed boiled sweets, and Frank was astonished to see how greedily the passengers scooped up almost the entire contents of the plastic tray; so that every few moments the attendant had to return to replenish the offering. This, he reflected, was a far cry from the tradition of frugality and renunciation which had always been associated with India. It was doubtless, he thought grimly, evidence of modernisation.

Frank tried to hide his anxiety when the aircraft juddered and shook as it took off. His seat belt was not working properly, and he had to hold it around his abdomen, because the buckle would not fit into the aperture. Prakash sat beside the window, and urged his companion to share his wonder, as the Rashtrapati Bhavan dwindled and the plan of the Lutyens capital became visible on the ground beneath them. Next to Frank sat an elderly military-looking Indian, who asked him a few questions about himself, and then proceeded to instruct him about India in a way that Frank found infuriatingly opinionated and patronising. Frank wanted to enjoy his friend's pleasure in the flight, and responded sparingly to the stranger's informative monologue. Of course, he was saying, the diversity and richness of India can scarcely be apprehended by an outsider. The British, he solemnly informed the foreigner, had bequeathed to India a perfectly functioning administration and an excellent communications system, both of which the Indians had proceeded to destroy. When the British departed, he said, there were no slums in his native Bombay; and now more than half the population was housed in the most wretched hutments. Of course, the real problem is that the Indian is fundamentally lazy, and won't work without some salutary coercion. He wants character. It was a mistake to extend democracy to every slum-dweller and beggar on the streets. Some educational qualification should be a prerequisite. Look at Singapore. If you spit on the road, you'll be caned. In this, Frank recognised the self-congratulation and lofty detachment of the inheritors of the imperial sensibility.

It was not long before the stranger was in full spate, openly asserting that the Muslims of India did not really belong there, and if they could not adjust to the fact that 80 per cent of Indians were Hindus, there was only one destination for them. Pakistan ya kabristan, he muttered with a leer, not realising that Frank could understand Hindi. Coldly, he said that he did not see any solution other than coexistence, as had been practised for centuries. Surely, he said, the essence of Hinduism is its tolerance and non-dogmatic quality. Ha, snorted his travelling companion, the Hindus have bent over backwards to accommodate the minority. In fact, the Muslims have become a privileged group. They have their own separate laws, they are constantly spoiled and appeased by successive governments. It is time for a firm hand, a strong man.

Frank felt he was being abused by the old man's intemperance; he was being taken advantage of because he was non-Indian, and politeness forbade him to say that he had never heard such an outrageous stream of prejudice. In fact, he wanted to say, Indians in his own country are on the receiving end of precisely the same kind of wilful incomprehension as the Muslim minority in India; but he could never have expressed any such thing in the company of his unwelcome interlocutor. Tourism, he was now saying, is the future of India. There is so much to see, the whole world will beat a path to our door. They will bring foreign exchange and we shall all be enriched in one way or another. Frank said nothing.

He turned towards his friend, who was absorbed by the effect of the spun-sugar clouds, the great bronze cumulus that reminded him, he said, of the Himalayan glaciers seen from Kalgotri. The light from a radiant sun gilded his skin and his eyes shone, polished amber stones in white enamel. The foreigner was pereptually amazed by his beauty.

The brief flight seemed to have lasted for hours. The military man gave Frank his card and insisted that he call on him next time he was in Bombay. He was, it turned out, retired from the army, and was now in the business of exporting shoes, which were made in Agra. As it touched down, the aircraft jumped along the runway. For a moment, Frank felt he would willingly have seen the whole thing go up in flames, as long as it finished off the offensive military man along with him and his friend.

He took the young man to one of the most expensive hotels in the city, the Mughal Sheraton. Even he had underestimated the cost, but his pride forbade him to flinch at the $150 a night. The staff were supercilious, and, it seemed to him, he intercepted a look of disdain for his young companion. On the floor of the lobby, the word WELCOME was spread in jasmine and red rose-petals.

They were shown to a chamber, where two vast beds on gilded wooden stands were flanked by a glass table, an expansive wardrobe and a view over the sequestered cloister of the garden. The young man was over-awed, and spoke little. In the hushed dining area, he chose only the cheapest fare. Frank was irritated by his modesty and self-effacement. He is behaving as though he had no right to be here. The other tourists had no such reservations: they entered into the complicit fantasies which, it seemed, were the object of the hotel's existence. Some were garlanded with mari-golds as they arrived; they were given velvet waistcoats and caps with glittering designs, kurta and kamiz, or diaphanous gold-bordered robes, before proceeding to their banquets of 'secret recipes from the Emperor's kitchen'. They spoke noisily, French, German, Italian. The hotel lobby flashed and exploded with cameras as the tourists took pictures of each other in their exotic wear, self-consciously storing up memories which they could no longer trust themselves to contain in their heads. Frank laughed at the pretentiousness of it all, but the young man only frowned. Outside stood limousines, taxis, cycle rickshaws, camels, so that the pampered guests could select the transport by which they would be ceremoniously conveyed through the streets of Agra.

Frank soon realised he had made a mistake. The whole excursion was calculated to distance him from Prakash, to emphasise the gulf across which they had reached out to one another. It was, he said by way of conciliation to his friend, a poor exchange for the hospitality he, Frank, had received at his friend's house; but the young man thought he was mocking him, and became even more sullen and taciturn.

They went to visit what Frank dismissed as the most pretentious tomb on earth. He observed that if Shah Jehan had really cared about the well-being of his wife, he would have spared her the ordeal of a fourteenth child, which killed her. Prakash did not understand his friend's sense of humour, and this time, thought he was disparaging India; he showed a powerful sense of slighted nationalism, as if any dismissive remark about the Taj Mahal were an insult to his country. Frank tried to make amends, by saying that he preferred the exquisite dome of Humayun's Tomb in Delhi, which he had always felt was a more perfect, if more modest, construction. This hardly redeemed the occasion. The young man looked at him, puzzled and said Don't you ever do anything but talk? Frank felt the young man's criticism keenly; and now it was his turn to fall silent.

They went by bus to Fatehpur Sikri, the melancholy capital built by Akbar in the sixteenth century, and abandoned only fourteen years after its completion. Their voices echoed in the red sandstone courtyard, surrounded by its high crenellated walls. An evocative, eerie place. A flock of parrots perched on the chhatris looked like an efflorescence of vivid green leaves. The fretted marble and the tombstones in the mosque dazzled their eyes in the afternoon sun. The roofs of the towers were covered with lichen, while purple and orange bougainvillea had invaded the crumbling edge of the city. The dust and grit swirled in the courtyard, polishing the stone so that it shone like glass. The foreigner winced each time a sharp stone cut the tender soles of his bare feet.

Outside, in the shadow of the deserted city, they found that a culture of mendicancy and servility flourished. Children living in the poor village at the foot of the palace had acquired the accomplishment of touching the hearts of visitors by saying 'No mother no father', and asking for money in all the principal European languages and Japanese. Around the monument, vendors of novelties, trinkets and mementoes: the degraded village in the shadow of the majestic ruin seemed to Frank a singularly appropriate metaphor for India: the ruins of a civilisation inhabited by its own estranged descendants.

He suddenly felt deeply, inexplicably sad. They returned to the secluded luxury of their hotel, reduced to an alienated and resentful silence with each other. Frank reflected that he had spent all this money in order to get closer to his friend, whereas, in fact, their companionship in this anomalous and monstrous place had never been less harmonious.

The hotel itself seemed to Frank the contemporary equivalent of the old Mughal capital at Fatehpur Sikri. It, too, was an enclosed fortress, a defensive architecture, a place of protected privilege. Within were replicated some of the excesses of the Mughal emperors whose name it flaunted: tourism, he felt, was a mass marketing of privilege formerly even more restricted than it is now; but it could never be extended to include the humble, invisible, exploited people who kept it all going.

That night, the young man slept alone in the great catafalque of a bed. Frank felt defeated, too demoralised to make any movement towards him.

The flight back to Delhi was also silent and constrained, contaminated by the distance between them. The young man no longer appeared to take any interest in the novelty of being in the air. Frank decided he could not delay his return home any longer. Within the next few days, he would be gone. For the first time, he felt comforted by the thought that he didn't have to stay here. He had always gratefully left his home, thinking that in a new country, in a different culture, he could in some way remake himself. Here, he had no antecedents, no ties, no one who could deny the version of himself which he chose to promote. But now, he felt a kind of relief at his departure. He thought of the friends to whom he could narrate the eventful encounters of his trip, and could imagine their envious interest as he passed round the photographs of Prakash. This cheered him: the prestige value of his relationship, in a status-obsessed culture. Almost immediately, he was overcome by regret and guilt at the thought that recounting, contemplating the relationship could be more important than living it and savouring its changing moods. That night, he was thoughtful and tender with his friend; and when the young man responded, Frank asked himself why he had, even briefly, relished the thought of leaving him.

Fourteen

THE DAY before Frank left, he was irritable and unsettled, beyond the normal apprehensiveness that comes before a long journey. He kept looking at Prakash, who wore an air of numb dejection; his face unusually immobile and expressionless. His friend was ill at ease. There was something new, something he could not define, in the young man's behaviour, in his unresponsiveness.

They walked in the white polluted sunshine, over the railway bridge where the people slept on the steps, wrapped like mummies in dun-coloured blankets. Because he was leaving, Frank saw the city and its people with unusual clarity. At one point, there was a boy of about fifteen with a refrigerated water-cart. It had been slightly struck by a car, and the boy watched desperately as the water gently flowed through a small puncture onto the burning road beneath; if it had been blood, it could scarcely have been more vital. He was so distressed by the loss of his livelihood that Frank turned back and gave him a hundred rupees. Even this did not rouse the young man out of his silence. Later, they saw a hijara, a eunuch, in a scarlet saree, raising his brawny arms aloft and clapping his hands at couples sitting around Connaught Place. Many gave him money; once regarded as an auspicious omen who never had to solicit alms, Prakash explained, their function has become degraded, and many of the hijaras in Delhi have become little more than aggressive beggars.

Nor did the young man raise his eyes while they sat in the restaurant. Frank became more and more uncomfortable and impatient. For God's sake, he wanted to say, this is my last day, why can't you show at least a little regret that I'm going; and then, when Prakash finally raised his dry expressionless eyes, he could see. He was grieving. The departure of his friend had rekindled a memory of another loss. He was mourning all over again; or perhaps, the departure had set up feelings that he had known long ago, feelings of deep absences and wounds which had finished by becoming familiar to him. Why, even his relationship with Frank, which must always be marked by separations, guaranteed that the same sentiments would be reawakened every time they parted. The young man had settled meekly into this perpetually interrupted relationship, as if he had sought out the company of an old friend. An old friend. How strange, thought Frank, that the sense of loss seemed more compelling, more necessary to the young man than the delight and mutual pleasures of their friendship. He thought he had glimpsed something significant about his relationship with Prakash; it had been structured in such a way that it would continue to produce this repeat of the unhappiness and pain of discontinuity. The feeling of irritation dissolved in a flood of tenderness.

As they walked back to the hotel, Frank slipped his arm through that of the young man, who walked with his hands in his pockets. He made no attempt to free himself. Frank was reconciled; he thought he had seen the depth of the young man's need. It made him strong, for he knew how important he had become to his friend, even if equally in this negative sense, as the instrument of familiar severings and partings. It strengthened again the conviction that Prakash was indeed gay, and that he had little to fear from any talk of marriage. He tended the image he had of him on the day before he left – the silent misery of anticipated loss; – and he was reassured; a reassurance, however, tempered by guilt.

Prakash went with him to the airport, although Frank had urged him not to. It seemed he wanted to savour the parting, as though by doing so, he would come closer to his own deep feeling of being bereft, abandoned, alone. Before they separated, Prakash looked at him and said I think I am a very bad person. Why do you say so? Because sometimes I wish I didn't have so much responsibility. I wish I didn't have to do my duty. I wish I could be free like you. That doesn't make you bad, his friend comforted him. These are only thoughts, aren't they? It's what you do that counts, not what you think. And you know that you'll always do what's right, don't you?

They said goodbye under the concrete awning in front of the departures concourse at Indira Gandhi Airport. Only travellers were allowed beyond the barrier for security reasons. It seemed that each passenger was accompanied by his or her extended family; although it was three o'clock in the morning, crowds blocked the entrance, and smudged the glass with their breath as they sought a last glimpse of those they loved. A curious mixture, nonchalant travellers who took the flight between Delhi and London as merely another tiresome journey in their busy lives, mingled with clenched and terrified migrants on their way to the Gulf as drivers, maidservants, cooks. These stood in a bewildered trance, not knowing what to do, which documents to present, which papers would get them past the next hurdle towards partings which tore their heart out.

Frank hugged his friend closely and said Write to me soon. Then the young man went back to the taxi, whose driver Frank had asked to take him to camp. What he did not know was that as soon as the young man got into the cab, the driver spat and refused to take him to his destination. He dropped him on the edge of the airport, and the young man had to walk the seven kilometres to his camp.

When he reached home, Frank experienced the excited anticipation of arrival, of meeting friends, of explaining why he was late for the beginning of term. This proved to be a pleasure that was soon exhausted. He lived in a flat in South London; what had once been a substantial Victorian house had been transformed into eight apartments, a plastic panel of lighted door-buzzers in the ornate weathered porch; inside, a public space with thin cord carpet and a bare electric light bulb, dead leaves blown in by the wind and piles of junk mail for forgotten tenants. The flats were separated by fragile hardboard walls, so that the living room was only one quarter of what had been a spacious drawing room.

The building smelled uninhabited; a faint aroma of gas and dust, the warmth of an airless summer trapped in unoccupied rooms. Frank looked without interest at the letters that had accumulated inside his flat, hoping that, miraculously, there might be a letter from the friend he had just left. Dust had settled on all the surfaces; he threw his bag onto a chair, and a mist of particles rose up into the autumn sunlight. He was aware, too, of how this place was a fitting expression of the depleted emotional spaces in his life; a depopulation of the heart. He shivered, and reached for a drink.

He called the nursing home. He was told his mother was fine, and looking forward to seeing him. He would go the next day. When he had replaced the telephone, he thought – perhaps still under the influence of the tenderness that united his new, elective family in India – he should go at once. Being exhausted and jet-lagged, he felt all the more virtuous in making the journey immediately. When he got there, she offered her cheek and said I didn't expect you till tomorrow. His heart had been full of all the things he wanted to say to her; not only did he want to repeat how much he loved her, but he had resolved to tell her about India, its splendour and poverty. He would speak of Prakash's family, he would tell her about the Taj Mahal. But she looked tired and frail; his overflowing feelings remained unexpressed, the stories of his travels froze. She was without curiosity; exuded a punishing and resentful silence. She had seen no one. Frank's brother had come once, but stayed only half an hour. He hadn't wanted to bring the children, because it might upset them, coming to a place like this. Frank took her hand; the flesh had swollen around the wedding ring, there was dirt under the neglected nails. Why, he asked himself, was it unthinkable that she should live with him? In India, he had known how deeply he cared for her, but when they met, everything returned to the old imprisoning silences, to – was it fear? – of feelings which didn't exactly forbid their expression, but forced them, as it were, underground, so that they could only peek out timidly from the safety of the metaphors and symbols which dissimulated them. She said You had a nice holiday then. Furious, he said It wasn't a holiday, I was working. Where is it you've been? I wrote to you. India. Oh yes, I believe I had a postcard. He had written to her every week.

He went home and wrote to Prakash almost immediately, with re- newed expressions of affection and friendship. He waited for a reply. A curious sensation: whenever he felt secure in the young man's affection, the intensity of his own emotion began to fade. But when a week passed, then two and three, and there was no letter, he began to feel afraid. What he now began to call his love for him was stimulated, and gained strength. He was seized by an urgent desire to hear his voice. He wrote to the young man again, asking him to telephone him on a certain day at a certain time, a collect call that would cost him nothing. When he had posted this letter, he was for a time, elated. Later, he reflected that Prakash scarcely ever used a telephone; certainly he would be unlikely to make calls from India to Europe without good reason. No call came.

Something troubled Frank. It was the young man's obduracy; his rootedness, his inability to transcend what Frank thought the superstition and irrationality of his religion, the powerful transmission of cultural val- ues that created an obstacle to his ability to break through to what Frank regarded as the essence of his being, his gayness. Whenever he was chal- lenged, he always deferred to Frank's interpretation of the world; he said he, too, was angered by the caste system, the oppression of women, he didn't believe in the numberless gods of Hinduism. Yet he would never eat chicken on Tuesday in deference to his protective deity, Hanuman. It was, he said, a kind of sacrifice, not so much to the god, as for himself, to show that he had strength of purpose. And in spite of what he said, Frank had seen him in the morning doing puja in front of the little glass shrine in his bedroom, the scarlet glow of the agarbatti and the white heart of a coco- nut gleaming in the early morning darkness. When Frank had wanted to stop at the harijan settlement on the edge of the village, Prakash had urged him not to. His mother's prohibition was still too strong, even though in all other cases, the young man expressed a lively awareness of social injus- tice, and his disgust at it. Frank knew the young man was torn, between what he saw as a recognition of his true sexuality and the obscurantist tug of his religion. For Frank it was clear which would win; the triumph would be that which he represented the enlightenment of identity, of defining oneself against a tradition, which, whatever its strengths, nevertheless crippled and inhibited. Of course, he was well aware of the malign side-effects of westernisation, the grafting onto India of a high-consuming middle class which only took further resources from the poor. But that, he rationalised, was economic and social domination. In the area of the heart, there was no real contest. Human psychology, he told himself, is not confined by ideology, is not structured by faith, is not mediated through creed or revelation; and so he rested in his sense of eternal values, which was all the more comfortable, for they were his own.

Yet his mother's mute reproachful presence, the lack of contact with his brother, the sister in Canada – Saskatoon, a place whose very name repelled him – the functional and forgotten friendships of gay pick-ups, how he could he offer this as a more desirable alternative to the sustaining network of humanity in which his friend thrived? Why did Frank need this victory? Why did he want to detach the young man from his roots, and what did he propose if he succeeded? He realised that the relationship had little scope for development: the young man was not going to emigrate to the West, even if that had been possible. For him, Frank occupied a role, many roles – a father-substitute, a friend, a confidant, to some extent a lover. So what did he expect? That he would remain in India, waiting for his visits, that he would be eternally available as and when the Frank appeared; waiting at Indira Gandhi airport when the flights from Europe arrived in the early hours, while people yawned in the long queue in front of immigration officials, and the mosquitoes were incinerated with a noisy crackle in the unearthly blue light of the Insectocutor? It was scarcely credible. But Frank would not let these doubts disturb the deeper knowledge he thought he had of the young man's needs; and of the conduct which he thought these must necessarily lead to.

After a few weeks a letter came, in the young man's less than adequate English. It said that his marriage would not take place this year, after all, and that he looked forward to seeing his friend when he came to Delhi. He was practising hard for his competition which would take place in Mumbai in a few months' time.

Frank was dissatisfied with this letter. He had never taken the talk of marriage seriously, even though he was well aware of its function in the lives of his friend's family. He tried to find some comfort in the news that it would not happen in the immediate future. He took this to mean that Prakash had been unable to go through with it; an experience with which he could readily identify.

He remembered his own engagement almost twenty years earlier. When he was only nineteen, before going to university, he had met a young woman through the town's Dramatic Society. She worked in a solicitor's office, and quickly became deeply attached to him; and for a time it seemed that her love would be enough to make up for his own deficiencies. He liked her very much. They had got on well. But now he recalled the torment when he tried to beat into himself some sense of enthusiasm, of sexual desire, for the unsuspecting and attractive young woman. He had cast his fiancée in the role of rescuer. He had appointed her to deliver him from himself, and he still felt hot with shame when he remembered how he had blamed and abused her when she failed.

He remembered the few months of arduous work of denial, when he had tried to banish the male images of his desire. He had finished by insulting the young woman. In the end, he succeeded in driving her away, without even telling her what he still saw, at that time, as his problem. She probably imagined that he found her repelling; she had, no doubt, accused herself, in the long tradition of self-blame with which Western women, too, had been accustomed to exonerate men for the wrongs that they do, calling their faithlessness weakness and excusing their mistreatment by saying they were simply following their male nature. Many years later, he had written to explain to her that the fault had been entirely his. He had received no reply.

As he looked again at the young man's letter, he felt that at least his friend was slowly becoming reconciled to what he was; but this was the only consolation he could find in the otherwise bleak little note. He told himself that letters do not have the same function in Indian culture, and that his own need to express everything in words was yet another form of wanting to dominate. But none of this consoled him.

Frank decided that he would not return to India for some time. Give the young man time to think over exactly what his choices were. He had never told Frank that he loved him. He had always been circumspect, in control of himself and his feelings; part of him clearly was pledged elsewhere. Frank had assumed this represented the power of his mother and the household of women in which he had grown. He had yet to emancipate himself from their influence. Somewhere, at the edge of this consciousness hovered another insight; that emancipation from the ties of kinship was not the project at the heart of the culture of the young man who had engaged his affections so strongly. And that idea came and went constantly; not even articulated, but as a sombre preoccupation that neither defined itself clearly, nor ever disappeared completely. This led to a restlessness and irresolution which Frank had never known: he had always prided himself upon knowing precisely what he wanted, and upon his ability to form strategies to obtain it. He was now condemned, and not for the first time in his brief relationship with the young man, to learn something new about himself.

He had the consolation of his work. He taught sociology in a college that had recently been raised to the status of university. A college of not much further education, he called it. Once, this had furnished him with great satisfaction; but now it had become insipid and savourless. He had increasingly tried to bring aspects of the Third World into his teaching; but since his students could expect no questions to be set on this aspect of the course, they became impatient and tried to bring him back to discussions about relative deprivation, crime, or the structure of the family. Only this last roused something like passion in him. Because his own family had melted away – how? he could never answer – he had become virulently anti-family. He took pleasure in the fact that one in four people were now living alone in Europe, and one in three in the United States. The remorseless rise in the number of divorces offered him a curious comfort for the broken associations within his own family; the ruptured relationships, the coldness of the brother and sister who had abandoned to him the care of the mother, who had shown such a clear preference for him, the last born. While talking to his students, he spoke with some warmth, even passion; he scarcely realised that in his exultation over the breakdown of the family he was actually addressing his distant friend; trying to detach him from the sense of place to which he nonetheless seemed to cling with such archaic, yet persistent force.

He went regularly to visit his mother in the nursing home. Her life had become strangely separated from his; she depended upon the staff of the home for everything, her food, her comfort, her social, and it appeared, even her emotional satisfactions. She had entered into their lives, their relationships, the lives of their children; the state of their marriages. She had set up a kind of substitute family to fill the vacant spaces in her own ill-furnished existence, an intimacy of strangers. He felt guilty. She looked at him with an affection grown distant, which gave him the impression that it was he who had died and left his mother stranded, bereaved.

Once her eyes had searched his face in the way that those of the mother of his friend dwelt on every feature of her son, but now she read his face in the way that people read obituaries on tombstones. He had achieved the emotional break with his mother after many years of struggle. He looked at her, white hair, pale face against the pillows, so that she almost merged with the sheets, only the bright eyes, blue as the twinkle of lobelia, sharply standing against the implacable monochrome of the bed. He found it difficult to believe she had once wanted to possess him, had stopped at nothing to keep him beside her. The conflict with his friend made him wonder afresh why his own identity had been able to define itself only at her expense. He promised he would come to see her more often. The picture of him and his brother, taken in the back garden when Frank was six, stood in a leather frame on the side-table; a smudge of white roses, and two little boys holding hands. As she drifted into sleep he felt once more the desolate aching of his love for her, just as people who have been amputated say they still have a powerful sensation of their absent limb.

Of course, he entertained his friends with the story of his adventures in India, and they were impressed by his account of the meeting with the young man. He passed around the photograph of him, and they agreed that such friendships were rare in this country. They spoke to him in terms of making a lucky catch, as though, he said to himself contemptuously, he had been fishing. They were fascinated by the sexual details, but they were not interested in long explanations about his psychology, his family circumstances, the conflict between him and Frank. They changed the subject, or yawned, and said how late it was getting, or helped themselves to some more prawn biryani.

It was almost six months before he returned to Delhi. In the end, unable to stay away, he had written to say that he had to come back in order to finish some work that he had failed to complete. This was true. He had had to plead illness to the charity, and promised to deliver his report in the spring. He had asked the young man to meet him at the airport. There had been two or three further letters, warm, affectionate, signed 'Always your friend'.

Before returning, Frank was excited and anxious. He no longer knew how he would feel when he saw the young man. In the intervening months, he had become more preoccupied with his life at home; his feeling of affection rose and fell, according to the degree to which he was involved in his work, with his friends. He told himself that after the initial resurgence of feeling, he had cooled. The relationship with Prakash was not, after all, essential to him. In fact, he had known him only a few months. He even thought he could accommodate the idea of his marriage. In spite of this, he no longer sought casual sexual contacts. But he remained, he thought, in control.

The flight was almost three hours late. He sat next to an elderly man who was travelling to Thailand, 'to see his Thai wife'. Are you married to a Thai? Frank asked. Not exactly. But I have a friend there who likes to call herself my wife. I leave my English wife at home twice a year. Oriental women, he explained, know what a man wants. They know how to care for him. Do you know what caring means? It means finding the toothpaste already squeezed onto the brush and waiting for you, when you go into the bathroom in the morning. Frank was repelled. He thought again of the women who served his young friend.

As the flight became more delayed, he found it difficult to suppress his agitation. Would he be there? Would he wait? The formalities with customs and immigration were interminable. His baggage was among the last to appear on the squeaking carousel. As he walked towards the exit, the windows of the airport building were a mass of dark faces: he was aware of the eyes, like a multitude of fragile night creatures beating against the glass, so desperate was the urgency with which they scrutinised the crowd in search of those they loved.

He was there, inside the airport, behind a metal barrier. Frank wanted to throw his arms round him; but he extended a hand across the wire mesh and said I'm happy to see you.

The young man responded passionately to his friend, and their relationship was easily restored. They slept in each other's arms; the young man smelt of buffalo milk and cardamom. A remembrance of the heart overwhelmed Frank; a memory that has nothing to do with the recollections of the brain, but is a physical response to the body of another from whom we have been separated. He was elated. Such a relationship must have long-term consequences. Prakash himself had always said that friendship was 'for life, at least my side'. Frank thought he had heard too many protestations that promised futures which were never fulfilled; but now he dared to hope, because this was a different culture, and one which took such promises, such vows, seriously.

Fifteen

IT WAS late April. The nights were already hot, and the sun oppressive by day, its heat intensified through metal, concrete, fabric. A desiccating wind scorched the city, full of dust and grit. The body became quickly dehydrated, and simply to be in Delhi was uncomfortable. There were few tourists to be seen. Delhi was extinguished by the heat. Only the gulmohar trees, which burst into blossoms the colour of molten metal, gashed a city bleached by sun.

The young man told his friend that he had come fourth in his race in the inter-services competition. He had not been quite fit enough; he had overestimated his own powers; already there were younger men who could out-run him. The thought of Frank and his friendship had, he said, been his only consolation at a sad time. As a result of his failure, he was now going to be posted to Kashmir. It seemed to the foreigner horribly punitive. The young man said I am in the army.

Prakash was up early next morning, moving noiselessly around the bedroom. Frank groaned, and pulled the sheet over his head. It was only six o'clock. They had been in bed less than four hours. The young man seemed unusually purposeful. He sat on the bed beside him, took his hand and said My marriage will take place on the tenth of next month.

Frank sat up, wide awake. You told me... I thought... You told me a lie. No, no, the first girl would not have been suitable. That girl's family have a lot of land. They are rich. It wouldn't have been possible. But another man came to my house. It is his daughter. My mother thinks she is suitable.

Your mother thinks... Frank managed not to speak what he felt.

The young man said, looking at himself in the glass, I am considered to be quite a good match. They have a little land and a shop in the town. We shall never be poor again. My mother is very happy. The horoscopes were good. Everything is arranged. The marriage will take place at her house, and then the next day she will come to my home. There, we shall set up a shamiana and about two hundred people will come. It is not really the marriage season, but it has to be at this time, because the wheat has been cut and it is not yet time to plant the rice. It has to be in the season when the land is clear of crops. If you like to come, I will be happy. But I think it will be too hot for you.

Frank was hurt and angry; first of all, he was offended by the clear indication that he was not really wanted at the wedding, and secondly, because he had come to Delhi – or so he told himself – simply to spend some time with his friend. Why ever didn't you tell me? I could have saved myself the journey.

It had all happened within the previous fortnight. Arranged marriages, explained Prakash, do not necessarily take a long time. He smiled. My mother has been preparing for this for twenty-six years, since the day I was born. When you come to my house, you will see many changes. He was strangely exalted, full of a new nervous energy. It was as though he wanted to precipitate the event; to hasten it, so that it would be all over as quickly as possible. From this, Frank concluded that Prakash was terrified.

He had much to do in Delhi. His mother had charged him with the business of buying sarees and lunghis to give to the wedding-guests; so many of high quality, and so many of cheaper fabric and design, according to the closeness of the relationship of the recipients; an extraordinary hierarchy in the priorities of kinship, reflected in the bestowing of gifts. Frank listened. He had learned through the language that there are words to express the precise degree of relationship in a vast network of individuals. Family means something sprawling and far reaching; so extended that its edges fray with distance; a bit like his own had once been, he reflected, before they had learned the superior wisdom of going their separate ways. But in Hindi, there were words for brother's sister's daughter, brother's brother's daughter, father's sister's husband – the actual words had always defeated him. He began to understand the social significance of marriage in this context; the individuals concerned were scarcely individuals at all, they were merely the symbolic bearers of union and continuity, almost arbitrary actors in the continuous drama of the generations. Frank felt himself foreign, overwhelmed by this unappealable reality, and perhaps – although he would not admit it, even to himself – by his exclusion from it.

He soon realised that to object would be both idle and destructive. He hated it, but he was not going to take on, single-handed, the kinship system of India. Even so, he had an obscure feeling that he had been tricked; although he could not say precisely how. It was not as if any promises had been made to him. He resented the young man; even when he said to him Nothing has changed. In fact, he even asked that their relationship should become pukka before his wedding; that is, he asked Frank to penetrate him. This made his friend uneasy, and he experienced a movement of revulsion. I can't, he said. Not before your marriage. I can't. But he said dutifully I am very happy for you. It was painful even to utter the words; and he wasn't certain that it was the right thing to say. Prakash suggested it might not be, when he sighed and said It means more responsibilities for me. He repudiated the notion of personal happiness; the family would be the beneficiary, and that was the main thing.

Of course Prakash was apprehensive. An outbreak of a skin rash indicated to his friend the depth of his fear – both of the ceremony, of which he would be the centre, and of the responsibility to his wife and mother. He didn't say so, but Frank guessed he was afraid of the sexual contact also. All day he was distracted; it was clear that his thoughts were in the little town where the preparations would be well under way. Frank went with him to the market, to buy bundles of sarees and lunghis. He found it very depressing. They carried them back to the hotel in the back of an autorickshaw. Then there was the mangal sutra to be purchased. The young man had with him all his mother's savings, sewn up in a little leather pouch which he wore inside his trousers. They went to a shop and spent ten thousand rupees on the wedding jewellery; an elaborate neck-lace with gold pendants, which the young man then sewed back into the leather pocket that had held the money. Frank watched him as he worked purposefully with the needle. He was touched, and and yet irritated be-yond measure.

Prakash wanted to keep up his training for the few days he was in Delhi. So each evening they went by bus – the young man considered autorickshaws a waste of money – to Lodhi Gardens, with their warm sandstone ruins, where the young man ran for an hour. He travelled in his training suit, which he stepped out of before running, leaving the pile of clothing with his friend. At each turn around the cool, fragrant garden, he waved to his companion, who had never felt more like a parent, guarding the boy's clothing and buying a soft drink from a vendor who, he was astonished to see, had created a kind of shelter in the bushes which was his home. The foreigner sat in the shadow of the Shish Gumbad, the great tomb of pink sandstone, stained a richer colour by the dying light, with the azure tiles around the dome which mocked the end of day with their unyielding blue. After an hour, the young man returned. In the gathering dusk, he brushed his friend's cheek with his lips, and then lay on the grass. The foreigner observed his body, his chest rising and falling under the singlet, his hands idly pulling at tufts of grass, the inconspicuous mound of his genitals beneath the green satin shorts. The black shapes of vultures perched in the trees, a sinister dark scribble on the indigo sky. From somewhere in the tombs, the voices of people could be heard, magnified by the great hollow interior.

Frank could scarcely believe what had happened. He had always called him by his name, mera dost, my friend; now the young man, with a weak smile corrected him: 'dusri ka honewala hun,' I'm about to become somebody else's. Frank felt an inner chill. Prakash was so preoccupied, so distant; even though at night he appeared to throw himself into their love-making with a kind of desperate zeal, his mind was constantly on the event that was now less than three weeks away. Frank said, punitively, If you had told me, I wouldn't have come. It's obvious that I'm making it difficult for you. No, the young man protested. I'm happy to see you. But next week, I shall have to go back and help. My mother cannot do it all by herself. Frank said I've heard of a condemned man; but having to build the instruments of your own execution is something else. Then, once more, he felt he was becoming hard and brittle, falling into the glib mockery that was part of the usual discourse of his gay friends at home. Fortunately, Prakash did not understand.

Prakash said to his friend Don't be sad. We're still friends. I don't change. Mera dil ka dost, my heart's friend. Frank asked How can you do it? How do you feel about sex with a woman? The young man said I want to have sex with a woman. What has that to do with it?

Frank could not resist the feeling that the young man had taken something away from him; his own emotions were more committed than they had ever been in any adult relationship. It had somehow stolen upon him, without his really being aware of it. He felt strangely abandoned, used up. He feared that Prakash had wanted to visit upon him the same feelings he had known in his father's desertion, his flight into death. He knew about bereavings; and he perhaps needed to inflict upon others a version of what had happened to him. He certainly had this strange preoccupation with partings, with relationships that could not be fulfilled. Was that why he had attributed to his friend the role of father, in order to work an existential revenge on the man he had never known? Certainly, it felt to Frank that Prakash had seen something within him that he had wanted, and had taken it from him.

They had joked that the young man had been looking for a father and had chosen Frank. You must be the only person in India who has chosen his own father, especially since I'm the wrong colour, he had said. But perhaps that was it. The fact that a less suitable father figure would have been difficult to imagine made no difference. It isn't who you are; it has nothing to do with the reality of your being, the depth or conviction of your maleness. It is enough to exist, in order to be the recipient of all kinds of projections and imaginings; to become a figure to fill so many absences and wants in the lives of others. They will do all the work. It doesn't matter. Was that it?

Are all our relationships like that, Frank wondered, are we always for others the shadowy embodiment of the dead, phantoms of those who preceded us? Had he served as an object with whom the young man could grow up, finish his woman-dominated childhood; mature and break out to form an adult relationship with his wife? Frank was stifled by the thought that the young man's life-project should perhaps have involved him in so incidental a way, when he himself had become deeply attached to him. In another context – with his students perhaps – he might have been flattered at this surrogate parenting; but as it was, he felt abused. Something had taken place between them of which he had scarcely been aware. Yet, surely, the sexual feelings were scarcely those of a son. On the other hand, had he not written in his letters how much respect he felt for him, had he not professed himself honoured and flattered by the friendship? Frank had ascribed that to a form of inferiorisation that had colonial roots – and indeed, had been ashamed of it, while not disdaining to take advantage of the young man's obvious fondness for him. But it had, he was compelled to admit to himself, made him uncomfortable; and he had always resolved to say so to Prakash; indeed, had done so, obliquely, in his admiration of him, when he told him how beautiful he was, when he praised the cinnamon-coloured face, the darker limbs, the crimson lips and translucent teeth; the cock with its dark roll of skin and pale tip like an acorn inside its shell, the muscular arms and the graceful curve of the back with the regular knots of the spine. That had been his indirect tribute to his friend, the compensation for his own superior understanding and intelligence, the alertness of a consciousness that, in the end, had been so small an advantage to him.

But this was different; it was as though he had spirited something away from Frank, who had come with his small gifts from the West – the tin of biscuits with the coloured picture of Balmoral on it, which had become a major item of the household, to be offered around whenever visitors came; the bottle of Courvoisier which had been placed on the table with plastic flowers in it, the gifts of soap and perfumes from the Body Shop, which the women had used so sparingly and with such care. His arrival had been a time of great excitement and pleasure; but it had all been within his gift, within his control. He announced the day of his arrival and the young man was always there. He had never bothered to find out whether it had been easy for his young companion to get leave, or what difficulties had stood in his way. He had always come away from camp and stayed with him, more or less at Frank's convenience. But now he knew he was not wanted at this symbolic moment in the young man's life. Of course, at one level, he could easily understand it – this aspect of his life really could not be integrated into the social and religious context of his marriage. But he felt rejected; orphaned again. Once more he had a strong sense of the disagreeable relativising of his own culture. This was something which Westerners rarely experience; normally it is the other way round: they are the bearers of change, enlightenment, excitement, novelty; symbols of the modern world of which the people of the South could usually only dream. And now he, with all the paraphernalia of advantage and superiority, was being expelled from the life of his young friend.

He suddenly wanted to get away. He would not wait until the young man returned to his village, for he knew Delhi would seem empty then. He said to the young man, as though he had picked up something of the Garhwali idiom, Delhi without you is like a meal without salt. That the young man understood well, and he smiled with pleasure. Frank could not bear to stay alone in the city. He thought how easy it would be to pick up someone else, to start a new relationship; but he didn't want anyone else. At the moment when the young man seemed on the point of leaving him he desired him, he wanted him, he loved him, more than ever.

When he said I have to go home, the young man made no attempt to restrain him. He went with him to the airline to change his ticket. He hoped Prakash might say 'Stay a little longer'; but he could think only of the family, and was anxious to face what was, after all, for him, the major event in his life. Frank felt keenly his isolation and exclusion. But, he reflected, why should he imagine that other people's lives stopped and started with his comings and goings? Even so, he felt betrayed by his friend, just as he felt his friend had betrayed himself by giving in to the pressures for marriage. At least, he thought, not yet. He might have waited a year or two. We could have had enjoyed ourselves, travelled around together. Why has he thrown himself into this convention, this stultifying orthodoxy? Perhaps, he thought, it is because I have awakened something in him which he cannot face. This is why he is rushing back into the open arms of his culture; arms that will soon close tightly around him in an embrace that is far from loving.

Prakash would not stay in the hotel once Frank had gone. So on the night of his departure he gathered together the sarees and the shopping, the new shoes the older man had bought him, and prepared to set out for the Bus Terminal to take the night bus home. Frank looked at his face, pinched and frightened in the warm night. He asked him how much the wedding feast would cost, and gave him the five thousand rupees that would be his gift. The young man didn't take presents easily. As he left the room, Frank had to ask him to give him a hug; which he did briefly, perfunctorily, before disappearing down the echoing staircase of the hotel under the burden of his wedding shopping. He paused on the steps and gave his friend a last look of helplessness, resignation and sadness; at least, that was how Frank interpreted it.

He returned to the hotel room which expressed that absence which only the departure of loved flesh and blood can give to a place; he smoothed with his hand the dent in the bed where Prakash had recently lain, looking up at the flaking ceiling and talking of a future that would also include him; and he imagined his dark head on the pillow, the curve of the eyelashes on his smooth cheek as he slept, the glint of silver between parted lips when he awoke; and he wept as though his friend was dead.

Sixteen

FRANK WAS overwhelmed by feelings of rejection and betrayal, although even as he formulated his reaction, he knew it was ridiculous. But he had been unable to leave India quickly enough. On a burning May night, when the searing loo wind seemed to have dehydrated the heat-blanched city, he left it gratefully, for what he told himself was the last time.

But no sooner was he back home than he regretted his haste. He had certainly over-reacted. He had wanted to punish his friend, but had hurt only himself. Why should he not have gone to the wedding? Prakash clearly wanted to keep his life with him apart from that with his future wife. That was understandable; he was to be integrated in the role as friend, nothing more. Yet that was already a great deal, in fact he had been absorbed by the family; the promise that he would go and live with them, had that been nullified by the sudden dramatic event of the marriage? Surely not. But why had he not stayed long enough to find out? He now wished he had not yielded to panic.

On the other hand, the fact that the young man had determined the nature of the relationship with a man from another continent, had chosen a foreigner – for it had been he who had taken the initiative – only added to the sense of its externality to his life, his real life. Yet there was nothing unreal or simulated about his passionate devotion to the older man, unless he was capable of a degree of pretence and dissimulation that he had concealed until now. Although Frank knew intellectually that marriage was an indispensable part of the young man's life, his duties, his obligations, he had no control over the emotions which had been released in him by the relationship; he was hurt and felt shut out of a life to which his access had been, he thought, privileged. These feelings of pain hardened with time into anger, and later, into a desire for revenge; but revenge for what? – for a cultural difference which Frank could not bear, for a Western sense of superiority, for an intolerance, which he would be the one to pay for in the end. Then he said to himself, have I spent half a lifetime trying to struggle free from one family, only to be devoured by another? They have been just as damaging to Prakash; why will he not recognise it?

He knew that the boy – as he thought of him sometimes, when he wanted to be diminishing – was gay; and he told himself that Prakash was also perfectly well aware of it. What Frank thought he could not accept was the pretence: the pretence in public that they were merely acquaintances, chums maybe, buddies – he shuddered at the thought of these, for him, reductive words. He hated the distance which the young man assumed from him when they were out together in the city streets, the announcement in his gait and demeanour that here were two friends, two Indian friends, even though one was not Indian and their friendship was not that of peers.

He resolved not to write to him. Indeed, he would be brutal, and crush the feelings he had for the young man. He would regain control of a relationship which increasingly preoccupied and threatened to engulf him in its unpredictable intensity. After all, he had not chased the young man; on their first meeting, he had thought he was a hustler, had certainly disbelieved in his sincerity. And, in spite of all his protestations, the young man had done very well out of him – the hotel bills, the shoes and the trousers, the sister's operation, the wedding feast... Perhaps after all, he was merely a more subtle player of a common gay game.

He would throw himself into his work. His work. How empty it all was. The college was being reorganised. That might mean dismissal. He hated the way in which the education system, like every other institution in Britain, was being reshaped on the model of an industry. The education industry. He became more estranged than he had ever been from the values of his own society. It felt more than ever like exile.

One event at college demonstrated the degree of deskilling to which lecturers were being subjected. A student had presented him with an essay which he recognised as part of a chapter of Ruth Benedict's *Patterns of Culture*. He had given him zero marks. His superior, who occupied a newly invented role as Department Education Manager, called him to his office and said that if plagiarism was suspected, it should go before the appropriate committee. By denying the student any marks, he had laid himself open to possible disciplinary action. But I know the chapter, he had protested. That is not within your competence. He had become the offender, not the student who had copied from the book. In this he recognised that students had to be cherished as consumers of education, or was it now customers, he thought bitterly; and customers are always right. He felt more estranged than ever from what he had always thought of as his profession.

As the days of the northern summer lengthened, so did his sense of boredom and detachment. His thoughts were constantly drawn back to the little house in the shadow of the mountains, the tattered hotel, site of their relationship in Delhi; and he was overcome by feelings of nostalgia, loss and regret. As the date of the wedding grew closer, he found it unbearable. He was seized by passions stronger than anything he had known at the time when Prakash remained constantly available to him. Now he thought about him together with his wife. He imagined the wedding night, the young man's discovery of his delight in a woman's body, and how he would bring to that encounter a wholeness which he had gained from, and at the expense of, himself, Frank. He could not evict this image from his thoughts; it occupied them obdurately, the wedding night, the young man naked, the shy seductive smile of the wife, as terrified as he was; and their triumphant coming together, which would certainly draw a line under the – was it adolescent? – relationship which this lifetime partnership had superseded. Frank experienced a mixture of indignation, grief and fury, which together had the effect of immobilising him completely.

He went to gay clubs, he went to Hampstead Heath to pick people up; he even sought to rediscover something of the excitement of the public lavatories that had been the place of his early initiation, but he found that most of them had been closed, or were boarded up and covered with violent graffiti. In spite of these excursions, he always returned home to the little flat at the top of the spacious Victorian house, morose and filled with a profound unappeasable longing. He almost took a flight to India; he imagined himself turning up at the wedding, confronting his friend, and in a dramatic gesture, bidding him make his choice. He saw Prakash forsake the bride and throw himself into his arms in front of all the guests. These feelings were succeeded by resentment and bitterness that he had been used and slighted. Prakash had been so deeply engrossed in his own feelings, he had not seen the harm he had done to his friend. Then he tried to harden himself and resolved not to write. The next day, he would write nevertheless, and then tear up the letter. He had placed the wedding invitation his friend had given him on the mantelpiece; an embossed card, red and silver. He threw it into a drawer.

As the day of the wedding approached, his fantasies became even more sharply defined and more obtrusive. He thought of the young man, dressed up in his wedding clothes; the woman, whom he had never seen, in her red dress; the coat with the money sewn onto it, the Maruti car with its diamonds of tinsel and marigolds, and the crowds of admirers and neighbours, as it made its way laboriously through the streets of the little town. He thought of the wife, more knowing than her husband, allaying his timidity; massaging his flaccid cock and guiding it into herself.

He could not remove these feelings of jealousy; he had thought himself an advocate of open relationships, of casual sex, of encounters without consequences; and here he was, condemned to learn yet more unflattering things about himself, to be taught sober lessons by this naive and callow young man whom he had permitted himself to trust, it seemed, a little too much.

It was as though all the tenderness and passion that had expressed itself between them had been cancelled by this act of treachery. He tried not to think about it; but this graphic picture – of the wife and her know-ing, dexterous capacity to overcome her husband's shyness – tormented him. He hated her. If only he knew what she looked like; he had seen no picture. The young man had given no inkling, apart from saying that she was twenty-two, a simple country girl. What did that mean? There are no simple country girls when it comes to sex, thought Frank, who had always been pleased to think of himself as an enthusiastic feminist; now there seemed no limit to the instruction he was doomed to receive, from what had seemed at the beginning like a casual encounter.

A card came from a resort, a holy city on the Ganges. The young man wrote I am happy now because I live with my wife in Rishikesh. The place where the Ganges touches the plains for the first time. He thought of their times together in Kalgotri, and a choking rage took possession of him, a jealousy that annulled every other feeling. How could he write anything so cruel and insensitive. I am happy, he had said. Was this a final signal to him that their relationship was finished? Was this his way of saying that he had taken all he needed from the foreigner, not only the money and the gifts, but that he had gutted him, in this accelerated and intense father-relationship, had wrenched from him a parenting that Frank had not even known he was capable of? On the card he had written 'Always your friend'. The foreigner had tried to find significance in that, but it offered meagre comfort.

It was a sad time. A letter followed, with a picture of his wife. She was dressed in a red wedding dress, her hands coloured with the sienna-coloured mehendi; on her head she was holding what looked like a vase of plastic artificial flowers. She was smiling; her skin was smooth and pale and her teeth regular; her face was rather plump, a faint hint of a double chin; she would be fat as she grew older, he thought. The letter again said 'Always your friend'. A fine return of friendship, he thought, and placed it in the drawer alongside the photograph of Prakash. But he kept returning to the picture, looking at it as though to find traces of the treachery whose victim he was. Nothing; the smile, the golden eyes, the skin made pale by the lights in the studio where it was taken. He threw it aside again.

He went to a gay disco in the East End; he felt the the noise and the light as violence. The people danced, detached from each other, puppet-like; a tableau of individualistic isolation, it seemed to Frank, who, although he felt increasingly ill at ease in his own culture, certainly had no place in any other. He talked to a young man wearing a striped matelot shirt, a pirate's earring, the baggy trousers of a eunuch and the boots of a mata-dor; a mixture of styles which appealed to him. The man had an angelic face, but his fingernails were bitten and ugly and stained with nicotine. He was friendly enough, and agreed to go home with the older man. As they were walking into the cool London air, he turned to his companion and said It'll cost you, you know. How much? The young man shrugged. Down to you. Not less than twenty-five.

He was, it turned out, unemployed. He had worked as a van driver, a messenger, and in a bar. He came from Bradford, but no longer kept any contact with his family. He was not disposed to talk, but was compliant and made himself agreable to the man he saw solely in the guise of punter.

The only time his beautiful face became animated was when he talked about money; then his eyes shone and his lips curved seraphically. When Frank asked his name he said they called him Chico. It was late, and he said he would stay the night; at no extra charge, he said virtuously, as though he were bestowing a rare gift upon the older man. In the morning, Frank went out to get some milk. When he came back, Chico had gone, with his wallet and its credit cards, and fifty pounds in cash.

Frank thought he deserved it, and told himself that he now understood why he had gone to India in the first place. Why was the young Englishman so brutalised, resourceless in comparison to his Indian counterpart? Why was the sensibility so different? Why these fragmentings and scatterings of identity in his own money-hungry culture, while his Indian friend remained anchored in a world that, if narrow, certainly had a depth that was absent from the celebration of surfaces which lay at the heart of Western society.

He couldn't forget; and he was unable to reconcile himself to the thought that his relationship with the Indian could never be restored to what it was. After a few days, he wrote to his friend. He had meant to be restrained, not to show how serious was the injury – to his pride as well as to his feelings, a fateful conjunction; not to say how much he cared for the young man who had voluntarily given himself to someone else, when it seemed their own relationship was still developing. He wrote a letter that expressed some of his passionate unhappiness; words of affectionate renunciation; a conviction which he was far from feeling, that Prakash would still need a friend upon whom he could always rely. He pointed out that where he lived was no further away by air from Delhi than the young man's home was by bus, and that if ever he wanted to see him or was in need, he would come from one day to the next. He posted the letter, afraid that he had been too open, revealed too much, demonstrated his dependency upon and subordination to the young man who had seen him as father. Was this, he wondered, also the fate of fathers, to see themselves overtaken, left behind, by their sons? It seemed to him he had had all the pain and little of the reward for this phantom, unchosen fatherhood.

The next day a third letter came. This one was brief and plaintive; he asked if Frank were angry with him. The young man said he had now written three times and was back in camp; waiting for a letter, looking out every day for the post. Frank felt a leap of hope in his heart. Perhaps something would be salvaged from the friendship after all.

He desperately needed to see him. He would go in the Christmas holidays. He wrote to the young man, saying that he had work in Delhi and would like to spend a few days with him. He also wanted to meet his wife. Would that be possible?

When the young man received the letter in which his friend had opened himself up, he was very happy. He wrote to say that nothing had changed. I want you as much as ever. We shall always be friends. He reminded Frank that when he said for life, he meant it. He had been puzzled by the curiously interrogative tone of his friend's letter, its reproachfulness and doubt. Perhaps people in your country say things without meaning them. I do not.

Seventeen

WHEN HE had said goodbye to Frank, the young man's first feeling was one of relief that his friend would not be at the wedding. He was overwhelmed by his generosity, the help he had given his family; and the release he felt in his arms was precious to him. He was sometimes puzzled by the unpredictable intensities of the foreigner, the demand that he should define himself exclusively in this way or that, preoccupations which could certainly do nothing to further their friendship. Frank had become a compensatory presence for Prakash: whenever he failed to win his races, when he felt slighted or humiliated, whenever his Rajput status was undermined by his family's poverty, the thought of his relationship consoled him. The only thing it could never do was eliminate the absolute necessity for marriage and children; just why his friend insisted that he should do the one thing that was impossible, he could never understand. Prakash thought of marriage as a duty; even a burdensome one, and something he wanted to achieve as quickly as possible. He imagined Frank would be pleased if his wife became pregnant within a few weeks of the marriage, for that would open the way for him and his friend to spend more time together. It would remove the pressure from Prakash, and at the same time provide the necessary social concealment which their clandestine friendship required; a married man with a pregnant wife is above all, beyond reproach.

Among the objections which Frank had advanced against the marriage had been the assertion that it would be unfair to Sunita, Prakash's prospective wife. This had troubled Prakash. But there was no doubt that he would grow to love her; they would evolve a sweet and open companionship, a shared upbringing of the child – he had made up his mind that one would be enough. In the running of the house, the acquisition of more land, they would be partners and friends. It was true he was apprehensive about his sexual duties; but that he should fail to produce children had never occurred to him. There was one secret shame which he was compelled to admit to himself; and that was that although he regarded it as his highest duty to have children, and indeed was resolved to do so, insofar as sexual and physical pleasure went he would have preferred to remain with Frank. This he had told him clearly enough. By his readiness to extend the house, to accommodate him whenever he chose to take advantage of the offer, he was admitting his preference. He could not understand why such a clear gesture was insufficient for his friend, who always seemed to demand something more. He did feel, in advance, a guilt towards his wife. He knew that she had led a sequestered life, had spent it all in preparation for her wedding. He felt that their sexual relationship might be less full than she might wish; but he calculated that since she would never have had experience with anyone else, and would be unlikely to in the future, she would have nothing against which to measure any obscure dissatisfactions she might feel.

Here, he knew, he was taking advantage of the privilege of men, and he conceded that his friend was right, though less so than Frank seemed to think. After all, his wife's work would claim so much of her energy – the fields, the home, the children. She had been formed for this, and this was what she expected. He did not doubt that he would be, in every other particular, honourable, gentle, submissive to whatever she wanted. Only that he would never be able to give himself to her completely remained to reproach him. There would always be one element of secrecy and silence between them. But then, he reasoned, he would be nothing like his sister's husband, who had been so cruel to her from the very day she stepped into his home, had preferred the companionship of daru, home-brewed liquor, to that of his wife; had spent his time gambling, coming home only in the early hours to beat and torment her. She had been fifteen at the time, little more than a child. He had felt a wild rage on her behalf, even though nothing had been said to him. He was then eleven.

But this had seemed to confirm to him his mother's disgust with men. Men were inconstant, unreliable, selfish. Men ran away: they escaped, going down into the plains, fleeing into drink or gambling or even death, as his own father had done, leaving women to survive as best they could. The young man always insisted that he wanted a girl child rather than a boy. The women protested that he was wishing misfortune upon himself. The mother remembered old ways in which girl children used to be disposed of: all it required was a single husk of paddy in the mouth of a new-born child. It would choke her, noiselessly, and by the following morning she would be dead.

Prakash felt that with a girl he could make up for the obscure wrong he felt he was doing to his wife; not a very grave wrong, since he had not chosen to feel as he did, but it nevertheless gave further advantages to him, the man. And in any case, a boy would make demands on his maleness which, he felt, remained too insecure and shallow-rooted. He feared that a boy would bring him face to face with all the inadequacies he still felt within himself, in spite of the healing relationship with the teacher and the sweet friendship of the foreigner.

It was the truth, as much as the falsehood, in what his friend said that made it so hard for him. And indeed, the wedding had been every bit as dreadful as he had anticipated.

The day before, his best friend from camp had arrived, and he had asked him to spend the night. His mother had wanted to know all about him, just as she had wanted to know all about Frank. When she discovered that he was from an Untouchable family, she was very angry. He can't stay here. He can sleep on the verandah. No, said the young man, he will share my bed. The mother had raised such objections, he thought she would make herself ill; but he couldn't possibly do this to the friend from whom he had learned so much, and to whom he was so attached. In fact, he thought, if his mother had known about his true relationship with the foreigner, the caste and background of his army friend would have become a minor problem. Once more, he was troubled by the growing area of his life which he could not share with his family. He had learned that individual destinies are not all the same, that needs vary, and the social patternings to which everyone deferred were acts of violence to many people.

In the end, he promised that he would keep his friend out of the kitchen; and in return, he made his mother promise to greet him with warmth and hospitality. There was no problem with Aruna; whatever he said she trusted implicitly. She took all her views and her outlook on the world from him, even though her mother spent a constant, though never winning battle, to bring her back to her own certainties. Before the wedding, there had been a vehicle with a loudspeaker from the Bharatiya Janata Party playing religious songs and propaganda about the necessity of destroying the mosque at Ayodhya, and reconstructing the temple that commemorated the birthplace of Rama. The mother had not questioned that it was necessary to destroy the mosque, by force if necessary, and to restore the site to its former sacred function. The young man and his sister had not argued with her. She was too old to change; she could not be expected to foresee the violence and disharmony that any such action would – and indeed did – set in train.

The wedding day was interminable. His mother was up at four o'clock in the morning, preparing for an event that would last at least 24 hours. He pulled the chadar over his head, but she was in the room in no time, urging him to prepare himself. He had sat up late the night before with his friend, discussing ways in which they could get out of the army. They found the life enervating and dull. Most men were living for the time – after twenty years' service – when they could retire with a pension. Even worse was the prospect of being transferred to Kashmir.

Fortunately, his friends in Rangniwas had helped with the wedding. The shamiana had been given by the parents of one of the boys he had trained in the stadium. A former school-friend had provided the car and decorated it with flowers, and the loops of winking coloured lights that decorated the front of the little house had also been freely given.

He hated the headdress and the costume he was obliged to wear; and being at the centre of attention was repugnant to him. He enjoyed being watched when he was running, but to be caught up at the centre of this endless, static ceremonial made him unhappy.

His friends were impressed by the bride, her soft and stately bearing, her smile and fair complexion. In the red and gold saree, with the bangles and anklets, she moved in a music of glass and metal, and with her small submissive voice and lowered eyes they thought everything augured well. Most had never met a woman unrelated to them; he was aware of their covert glances of appraisal and embarrassment. He was the first in his circle of childhood friends to marry, and they teased him, envied him openly. He didn't enjoy their banter, and could not enter into it. He blushed and fell silent, and then they felt sorry for him and hugged him affectionately.

The bride came from a large family, and the young man's friends were easily outnumbered by them. His mother looked tired, self-effacing and ill at ease in the public throng, who were trampling her herbs and compacting the earth which she would have to dig and hoe afresh before the rains came. The day was unbearably hot; fortunately the shamiana was open at the top, and the stars hung low in the sky, as though they, too, were part of the celebratory decorations.

With the money from the foreigner they had been able to provide a respectable meal, and furthermore, wholesome and well-prepared. The previous week all the guests at a wedding in the town had been stricken with food poisoning, even before the conclusion of the wedding, and forty had been detained in hospital. The mother had gone to inspect the fare being supplied by the caterer, and had satisfied herself that it was of the first quality.

As the night wore on, the young man watched the young men dance to the sound-system which another classmate had offered. They were determined to enjoy themselves. Although no liquor had been provided, many of them had brought beer and whisky, and when they started to dance, they did so with an uninhibited exuberance, whirling and gyrating, showing off to the young women who sat apart, in clusters, whispering together, the mysterious cadences of their secret otherness.

Prakash felt his eyelids close with fatigue and the stress of the day. He could find nothing to say to his bride as they sat on the silk cushions under the stars. This scarcely mattered, because they were caught up in a celebration that bore them along despite themselves, actors in an ancient drama in which all the roles had been distributed for eternity. It was five o'clock in the morning before they were alone; and both were so tired, they fell asleep almost instantly as an ivory sky took on the first golden tinge of a metallic May sun.

After two days of awkward politeness under the vigilant inattention of the mother's gaze, they took the bus towards Rishikesh. The first night they stayed in a small hotel which usually received pilgrims. So far, there had been no mention of sex. They had slept in their usual nightwear, neither undressing in front of the other.

The young woman was delighted by Rishikesh. Here, the Ganges strikes the plains, the clean many-fingered streams that fall down from the Himalayan glaciers pour their ribbon of cerulean blue between banks of sparkling white sand. In the evening they went to the shore, where the beggars and holy men sat. They bought some candles and a little wreath of marigolds, which they set on a teak leaf stuck together to form the shape of a tiny boat, and they lit the candle and sent the fragile vessel down the river. For a moment, the river was alive with lighted tapers; but eventually, capsized by the current, they were extinguished. She smiled and clapped her hands, and the young man was moved by her happiness.

They went back to the hotel, feeling more relaxed than they had yet been. They undressed, shyly, their backs turned to each other. He looked at his wife. Her breasts were generous, with dark nipples; he admired the convex shield of her stomach, and the mysterious fold of flesh beneath, with a luxuriance of pubic hair. He had shaved all his body hair and felt slightly embarrassed by the gesture: he was not quite sure why he had done it. He vaguely felt it had been a kind of attempt to purify, to de-sex himself in some way. His cock was shrunken and unexcited, his throat dry and constricted. She smiled at him and held out her arms. What he did not know was that her mother's sisters had given her the benefit of their accumulated experience, and had instructed her carefully. Men, they said, are always timid in the presence of a woman's body. This is because they are spoiled by their mothers. They need help in thinking of women in another way. Do not expect him to take the initiative. You must go more than halfway to meet him.

This was why she kissed him fully on the lips, parting his clenched mouth and exploring him with her tongue. She caressed his back, his buttocks, his thighs, forbearing to touch his cock, as the older women had told her. Little by little, she felt him stiffen against her, and then, with a deft gesture, she took it in her hand and guided it into her body.

He was surprised by the ease of it, the enclosing flesh and the instinctive rhythms of their joint desire. All the anxiety and trepidation disappeared. He held her tight and closed his eyes. She laughed with wonder at her own cleverness; and he with his gratitude to her. Whatever else happened, he knew then that they would be the best of friends.

The next day they went on a trip to Hardwar, and from there, still in the first flush of pride and success with his wife, he sent a postcard to his friend; the postcard that had caused its recipient such anguish,

Eighteen

THE YOUNG man continued to repeat to his friend that nothing had changed, but the foreigner knew better. He had changed. He could not accommodate the idea of this vulnerable young man with the image of the Indian patriarch. He had told his astonished friend once more that it was unfair to the woman; and injustice towards women was something the Frank had known all about. But he felt his argument falter; it sounded more like special pleading than any true concern for the woman he had not met. He had looked at the photograph of her and felt an immense pity for her artless marriage-pose, and great compassion for her in the troubled relationship which, he anticipated, her marriage would surely be.

Frank's jealousy waned a little under the influence of the affection-ate letters from Prakash. Within two weeks of the honeymoon he had returned to camp, and was waiting for the posting – perhaps to Kashmir, perhaps to Assam – that would come soon. He wanted to see his friend again.

Frank arrived soon after Christmas, when Delhi was shivering in a blanket of smog that scarcely thinned even in the afternoon. People wore heavy shawls and blankets. Fires were lighted by those who lived on the streets, and the smell of woodsmoke, added to vehicle and industrial pol-lution, created a clammy, choking atmosphere.

The young man greeted his friend almost casually, as though they had separated only the day before; and the dialogue between them was resumed where it had been left at their last meeting.

Husband and wife, the young man explained, means not so much a relationship as a role: she was to be his wife and a mother to the children they would have, a daughter-in-law and sister by marriage. This, he gave Frank to understand, provided a rich social and affective texture in which she would express herself. What did she know of sex or love? She had never known another man. In any case, he said, love comes later. I shall learn to love her.

Frank protested that in his country people married for love. Then what do they divorce for, asked the young man. Surely, a marriage that has been arranged by loved ones has more stability and more affection than those which flare up from passion and then die.

But look at the women here, abused for not bringing enough dowry, the women whose lives are made a misery by their in-laws, what about all that, the burnings and atrocities against women? The young man said he understood why such cases appealed to the people of the West; what you don't hear is the millions and millions of people who marry and learn to love and live together and bring up their children quite happily. He said I am not going to burn my wife, nor complain about her dowry. Love grows out of familiarity and dependency; then it is warm and unshakeable. Love born of passion consumes itself, and sometimes burns up the people with it. Frank looked at him in astonishment. How did he know these things? From where could he have gained such insights? He forgot that the subordinate often have a knowledge of those who dominate which the latter are denied. They returned to the discussion again and again, always inconclusively.

Frank still hoped that sooner or later he would hear the story of his friend's dissatisfaction with marriage, the sexual disaster of the wedding night. He anticipated that the young man would tell him he felt trapped, unhappy; he would beg for help in order to leave India. Frank felt an access of strength and power once more, and he was comforted,

But the conversation which he had rehearsed to himself did not take place. No avowal of unhappiness came. The young man assured him his wife was a good woman. He liked her; but then, he would expect to. He could not imagine that his mother, after the tenderness she had shown him all his life, would suddenly turn and become so cruel as to choose someone unsuited to him. They still did not know each other very well, they could not yet speak freely together, but everyone was pleased. The young man said that in his affections his mother still came first, his sister second, and then his wife. He admitted that the wedding had been an ordeal: it had gone on through the night, the most auspicious time having been declared by the astrologer to be three in the morning.

The young man asked his friend about pregnancy. How long does it last? he said. Is it ten months? Frank gasped at his friend's ignorance; or was it innocence? The young man set his head on one side and said I will have more responsibility now. Frank didn't seem to understand that this was his way of begging for his support and love. He said brutally, Well you chose it. I think you might have learned some of the elementary facts of life. Like how long a pregnancy is. Then he regretted his words: the wife had become pregnant after the honeymoon.

Prakash had taken him at his word, and promised that they would go together to Rangniwas. The family were expecting him. The night before, there was an important international athletics meeting in the United States that was being broadcast by Star TV. Prakash set the alarm for two in the morning. Frank groaned, and thought wearily of the overwrought TV commentary, the sleepless night, and the exhausting journey that awaited them, the tension of meeting the new wife. When the alarm sounded, his friend turned on the television and then came into his bed, He was more affectionate than he had ever been, and made love ardently. Frank was surprised. It was one of the most agreeable moments they had ever spent together.

They travelled to the little town, along the now familiar road. The young man slept in the bus; when his head rolled onto Frank's shoulder, he felt angry at what he still saw as his friend's renunciation of the sweetness of their being together. He shook himself roughly and the young man withdrew. Frank felt sorry and gently brought Prakash's head to rest on his shoulder. But this time, it was the young man who detached himself brusquely.

In the countryside the days were still warm, but the nights had taken on a distinct chill. A cold, dry wind blew from the mountains. The rice on the land which surrounded the young man's house had long been harvested; the arcs of red and yellow with their graceful necklaces of grain had gone, and only straw-coloured tufts remained in the dry earth.

The house had been improved: an ornamental window, without glass, but a metal grille to keep out the the birds. The structure had been painted a dazzling white. A little garden had been made in front of the couple's bedroom, with canna lilies, marigolds and asters in full bloom. The creepers had almost covered the house: cucumbers and great ridged orange pumpkins. On the roof deep gold spindles of maize, scarlet chillies and vegetables drying in the tepid sunlight. Frank contemplated the ripening harvest of the fields, and then his friend, who looked, he thought, a little older; as though he, too, were part of the timeless landscape of growth, death and renewal; as indeed, he reminded himself, we all are. Only he accepts it with such ease, and I can't.

The young man had had a bathroom and lavatory added to the house; bare concrete chambers without running water, but at least they afforded some privacy. The borders of the field were ablaze with wild flowers and pink silwari grass, In the orange light of evening a layer of mist hugged the earth. As they walked, yellow flakes of sarsoon, mustard petals, clung to their shoes, and the fragrance filled the cool air. Frank for a moment felt lulled; yes, I could live here.

The women are there to greet them. They smile and make Frank feel welcome. They make no reference to the help he has given them. The sister looks well; she is still thin, but her face is mobile and cheerful, and she is energetic in her welcome, running to make tea in the kitchen by the light of a candle.

The young man takes Frank into his bedroom. Part of the wife's dowry has been a big wooden bed with mattress, an upright wooden sofa with cushions and two chairs to match. There is also a television, which sits under a sequinned shroud on the table, waiting for the electricity to come to the house, which will call it into vibrant life. But not yet.

Sunita appears. She is wearing a dark red saree, bordered with silver; a dramatic contrast to the shabby blouse and saree of her mother-in-law and the dingy colours of her sister-in-law, who seems to express her own deep sadness and exclusion through the neglect of her person. Aruna is a woman who no longer has any hope for her own life; a pitiable figure, although she laughs a lot with an uncultivated rough country charm. Frank likes her more and more.

The wife is attractive, slightly fleshy; she wears anklets, silver medallions on a chain which make a light chinking sound as she walks. Her movements have a kind of indolent grace, although in fact she moves quite quickly. Her hips are broad, her skin is rather pale, her face round. She speaks sparingly and is self-effacing; her voice is high, like a little girl's. Frank reflects that she has been practising all her life for this moment of consummation. She smiles shyly, and goes away to prepare some food.

She will desert the conjugal bed in favour of her husband's friend. This is considered quite normal, the young man reassures him. What do you think of her? Frank observes that the young man looks at her through his lowered eyelashes as she busies herself in the half-light in the kitchen; he cannot tell if it is a look of appraisal, desire, revulsion. They scarcely speak together in the presence of the family; and since they will spend no time alone while Frank is there, he can make no judgment on the relationship. He finds this tantalising and disturbing – is it because their relationship is so good they won't show it off, or so bad that they cannot bear to display it? Is it, he thinks, because it isn't a relationship at all, but a role into which both, knowing what is expected of them, fall, graceful and accepting?

The mother comes into the bedroom and sits with Frank and her son. Aruna helps the wife in the kitchen. The mother takes up her monologue where she left it last time she saw Prakash. Frank is convinced she does not talk like this when she is alone with the women: a thin filament of lament, of weariness and sadness. It is clear that it is not enough for the young man to have provided her with a wife and a child. She wants him back home. This is your place. Frank agrees. Prakash wants to leave the service, he wants to come home. But there is no work. He would like to be a teacher of phsyical education in a local school.

The young man is being transferred to Kashmir. The mother says I didn't work as I worked for you to go and leave your bones in Kashmir, and your wife and mother to weep for you. I'll be in camp, says the young man. But it is a withdrawal of privilege. He will not be able to go out of camp, because of the danger to army personnel. He will practise, eat and sleep. He says that if he can find a way of coming home, he will do so. The mother turns to Frank directly. Can you help him? Frank says he will be only too happy, if the young man can find some work. He will help him open a business, anything. The young man looks at the floor.

Suddenly, the mother interrupts he ritual lament and talks more vigorously. Now the subject is her daughter-in-law. She doesn't work hard enough. She doesn't know the meaning of work. She is slow. She has not lightened our work at all. Quite the oppposite. Everything she does has to be done all over again. There is something about her I don't like.

Both the husband and the sister defend the young woman. That was your life, they say to their mother. You had to work, for our survival. Nobody has worked as you did. Nor should they have to. It is different for her. Anyway, what doesn't she do properly?

She doesn't work hard enough, says the old woman obstinately. The wife brings the food. A lock of hair falls over her face in the yellow light from the kerosene lamp. She is about to turn and go, when Frank asks her to sit. She is one of eight children, with four brothers and three sisters. She has never worked, except in the home, helping bring up the family. She has clearly been schooled to discipline and acceptance; a long apprentice-ship in subordination. Life is suddenly different for her. How lonely she must feel. The sister-in-law tries to make up to her for the mother's hostil-ity. But even this does not surprise her; it is part of the expected ordeal of adapting to this new family, strangely depleted, a family without men, from which her husband will remain absent for months at a time. Frank feels great pity for her, a pity which he will later use to hurt her even more.

They sleep early, By ten o'clock the small house is quiet. The two men lie in the marriage bed. The young man creeps into his friend's arms, Frank hears the sound of night creatures, birds that shrill in the dark, the scrabbling of rats, the hum of insects, even, it seems, the mites attacking the wooden chairs, the mildew of the rains eating the fabric of the house. It is, he thought, like listening to time.

Frank cannot sleep. He hears in the night the sound of cattle som-nolently crushing grass, the chirping of crickets, like a nocturnal shrilling of distant telephones. At one point, Prakash's mother cries out in her sleep, a dream of old insecurities, as she begs a moneylender for credit or a doctor for medicine for her children. Prakash gets up, and Frank hears him soothe the old woman back to sleep; words of comfort whispered in a homely dialect; and he feels excluded again.

The women are up before dawn, engaged upon their endless labour. They water the animals, gather fodder, fetch drinking water. The wife sweeps the verandah with a brush of soft twigs, then she washes the floors, the clothes. The young man, stung perhaps by Frank's observations on the work of women, fetches some water and warms it for his friend to take a bath. In the early morning, the fields, silvered with dew, are full of women working.

Nearly everything is made at home. They grow almost enough rice, there is wheat and maize, and they never have to buy vegetables. A minimum of requirements is bought in – they buy salt and sugar, kerosene and rice from the ration-shop, although at six rupees a kilo it is of poor quality. Potatoes and onions are drying on the floor of the room where the women sleep. The young man makes breakfast, omelette and chappatis.

Frank wants to go back to Kalgotri, which he has never seen when it is not raining. He observes the young man fall into a male stereotype at home. The women sit and look at him all the time, waiting for him to express some need or wish that they instantly fulfil. Frank finds it unbearable, and he wants to talk to him alone.

They find a taxi that is being run by one of Prakash's former colleagues, a sportsman who left the service and bought a Maruti Bahin. He says business is not good. Fifty rupees a passenger, five passengers, but some days they make only two trips up the mountain and back. It is too competitive. Later, in the hill-resort, they take the funicular railway to the view of the Himalaya. The glacier is not quite visible in the autumnal haze. The young man who tears the tickets was also a sportsman, a javelin thrower. He has come home, and this is the best work he can find. He grimaces at Prakash to indicate that the doesn't like it.

Prakash is quiet. He has seen the fate of his peers. He will not leave the force for something so insubstantial and unrewarding. They meet another friend, a young man who runs a flour-mill. He is the only earner in his family. He has a hard time making a living. The army has always been a way out for many boys from the hills; but it makes it impossible for them to return, unless they will accept some menial, ill-paid work.

They visit the old colonial hotel. It is cold in the hills now, but the sun shines through the big window and illuminates the archaic dusty interior. Frank says to him suddenly Now you have to choose.

Choose? You can't lead a life like this. You either have to come home and live with your family, or you come with me. I want you to live with me. That isn't possible, said the young man. If you could choose what would you do? I can't choose. Yes, you can. Anyone can. You can send money home. From where?

Frank doesn't reply. The young man looks at him. Of course, he is torn. He feels the pull of freedom, of what he thinks the West is like; but the tired body of his mother and the young body of his wife tug him in another direction. Frank, the foreigner, feels the upsurge of jealousy, which he rationalises by calling the young man a hypocrite. It is, he says, the pretence he cannot bear. He says his friend is hiding from himself; is marginalising a relationship which to him, Frank, has now become central, obsessive even. Frank remembers the postcard he had received from the honeymoon resort. It was gloating; had made him feel superfluous, inadequate. The young man was flaunting a maleness in which he had, until he met his friend, been deficient. The still unappeased desire for revenge flared up once more. He said You want the best of both worlds. Well you can't have it.

It isn't the best. I don't have a choice. Frank will not listen. He says Everyone has a choice. You don't understand. I understand that you manipulate everything and everybody to get what you want.

They went back to the house in the gathering dusk. Frank saw Sunita crouched over some twigs, kindling a fire in the kitchen for the evening meal. Suddenly, he is agitated by a desire for revenge and destruction. He kneels down beside her, and blows to quicken the twigs into life. He says Your husband has not told you everything. She pauses in her work, turns up the yellow light from the kerosene lamp, which is hissing faintly. It illuminates her face from below. To Frank, her dark eyes seem to express triumph. The sound of crickets and birds comes from the field. I think you should know what has been happening. She does not speak. Prakash and I... He swallows hard. We have been together. I love him. We have a relationship. We make love together. He doesn't want me to tell you. I thought you should know.

It sounded false, wrong. It didn't even ring true. The young woman looks at him with a sad smile. She has replaced the lamp on the floor, and her face is a dark oval; only the teeth an arc of silver. All she says is I have four brothers, what are you telling me? Frank, abashed, turns to go. In the doorway, he meets the young man. In his eyes a look of incredulous pain, and a reluctant farewell that seems to reach him across the immense distance of their unbridgeable cultures.

Prakash accompanied Frank to catch the night bus. At the bus stop, he said Why did you do that? Frank said I cannot stand your duplicity. If you would deceive her, you would deceive anybody. You would deceive me. You have deceived me.

The young man looked at him with his clear amber eyes. It isn't deceit. Life is not so simple. Why do you want everyone to see things the way you do? I meant it. You could have lived here. You would have been welcome. We owe you so much. Why have you thrown our friendship away? You must be very rich if you can squander such precious things so easily.

Why can't you face reality? Frank said to the young man, who replied I am not the one who left my home to look elsewhere.

The bus came; the rattling snub-nosed bus that would take eight hours to reach Delhi. Frank gave his hand to the young man, who shook it warmly, and looked at him searchingly, but now, it seemed, a stranger was looking out of the shining amber eyes; the stranger he had always remained. Frank felt his had been another alien presence in India, which had changed nothing. Defeated, he climbed inside the bus. Prakash stood by the open window. He didn't speak again, but Frank could see that he stood and waved on the dusty margin of the road until the bus was out of sight.

Frank returned to a wintry London. In the months that followed, he went back to the old cruising places. From time to time, he thought he caught a glimpse of his friend – a flash of dark skin in sunlight, an athletic body running across the grass, a sudden smile; but of course, he was not to be found there.

A letter came from Kashmir, already two months old; plaintive, unhappy, begging for help. Frank cast it aside. After that, silence.

* * *

Glossary of Hindi Words

p. 10   pakka: (in this sense) stone-built. Literally 'cooked' as opposed to 'kacha', raw.

p. 11   pailag: a greeting, where homage is paid to a superior by touching his or her feet.

p. 11   karvi: an orange-coloured flower.

p. 16   frangipani: a sweet-smelling flowering tree.

p. 16   kharif: the wet-season crop, usually rice.

p. 18   Lakshmi: goddess of wealth.

p. 20   terai: cultivated land on the hillsides.

p. 21   nalla: stream or small river.

p. 22   mehendi: a henna dye, used for decorating the hands at the time of a mariage.

p. 25   kabbadi: a boisterous Indian game.

p. 27   khadi: homespun fabric.

p. 30   brinjal; aubergine.

p. 30   chadar: bedsheet

p. 31   channa: chick-peas.

p. 32   chacha, mama, kaka: paternal/maternal aunts and uncles.

p. 34   puja: religious observance, worship.

p. 40   chawl: workers' tenements, usually brick-built.

p. 41   dalit: Untouchable (literally, oppressed)

p. 43   jhuggi-jopri: slum hutments.

p. 44   Naxalites; an extreme left-wing group committed to violent change.

p. 45   gulmohar: a tree with flame-coloured blossoms.

p. 45   ratkirani: (literally, queen of the night), a night-scented jasmine.

p. 46   beta: son.

p. 49   bigha; a measure of land, approximately sixth of an acre.

p. 53   jamun: purple fruits of trees that line many streets in Delhi.

p. 57   'brown sugar': a heroin derivative.

p. 62   lakh: 100,000.

p. 66   Vande Materam: the Indian National Anthem.

p. 80   hamal: cart-puller.

p. 88   dada: slumlord.

p.88   bulbul, shintola: Indian birds.

p. 111   kabristan: cemetery.

p. 113   chhatri: a dome or cupola.

p. 124   shamiana: a tent.

p. 126   mangal sutra: wedding jewellery.

A WOMAN'S LIFE

Syphilis, to the first half of this century, represented much what AIDS has to the past fifteen years; except that it remained the object of a rigorous taboo, a private and lonely torment to the individuals it touched. Those who suffered from it were, at that time, in no position to struggle against the public shame which they incurred. It was believed, as so many diseases have been, to be a retributive, even divine, visitation.

My mother's life was shadowed by its secret ravages, which went far beyond its damaging physical effects. This story shows the response of one woman to her husband when he contracted syphilis. I offer this account of her bravery and loneliness, with affection and tenderness, and in the hope that the time may come when no sickness, no leprosy or plague, no syphilis or AIDS will ever again be thought to be deserved by those affected by it.

Jeremy Seabrook
New Delhi/London
July 1994 – July 1996

One

MY MOTHER'S whole life had tended towards the complete physical immobility which claimed her in the end. She had always been afraid of
going away, of new places. Leaving home, even for a holiday, filled her
with anxiety. At such times, she would walk round the house, checking
the chrome ears of the gas-taps and rattling doors she had securely locked
a few minutes earlier. Later, she became terrified even of going outside the
house, then of going upstairs, and finally, of leaving her chair of pink
uncut moquette with its sheltering wings, the clasp of its strong wooden
arms. At last, rigid with arthritis, yet shaking with Parkinson's disease –
immobilised yet in perpetual movement – she could do nothing without
help.

But to remain in one place was not what she really sought, for this
brought her neither peace nor security. The longing for stillness had at its
root a deep inner turbulence. If I leave the house, she thought, I might
have an accident, I might fall down, I might be forced onto the mercy of
strangers in public. Something terrible will happen if I go away; as though
her presence in a place were a guarantee of her power to control everything that happened there. For she had a horror of the unexpected, the
improvised, the sudden. This was in part the other side of her need to
keep up the illusion that she was the prime mover, not only in her own
life, but in the lives of those who depended upon her. And dependency
upon her was what she most wanted.

Even when she was completely paralysed, the anxieties did not re-
cede. Quite the contrary, they assailed her powerlessness with even greater
insistence. In the nursing home where she died, her questions were 'What
if the nurses drop me, what if someone breaks in, what if they don't hear
when I cry out in the night?' Her desire to be at rest physically was revealed as merely a metaphor.

Her life continued to be cramped and controlled by fear until she
died. And indeed, that fear led her to cramp and control others; as though
she were merely the medium through which an almost abstract fear worked
upon me and my brother.

An intelligent, able woman, she had always believed that she was
handicapped by her lack of education; this served as excuse for all her

153

failures, and in the end became a veil for what was a truly disabling agoraphobia.

She had been taken out of school on her fourteenth birthday to work in a brush factory. She worked a treadle that pulled the bristles through the wooden base of the brush. She was rescued by the authorities, because it had become the law of the land that children were to stay until the end of the term in which their fourteenth birthday fell. Her schooling was, therefore, prolonged by this benign legislation for a further six weeks, an interval which somehow qualified her for employment in the office of a boot factory. This was a rare privilege, for her twelve brothers and sisters had, without exception, worked on the shop floor.

Whenever she spoke of her schooling afterwards, she remembered that during sewing classes, it had been the custom to have one pupil read to the others as they plied their needles, it being considered prudent not to allow the minds of young girls to stray too far during the long hours of plain stitching. She was invariably the one chosen to read; and for the rest of her life she could recall by heart the *Idylls of the King* or long passages of a work called *Joy's Jubilee*: the story of how a little girl spent the Golden Jubilee of our beloved Queen Victoria. As a result, her ability to sew remained limited; although this did not prevent her, when we were young, from sitting long hours by the wasting fire late at night, darning our socks across a pink wooden mushroom.

In fact, she was never good at any domestic tasks, although her role as woman compelled her to claim certain competences, the absence of which would have been, at that time, a source of great shame. She never liked cooking, although everything she prepared was always of the finest quality, even in the frugal post-war, full of some mysterious quality she called 'goodness'. Mealtimes were functional, even lugubrious occasions, not to be associated with pleasure; a time for silent, concentrated absorption of the elements that would make us grow big and strong.

She had always seemed to me a sombre, saturnine woman, enclosed in her own perpetual terrors which she tirelessly sought to communicate to my brother and me, so that we could share the bleak prospect of the world onto which her melancholy character looked. As far as I was concerned, it was redundant effort, and it only created resentment in my twin.

It wasn't until she was into her eighties that I heard her laughing uninhibitedly at one of my cousin's jokes, stories I would never have believed she could even understand, let alone sanction with her rusty laughter.

One day when I visited the home, her eyes were overflowing with tears as my cousin was telling her a story about a middle-aged couple who got married. 'It came to the wedding night. He got undressed quickly and got into bed. She was taking her time over it, puffing and wheezing as she took her blouse off, her slip, her knickers. He said to her "Come on, woman, hurry up." "I'll have you know," she said with dignity, "I've got acute angina." "Thank God for that," he said, "cos your tits are horrible."'

She had almost never spoken to us about sex; just a few sharp words about keeping ourselves clean and treating women properly. She no doubt thought this did not need to be stressed: her whole life had been an object lesson to us in the abuse of women.

ONE DAY when I visited her in the nursing home, I found her in a state of high agitation. 'Look,' she said excitedly, 'see who's sitting over there.' In the dimly lighted parlour, with its wooden panels and displays of artificial delphiniums, across the room, between an incontinent tv set and some noisy parakeets, sat an old woman with pale watery eyes and an aureole of wispy silver hair. She appeared to me an unremarkable newcomer to the wraiths assembled around the walls beneath the parchment lampshades. My mother made an exclamation of tetchy annoyance. 'Don't you recognise her? It's Pearl.'

Pearl had been one of her husband's fancy-women; although the term, always something of a hyperbole, now sounded downright cruel. But it gave my mother a moment of rare exultation, because Pearl no longer had any memory. 'She doesn't even know me,' said my mother contemptuous and triumphant. 'She's lost her senses. Not that she was ever burdened with too many even in her prime. She's been telling people "I was engaged to Sid Seabrook." If she was, he never told her he happened to be married to me at the time.' Pleased by her former rival's descent into dementia, she nevertheless regretted being unable to let her know she, at least, was still all there.

Pearl had been married to a policeman, and Sid had once taken our toys to give as presents to her children. Not only did he rarely give us anything, but he actually robbed us on that occasion to impress strangers. The stolen toys were little wooden wheelbarrows in which we carried around the animals of the neighbourhood, a duck, a cat, even a pig. One day we had gone out with Sid, and after a couple of drinks at the Fox and Hounds he had taken us to Pearl's house. And there, we had seen our vanished toys in the backyard. If we had known who had made these finely crafted objects, we might have understood why Sid had given them away. As it was, we ran home to our mother to tell her what we had seen. She went to the house to rescue them. Strangely, once retrieved, we never played with them again. The paint chipped and blistered, and they were eventually used to light the fire.

ILLNESS BECAME my mother's identity in the end. There was a tradition among working-class women that they never really recovered their health after the menopause. For many, it might have been mourning for a sexuality that had never been given the space to grow and flower. For others, it was a fretting for affection that remained undisplayed by their men. They suffered, a non-specific but pervasive ill-being. Perhaps the visceral vagueness of their disorder marked a final break with children, because it often seemed to coincide with their marriage, their departure from home, their move to a new job in another town. This malaise became worse in the later years of the century, as those ruptures became more definitive. Their young began to articulate a need to distance themselves from their parents, as though departure were also a liberation, whereas in the past they had merely moved to a neighbouring street, even a few doors away, in order to be close to their mothers. But now, the young worked away, and could return home only twice a year – at Christmas and in the summer. They paid for a telephone 'to keep in touch', and would call once a week. They sent school photographs of the grandchildren, smiling against a blue oval background, which stood on the little table next to the red cyclamen that wilted in the heat from the gas fire. The old women would talk about them to callers, even the home help and the gas-man. In the vacuum created by these separations, what could be more natural than that the illnesses should become more florid and without remedy? What had been a vague sense of loss of vitality, of feeling less than well, became a central feature of their existence.

My mother developed a mystic communion with her illness; as though she were listening to the brittleness of her bones, was watching the falling of the flesh, tasting the sourness of age. It became a bond, tighter, more exclusive than any other; a lonely unreachable thing, protected, as we had been protected as children. Indeed, her illness became the defining identity of her later years. It is a harrowing experience, to see yourself supplanted in someone's affections by a sickness. In the tenderness with which she dwelt on every detail of what was crippling her, I recognised the obsessive concern which she had once shown us, itself a crippling disease, which affected her and us alike. She sat in the winged armchair, listening to the progress of the illness within, responding to the silent disabling of her being as though to an invisible lover. She certainly had no wish to die at that stage: she had her illness to take care of, to cherish and keep from harm.

IN ALL fairness, this bonding occurred only when all others had failed her. She had tried her best to keep my brother and me close to her, and would have preferred us to accompany her into infirmity. And she had been very successful in attaching me to herself. For many years, my feelings had been caught in the trap of her possessiveness, and their efforts to be free easily thwarted.

When I finished university, I went home and worked in North-ampton Central Library. There, I became friendly with a young man of about nineteen, who represented the first contact our town had with what it called – already belatedly – beatniks. That is to say, he grew his hair long, wore old jeans and was a member of CND. He was a gentle and sensitive man, and his beautiful face blushed readily, a rich pink beneath the still golden hair on his cheeks. I harboured feelings for him which I could, at that time, scarcely acknowledge. One Saturday afternoon after work, he suggested we should go to London for the weekend. 'Why not,' I said; although in my heart I knew very well why not, even though I had been at Cambridge for three years, and had spent summers in France and Italy. Of course I would go with him. He had friends with whom we could crash for the night. 'I'll come round for you at six o'clock. We'll hitch a lift.' It sounded dangerous and exciting, and implausibly independent.

My mother opened the door to him and said coolly, 'What did you want?', even the tense she employed indicating the unreality of his plan. He said, blushing, 'Jerry and I are going to London.' 'You'd better come inside'. She didn't invite him to sit down, but said to me, 'What's this?' 'We're going to London.' 'Who is he?' she asked me, 'and why is he dressed up like some bloody street-Arab?' She turned to him, 'What are you, some kind of tramp?' Then to me, 'He's dressed the way we had to dress when we were kids. We ran around in rags, with our arses hanging out, because we were poor. You, I've given you the best of everything, Chilprufe vests and Crombie coats, even when I've had nothing, just so you should never have to go through what we did. When we were young, our mother put us to bed at three in the afternoon, and she hung sacks at the window so we should think it was night and not feel hunger. And you,' she turned back to me, her olive eyes fierce with a rage I had rarely seen, 'all you can think of is getting back to what I've given my life to keep you from.'

To Jack Williams she said, 'He's not going to no bloody London. I don't know who you are, or who your mother is, but if I couldn't send you out looking any better than you do, I'd bloody well keep you at home. He's not leaving this house and that's all there is to it.' Jack Williams blushed more deeply than ever, lowered his eyes so that the long lashes caressed his soft cheek, and slipped out of the front door. I did nothing to stop him, although I felt how ridiculous it was. But her passion was overwhelming. Her whole body shook with emotion. In vain I told myself I was 21; that it required minimal insight to understand that this scruffy young man was middle class, and that she would always be the first, in all other circumstances, to assert that appearances were deceptive.

But that really had nothing to do with it. I knew, as well as she did, that I did not hanker after the poverty from which she had delivered me, but that my affections might have wandered, poor starved things, hesitantly and timidly, beyond the narrow overgrazed pastures on which she alone permitted them to feed.

Later, the same evening, when the intensity of anger had subsided, we sat beside the dying fire. She poked the coals restlessly, causing them to collapse and flare in a last burst of flame. The air was heavy with resentment, remorse and, on my part, an obscure double feeling of guilt, that I had upset her so, and equally, for both our sakes, that I had been unable to stand up to her.

She said, 'I only want you to be happy.' The key words were 'I want'; she didn't even recognise that my supreme gift lay in being miserable, and she should have done, because it was part of her involuntary legacy to me. I understood through her the terrible insecurity that makes us want to dominate others.

Her insecurity did indeed come, in part, from growing up poor. But 'growing up poor' had become a reason, an explanation, and an excuse for everything. To her, it was perverseness that drew me back to the poverty that had scarred her. She had dwelt so insistently on the horrors of her childhood that I became fatally fascinated by them. Her power over me was so complete that she had actually implanted her own memories in me, and then she blamed me for not forgetting them.

That feeling must have been made worse by her position as youngest of twelve children. She had had to struggle for space in the crowded houses where the family seldom stayed for long, because they were always being evicted for not paying their rent. She often claimed that her mother had called her 'the flower of my flock'. When I said this to Aunt Em, her sister, with whom we went to live when I was ten, she vigorously denied that Gran had ever said any such thing. 'Our mother never made fish of one and fowl of another. She treated us all the same. Glad must have made it up,' That was as close as Aunt Em ever came to criticising her sister, the sister who found fault with her all the time.

WHEN MY mother was nine, the family had lived in Alliston Gardens, at that time one of the most shameful streets in the town, being one of the few from which the respectable working class was almost entirely absent. It was a long crescent of three-storey houses with basements (or 'under-ground kitchens' as they called them), occupied by the most recent migrants to the town, and by the most feckless, those who were such notorious defaulters on rent payment that they could find no other place to live. Of her father, my mother said, 'He'd drunk the house away and all the furni-ture'; an image which puzzled us as children, as we tried to imagine the liquefaction of such solid objects. 'All we had was a few crates and some old blankets. I used to walk the long way round to school, so nobody should see where I came from. It was a humiliation to be living there.'

Alliston Gardens was still standing in the 1960s. I went to see the place where she had lived: worn cobblestones etched with bright moss; chocolate-brown painted woodwork, broken windows; buddleias had taken root in some of the walls, which attracted red admiral and peacock butter-flies. Some people had left their belongings strewn in the basements – old photographs, broken clocks, Windsor chairs. Curtains, faded by sunlight, flapped at the broken windows which had shredded them.

When my mother lived there, the room above theirs was occupied by a man and a woman who quarrelled all the time. One day, my mother was alone in the house because she had been away from school with scar-let fever. Her mother had gone out – on those errands of survival which are still familiar in the urban areas of the Third World – to gather wood for the fire, to scavenge rotten fruit around the market stalls, or to buy some penny bloaters for a meal. Whenever I see women pushing a cart in Bombay or Manila, scheming, contriving to earn something to feed the children, I see in them my grandmother and her desperate strivings.

My mother was afraid of being alone. She heard footsteps on the uncarpeted stairs, and opened the door onto the landing. In the dusty light from the landing window, she could see the neighbour from upstairs. He sat on the top step, leaning against the worn dado. He called out to her. 'I want y' a minute, m' duck. Come up here.' His voice was soft, quite unlike the tone they were accustomed to hear through the walls at night, as she and her sisters clung together in fear under the blanket. She hesitated; but being an obedient child, went slowly upstairs. He said to her, 'I need somebody to polish my middle leg.' She could see his trousers were unbuttoned, and the bruise-coloured tip of the cock with its red eye. She flew downstairs, but he followed her. He seized her hair and turned her round to face him. Shaking her violently, he said, 'If you say a word, I'll slit your bloody throat.' She didn't speak of it until many years later; but this image of sex haunted her into adult life.

All her references to sex – rare enough – were disparaging. On one occasion, my brother and I, with an older boy, had seen the father of another of our school-friends masturbating in his front garden. It was a late summer twilight, and he stood on the crazy paving between the hydrangeas, gently manipulating his erection. He beckoned to our friend, who immediately turned and ran home to tell his parents what had happened. We were more discreet, and said nothing, possibly because we knew that such things did not fall within the ample range of confidences we were daily expected to make to our mother.

The other boy's parents, however, seemed to think some decisive action was called for. They came round to our house, dressed up rather incongruously in what looked like their best clothes, to discuss the matter with our mother. We were banished from the room, but we heard the inflections of a long, fierce conversation between the adults. 'It ought to be put in the hands of the police.' 'I'm not having no child of mine in court.' 'What he needs is a bloody good pasting, one he won't forget.' There was a silence. 'I can't hit him,' protested the father of our friend, a generous, sweet-tempered man. Our mother said decisively, 'Well somebody's got to do something. It'll happen again else, and there's no telling where it might end.' This suggested that sex was both sinister and damaging; which, in her experience it had been.

She repeated, 'Somebody's got to do something.' The silence spoke of the reluctance of the designated somebody. 'As a man,' she said, 'it's your duty.' His wife said acerbically, 'Don't you tell my husband what his duty is.' 'Well, is it or isn't it?' 'Jim, it's your duty to go and have it out with him.'

Wearing our pyjamas, we came back into the room, and were not sent away; perhaps we relieved the tense stillness between the two women.

What the woman didn't ask our mother was where her own husband was, and what she thought his duty might be in all this.

Jim went. The walk was no more than ten minutes across the rough piece of land with its wild grass and late summer growth of golden hawkweed and white yarrow. Our mother made tea. She paced up and down, as though to demonstrate that her sense of outrage far outstripped theirs. She would, perhaps, have offered to go herself, but since it was their son who had been the object of the man's intended indecency, she held herself in check. She rattled the spoons in the saucers, determined that her indignation should not perish for want of fuel.

When Jim returned, he was smiling cheerfully. 'It's all right.' 'How can it be all right? After what he's done?' Jim said sagely, 'It was the War. Done this to him. It's left him with a kink. The things he saw. Out there. In the East. He can't help it.' 'You didn't give him a bloody good hiding?' 'Do I look like somebody who's just given a good hiding? He told me he's under the doctor with his nerves,' 'You mean,' our mother said slowly, 'that he's going to get away with it? Never.' 'He's assured me that it will never happen again. It was a momentary blackout. He has no recollection of it whatsoever, although he knows he's liable to do strange things when he gets these attacks...'

The women were both angry now. They spoke almost as though Jim had been the one to expose himself on the doorstep. My mother implied that anybody who would close an eye to such things might be capable of doing them himself, That was enough for Jim's wife, who hastily decided it was time for them leave. To us, our mother said, 'Go to bed and forget it.' Somehow, though, like all the things which she exhorted us to forget, this remained, curiously indelible, in our memory. At that time, we could have known nothing of the reasons for her vehemence over sexual wrongdoing; but that only made the intensity of it the more unforgettable.

The incident didn't quite end there. Next day at school, our friend was asked why his father was walking round and round the piece of waste ground that separated our house from that of the delinquent. He clearly had not even confronted him at all.

IN POOR societies, the majority of women are oppressed by their role as comforters of men. It is their function to console for men's powerlessness, to redeem their social impotence in the presence of injustice, poverty and exploitation. Women become the victims of victims, recipients of cruelties which men experience in the workplace, in their relations with authority, police, employers, officals.

As societies become richer and more secure, the role of women tends to change into that of servicers of desire; and although that is never absent from the earlier period, it does not dominate when want, hunger and fatigue rule the lives of the poor.

Most of the women of my mother's generation spoke slightingly of sex, when they spoke of it all. They would say they couldn't wait for the time when they could do their bottom button up for good. They submitted wearily to the Saturday-night chore, and said they supposed you didn't look on the mantelpiece when you poked the fire. They would try to avoid the kisses that smelt of insincerity and beer, and clench their bodies against what they felt each time as a renewed invasion.

Our mother never entered into this kind of collusive intimacy with the other women on the estate. This always set her apart from them. They saw it as a sign of superiority and strength. And accordingly, they would come into the shop, and in a few words, reveal the depths of their loneliness, their dissatisfaction, their despair, sometimes more shocking than the physical bruises which they also sometimes exhibited to her, beneath the pinafore or the sleeves of their dress.

One woman, a thin, dark-haired creature, so nervous her hands were ever still, one day said to my mother that her husband had never 'consumed' their marrriage properly. They had been married fifteen years. What could she do? Our mother asked the woman, 'Has he never made any attempt, you know? She replied he had never touched her. A kiss on the cheek every day. She thought he loved her. But never in that way. She imagined perhaps that he didn't like it, But at heart, she feared it was her fault; she was afraid that she inspired revulsion in him.

Then one day, excitable, her hands fluttering, she came into the shop, and stood waiting until there were no other customers present. She had met another man. At the bus stop, she said, full of shame. He had been visiting his sister who lived on the estate. They had fallen into conversation. He was married, but unhappy. He had taken her out for a drink one Saturday dinner-time. Somehow, before they knew what was happening, both had confessed their unhappiness to each other. They had met in town, discreetly, two or three times. They had instantly recognised the urgency of repressed desire. Only they had nowhere to go. What could she do? There was no place, there was no time. Women had to account for themselves to their men; for them time was an impermeable invisible mesh which kept them captive to preparing the evening meal, being at home whenever he got in, as though they were an extension of the shelter itself: all houses were, as it were, tied cottages, Women might visit relatives, but these would certainly not lend themselves as alibis for infidelities which they themselves had no opportunity to explore. Where could she go with her man-friend? She had had no experience of sex. There was a hoarse urgency in her questions. It was impossible that she could go out in the evening without her husband, just as she would never dream of going out with him. She had heard of people who went to hotels, but it would cost a fortune, and she didn't know how to behave, she would be sure to give herself away. Anyway, what excuse could she give her husband?

Mother leaned over the counter and whispered something to her. Another customer came in. The woman lingered while the newcomer was served. Then my mother passed something over the counter, dull metallic. It was the key to the henhouse that stood on the waste ground close to where we lived, all moulted feathers and blanched shit.

'DON'T EVER let me go into a home', she had implored us as children, embracing us intensely. 'Whatever happens, don't put me in a home when I'm old.' Terrified, weeping, we made solemn promises that we would never, could never, imagine doing anything so heartless. At that time, the prospect seemed remote. It was far more likely that she would be the one to abandon us in the way she professed to dread. After all, whenever we misbehaved – infrequently – she had threatened to send us to live with Mrs Jones, a notably slovenly mother on the estate, whose children roamed the streets late at night and stole sweets from the tobacconist's shop on the corner. Occasionally, she said she would give us away to the gypsies.

Since we believed what our mother said, because she was always declaring her loathing of lies, I once thought it wise to look into the living conditions among the gypsies, into whose punitive custody we might one day be delivered. They camped on the verge of the road which led to our school, battered wooden chambers on wheels with painted hoods in front and shafts for the horses, and all around them, scratched armchairs and zinc bathtubs. I approached a woman seated on the stump of a fallen tree that was covered with buttery fungus. I looked into her unsmiling eyes, and explained that my mother was contemplating a future for me in her care. 'Oh is she. And what are you good for?' Not understanding her question, I said, 'No, it's because I'm bad and make her cry.' 'What makes you think you'd be wanted here?' This had not occurred to me; that the function of gypsies might not be as receivers of naughty children came as a surprise; and the thought of being repudiated by such outcasts an ever greater shock. 'Can you catch birds, can you skin rabbits, can you ride a horse?' I told her I was sorry, and left her, pursued by the fierce barkings of a half-wild dog covered in sores.

But it was into a home that she went in the end. At the time when she extracted from us the promise that we would never abandon her into the care of strangers, a home was perceived as the most shameful destination imaginable: a public admission that people could not look after their loved ones, or worse, that the loved ones themselves were not sufficiently deserving to be cared for by their kin.

When it did come, the context in which such things occurred had changed, and it appeared the most natural thing in the world. Indeed, she herself welcomed it. All past promises and protestations were cancelled. It had been a slow decline in the house which she and my aunt had shared for thirty-five years, as she became steadily less capable of coping with the familiar objects and the new appliances that had been installed specifically to help them answer their modest needs more easily. They would sit and wait for the community nurse to put them to bed, in the beds that had been brought downstairs into what had once been the front parlour, with its dusty moquette, the leggy geraniums in the hearth, the photograph of my aunt's long-dead husband. They would fidget like children, incapable of doing anything for themselves, and hating the dependency which the years had forced upon them. The arrival of the nurse was often delayed by whatever misfortunes she had found in the houses of the other old people on her rounds: an old woman had fallen and broken her thigh, and she was unable to reach my mother and aunt before eleven o'clock, so that their heads drooped forward in sleep; or she might come at seven-thirty, while the sun was still shining on the houses behind and throwing its red-gold reflection into the room, because on certain days this was the first call on the evening's journey.

My mother and aunt sat captive in their chairs, watching the thin loops of cobwebs tremble in the fumes from the gas-fire, observing the dust settle on tables they had once prided themselves you could see your reflection in, seeing the brass ornaments tarnished by the sour breath of age. Meanwhile, the upstairs had been shut off; the rooms became mildewy and decayed, the window catches rusted, the air of perpetual winter trapped in the unused spaces between the cold walls.

When the nurse came, they would relax and smile in welcome at her. Mostly middle-aged women, the nurses put them to bed with as much tenderness as their busy schedule permitted, trying not to catch the vest in the hairpins, and rolling down the stockings neatly, so they would be ready for the morning. They gave them a hot water bottle, warmed some milk to drink with their sleeping-tablet before turning off the light. Sometimes, they gave the old ladies a goodnight kiss, before letting themselves out of the darkened hall.

Although the move to the nursing-home was in the beginning a relief, my mother was quick to insist she was not happy there. But she had never been happy anywhere, so at least this was of a piece with the rest of her life. The first home had been the residence of a boot-maker, who had made a fortune out of military boots in the First World War; a red-brick gabled house, surrounded by the kind of sombre evergreens – stiff holly, sculpted laurels and funereal cypress which traditionally screened the conspicuous luxury of the rich from the gaze of passers-by, many of whom they probably employed in their factory.

She couldn't settle. Although until this time she had read eagerly and extensively, she no longer felt sufficiently at peace to open a book; and in any case, there was no one to turn the pages for her, so what was the use. Nevertheless, she took with her *Bleak House* and *The Mill on the Floss*. The care workers would come in, pick them up and say 'Fancy anybody being able to read that'. She had placed the books close to her as a warning to staff members who infantilised the residents, that she, for one, still had her wits about her and was not to be trifled with. It worked, too. They treated her with respect. She would not watch television: loss and grief were too interesting to permit of such trivial distraction.

Whenever I visited her, I stored up tales to tell her, incidents and fragments of gossip to amuse her; but they froze in my mouth. She treated anything from the outside as insignificant, and an intrusion upon her unique and inconsolable descent into old age. I would sit, holding her arthritic hand, the middle finger of which was bent back upon itself, wondering how I could hasten the passage of the three hours I would spend with her. Everything I had wanted to say was crushed by the weight of that immobilised source of power within her, which seemed all the more concentrated for its enforced stillness. One day, when I was searching for something that would rouse her interest, she looked at me and said, 'If it wasn't for you coming to see me, I shouldn't care if I never woke up again.' Perhaps it was the fact that I continued to respond to her influence that made of me so desirable – if so wretched – a companion. It demonstrated that she had not lost the ability to reduce me to dumb acquiescence.

I couldn't believe when another of my cousins said, 'We like to go and see your Mum. We have a laugh with her.' 'What do you laugh about?' I asked incredulously. 'She has us in stitches. She tells us all about the staff, the other patients, the visitors.' In the home was a woman who had formerly been employed as a guide at Althorp House, the home of the Princess of Wales. She would intercept visitors at the threshold of the nursing home, and request them to be patient until the whole party was assembled before she could show them round. Some people, impressed by her authoritative manner, waited for the absentees to appear. Indeed, she would conduct people from room to room, an accomplished mistress of ceremonies. One day, my cousin asked her if she could tell him where the lavatory was. She looked at him appraisingly, and said, 'I suppose there must be somewhere for the workmen to go. I'll make enquiries.' This reminded my cousin of one of his workmates, who had been a fitter for the Gas Board. One day, this man had been repairing the gas system in a big private house in Northampton, and he had asked the householder if he could use the toilet. 'Certainly not,' she had replied. In revenge, said my cousin, he shat under the floorboards before nailing them down. My mother again laughed, that rare unfamiliar evidence of a sense of humour, any display of which she had withheld from me or my brother.

One day, when I had spent the whole day with her, she said proudly to one of the staff, 'I've had a companion today.' To be described in such impersonal terms was very sad; not only because it had made the day special for her, a contrast to the long companionless days which were usual, but also because it made me feel like the vicar.

On another occasion, she had heard some of the staff talk disparagingly of one of the other residents, a woman who was confused, and thought one of the care assistants was her daughter. My mother let them know she had heard every word. One member of staff said to her, 'You're too damn sharp for your own good, Gladys,' She retorted, 'What do you want me to do, lose my senses like the rest of them, so you can do what you like to us?'

A shrewd survivor, she made friends with many of the employees of the nursing-home. They liked her, they talked to her. She knew all about the efforts management were making to save money, about the levels of occupancy and shortages of qualified staff. She knew precisely how much money was allowed per head for meals, and she expressed her own views about agency staff who were sometimes employed for night duties. They called her room the Board Room, because that was where staff spoke their grievances; grievances about which nothing could be done, because, of course, there was no question of a union.

Sometimes my visits felt like an intrusion into the conspiratorial relationships with those she saw daily, These had become more real for her than relationships with the family. She listened avidly to the details of their lives. One woman had been on holiday with her husband to celebrate the 38th year of their marriage; on the last night, he told her he was leaving her. Others spoke to her about their debts, the cost of their daughter's wedding – 'I know the wedding's going to be sumptuous, Glad, it's the bloody marriage I'm worried about'. They told her stories of their children's successes, their miscarriages, their divorces, even their lovers. Perhaps they sensed that my mother's supreme ability lay in her gift for keeping secrets. She had, if they had only known it, kept her own long enough, even though it had corroded her spirit for half a lifetime. When I saw her with the care assistants, she reminded me of the sympathetic and collusive shop-woman she had been when I was a child.

'WHY EVER DID you marry Sid?' I sometimes asked her. If she had set out with the determination to find someone completely at odds with her nature and temperament, she could scarcely have made a more perfect choice. She always said quite simply, 'I assumed everybody was the same.' She meant that the working-class culture in which she grew was a formidable arranger of marriages. The idea of 'choice' had few of the associations it has now. She said she had no idea that people had different needs. To her, a good wife or husband, a good mother or father were all public roles. This implied a certain kind of behaviour, a code of conduct, the observation of certain duties, not forms of satisfaction and personal fulfilment which depended upon individual and sometimes incommunicable wants and desires. These would have seemed impossible luxuries in the poor, enclosed world of her youth, in which the great majority of people worked in the same feral-smelling shoe factories, lived in the same small terraced houses, drank and sang in the same bleak pubs, grew tart rhubarb and prize dahlias in the same allotments, went to the same cinemas to see *The Garden of Allah*, were married in the same church or chapel and were buried in the same graveyard.

She said, 'I thought you just got married, and that was it. I supposed everybody's life was the same. I knew there were good husbands and bad husbands. My Dad was a swine to our mother. He drank and knocked her about. He kept her short on money and long on kids. I thought a good husband was somebody who didn't smoke and drink, always worked and gave his wife enough money to feed the children and provide properly. It never occurred to me that two people might not get on sexually. I thought you just did what you had to do to have children, and that was it. I thought it was the same for everybody. I learned different, but it was too late by then.'

In her crowded childhood family, there had been little space for sharp psychological differentiation. She knew, of course, that the character of people varied – some were kind, others mean, some short-tempered, some jealous, others generous, some reserved, others unhappy. But all this was contained within fixed roles – husband and wife, brother and sister, father and mother. Indeed, these roles were the principal influence upon individuals, served them as known guide and discipline, and more or less kept their conduct with certain strict limits.

It was her fate to see, within her lifetime, the decay of this culture and the relativising of its values. Her generation was to form the human bridge that transformed roles into relationships. From a public recognition of clearly defined roles, to the private realm of secret, and often, unavowable satisfactions; from one extreme, as she said, to another. Few things can create more anguish in a human being than to see their beliefs, their world-view undermined, their values and way of life laid waste and destroyed. In fact, the trauma this imposes upon traditional societies – tribal people, Adivasis in India and indigenous peoples in previously remote forests, when they come into contact with the more powerful values of the dominant global society, is itself only just being understood. That a similar process occurred only recently within the heart of Western society itself, and within living memory, has been almost completely ignored.

Part of my mother's suffering was not hers alone, was not merely the consequence of her own strange and aberrant sensibility, but was shared by millions of voiceless people. It had its origin in the collapse of a collective value-system which had developed in the industrial period as a protection against some of the rigours of industrial life, and its replacement by an extreme individualism, which is the more damaging for being unable to recognise itself as ideology, but declares that it is the essence of Life itself.

What all this meant when she was in her early twenties was that she was quite unable to distinguish those who might from those who would certainly not be a good match for her. Later in life, she always prided herself on being 'a good judge of character'. This consisted in distrusting everyone, and the assumption that they would inevitably, one day, disappoint, cheat or betray you. In the end, most of us prove unworthy in one way or another; this enabled my mother to declare triumphantly that she had always known, she had never liked them from the start. The truth was, she never liked anyone from the start; so this gave her an enormous advantage in her long-term judgments, and placed her above those gullible souls taken in by appearances.

She lived through the dissolution of the extended family. We grew up among hosts of aunts and uncles, and our lives were crowded with cousins. Each birthday brought more than a score of cards and presents. Sometimes, at holidays, when we went for a picnic, a whole field seemed filled with those related to us. With the passing of time, they all went their individual ways, followed strange paths which mysteriously separated their destiny from ours for ever; so that even those whom we had seen daily as children eventually became strangers to us.

In spite of the depleted family group in which we were raised, my mother maintained a traditional diffidence to those she called 'outsiders', which referred to those not related to us by blood. She was suspicious of those who were not our kindred, that despised archaism from whom it became our object in life to liberate ourselves. She spoke as though the whole world were scheming or clamouring to gain admission to the secret, closed and depopulated sanctuary of our family life. Families had been all-in-all to each other, sites of fierce quarrels and jealousies no doubt, of battles and rivalries which sometimes went on for years; but as soon as any outside threat appeared, they showed an impregnable solidarity and defensiveness. 'They're still your own,' she said to the mother whose son had been arrested for stealing lead from a church roof. Blood remained, for the time being at least, thicker than water.

SID HAD grown up – or had perhaps failed to grow up, according to her exhortations to him to do so – in a little country town just across the Buckinghamshire border, where his parents had a slaughterhouse and butcher's shop. The town was at that time a somnolent country place, with its distinctive raw accent, the rows of tumbledown cottages, and meadows of wild flowers, where women still made lace on the threshold of their houses, rattling their bobbins and placing their pins on the crimson cushions on which they worked, and children bathed naked among the bulrushes and blue irises in the river. Market day still sent ripples of excitment into the surrounding countryside, as people set out their home-grown produce – sour green apples, hard pears that would be placed in a linen-drawer to ripen during the autumn, blue savoy-cabbages, potatoes encrusted with earth; pea-pods to which a faded grey flower still clung.

Sid was very attractive as a young man, and was said to have borne a strong resemblance to Henry Fonda, whose flickering image sometimes passed across the grainy screen of the little lop-sided Electric Cinema in the High Street. Sid was admired by many young women. He became the object of their dreams and fantasies, like the cinema screen whose shadows he recalled; and they projected onto him their own desires and imaginings with such persistence that he sometimes found it difficult to distinguish between their dreams and his real being. Like many physically desirable people, he longed to be wanted for himself, even though a sense of his own authenticity escaped him.

If Glad intrigued him, it was because she didn't seem to notice his good looks, but gave him to understand that she saw something beyond them. She did not appear intimidated by him, she did not blush and lower her eyes whenever they met. It seemed perhaps to Sid that she had discerned in him something profound and appealing, some quality of mind or spirit which others had not observed; and suffering as he did from the fanciful imaginings of most young women he knew, he was anxious to discover what it was.

They met in Olney High Street, when she was visiting one of her sisters, whose family lived in a tiny ramshackle cottage, one of a row of eight which shared a communal backyard. Glad was perhaps more alert than her sisters, perhaps because she was not pretty, and had to work harder to attach people to herself. She learned later that despite Sid's longing to transcend what he experienced as the burden of his good looks, he wee nevertheless deeply dependent upon the constant attention and flattery which these earned him. In fact, the feeling of inner emptiness existed quite independently of his appearance; and to be alone with it was a terrible ordeal, which he would do anything to escape from. Later, he accused her of creating that lack of substance, of diminishing his self-esteem. She had seemed at first to offer the possibility of achieving a sense of himself and his worth beyond the adventitious satisfaction he derived from his beguiling dark eyes and soft crimson lips; and when she failed to provide him with it, he accused her of betrayal. He wanted her to rescue him. When she couldn't, he blamed her, not only for the false promises which she certainly never made, but also for being puritanical and denying of life; which she certainly was.

In order to distinguish herself, the youngest among so many brothers and sisters who grew as profuse as flowers in a summer field, she required a special destiny. She had no idea of how special it was to be, as she entered the unknown territory of a relationship while still believing she was passing into the familiar landscape of a revealed role.

THEY TOOK a mortgage on a butcher's shop, on a new estate on the edge of Northampton. It was one of a crescent of ten shops, pebble-dashed, white-washed, flat-roofed, modern, even futuristic, and inspired by a mixture of California and a series of hot summers in the 1930s. Inside, the shop floor was of black and white tiles like a giant chessboard, while a huge black refrigerator hummed and purred night and day, protecting from putrefation chilled Argentine beef and spring lamb. In the shop window were diamond-shaped sheets of greaseproof paper and gleaming steel rails, from which haunches of dismembered animals bled gently onto the white-tiled display counter beneath.

Glad had always loved reading. In the evenings, when the shop was shut, they sat in the comfortable living-room behind, and she offered to read to him, recalling the popularity of her readings in sewing classes. He agreed, but without enthusiasm. He preferred the more immediate excitements of the radio. She took one of her favourite novels, *Comin' Through the Rye*. 'You'll like this.' After she had been reading for five or ten minutes, she glanced up to see how he was enjoying it. He had fallen asleep. She felt abandoned; a foreshadowing of desertions to come. She shivered and closed the book, rattled the poker in the embers of the dying fire.

It soon became clear that Sid had no gift for shop-work. She knew how to please and flatter the customers. Sid had no time for their stories. He was not interested in exchanging gossip, listening patiently to their confidences. When he was serving, fewer people came into the shop. Before long, his function was reduced to carrying and cutting up the carcasses of meat that were delivered from the wholesaler every Tuesday, cleaving the maroon-and-yellow sides of beef, opening up the stiff white and rose cylinders of lamb to expose the white suet and the chocolate-coloured kidneys. She attended to everything else. They agreed it would be better if Sid found a job; their income would increase, and there really wasn't enough work for two people in the shop.

He hired a lorry, and was soon delivering loads of bricks, timber, sand, or manufactured goods from factories to distributors. For him, it was a release, not only from the confinement of the shop, but from the claustral relationship with Glad. He began to work long hours, unpredictable journeys that took him to Walsall or Liverpool. The irregularity of the labour justified lengthening absences from home.

At that time, in the late 1930s, it seemed to her she spent most of her time waiting for Sid to come home. She moved restlessly through the house, glancing at the clock, wiping down a surface, cleaning the shop-floor again. She worked late, cutting up the orders for the next day, so that frequently the lights shone out onto the wet road until nine-thirty or ten at night. Sometimes she stood on the doorstep, looking for the cone of light from the headlamps cutting through the darkness. Sometimes she became angry, and no longer tried to keep his dinner appetising, but let it burn up in the oven; then, overcome with guilt, she would throw it out and prepare something fresh for him. The sound of the tyres on the gravel beside the shop always filled her with such relief that she would run to the door to open it for him, fill the kettle with water for tea, rush to greet him, animated by the pleasure of seeing him, even though they might have parted only that same morning.

Yet her eagerness evoked little response from him. He would be tense from the long journey, his eyes still fixed on the long ribbon of road and the night-creatures that sometimes burst against the windscreen of the cab. Why was he so late? There had been a puncture. He had seen an accident. As soon as he was home, and no longer in movement, he became surly and irritable. He was tired, he didn't want to talk. What else happened? she would insist. Nothing. What about the accident? What accident? The one you saw. He would shrug. A man knocked off a bike. An ambulance, A red blanket, A face in pain. It happens all the time.

She herself was always full of news. She soon acquired a rich store of information about people on the estate. She knew who had moved away without paying rent, whose wife had been seen up an entry with the coal-man, whose barking dog had been poisoned by a neighbour. He showed no interest. She had, she felt, so many things to tell him, but they remained choked inside her like badly digested food. When she had set his food on the table, she would fall silent, pick up her book. But she wasn't really reading. She would look up shyly at him from time to time, and if he looked at her, smile. This worsened his mood, and he would turn away. 'Leave me alone,' he sometimes said under the unspoken reproach of her eyes. She felt how unreachable he was, She was well aware that he could not follow her thoughts and ideas. Her intelligence, her perceptions were closed to him; but here were feelings locked away, she felt, fugitive, hidden. He was absconding emotionally, there was an absence that should not have been there.

Yet she thought about him obsessively. The details of his body, the thickness of his thighs, the bud of his penis in repose, the herringbone of dark hairs from the stomach to the groin, the creased crimson sack of his balls. Sometimes, cutting the meat, she would be thinking of him, and the knife would slip, gashing her finger, so that her own blood mingled with the dark red trickle that oozed from the chunk of beef on the block.

Later, his comings and goings became even more unpredictable. There was a load of wood, a delivery of sacks of freshly-dug potatoes, some bricks urgently wanted on site. If she asked him where he was going, his replies became evasive – the kind of vagueness with which the curiosity of children was checked: 'Two fields the other side China' or 'To see a man about a dog.' She felt patronised, insulted. Everything was wrong. She wondered why; but eventually became so tired from her work that she no longer waited up for him; and it might be three o'clock when she glanced at the noisy Westclox alarm in a shaft of light as he opened the bedroom door and crept into bed beside her, taking care that his body should not touch hers at any point.

His remoteness was the first inkling that something was badly wrong. She made all the excuses that women know, know instinctively, know by heart, even though they have never heard them spoken before. You can't expect men to feel in the way that women do. They don't know how to show their feelings. This is their loss. They have their own rhythms, which are not ours. They don't like to be tied down. It takes time.

But how much time! Two years, three years passed. Until this time, she had felt herself secure behind the counter in the shop. This was an unassailable position, one from which she could listen sympathetically to the confessions and confidences that came from the women she served. She had a role. She was on show. She was always there, was known to be discreet, sympathetic. Women sensed that nothing they told her would go any further. She looked at them with frank eyes the colour of amber in the morning light; and these suggested depths of compassion and understanding which few could resist.

She had been secretly gratified by the stories they brought to her, tales of infidelity, unhappiness and grief. One woman's husband had stolen female garments from a washing line. Why, she asked my mother, aghast, why had he done a thing like that? He was a normal man. He worked on a building site. They had a proper married life. Why would he want to steal women's underwear? She had found a pair of silk panties under the mattress. At first, she thought they had belonged to another women. 'Well, they did, but not quite in the way I thought.' Later, he was seen actually unpegging a slip and some knickers in the green January twilight, and was followed home. Caught red-handed with the articles concealed beneath his overalls. The man who had apprehended him went straight to the police. 'What is it Glad? Why would he want to do a thing like that?'

My mother listened gravely and counselled. 'It's an illness' was her judgment. 'He can't help it. he needs some sort of treatment. It'll do no good going to court over things like that. It's not as if there was any injured party.' She was extremely sympathetic in her response to irregularities in the lives of people which did not touch hers; it was only for domestic application that she deployed her inflexible and punitive puritanism.

The man did go to court, His name was published in the local paper the equivalent and refinement at that time of the pillory – which duly exposed the shame of wrongdoers to the community. He received letters signed 'from a well-wisher', which advised him to leave the estate. The woman came into the shop to tell my mother they were indeed leaving. 'You've been the only friend I've had.' Mother did not repudiate the compliment. 'I shan't forget you.' Glad smiled and said, 'Yes, well you know where to find me if you want me.' The unhappiness of others made her feel safe, untouched by, and somehow sheltered from, such afflictions.

There was another woman whose husband, on their wedding night, instead of making love to her, had beaten her up. It was a nightmare, she confessed, looking down and clenching her hands so tightly around the parcel of meat that blood came through the newspaper. 'As soon as we were alone together, he turned. I couldn't do a thing right. We went to the hotel, had a drink. After he'd had one or two drinks, he started sneering at me. I felt scared. I'd known him over a year, but I felt I'd married a stranger.' 'We all marry strangers,' said my mother with authority. 'When we got into the room, he started on me. He slapped me, pulled my hair. He said I wasn't a virgin. He said I'd tricked him. I tried to be affectionate, but that only made him more angry. I said, "I've never been with a man." He said "What have you been with then, women?" Why does he hate me?' She wept, and her tears mingled with the blood from the meat. Glad leaned over the counter and said, 'It's not you m' duck. He might be impotent. Had you thought of that?' 'Oh.' 'Why would he carry on like that? He was scared, frit to death. That's why he had to accuse you.' 'Yes. Yes.' It struck the woman as a revelation. 'I thought it was me.' 'Yes', she said, 'women always do. It's him. Make no mistake.'

How did she know? From where did these insights come? Perhaps she had already learned from her own anxieties, the lonely hours she had reflected during Sid's absences, on the sorrows of all women, sorrows from which she, at that time, was learning that she, too, was not immune.

But it was some months before those empty spaces in her own life, filled then only with formless fears and amorphous imaginings, began to assume a clearer shape. Her fascination with the stories of others helped her to keep her own anxieties at bay, even while, below the level of conscious reaction, she was already preparing herself to deal with something far worse than anything her customers had confided to her.

Two

HER ANXIETIES at first focused on the possibility that he might die. The lorry was unsafe. She saw it swerve as his eyelids closed with fatigue, glass and metal against a tree by the roadside. There lay the body she loved, pierced by metal, the bone through the flesh. These images were so vivid that she sometimes tensed herself, half-expecting the call from the police, the telephone bell, the urgent knocking on the side-door.

She thought of other horrors. Hardingstone, the neat sandstone village to which she had walked over the fields as a child, had been the site of a particularly gruesome murder only a couple of years previously. Known as the 'burning car murder', the victim had never been identified. Once, when my brother and I were young, we had been to see the grave, marked with a plain wooden cross, inscribed To the Memory of an Unknown Man. The murderer had taken out insurance on his own life, had picked up a stranger, and had murdered him. He set fire to the car, and, hoping the body would be identified as his, had his girl-friend claim the insurance. The identity of the victim was never traced. No one claimed him, no one missed him. That always seemed to the people of Northampton – anchored, rooted, belonging – an unimaginably cruel fate.

Whenever Sid was late, it was to such events that her mind sped. Later, I learned that a good deal of her terror of leaving home came from this overwhelmingly vivid apprehension of the worst that could happen; an ability to imagine every possible disaster. If she walked down the street, a car would mount the pavement and kill her. If she went abroad for a holiday, some rare tropical disease would single her out and bring her down. Nor were these fears solely for herself. When I went to India for the first time, she was certain that she would never see me again, and begged me not to go: she had foreseen a plane crash, she had imagined me convulsed with typhoid, dying of malaria on the streets of Bombay. Again, much of this I understood as metaphor, the fear of what would happen were she to let go, to surrender control, to express the depth of her anger, the extent of her frustration. The whole world would go up in flames. The material imagery of her terrors was a displacement, a projection of the violence within; a violence, not of illness or accident, but the furious ferment of emotions repressed and energies which had to be contained, since there was no vehicle licensed, as it were, to bear them. It is not surprising that the urge to create and to act in the world and the severe denial of it, led to what was diagnosed as 'depression'. The unquiet composure was symptomatic of powerful, conflicting impulses within; the motionlessness and melancholy were deceptive, not what they seemed.

At night, when Sid didn't come, she would walk through the house and shop. Whenever there was a thunderstorm, she took down the steel choppers and knives from the rail and hid them, so they would not attract the lightning which filled the white tiled shop with its unearthly blue radiance. She would sit and stir the scarlet embers with the poker, and read signs and portents in the dying flames, strangers coming in, coffins and cradles, according to the shape of the cinders, the likelihood of frost; memories transmitted from distant childhoods, not her own. She was the repository of a great deal of folklore and popular belief that died with her, the long oral memory of the life of countrypeople which her family had remained until the generation before. She was the necessary agent of betrayal of that tradition, which had ceased to live; and that defection only added to her burden of guilt and anxiety.

She more rarely opened a book now; and if she did, the print blurred, as her eyes fixed themselves, not on the page, but on the internal images of their life together – a mere four or five years, but already so changed from the hopeful day when she had stood in the backyard in her cloche hat behind a bunch of white roses, and Sid's dark hair had shone like satin, and her arm had rested trustingly in his. She sometimes sought out the photograph, as though, by looking at it, she could track the feelings that had decayed so swiftly since that bright July day when she had smiled her pallid smile, framed by the zinc bath on its rusty nail, and next door's cat basking on the wall.

She knew that sexual relationships cool with time. You know that the intensity of the beginning cannot be sustained. If it were, you would simply never be able to get on with your life, do a day's work. The demands of the world would go unheeded, and society fall into an even more ruinous state than it had reached already. For the first twelve to eighteen months, Sid had not objected to her obsession with him. On the contrary, he was flattered, and it made him feel safe. It suggested to him that she might be able to keep him from whatever it was that he feared most inside himself. She offered distraction and security at the same time. They would be seized by the desire to make love at any time of the day. They had once even shut the shop on a Saturday afternoon, the busiest time of the week, and customers had angrily rattled the shop door while they giggled together upstairs. They had been overtaken by strange urgencies, at any time of the day or night; although her own enjoyment had always been impaired by the fear that it would not, could not, last. She had always had a strong sense of sexual inferiority, had never believed herself to be desirable. That she could attach Sid to her seemed to show her she had been mistaken. She did not see that his fascination with her came from her apparent desire for something in him that transcended the obvious, the physical, and which, alas, did not exist. But for as long as they continued in their happy misapprehension of each other, everything went well.

It was perhaps understandable that her relationships would be obsessive: what she lacked in breadth of experience, the scarcity of legitimate conduits for her affective life, only added to the intensity of her feelings; and she poured into her husband all the choked impulses and smothered exaltations of her mind and spirit. If her life remained narrow, it was certainly not superficial and did not lack depth. But the strength of her desire – and not merely sexual – was onerous to Sid.

None of her sisters had ever spoken with any enthusiasm about their sexual experiences. The women on the estate, too, had come into the shop on Monday mornings, raised their eyes in a resigned appeal to heaven from which they expected no succour, and complained they were black and blue after the weekend mauling. They expected so little, and were therefore scarcely disappointed. Perhaps that was why their children assumed such overwhelming importance in their lives. The women often used to say 'I live for my kids. If it wasn't for them, I'd walk out on him tomorrow.'

She said nothing to them. Although she knew that sexual intensity fades, it was the speed of its dying that frightened her. His loss of interest in her was too rapid, and took her by surprise. It seemed almost as though her true feeling about her undesirability had communicated itself to him; she had been right after all. And now he, too, had perceived it. She tried to take comfort in her intelligent woman's rationalisings. But it wasn't that. She could scarcely not observe that he was taking care to make himself look good, whenever he went out 'for a drink', that apparently most innocent of male outings, which she knew implied a comradely pooling of male dissatisfaction, an outlet for the discontents of monogamy. Yet until this time, he had never had friends: he had enjoyed the company of what she disparagingly referred to as his 'pals', a relationship that implied superficiality and exploitation. These were the people with whom he was going to do business deals; which meant, for the most part, lending them money. He was going into the timber business, and installed a saw-bench and engine at the bottom of the garden. It soon fell into rust, and was dismantled and sold for scrap by one of his associates. He was going to earn money from keeping fowls. But the hen-run was soon neglected and harboured rats. They had to get a neighbour's dog to destroy them. The hens became diseased and died. He concluded drunken deals with a solemn pledge which he had forgotten all about by the next day; but somehow his partners, although equally drunk, always remembered; and frequently they called on our mother to honour promises he had made – a loan of a hundred pounds, an investment here, some capital outlay there. They rarely repeated the experience.

When she observed the extent of his disengagement from her, she said nothing to him, for fear of what she might learn. She told herself that she was being morbid, unreasonable. She was always accused of looking too much on the dark side. This meant she had inherited the sombre, lugubrious sensibility of her mother's family, which was a secular residue of a former religious fervour, with which they had spent their days contemplating the brevity of life and the certainty of suffering. The old aunts had liked nothing better than to sit in the churchyard, where they knew the inscriptions on the gravestones and the Gothic verses by heart; and for as long as this remained attached to a religious tradition, it could express itself cathartically. Only when the religious associations had decayed, it appeared as an individual affliction, a personal attribute which was a kind of curse.

She saw with a heightened clarity all the places they had visited together, transformed by the intensity of her feeling for him. He had had a motorbike, and they had gone into the forest; the forest – site of childhood picnics and Sunday-school games of hide-and-seek – had never been so vivid, the red campion had never looked so pink, the ladysmocks never smelled so sweet, the buttercups had never shone as they did that May. She told herself that people remain faithful to each other because they are grateful for what that person has done for them. You feel you have been loved, and that makes for commitment beyond desire. That love becomes a milder feeling, but still coloured by gratefulness and affection. The urgencies and appetites become less powerful as the years pass. It would be foolish to try to recapture it, because by the nature of the change it works in you, it can occur only once. To have been loved is to have been transformed. To remain with him who has been the agent of such a liberation seems natural.

Of course, she reflected, you can find novelty and excitement in others. She knew she was capable of responding to other men, but it wouldn't be the same. It would be foolish to jeopardise what you had gained in life. She wouldn't dream of throwing everything away on such a doubtful gamble. She assumed that he must feel the same. Her own feelings were so powerful, she could not believe they were not mirrored in him; in fact, it seemed that their very strength could not fail to evoke an equally strong sentiment in him. She projected her own emotions onto him, and then mistook these for his answering mood,

On the evenings when he was at home, they would sit on opposite sides of the fireplace; and he would flee into sleep, or at least, the pretence of it. He closed his eyes to get away from her obsessive searching regard. But she couldn't help it. She would sigh, turn away and pretend to read; yet she could no longer concentrate, the words on the page that had once been so vivid and enthralling ceased to engage her. She had been such an avid reader. She had learned much from what she had read; so much indeed, that she had to feign ignorance, so as not to express, however inadvertently, in his presence, her superior understanding. She had to pretend that she accepted all things at face value; indeed, there was no limit to the violence she did to herself in order to accommodate him. She deliberately unlearned all that she had taken from reading the novels of the nineteenth century – George Eliot, Dostoevsky, Tolstoy, Dickens, Thackeray – so that she could pretend to herself that all this was only fiction and that real people could behave as Sid did, and still love her.

The jealousy that had always been in her began to express itself. Because of her position as youngest in the family, she had always had to struggle for recognition, even for affection. She felt that the others were preferred, because they had all arrived before her. She had been sent for as an afterthought, and in twelfth position, as a very distant one at that. All the space available in the affections of the family – space no more commodious than the succession of cramped terraced houses where they lived – seemed to be occupied when she arrived. She prowled around this already complete entity, searching for a way in. This left her with a need for exclusiveness, to be uniquely distinguished, and especially, to be loved without rival or threat.

There are certain things which we try desperately not to tell ourselves; but once uttered, we never cease to repeat them. At last, she spoke to herself that which she had resisted for so long – he had found someone else to love. She looked at her body in the wardrobe mirror, and hated it. She tried to imagine what qualities his new woman could have, which she herself lacked, It couldn't be intelligence; but then, he hadn't been looking for that even when he met Glad: what he liked was the idea of vanquishing intelligence. The distinction of being clever was no longer a consolation to her. She longed to be beautiful, with a fierce resentful yearning; so much so that sometimes she imagined that she was and for a time held herself in the way that she had seen people of great physical perfection do, looking neither to right nor left, secure in the looks of envy, desire or admiration that they attracted wherever they went. Then when she caught sight of her prominent nose in the glass of the scales in the shop, or saw her reflection in the darkening shop window at night, she was compelled to return to the plain, undistinguished figure she was; hunched, apologetic, humble.

She might have been comforted to know that Sid was not preoccupied with one woman, but with women, all women. The presence of any individual woman he happened to meet actually erased all memory, filled his consciousness so completely that nobody else existed. In this way, he was subject to strange exaltations and intensities with strangers, who preoccupied him to the exclusion of everything, even his work. A woman had only to appear to smile at him in the street and he would pursue her, in order to discover the meaning of her glance; and was frequently confronted by an indignant stranger who asked him how he dared to follow her, and threatened to call the police if he didn't leave her alone. Sometimes, however, enchanted by his apparent charm, they did not repel his approach. His erratic comings and goings, the faulty deliveries of goods, the missed appointments, were not so much a criticism of his wife, as a symptom of his own disorder; but the comfort, if it was one, that this knowledge might bring, was denied her, and she continued to be overwhelmed by feelings of rejection and inadequacy.

She had tried so hard to overcome the disadvantages that undermined her: by reading, by changing her voice so that she no longer spoke with the raw regional accent, but had acquired a neutral English that made some people see her as stuck-up, pretentious. She had wanted to provide herself with qualities that were remarkable, and with these she would obtain for herself what her natural physical endowment could never guarantee her. Now, she sometimes quoted Shakespeare, Wordsworth, Shelley, to herself, while she was waiting for him to come home; only these were sterile consolations now, had no power to regain her power over him. She could not prevent her memory of the pictures she had of Sid in her mind – smiling at her, looking at her with desire – turned upon someone else. The images of her brief happiness came back to her like an assault, a reminder of what had failed to be fulfilled. While he was away, she simply longed for him to return; on any terms, it seemed to her then. But as soon as he came in, she could sense the ghostly presence of whoever he had been with, who had drawn him away from her; and this prevented any intimacy or familiarity between them. And when he looked at her, she saw in his eyes the cruellest of all questions, why are you not someone else? That she had failed him was the unspoken assumption; it was not a question of how he had failed her, repeatedly, heedlessly, without compunction. Responsibility for what had happened was always hers.

My mother was not exactly embittered by her experience with Sid, but it made her sadder. Her experience merely reinforced her melancholy. Perhaps that is the nature of experience: it helps what we are to unfold more readily. She used to say that as you grow older, you become more like yourself. It isn't that we choose experiences that correspond to our underlying nature, but rather that these merely enable our underlying predisposition to express itself. It was a very fatalistic and pessimistic view.

SOMETIMES, WHEN I went to see her in the home, she would look at me between the arthritic fingers splayed across the side of her face, and say 'I hate every minute of it.' She spoke with a curious vehemence, and it gave me a shock of profound recognition. I knew, not so much what she meant as how she felt. Because of such moments, it became possible for me to reconstruct her story, even though she had given me only the most spare details. There is no point in blaming her for this impersonal inheritance

181

that flowed through her family for generations, a sombre anticipation of the worst, and one that was never entirely misplaced, for often, in their bleak, poor lives the worst did indeed happen.

When she said she hated every minute, she meant that she could not live comfortably in the present. She was never at ease with life, never at home with herself. She struggled against time; not in the sense of trying to arrest its progress, but simply to get through it, as though it were an alien element in which some malign force had compelled her to live. Her life was always displaced into past or future, because she found the moment unbearable; so damaged by fears of the future, so haunted by pleasures of the past, pleasures that had not been at all agreeable then, but could be savoured only once they had been safely negotiatied, were finally free of contamination by a dangerous and unreliable present. The present was a hostile territory to be crossed, even though the future offered no sanctuary. Indeed, as she got older, the future became more and more depleted – and in truth, it had always been invaded by much uncertainty; its greatest benefit was that it would contain her sons as the adults who would look after her. The past became the place where she dwelt; not, of course, a real past, because it had been too cruel at the time, but a past which she had safely come through, and which was beyond impairment or loss. As she grew older, she used to say that her happiest times were when we were children, still dependent on her, tractable and docile, with the promise of a future not yet spoiled by its realisation. With her, I could also understand the roots of nostalgia: this is a celebration of the irrecoverable, and part of that celebration is that we have lived to tell the tale. Nostalgia is a festival for survivors.

When I was with my mother, and felt the samenesses of our consciousness, I thought of George Eliot, who had written of Nature as a great tragic dramatist, binding people together by flesh and bone, yet dividing them by more subtle and painful differences of sensibility which jar at every moment. In some ways, to be united in a shared sensibility, but divided by gender and generation, is even more painful. I was bound to her by common feelings, an intuitive apprehension of a shared predicament, a sense that we possessed identical, and sometimes burdensome, characteristics, She never needed to explain things to me, and this accounts for the fulness of the silences between us, Perhaps this was why all the stories and gossip that I saved up to tell her remained unspoken. All these things were trivial diversions from the reluctant communion forced upon us by the knowledge of what the other was feeling. When I remember the hours passed in her company, so much of it was was of speechless being together. Nowhere else have I ever found the boundaries of self so fluid and indeterminate; I felt ghost-like, porous, as though she inhabited us both.

She could perhaps contemplate with serenity the perpetuation of the melancholy existence that was hers, and which would continue after she was dead. It assured her, not exactly immortality, but a longevity not vouchsafed to most people. She was more like my real twin than my brother ever was. He remained remote and inaccessible, estranged by the personality that neither she nor I ever understood. That was perhaps the origin of his bitterness against us; although in fact, what my mother and I shared was not really a consolation to either. The truth is that because of the mystery and distance of my brother, she actually preferred him to me; although it never appeared so to him, who took the unsought, indeed, frequently unwelcome, collusion between us as a conspiracy against him; and he dealt with it in his own way, which was to cut himself off from both of us in the end.

When she spoke – however briefly – of how she had waited for Sid to come home, straining to hear the sound of his lorry, his footsteps, his key in the lock, I could immediately imagine the agitation and conflicting feelings that she must have known at such times. I, too, seemed to have been waiting all my life for people to arrive – for my mother to come to bed when I was a child; for friends who had promised to call for me when I was adolescent; for a loved one to come home as an adult. It seemed that I was always listening for the phone to ring, waiting for the post to arrive, expectant, anxious, unsettled. I could well imagine her impatience and emptiness, inventing things to do in the uncertain spaces between waiting and meetings that sometimes never happened.

She was in her late sixties when she became afraid to leave the house. There had been an incident in a big store, where she would hunt for bargains with her sister; one of those austere pleasures of people who have been brought up poor, and who take enormous pleasure in buying some unnecessary article for next to nothing – a new tea-towel, a box of handkerchiefs, a cardigan: this is as close as they come to extravagance. A boy on a skateboard had been riding the wooden floor of the old-fashioned shop, and had crashed into her, damaging her foot. What, her sisters asked, were children doing on skateboards in a shop? But then, what were children doing listening to music, eating fried chicken out of a red and white striped box, dripping the liquid from melting ice lollies onto racks of garments. The accident was not serious, but it undermined her already impaired confidence; and after that, she left the house only rarely. It became magnified in retrospect, and the symbol of all the dangers that lay in wait beyond the confines of the little house.

For many years, her outings had already been reduced to the half-mile walk from the house into the centre of town and the market-place; an itinerary which she followed almost every weekday. She had followed the same path for almost twenty-five years. Although it might have appeared eventless, it was nevertheless packed with significance for her. She passed through the churchyard, where the old boot and shoe masters lay in competitively ornate splendour beneath the horse-chestnut trees. She would pause at the library where, under the death-mask of John Clare, the old women fought each other for possession of love-books about the exotic lives of society hostesses and surgeons. Then on to the market square. This was always thronged with people she knew – girls she had worked with, women whose weddings she had attended, people who had lived next door at one time or another during their frequent removals. Nothing could have been less threatening than looking for items she did not need in the sales, exchanging banter with stallholders, monitoring the progress of an illness or the decline of a marriage among the clusters of people that formed and separated on the cobbles of the market square, shopping for fresh produce, windfallen apples, new potatoes, squeaky pea-pods, carrots still attached to their bright green plumes.

Eventually, these benign scenes became fraught with terrors for her, Even when she did go into town, it ceased to be a pleasure. She would not linger, anxious to return home and close the door. She would sink into her chair with a cup of tea, alone with her reflections on what had happened to her, reworking a past that seemed to have robbed her of everything; even though, as she said, she had started out with nothing and finished up with little more.

Occasionally, she would sit on a bench in a recess in the path that led towards town. Strangers who sat beside her would often ask her what was the matter. Her face, in repose, always wore an expression of such misery that people often concluded she had been abandoned that same day by a lover or husband; when she stood in shop queues, or sat on the bus, she looked as though she were on the point of losing a struggle against overwhelming grief. One day, an old man who sat next to her said, 'Cheer up my duck, it may never happen.' She turned her sad gaze upon him and said, 'Oh yes my duck, it already has.'

She fled to doctors to assuage illnesses they could not diagnose, fears they could not recognise, a nameless pain which only illuminated for them the limits of their competence; and, as a result, they sometimes became impatient with her persistence. She found relief in dependency on diazepam, nitrazepam. Tranquilisers and sleeping tablets, even though her life suffered by this time from an excess of tranquility and a surfeit of sleep. But it didn't really matter, she said. Since the turbulence and anxieties were all generated internally, it was as well that it should be stilled by chemicals, medicines, something administered externally. She said grimly, 'The only thing wrong with me is being who I am. There's only one cure for that, end it comes soon enough anyway.'

She did later find comfort in a psychiatric hospital, the extensive grounds of which stretched to the bottom of our street. It was a private hospital, and the fact of her referral as one of the few National Health patients did much for her flagging sense of self-worth; made her feel very special. It was surrounded by a high wall; but inside, expansive lawns were shaded by luxuriant copper beeches, and spacious private rooms with high ceilings and ornamental plaster cornices. The hospital was occupied by famous people – stars from tv who had had nervous breakdowns, titled people who had tried to commit suicide, the children of the wealthy, addicted to drugs. Some of them befriended her, talked to her of their wretchedness, their ruined lives. This was possibly of even greater therapeutic value than the treatment she received. She said shrewdly, 'When monied people say "Wealth doesn't bring happiness," it is probably the only truthful thing they say; and funnily enough, it is the only thing they say which the poor don't believe.'

Later, there were numberless admissions into the general hospital. There, she felt secure, and sat cheerfully in bed, grey against the implacable whiteness of the sheets and the silver paint of the bedframe. The wards consisted of long double rows of identical beds. It was popularly believed that patients were moved closer to the door according to the severity of their illness; while those convalescing proceeded towards the glass balcony at the opposite end of the ward. In this way, you were able to monitor the progression of your own and other people's illness according to your position. Just inside the door were the terminal patients, surrounded by screens, and visiting hours for them were not limited; their closeness to the door enabled them to be wheeled out when they died with minimal disturbance to others. All this always revived her spirits considerably.

The truth was that she loved being with people when compelled into their company, but by choice, perversely, she shunned them. In hospital, she became expansive and sociable; and was often kept in beyond the strict term of whatever was wrong with her – itself often obscure – because she cheered everyone up.

MANY OLD people, especially women, imagine they are being robbed. They will often fix upon an individual, perhaps one of those on whom they have become dependent, and accuse her of stealing from them, clothing, money, even things of no value at all.

In the year before my mother and aunt moved to the nursing-home, they were looked after by a woman some twenty years younger than they, but who at times appeared more infirm than either of them. Grace smoked incessantly, she was thin and didn't eat properly, although she had always placed mountains of food before the men in her family. She became very attached to my mother and aunt; and arrived at the house before half past seven in the morning to get them up and make tea. She would be wearing thin plastic boots through which the snow had seeped, sparse hair clinging to her scalp, hands numb with cold. She was animated by a compelling need to look after others, and, it seemed, to neglect herself; a terrible expiatory activity of women with little self-esteem. She was always scouring and polishing, putting carpets straight, adjusting curtains; as though she had been called to a work of perfection that no human being could ever attain – a doomed, semi-religious undertaking, which, in the era of decayed faith in which she lived, had become a personal obsession.

For a time, my mother rejoiced in Grace's devotion, for it was this that had permitted them to stay on in their own home for a little longer. After a few months, however, she began to wonder at Grace's zeal, and to doubt the disinterestedness of her concern for the two old women who were, after all, strangers to her. She became convinced that Grace was taking things from the house. When she came in the morning, her bag was empty; when she left, it was bulging. My mother swore she had seen her, in the kitchen, rubbing the laundry-mark from the towels, although by that time, my mother was unable to move from her chair. She insisted that everyone who visited the house should go and check the wardrobe, to see that all her clothes were intact. She had a cache of garments passed on from her niece, things she had never worn and now never would; but to maintain them in a state of readiness for future events and high days which she would never see became one of her principal interests. She was certain that Grace was taking them.

In fact, she knew she was being robbed. She knew it with absolute certainty. Grace couldn't be trusted. One of her boys had been in court for stealing a car. When anyone said, 'Why would she steal anything? She is well paid for the work she does, why would she risk losing that for a few old clothes that are scarcely worth money?' my mother became very upset. Instead of answering, it instantly became a question of loyalty to my mother. 'You're taking her side against me. I'm on my own. Nobody believes me. But I know.' Anyone who contested her became an enemy. And in this way, she retained a sense of being special, endowed with unique insight and understanding; lonely, cut off, but distinguished from everyone around her, as she had never been as a child when she struggled in vain for supremacy over her older sisters. Sometimes, exasperated by her accusations, I would say to her, 'How can you know what you haven't seen?' She would reply, 'Don't ask me. I just know'; implying, as she had done when we were children – and to our great terror – that she had been granted insights not quite of this world. Later, we realised that the suspicions were probably simply further side-effects of the drugs – or medication, as she preferred to call it – that she had been prescribed for years.

Grace knew nothing of my mother's distrust, but gradually she began to behave more and more coldly towards the woman who had conceived a genuine affection for the two sisters. Where once, in the morning, mother had greeted her with gratitude, her presence showing that the long wakeful night was over, she would now barely acknowledge her. Even when the two old ladies were in the nursing-home, Grace continued to visit them, always taking some little treat for them to enjoy. One day, the matron went in to my mother and said, 'Grace has come to see you,' to which my mother responded, 'Well I don't want to see her. Don't let her come near me.' Grace, who had been waiting behind the door, heard this. She left the bunch of pink roses she had cut from the bush in her garden and fled. She never visited again. My aunt wondered what had happened to her, and asked me to go and see if she was all right. My mother never said anything. Not long after, Grace died of the cancer that had already been within her when she was looking after the two old women, who both outlived her.

In this way, the refusal of others to support her conviction that she was being robbed became another demonstration of her assertion that in the end you are on your own. It was a lesson in existential desolation, proof that you will always be deserted at last, even by those who say they love you. But her adjurations were also metaphor; nothing she ever said or did was to be taken at face value. To me, she was saying indirectly, 'You will not come with me. You too will abandon me in the end. You will go on living when I am dead. You will not even keep me company through the diminution and loss of my old age; whereas I came through everything with you when you were a child.' Of course there was no mystery in the meaning of these parables and stories of theft and loss. Her hold on the world slackened, her apprehension of her surroundings became more clouded. But apart from these obsessions and the mild paranoia they expressed, she remained completely clear. She was quite firm that this was not the onset of dementia – she had seen too many old women whose own children had become strangers to them, who had been unable even to name their own offspring, and she certainly had no intention of letting that happen to her. In order to persuade people that her mind was still lucid, she would quote the long speeches of Polonius, or Gray's Elegy, uttering the verses with great fluency, a child once more sitting bolt upright at a desk in a chalky Edwardian schoolroom.

Above all, the memory of the significant time came back, when her purpose of being a mother had flooded her whole being, had required neither reflection nor apology. She would say, 'I had to be mother and father to you as well,' a blithe assertion of her capacity to transcend gender roles. And she had indeed shown a formidable capacity to unite features normally separated in the sexual division of parenthood. She had controlled us with a powerful discipline that required no physical chastisement; she had loved us with a suffocating intensity; she had provided both moral instruction and entertainment. She had read to us a great deal; and sometimes in her haste to have us grow up, so that she might share her life with us more fully, she had misjudged our capacity for understanding. When we were about eight, she had begun to read aloud *The Scarlet Pimpernel*. I had been terrified by the mention of smallpox, which added yet another deadly disease to the list of those which I feared might remove her from us; and she had to put the book away, because even the sight of it made me howl. We had sat long evenings by the fire, when, in an attempt to cultivate our minds, she would permit us to sit up late to hear some new soprano on the radio sing the popular classics. She had washed us both in the same water from a chipped enamel bowl on the carpet; over which she always made a cross with her finger before starting on whoever had second turn – this, she told us, was to make sure the devil didn't get us. All the old superstitions and prejudices from the country childhood of her parents were offered up to us, partly to amuse us with their antiquity, partly in order to pass on to us the rags of what was a decayed popular animist faith.

I can now see her whole life in terms of continuous dispossession. The extended network of kin among whom she had grown had frayed and torn so readily, leaving her deserted. The nuclear family which had succeeded it fell apart even more readily. The money which she had laboured to save from the shop, and which was to have given her security in her old age, was all used up within a few months on nursing-home fees, and she was compelled at the end to depend upon the welfare state; and although she always professed herself a socialist, she hated what she saw as dependency. Even the sons she had made promise they would care for her, who had sworn they would provide gold and silver cushions for her to sit on when she grew old (did we really make such an offer spontaneously, or did she plant it within us?), failed to redeem their pledge, and had abandoned her to the indifferent hands of professional carers.

MY MOTHER always said that the happiest time of her life was between the ages of 18 and 24. Significant years: at 24, she had met Sid. This provided a sad contrast to my aunt, who serenely said that she had been happiest between the ages of 26 and 48, which were the years she spent with her invalid husband, whose nursing became for her a source of contentment impossible to describe. He had contracted TB when he was in the Navy, taking White Russian refugees on board off Novaya Zemlya during the Revolution. He was sick when she married him, and in defiance of all medical forecasts which assured her that he would be dead within two years, she actually prolonged his life by ten times that span. Her love for him, and her ability to attach a dying man to life for such a time, gave her the reputation of a worker of miracles. It was not easy for my mother to live up to this model of satisfaction, love and duty.

Indeed, it became the source of an intense rivalry between them; a competitiveness into which Aunt Em resisted being drawn; but she was no match for the rules of living laid down by her sister. Aunt Em's husband died soon after my mother and Sid were divorced. Mother, alone in the shop, found herself cheated by such helpers as offered themselves, all men, who seemed to expect for the assistance they gave her, wages not only in cash but also in kind; and in a form which she would certainly never grant them.

It was a matter of course that we would go to live in the little terraced house with Aunt Em. Their companionship lasted for thirty-five years, far longer than the time either spent with her husband. It seemed each would assuage the other's loneliness, provide a consolation for the hurt both had sustained. But Aunt Em's pain had been a consequence of the loss of death; my mother's of a voluntary desertion by her husband. This set up a torment of jealousy in her, a competitive need to have suffered more, and a long punitive attempt to redress the balance in her own favour. Aunt Em, uncomplaining, mild, patient, was the last person to enter into such emulous relationships.

Our mother also feared that her sister might establish too powerful a bond with my brother and me. It became her object to intercept any such possible intimacy; and this she did by disparaging to us our sweet uncomprehending aunt. Em didn't have her intelligence. She couldn't hold a proper conversation, wanted only to gossip. She had a group of friends who were snobbish and insufferable, and she was trying to rise above herself, especially living as we did, in West Street, in a two-up two-down row house with an outside lavatory and a po under the bed. On Tuesday afternoons, these friends ('pals' was my mother's scornful word for all relationships with non-family; a singularly inappropriate term for the genteel trio who came to the house, with their perms and brooches and lavender water) would come, ostensibly to play bridge in the front parlour, which until then had been Uncle Frank's bedroom. ('Bridge,' said my mother contemptuously. 'Who do they think they are, ladies-in-waiting?') In fact the card-playing was merely a formal pretext: my aunt had great power to draw people to her; over the cards, they talked of their lives, their friendships, which had begun in shoe factories thirty years earlier. Our mother would offer to take the tea in to them, slopping it over the edge of the cup, placing the milk bottle instead of the jug on the tray. Not long after we went to live there, the Tuesday afternoon meetings ceased.

Once a week, Aunt Em would wash my mother's hair over the kitchen sink; a towel round her shoulders, a spume of lather, and then jugfuls of warm water to wash the soap away. One day, she forgot to dilute the nearly boiling water with some from the cold tap. The nape of my mother's neck was burned. She never forgave her sister; blaming the accident upon her carelessness, her inability to concentrate, even upon a desire to hurt her. This even became another symbolic incident in her long, slow decline: from that moment she had 'nerve trouble', and began to suffer; the grave opened beneath her and she trembled upon its edge for the next thirty-five years.

Glad became special in her capacity for suffering. Being clever, and able to suffer, were what she excelled in, and together, these became the source of her distinction. Nobody understood as she understood, and nobody suffered as she suffered. In the end, she merged with her illness. The illness became both identity and a profound unreachable relationship. It gave structure and meaning to her day, as her children once had; and the row of pills in little brown plastic containers on the mantelpiece, the red one, the blue ones, the white ones, succeeded each other as the hands of the clock marked the passage of time.

WHILE OUR mother served in the shop, I sat in a corner of the black-and-white tiled floor, reading the old newspapers which people brought in for use as wrappings. The estate where we lived gave the first hint of the kind of mobility that was to become more widespread after the War. People from Wales, the North-East, Scotland had fled the recession of the 1930s. At that time, they seemed strange and out of place in our settled town, with its distinctive regional voice, half-rural, half-urban, from its staple industry of tanning and leather work. Many people on the estate had newspapers forwarded by relatives from their home town so that they could keep in touch; and as I looked at the old papers, I knew that Wilson, Keppel and Betty were appearing at the Glasgow Empire, that Douglas Byng could be seen as Mother Goose at the Newcastle Theatre Royal and that Charlie Cairoli was on at the Swansea Grand. I spent hours in the shop, half absorbing regional news about knifings in Glasgow, decrees nisi granted in South Wales and the apprehension of an arsonist in Gateshead who had burned three sheds on the allotments there.

This was a savourless pastime, and the real instruction was to be derived from listening to what passed between my mother and her customers, especially the women. For many years, the significance of the whispered stories escaped me. I was aware of a murmured hum of sympathy emanating from my mother, which encouraged them to unburden themselves of their anxieties and troubles, which they did, sometimes uninhibitedly. The shop was filled with the sound of the purring of the fridge and a long susurration that told of the pain, loss and grief of women.

Mrs Graham was a thin, gaunt woman, whose hands constantly played with the purse she held in front of her apron. She wore her hair in a twist of scarf that emphasised the oblong shape of her head. She had slippers of dingy fleece and no stockings, so that a network of tiny blue veins could be seen at her ankles, like the tributaries of rivers that we drew in geography lessons.

She always talked to my mother with a breathless, suppressed urgency. When another customer appeared in the shop she would change the subject and laugh loudly, displaying large grey teeth, as though enjoying herself so much that she could not bear to leave the place of entertainment. She would move from one thin leg to the other until the customer had been served, so that she could resume her lamentation. Indeed, customers who came in when she was there felt they were unwelcome; and they would be dispatched swiftly, making way for the pressure of the confidences which Mrs Graham could barely contain.

She had got up one night and found her husband in the room of their only daughter; a girl of twelve. He told her that he must have been sleepwalking, and didn't know where he was. At first, she believed him. When it happened a second time, she also gave him the benefit of the doubt. She was working in a boot factory, tiring work, for which she had to get up at six in the morning. She had fallen into the habit of going to bed before ten o'clock. She resolved to stay awake to see what happened. Three nights in succession, her husband crept out of bed soon after midnight, and into their daughter's room.

She was repelled and incredulous. They still had what she referred to as 'a normal married life'. She tried to pretend that she hadn't noticed. She told herself that he was merely comforting the child, who had always suffered from nightmares. But the suppressed knowledge made her ill. She developed a nervous tie, that convulsed the side of her mouth. Her hair began to fall out. 'Look,' she would say, 'it's coming out by the handful,' and tugged at a black curl that came away in her hand. She couldn't talk to him about it, and did nothing. She confessed to my mother that she loved him. She loved her daughter, too, of course. But she was afraid that if she confronted him, he might leave her. If she went to the police, there would be a court case, a scandal, he would go to prison. She didn't know which way to turn. She tried to tell herself that he wasn't doing anything to the child that any normal father might not do; he was just cuddling her.

For two years she said nothing to her husband. 'What am I going to do?' she kept saying, but expected no answer, for she was immobilised by fear and revulsion. Glad said it was not fair to her daughter to let this carry on. It could ruin her life. 'I know, she wept, I know. It's just that I don't want to lose him, and if I said anything I would.' 'It's better to lose him than to see your only child's life wrecked,' said my mother, who never had any doubt as to where her primary allegiance lay. The woman accepted the continuous chiding. It made her feel worse, because she knew that what my mother was saying was right; and the punishment she thus received from her helped allay the guilt over the silence she maintained.

When the child was fourteen, she became pregnant. They said she had been attacked by a man in the woods. There was a story in the local paper, with a picture of the stricken parents. The woman stopped coming into the shop: the family disappeared from the neighbourhood one night. Where did they go, I asked my mother. 'High Street China' was her evasive reply. Then she said, 'You shouldn't be listening to grown-up conversations.' I assured her I never listened to a word, I was too busy reading the papers.

Beneath the surface decorum of the estate, a life of secret disorder and chaos emerged from the conversations that took place in the shop, the whisperings that produced little mushrooms of cold breath in the damp air. Not all the tales were as sad as that of Mrs Graham. Tessie's husband had died in another woman's bed. He had been visiting her, if that's the right word, said Tessie grimly, for several years. One day, in the widow's bedroom, he had complained of feeling tired. He closed his eyes, and died in the double bed. The widow was a thoughtful, prudent woman, who had not wanted to cause pain to Tessie who, in any case, she claimed as her best friend. Somehow, she had dressed, him, dragged him downstairs, seated him upright in a chair. Tessie said how she admired presence of mind like that at such a time. The widow was a small woman, no longer young, and Tessie's husband weighed over fifteen stone. Tessie could not imagine how she had managed to lift him, replace his clothing. Had the neighbours heard the rhythmic bumping of the corpse on the stairs? How had she carried him to the armchair, where he was found by the doctor? Even more admirably, she had prepared a cup of coffee, which she placed, half-empty on the table beside him. Only then had she alerted the doctor, sent for an ambulance. The coffee was her alibi, a signal of regret and respect to Tessie, who had to be fetched from the factory where she was working. Indeed, Tessie admitted that nobody, including herself, would have doubted the innocence of her husband's visits, had she not found him with his boots on the wrong feet.

THE (NON-BUSINESS) transactions in the shop were echoed in what passed between my mother and her sisters on Thursday afternoons. For then the shop was shut, and Aunt Em, Aunt May, Aunt Laura, and sometimes Aunt Win or Aunt Het would visit; a moment of peace before the two busiest days of the week. I hurried home from school because Aunt May always brought something special for tea, some pieces of unidentifiable wartime confectionery, made with simulated jam and artificial fat, false icing and imitation cream. This was not the real treat, however, which lay in listening to what passed between the murmuring giantesses above me. I was supposed to be playing with plasticine, and I kept my eyes on the ric-rac pattern on the carpet, the brown and orange crescents and zigzags, In the presence of adult conversations, children are assumed to be without senses or intelligence. I acquired a functional absence; which meant appearing so self-absorbed that they occasionally broke off to say, 'Look, he lives in a world of his own.' This was true, but it was a world composed entirely of images, allusions and suggestions taken from their conversation, evocative, and comforting as the ripple of the wind in a grove of protective trees.

As they spoke, whole networks of relationships sprang into existence. They conjured great ramifying genealogies out of a funeral that had taken place the previous week; evoked the rise and extinction of whole families from a piece of gossip overheard on the market. They knew, it seemed, everybody in the town. They were aware of the state of everyone's health, marriage and financial situation. It was a time of considerable information exchange: people's life stories were amended and modified according to most recent data; whole lives reassembled out of surmise, speculation. There was something wonderfully imaginative about the zest with which they passed in review the fate of others. Their conversations were dramatic and theatrical, creative yet ritualised. At times they spoke with a choral, elliptical gravity. These were stylised performances, their own versions of poetry and art:

I see Miss Coombs died.
No age, was she?
She didn't want to go in the family grave.
Why was that then?
She wanted to go home to Naseby.
Is that where they come from?
Oo yes; ever such a big family of them.
She used to say 'The earth as bred me is the earth as'll carry me home.
She's got a lot of people belonging to her out there.
Where do they lay?

In the churchyard there.

I think she left the rent of that little house to Miss Maynard.

Oh?

Well I seen her go in there a-Tuesday. I reckon she's left the rent to Miss Maynard for life, then it'll go to the church.

Funny how thick they were.

Cheese and cheese gal?

Oh I shouldn't think so. Big churchgoers they were.

How do you know she's left the rent to her?

I could tell. The way she let herself in. She'd got a key.

They then rehearsed all the iniquities of men; although Aunt Em never took part in that part of the conversation. Whenever they referred to 'the family', it always meant their mother's family. Their husbands were without antecedents. Somebody's husband had been seen up a gitty with some wench, somebody else had got thick with a woman who was known to 'let her front room out', another was said to be seen dinxing all over town with a woman dolled up like a whore at a christening. Once, a man 'made a suggestion' to one of my aunts, as she walked home through the churchyard one night. She turned round and told him he could piss his tallow where his beer went; an expression that shocked but delighted them.

Much of their conversation was extremely morbid. It hovered around deaths and secrets of parentage revealed by pieces of paper that fluttered down from behind a clock when an old woman's house was sold up; around sudden revelations about illegitimacies, and half-brothers and sisters, and stepfathers that rendered wills invalid, made paupers out of those who had confidently expected to come into a fortune, and visited riches upon those resigned to a lifetime of poverty. They dwelt all the time on their own extinction; the brevity of human life stood them in the stead of decayed religious beliefs, and was a consolation for an eternity which had been stolen from them.

WHEN MY mother was young, if she ever thought about her old age, she probably anticipated it as a time of contentment and serene fulfilment; although since neither of these were conspicuous features of her young life, it is unlikely that even the most favourable fate would have provided them as she grew old. But for her, old age was still a repository of valuable wisdom and experience, a resource and comfort to the next generation. But that was perhaps because extreme old age was a comparative rarity at that time. By the time she reached her eighties, life expectancy had increased dramatically, and old age no longer had the same distinctiveness. In fact, the papers were full of stories about 'our ageing population'; they had become a problem rather than a source of helpful experience. The old were less frequently likely to see their eager descendants gather round to listen to the stories of hardship overcome, of the mean years cheated by their own resourcefulness and creativity. The old were both more numerous and more alone than they had ever been; their wisdom devalued, their accumulated knowledge of little account. The reason for this was no secret: while people depend upon the sagacity and discernment of those who have preceded them in order to survive in the world, this remains a hindrance to the expansion of a busy market system, always eager to supersede non-monetary ways of answering need by its own version of these formerly free transactions.

She was denied even the modest hopes for the future which she had permitted herself. One year, in my early thirties, I went back home to Northampton, to write about the changes that had occurred in the town since I was growing up. How easily I fell back into the role of child, permitting them to set my meals in front of me, to make my bed, to wash my clothes, even to see my aunt emptying the po into an enamel bucket each morning. When I think about it now, I feel deep shame. Then, I told myself that if I had interfered with their arrangements, they would have felt slighted: the self-serving excuses were always at hand, and at that time, I still reached for them readily.

One afternoon in late summer, I sat in the garden under the pear tree, where the wasps circled the fruit in the late sun. In the window of the living room I could see my reflection, which was suddenly interrupted by the appearance of a pale blur of face on the other side of the glass. I went indoors to see what she wanted, and found her in tears. 'What's the matter? What's wrong?' 'Nothing.' 'What is it?' I put my arm round her thin, rather hunched shoulders; those shoulders which are now my own. She said 'I was watching you. Sitting there. I thought, what a waste, what a waste. I wanted you to give me children.' I withdrew; all that I heard was I want and give me.

It would have been incomprehensible to her generation in their youth to see old age as a major source of employment. She and her sister were bewildered by the succession of Maries, Angeles and Samanthas, who visited the house to put them to bed, community nurses, many of whom they never saw twice. They lived to see an army of professionals concerned with the management of old age – wardens of sheltered homes, home helps, the geriatricians, researchers into the ageing process, as well as all the prolongers of youth, those chasing the 'grey pound', the makers of treatments and preparations that banish wrinkles and ward off disease, the builders of discreet retirement homes in enclosures called The Pyghtle or The Retreat, the providers of off-season holidays for the elderly which allowed them, at the expense of the council, to sit in rainswept glass shelters in Brighton in mid October.

More than this; my mother observed that the dereliction and infirmity of extreme old age had become someone else's business opportunity. Nursing-homes had become so profitable by the mid 1980s that even hotel and property companies were investing in chains of them, just as they had earlier invested in shopping malls or fast-food outlets. My mother swiftly perceived that the old offered prospects for the rapid recycling of their life savings to a new generation of entrepreneurs. The workers employed in these undertakings were often underpaid and inexperienced. Their lack of skills was simply a reflection of changed social attitudes towards the very old. 'Stick a frilly cap on their head and a badge on their jumper and call them a carer', she said scornfully. 'Who's going to care about anything for three pound an hour?'

Sometimes, when I went to see her, she would be sitting in the public lounge. It was impossible to be unaware of the significant social function of those cramped circles of high-backed chairs around the walls, the zimmer frames, the persistent odour of urine and disinfectant, the television playing Australian soap-opera, while heads fall forward on wasted chests, and hands continue to work away as though still at the bench or lathe they had abandoned twenty years earlier. For their fate is our future: the effect upon us of their immobility, of their confusion and helplessness is to make us realise how short the time is, and how we must hurry, hurry, to live life to the full, the brief years that stand between us and the catatonic stillness of the afternoon hours, when the summer breeze inhabits the net curtains and the geraniums blaze in their hanging baskets, and the old people sleep their shallow after-dinner sleep. Their purpose is to urge us on to even more heroic feats of enjoyment and living than we have known already. Our very pity for them, the scantness of their needs and wants, propel us into a resolve to fill the hours that remain to us with yet more of the pleasures and treasures that this society affords.

'You needn't come every week', my mother and aunt used to say to me. 'You've got your own life to lead. You can't be running up here every five minutes. We're all right.' Your own life to lead – a language of permitted disengagement, as though my sweet aunt and sad mother were not part of that life. Why is it so difficult for us to look after those we love, simply because they are old? Is it because families have become so depleted – often single individuals, people separated by the necessities of work or simply by the desire to be elsewhere? Is it true that there are fewer self-sacrificing single women who fulfilled such roles in the past? And were these often assisted by a more ample circle of kin and neighbourhood, which at least offered them both recognition and occasional relief from the duty of watching over the old? When it falls upon one person – nearly always a woman – she often becomes socially isolated, and the caring then becomes an intolerably lonely experience. My cousin, who nursed her mother until she died at ninety-three, said she never once slept soundly during the last twenty years of the old woman's life. Her attention was always alert, listening, anticipating, imagining cries in the night; her sleep haunted by images of her mother on the floor, rigid with a stroke, calling out with voiceless terror. She said, however, 'It was a privilege to do it. I don't regret a minute of it,' even though it used up so much of her own life. And now that more and more people live on into their eighties and nineties, their children discover that the years of their own retirement are claimed by the need to nurse them.

Perhaps the cruellest breaker of duty and commitment to a diminished circle of kin is economic necessity, the obligation to pursue a career, to earn a living. This brings us to some harsh confrontations with ourselves. I could plead my work in the presence of my mother's entreaties not to put her in a home; but what work could possibly be more important than the cherishing of my mother and aunt, to whom I was tied with such a profound and sorrowing helplessness? There is no answer to that, except the knowledge that it would be unbearable to spend the days preparing meals, feeding them, getting them onto the commode, holding the drink that shaking hands can no longer convey to the lips, and then listening half the night for the changing rhythms of breathing in their disturbed sleep. The question is, what has happened to us, how have our lives become structured in such ways that what ought to be the most natural course of action in the world now appears to us an intolerable sacrifice and torment?

Yet the professionalising of care for the old is still at a rudimentary stage. They are infantilised and depowered, expected to be good, docile and grateful, even though they may be paying the market rate for the care they receive. They are 'naughty girls' or 'bad boys' if they fail to conform to a stereotype of resignation and gratitude, expected to be, not only obedient, but also, for preference, insentient. My mother became like the rest of the very old people in the home, self-effacing, saying that she had lived too long and excusing herself for not having died earlier. In this way, her feeling of helplessness and superfluity, my sense of guilt and shame, and the competence of the professionals, all merge in a collusive unspoken assumption that this is the best of all possible worlds, even though, at a deeper level, we all know otherwise.

HER SISTER May was there again, and it was Wednesday. Glad was annoyed. Didn't she know that Wednesday was the busiest day of the week? Thursday was her day for visiting. That was when Aunt Em left Uncle Frank for a couple of hours, and Aunt May brought cakes for their little tea-party, exchanged an account of all that had happened since their last meeting, an affirmation of the continuity of lives bound together until they died.

But this particular week – it was June 1938 – she had already come on the Monday. And although she lived on the same estate, barely ten minutes' walk away, she would never have done so without good reason. Their visits were highly ritualised, and a call outside of the normal rhythm of their intimacy meant that something dramatic had occurred. Restless and agitated, May had been on the verge of saying something, but Glad had not encouraged her to speak. Sensing her sister's hostility, May had gone away again. My mother saw her through the kitchen window, a felt hat on her head, an apron over her skirt. It was still the custom for women to wear their hat at home all the time, as though permanently expecting to be called away suddenly; although in fact, they rarely went anywhere.

Aunt May was like my mother, strong-willed, dominating, self-righteous; but equally, upright, honest and completely incorruptible. As a child, I was always terrified of upsetting my mother, who let it be known that her love for us, indeed, her life itself, depended absolutely upon our complete obedience to everything she demanded of us. I never dared put this to the test for fear it might be true. This meant I sought never to vex or oppose her in any way. Occasionally, therefore, whenever I was left with Aunt May, I would misbehave, challenge and defy her, as the closest I could get with impunity to breaking the absolute taboo on contradicting anything our mother said. Aunt May would look at me sometimes with a troubled frown, believing that I was spoiled, that I needed a damn good hiding. There was no physical resemblance between the sisters; it was a moral and character similarity, but so striking that people often mistook one for the other.

May had something to tell that she could no longer keep to herself, however strong her sister's resistance to hearing it. Glad protested that her hands were full; there was a shop full of meat to be cut up. The delivery note didn't correspond to what she had actually received in the shop. May was insistent. 'His lorry has been parked in the same place five nights in a row.' Glad shrugged, and said that his lorry had been seen parked outside half the houses in the county. 'Not outside this one.'

Something in May's efforts at breaking the news gently had caught Glad's attention earlier in the week. The women of the estate were always vigilant, quickly on the trail of any irregularity of conduct, especially if it were of a sexual nature. It was always their duty to report anything they heard, or saw, or thought they heard or saw, or that anyone else heard or saw, to the injured party, which they always did with great ceremony and relish. Glad imagined that Sid had become less prudent in his promiscuous affairs, and, emboldened by her apparent indifference, had sought consolation closer to home than before. But there was a seriousness in May's voice that compelled her to ask, 'Where was this then?' 'It was outside the doctor's. Five times in a week.' Glad tried to make light of it, saying it was a pity her sister didn't have anything better to do than keep count. 'There must be something wrong with him.' Glad said, 'I knew that the day after I married him'; but she was troubled, and spoke simply to delay the disclosure, to make time to prepare a reply, to provide herself with a response behind which she could hide her real reaction. 'He's sick, Glad. Why else would he be at the doctor's every night?' 'What is it then?' 'How should I know?' 'Then what are you doing here?' 'I think you should find out.' 'May, my duck, I'm past caring.' 'You should care. It might affect you.' 'What?' 'He might have caught something. Something dangerous.'

May had spoken what Glad already knew, and that made her angry. She had once become aware of a terrible itching in the groin, and had discovered that he had given her crab lice. She had washed herself in almost boiling water, which scalded her flesh but had not removed the lice. When she confronted him, he denied it. He even accused her of going with another man. 'When would I have a chance to do that?' she had cried. Sid always refused to hear anything that he didn't like. He would point-blank refuse to acknowledge the obvious. He couldn't bear to be thought culpable in anything. What was worse, he could never accept the consequences of his own actions. He would extricate himself by the most elaborate and far-fetched excuses which convinced him, but left everyone else wondering at his infantile efforts at evasion. Glad had learned how not to know things from him. To her sister she said, 'Well it doesn't matter to me.' 'Does that mean you don't have anything to do with him that way?' 'You mind your business.' 'It is my business.'

It was, too. My mother's sisters had a keen sense of duty towards one another. This led them to what would appear now as unwarrantable interference in each other's lives, and would lead, in most families, to an irreparable rupture between them. If one of them was believed even to be contemplating any departure from the path of marital virtue – no matter how unhappy she might be in continuing to pursue this – they would regard themselves as perfectly justified in warning her to desist, in ordering the potential adulterer off, even in telling the tyrannical husband. This led to some fierce arguments and quarrels; but these never lasted long, for the feeling that each was there to keep the others from harm was always stronger.

May said, 'You can catch it off cups. The lavatory. I know. I know a woman who got it, and she had never been with a man.' 'Well, if you're interested, you ask him.' 'All right,' said May, 'I will.' 'Don't you bloody dare.'

May went away. She had done her duty. She had articulated what Glad had been secretly saying to herself all the time. That week, Sid had not been out at all. When he came home, she laid the table, and placed his meal before him. She sat down at the opposite side of the table, her face flushed with embarrassment, her eyes pleading for a plausible explanation, an excuse; and when none came, she asked why he had been visiting the doctor so frequently.

His first response was to ask why she had been spying on him. Her eyes never left him alone. They were everywhere. He couldn't even sit down in the evening without feeling her stare burning into him. What was the matter with her; why wouldn't she let him be. She persisted, 'Is there something wrong?'

He now became tearful. He hadn't wanted to tell her, because he was afraid she would worry, He had been to the doctor, because he had an infection that wouldn't clear up. He thought perhaps he had caught it from rabbits. It was his habit on Sunday afternoons to go rabbiting; chasing the creatures from their warrens with a ferret, and then catching them as they fled from the other holes in the grassy hillside. He brought them home; she skinned them and sold them in the shop. Sid then took the skins to the rag-and-bone man, and received threepence per skin, which he used for drinking money. The doctor had advised him not to go rabbiting for a little while. There was a rash on his body. Some sores. It would soon clear up, but you have to be careful with wild animals.

She had been so anxious to hear good news that relief overrode everything, including her usual suspicions that the worst had happened. May was a prophet of doom. She had never liked Sid. Who could know what her motive was in bringing these melodramatic warnings to her? Bloody witch, she would have a go at her when she came round tomorrow afternoon. Glad felt elated. It was nothing.

Sid didn't go out that evening either. She prepared for bed. He had started to sleep in the spare room, because, he said, he arrived home at all hours, and didn't want to disturb her, when she had to get up so early in the morning. She lay still in the big double bed in the room over the shop, and waited to see what he would do. She heard him come upstairs. He knocked on the door; and she smiled at the quaintness of his decorous respect. It had been a long time since they I slept together. He came in, but seemed in no hurry to get into bed with her. She looked at his face. There were creases at the corner of his eyes that she had not noticed before, a greater roundness in the familiar face, and the hairline was beginning to rise on his forehead. He sat on the bedcover, and took her hand.

She began to tremble, a shiver of apprehension. He had been moved by her readiness to believe him, and, overcome by a guilt he had to discharge somehow, he began to talk to her. He said, 'Glad. It's something else.' 'What?' 'It wasn't from rabbits.' She understood at once, as indeed, she had understood even when she was covering her understanding with the brief gaiety of the evening. Harshly, she said, 'No, I never thought for a minute it was.' She waited. A heavy silence formed between them; an impenetrable tension that would never again leave them. 'Well?' 'I got it from a woman.' 'What is it.' 'The doctor says,' he began, as though trying to evade the responsibility for what he was saying, 'it's sexually communicated.' 'Oh.' 'Yes. He says it's something called' – he pretended to search for the word, as though it was unknown to him – 'syphilis.' 'Oh my God.' She threw back the bedclothes, and shaking, threw a dressing-gown around her shoulders. 'I think we'd better go downstairs.'

Overwhelmed by anger and disappointment, at that moment she knew that their sexual relationship would never again be renewed. A sense of desolation swept over her, a shock of terrible exclusion. She had never thought of anyone else; it had simply never occurred to her. She had not wanted anyone else. Women, she thought contemptuously, full of self-hatred, they commit themselves to one man, the wrong man, always the wrong man; all men are the wrong man; and then when it turns out a disaster – and when doesn't it? – we're left stranded, with our feelings stuck to them like flies on sticky paper.

Now, she felt, she had been stripped of everything; even though much of what she had lost was already long gone, and even that had been illusion. She looked at him, and the wave of desire that had shaken her an hour earlier had spent itself. His teeth shone in the darkness. The whites of his eyes were clear, his dark hair glistened, iridescent in the light from the landing. In spite of what she had just learned, he looked more beautiful than ever. He would never touch her again.

He had been ill for two years, but had refused to recognise it. During that time, his life of nomadic eroticism had been uninterrupted, as he travelled across the country in his lorry. Many of the names and addresses of the women were false; others were untraceable. The hospital almoner had tried to compile a list of all those he could remember. There were 17 or 18; many others he couldn't recall. The almoner had undertaken to write to them, informing them of the risk they ran, and advising them to have an urgent check-up.

The syphilis had already passed into its tertiary stage. There was tissue loss to the roof of the mouth and the mucous membranes. He would have to undergo a course of injections, a mixture of arsenic and mercury. That would ultimately halt the damage, although the destroyed tissue would never be restored. The infection could eventually be cleared, but it would not be over quickly. He would attend hospital three or four times a week. He would have to give up work, at least in the early months of treatment. He must on no account have sexual relations with anyone. He was frightened, as much by the prohibition on what had become, for him, an addiction. He wept, and she sensed it was for that he was weeping. Not for her, not for the wrong he had done her. 'Glad, what am I going to do?'

Her first feelings were suceeded by a mixture of guilt and anger. How little she had been able to help him, driven as he had been by this strange male impulse to go from town to town, from woman to woman, in search of what she still felt, despite herself, she ought to have been able to offer him. What was wrong with her, that she had been incapable of stilling this compulsion, which she surely felt also, but for which she had never dreamed of seeking alleviation elsewhere? It led her to confront new depths of inadequacy and feelings of worthlessness .

But there were limits to the self-abasement to which she was prepared to descend; and this restraint later helped her to reconstruct her life, although not in ways which she at that moment could possibly have anticipated.

The doctor summoned her to hospital for tests. After an unbearably tense and anxious two weeks, she was informed that there was no trace of infection in her. She was relieved. She had remained unpolluted by the sickness that must have affected so many of the women who had welcomed his story of being a loner, an unattached wanderer on earth; and probably, she thought grimly, their husbands also and their other boy-friends... Her own immunity at least, gave her a kind of moral advantage, however insubstantial and unhelpful to the problem of how she was to lead the rest of her life.

During those two weeks of waiting, she pondered what she should do. She apologised to her sister, who wept and comforted her. From that time, until her death from leukaemia in 1964, May was to be her only confidante, the only repository of a secret which would remain with my mother until she told my brother and me some thirty-five years later. For a few weeks, she was numb and tearful. It seemed to her that her own position was without remedy. But within a short space of time, encouraged by her sister, and by the will to survive and the reservoirs of energy she found within herself, she had begun to devise a strategy, which she at once sought to put into practice.

Three

SHE WAS already thirty-four. Her first thought was that she would now never have children. There had been one miscarriage three years after her marriage to Sid. She had not conceived again, and in any case, soon after the miscarriage, their sexual relationship had waned. She sometimes wondered if that experience had repelled him. It had been sudden and unexpected; she had barely had time to realise she was pregnant. She had woken one morning with severe pains, and was serving in the shop. It was a cold February morning. She went to the kitchen to make herself a warm drink, and as she sat on the sofa, the haemorrhage occurred. He had come in from the shop, where customers were waiting to be served. He panicked, and fetched some newspaper which was used for wrapping meat. Then he called the doctor. He had looked at her, she recalled, as though from a remote distance; not merely the distance between men and women, that great gulf that permits perpetual renewal of sexual desire, but with something new in his regard: a contempt for a woman who could not even hold his babies.

She thought at first she might wait until Sid recovered, and then try to take up the sexual relationship again; but she shuddered at the idea. Not only was it an unreliable expectation, but she herself was now repelled by him; the good looks and slender body only mocked the inner decay; she had begun to identify him too closely with the sickness that had literally begun to consume him.

He stayed at home. He lay on the sofa, and played at being an invalid. He lacked conviction, and in any case, she would have none of it. This was an illness to be punished rather than nursed, and she went about it with avenging zeal. He didn't know what to do with himself; completely without resource, he read the first page or two of some Westerns by Zane Grey, he looked at the horse-racing column in the *Daily Mail*, he stood by the window, like a child whose parents had forbidden him to go out to play.

The truth was, he didn't trust himself to go out. He was possessed by his own sexual needs; and he stayed by his wife, trusting in her vigilance to exercise a control over him which he was incapable of supplying for himself. He felt her strength and endurance, and he placed himself in her custody. Infantilised, dependent and resentful, it now became his turn to watch her, although with a very different regard from that she had once turned on him: expectant, waiting to be told what to do. I later came to feel that she learned to be a mother through her later relationship with Sid; and my brother and I were the recipients of the same kind of remorseless care with which she had tended him. One day, Sid even pathetically asked her to read to him. She said 'Only one thing I'll read to you and that's the bloody riot act.'

His lorry stood unused on blocks beside the shop. The oil spilled in rainbow splashes onto the gravel; little pools of ochre rust formed beneath the mudguards. Reproachful, it remained, a symbol of his wandering desire, the vehicle of his nemesis. He covered it with a tarpaulin, as though the fault had lain, not within him, but with the mobility of the truck.

He decided he would clear the garden. The roses had been neglected for many years. The shoots and suckers that should have been pruned had spread in wide arcs, and the flowers had become thin and papery, ghosts of the rich white roses she had planted when they first came. Whenever she went out to the dustbin to empty the ashes from the grate, the thorns hooked her clothes, tore a long stitch of wool, or sprang back against her hand, leaving a dotted line of tiny bloodclots on the flesh.

Sid tore up everything that grew in the garden, and raked the bare earth. She watched him from the window, tearing violently at cowparsley and hogweed that had spread where the lawn was to have been. The sweat silvered his face and drenched his shirt; in his exertions she saw a labour of vain and ineffectual atonement, and she was not displeased. Although by a curious reversal, it was now his company that became irksome to her, and she reflected on the distribution of power in relationships; the swiftness of the change was certainly unsought by her, but she took such consolation in it as was available.

His life apart began. She told him she would look after him until he was fully recovered and able to work again. After that, she made no promises. She expected to be left free to do as she pleased with her life. This condition was accepted without protest. He could have no idea of what she intended to do. He was grateful. It was, and he acknowledged it, more than he had any right to expect. He said to her, 'You're a good woman.' She said, 'Don't soft soap me. You'll see how good I am by what I do. Judge me then.'

She behaved dutifully towards him, as though nothing had happened to disrupt their marriage. She emptied the zinc pail that stood by the sofa, into which he coughed the mucus and slime that came from his damaged mouth. She said the smell of it remained in her nostrils until the day she died, She washed it down the outside drain with half a bottle of disinfectant. She set aside for him a separate plate, knife, fork and spoon, and tied red warning cotton around the handles, so that no one else should use them. She would not go into his bedroom, and left him to wash his own sheets, which he rarely did. The room became rancid and feral; the rain came in through one corner of the roof, and mildew spread in strange bluish blossoms on the pale wallpaper.

At first, Sid could not believe his good fortune. But then, he said to himself, he had always underestimated her. Sometimes he was disturbed by a new resoluteness about her: the way she worked in the shop, the efficiency with which she cooked bland but nourishing food, kept the house clean, pursued her weekly timetable of penance and self-punishment. It was clear that she had made a decision, although whatever it might be, she did not communicate it to him. She asked nothing of him. His life became tedious in its leisure, a little clouded perhaps, by the apprehension that she had made her accommodation with the situation without reference to him, without consulting him in any way. But apart from that, his life was easier than it had ever been. He had entrusted his weak will to her, and she was happy to be its gaoler. With so little to do, the vacant hours would normally have been filled with plans for sexual adventures. He was thankful that her ubiquitous presence relieved him of this compulsion, although, at times, he also became resentful, and blamed her for the superintendence of his life. Then she would say, 'Nobody asked you to stay, Sid. You're free to leave whenever you like.' And the prospect of formless and unlimited freedoms filled him with dread.

At that time, she, too, lived under a secret terror: that one of her customers might discover the truth about Sid's illness. Even worse, she feared that he himself might threaten disclosure, and with it, the ruin of the business, if she vexed him in any way. Part of her conciliatory response showed her desire not to provoke him. She needn't have worried: it never occurred to him to do anything that might disturb the relative calm in which they lived. He was certainly not malicious or vengeful; less so than she was; but then, as she said to herself, he had no reason to be.

To those who asked about her husband's indisposition, she said he had ruptured himself while unloading the lorry, and would be at home for some time. Three times a week, he went to the hospital and sat wearying hours in a bare distempered room, along with other sexual miscreants, to await the injection of a punitive quantity of poison into his veins. Afterwards he felt dizzy, light-headed. He had been ordered not to drink, which was in many ways an even greater privation than the prohibition on sexual activity.

He talked to his wife more than he ever had done. He listened also. He turned his attention to the social and political issues of the time, things which he had until that time disregarded, as being no concern of his. He asked her opinion: did she think the unemployed didn't really want to work? She said, 'You should know.' One day, he expressed some admiration for Hitler, and was astonished by the vehemence of her reaction. 'Why, he said, it seems all right to me. You've got to hand it to him, he's put his country on the map.' Among the multiple differences between them, the political seemed to her too trivial to argue with.

In the evenings, when the shop was closed, she would come into the living room and sit in the chair by the fire. They were forced into a kind of conviviality that had never occurred in the early years of their marriage. At times, there was even a fragile security, a familiarity that was almost comforting. Sid, incapable of keeping secrets, needed to confide in someone, and he had no one else to talk to. Little by little, as he spoke to her, she was able to piece together what had happened.

HE HAD met a woman in a pub in town. 'A blonde with a navy-blue parting,' he said, borrowing an expression Glad would use. She was almost ten years older than Sid, a widow. She was, according to him, lonely, having buried her husband only recently. 'Where,' said Glad, 'in the back yard?' She had invited Sid to the little terraced house where she lived with her daughter, who at that time was not yet sixteen.

Whenever Sid visited, the daughter was always there. The mother never sent her out of the room. It was almost as if she welcomed the younger woman's presence; and the girl didn't make herself small, or sit in a corner. She would leaf through a magazine, do her nails, occasionally focusing on something outside the window, so that the sun, reflected on the red brick of the houses behind, gilded her face and her distant blue eyes. It seemed that the mother, uncertain of her own ability to attract him, kept the daughter close to her, as though to take from her a borrowed glamour. This, she appeared to be saying, is how I was, or perhaps that she, too, is available. And then, in a curious way, the daughter seemed to be chaperoning her mother; chasing away, or perhaps diverting her possible lovers.

It was only later that the mother appeared to notice her. But by then it was too late. Sid had already infected the girl with the disease he had taken from her mother. Then, when their relationship had been made transparent by the spread of the infection, the mother threatened to expose him for having had sexual intercourse with a girl under sixteen.

He couldn't believe it. A mother who would knowingly transmit a disease, and then permit him to pass it on to her own daughter, just to get money from him. He was genuinely shocked by the degree of cunning and depravity he had encountered. Somewhere, he had retained an element of country innocence. He was certainly capable of concealment and denial, but not of such labyrinthine deviousness. He gave the women all the money he had – a few hundred pounds. Then he had stolen from the shop. Glad had noticed a falling off in the weekly takings, and had worked harder to bring the money back to the level from which it had declined. She listened to his story but said nothing, checked herself from the anger that swelled up within her, when she learned that she was having to make good the money her husband was paying in blackmail.

He was thankful when the two women left the town; to try their game somewhere else, he imagined. His symptoms abated. A lesion that would not heal had eventually disappeared. He had taken some patent medicine that claimed to cure sexual diseases, and he thought this had done the trick. The sore had vanished, and he assumed this meant he was all right. He didn't like to think too much about it. At that time, he was angry with his wife. If she had been more responsive, if she had enjoyed his body, this would never have happened. He blamed her for her inability to rescue him from his own devouring sexual need.

She always managed to make him feel shame. Why should she? Why was she so contained? If she wanted sexual contact as much as he did, why could she conceal it, as he never could. He thought he despised her, yet in spite of his contempt he respected her. He resented her self-sufficiency, her continence. It made her curiously unreachable. She knew him better than he would ever know her, but that, he told himself, was because he was open, while she was always hiding herself. He felt known by her; he was vulnerable, uncomfortable. Occasionally, he had hit her; a cup of tea splashed in her face, a back-hander that had left a crimson flower on her cheek. She had not even flinched. One day, he said to himself, he would give her a blow that would knock her down. He would beat her until she cried. He had never seen her tears. She had seen him turn on the waterworks countless times, tears of self-pity, humiliation, frustration. Perhaps that was it: a woman whose tears were unseen remained mysterious, unknown.

When he had told her everything, she remained in a state of outward repose, calm. She didn't express outrage, either at the duplicity of the women, or at his conduct. She was as imperturbable as if they had been talking about some trivial item of gossip from the shop; and this encouraged him to reveal himself further.

Afterwards, he was afraid of her quiet resolve. What, he wondered, would she do? He thought she might be planning some terrible revenge. Would she kill him? That was it. He became convinced that she would murder him. He imagined the cold rage that would make her seize a butcher's knife, one of the cleavers hanging from the steel rails in the shop; he would wake up one night and see the blade in the moonlight as it cut the darkness before the mutilation, the pain, the emptiness of death. He thought she might poison him. And sure enough, one day, the dinner tasted strange. Bitter. 'What have you put in this stew?' 'What?' 'It tastes funny. What's in it?' 'Carrots, onions, potatoes. Nothing unusual.' She tried another mouthful. 'Yes, you're right.' She went into the kitchen. He had left some daffodil bulbs in the kitchen that he had taken up from the garden, and she had absently peeled them and unthinkingly cooked them. He said 'I thought you wanted to poison me.' She said 'No Sid, you're the poisoner in this house.'

ONE SUNSHINY morning, she stood at the kitchen window, washing up. The window was open onto the field at the side of the shop; dazzling with bright buttercups and the pale moth-like flowers on the blackberry briars. She looked up, and saw a man at the window smiling up at her. He had a full, rather fleshy face, with a moustache and receding fair hair. Surprised, she recoiled a little and some greasy water splashed her apron. Could he trouble her for a bucket of water? Instead of coming into the garden to give her the bucket, he lifted it up through the window. His eyes were dark blue. He told her he was working on the building site. The tap had run dry and water was needed for cement.

He came back several times during the morning, He was working on construction of the new roadhouse, about two hundred yards up the road. He had actually designed the building, but didn't believe in asking other people to do work he couldn't do himself. He had begun his working life as a labourer, and still enjoyed the exhilaration of manual labour, the satisfied exhaustion it induced. The building was, he told her, to be a completely new idea of a drinking place, the pub of the future. There would be a winter garden with palm-trees and exotic shrubs, a lounge and a car park. People would no longer have to drink in joyless spit-and-saw-dust street-corner pubs, but could enjoy their leisure in more spacious surroundings. We were about to enter a more sophisticated age, where working people would not be condemned to a miserable comfortless existence, but would begin to demand things hitherto reserved for the rich. What had always been seen as luxuries, too good for the common people, would become the staples of daily life. He spoke with animation, a quiet passion, which thrilled her.

Impressed by his enthusiasm, the vague plans that had been forming in her mind took concrete shape there and then, She was aware of his interest in her; the effort he took to explain what he was doing, the smile that illuminated his face when he met her eyes, She decided on the day of their first meeting that she would have a child with him. All she said was

'Isn't your idealism a bit misplaced? After all, it's only a pub.' 'No, no. This is the relaxation of the ordinary man. Why should it be without dignity or comfort.' 'But drink.' She grimaced. All the men in her family had been a little too fond of milk from the brown cow, and had denied their families the necessities of life in consequence. She said, 'Don't tell me of the pleasures of the common man, or I might tell you something of the sorrows of the common woman, because it's at her expense that he enjoys them.'

Now it was his turn to be impressed. She said to him, 'You're an architect?' 'No,' he corrected her, 'I'm a builder.' 'Won't they think it funny,' she asked him, 'to see you fetching and carrying water like this?' He said severely, 'There is nothing dishonourable in labour, however humble it may be.' 'Oh yes there is. You should have seen the factory where I worked when I was fourteen. It was dishonourable all right, and so was the reward for it.' He said to her, 'You talk like a socialist.'

She had never thought of herself as a socialist. But she recognised the truth of what he said, and she said, a little defensively, 'What if I am?' It pleased her to think that she might have a place in a scheme of things that seemed to be the prerogative of men; that she, too, could be part of a movement, not simply a clever woman, alone and silent, with no point of contact with anyone else who shared her view of the world. It opened up a possibility of belonging, of being part of a wider struggle for more general social ends, rather than simply the effort to survive in the shop, to manage the disaster of her marriage as best she could, to survey the desolation of her life as though it were a place apart, detached from any social or political context.

In the days that followed, he returned to the kitchen window, no longer with the pretext of asking for water. She enjoyed the insolence of his approach: even while she was at home, with her husband dozing by the fire which his condition required, even though it was the middle of June. He brought her a copy of George Bernard Shaw's *Intelligent Woman's Guide to Socialism*; *News from Nowhere* by William Morris, and a compilation from Robert Blatchford's *Merrie England*. In return, she gave him *David Copperfield* and *The Mill on the Floss*. She told him that the character of the aunts in George Eliot's novel were just like those of her family; that her native Nuneaton was not far from where her own family had come from, Long Buckby in the north-west of Northamptonshire. They had the same sensibility, the same mournful, superstitious nature; they even spoke in the same country idiom.

For the first time, she experienced the delight of a relationship born of affinity and sympathy, rather than of sexual attraction; although the latter was certainly not absent on her side. Later she denied this, and declared that she had seen him only as an instrument in the fulfilment of her project. But that was after he had proved himself as unreliable and treacherous as the rest of them (as though through Sid and him she had known all men; but then, perhaps she had).

He asked her to meet him in town one evening. She thought that Sid must wonder why she stood for so many hours at the kitchen sink; but if he did, he said nothing. She didn't hesitate. She promised to meet him the following Tuesday, when the shop would be shut, in a cafe in the centre of town.

In front of Sid, she was irritable, because for the first time, she, too, felt guilty. Was she not doing the very thing which she had accused him of? During the four days between the meeting and the assignation, she resolved several times not to turn up. It was only by recalling her deeper purpose that she was able to keep the appointment.

'Where are you going?' Sid asked her, when he saw her on the Tuesday morning in a state of unusual nervous excitement. She tried to force a little dried-up lipstick out of its long unused sheath. 'I'm going to meet a friend,' she said. 'Who is he?' 'No one you know.' 'It is a he then?' 'Not half as heathen as you,' she answered. She told him she was going to town to meet Louie, who had been one of the bridesmaids at their wedding. 'Bloody horse-godmother,' he called her. She had stopped seeing all her friends after their marriage, Sid didn't like any of them, and that had seemed sufficient proscription for her at the time to have given up all contact with them. She came to realise how conventional her behaviour had been; only the irregularity of her situation now helped her to an understanding of the orthodoxies she had to transcend, if she were to determine the course of her own future life.

They sat in a discreet alcove in a restaurant in the centre of the town. She had never been in such a place; to eat out was an extravagance from which, she felt, people like herself were excluded. She protested that it was too much ceremony for anything so simple as merely eating. She hated the loss of control over preparing food, which she expressed in an anxiety about the state of the kitchens. Her real fear was exposure in a public place, and uncertainty as to how to behave. He laughed at her fears, and ordered lunch of chicken, peas and new potatoes. She took a glass of wine which, she said, tasted of rusty nails.

Afterwards, they spent the afternoon together, sitting in the church-yard, where the sun glinted through the splayed green leaves of the horse-chestnuts. Crisp dry furls of holm-oak fluttered down and caught in her hair; he removed them with his fingers. He said to her, 'Tell me about your life.'

She talked, not about what had happened or the reason for her estrangement from Sid; but she made it clear that there was no longer either affection or a sexual relationship between them. 'What about you?' she asked. 'You're married, aren't you?' 'How do you know?' 'You have marriage-lines all over your face.' He told her that his wife was an elective invalid. She used her frail health as a reason to withhold from him what he wanted; what, he said, a man needed. She shuddered at these words, but she had already committed herself in advance. In any case, she really did like him, and could see in him an agreeable companion, a man she could meet as her intellectual equal: new areas of shared experience opened up to her through him. She was learning how unreflecting her marriage to Sid had been, how superficial her judgment on what people wanted from each other, how imprisoning the traditional roles of husband and wife. Joe gave her to understand that he was not prepared to jeopardise the security he had. 'What are you looking for then?' 'Friendship,' he said.

And they did become friends. Friendship between men and women who were not related to each other was forbidden in the streets where she had grown up. Social needs were almost completely taken care of by the family; the only function of friendships with outsiders was to look for a wife or husband. A certain cordiality might be established with brothers and sisters of the potential husband, but any incipient friendship with someone of the opposite sex was an immediate object of suspicion.

She talked with Joe about politics, about the war that would soon come, about socialism, about the better world which he did not doubt would ultimately triumph. He believed that nothing was too good for the people, and that the real problem with the working class was that it had never asked enough, either of life or of the economic system. She said, 'Yes, but is what the rich have what the poor need? Doesn't their wealth depend too much on violence? Wouldn't wealth itself become something else if it were more fairly shared?' Joe had a reputation as a communist. At the same time, he was intensely individualistic. He was a craftsman who restored churches in the countryside. He took her to some of them, the weathered gargoyles he had reconstructed, the fine tracery he had reno-vated. She said, 'Fancy a communist working on so many churches.' He said, 'Beautiful things don't belong to the rich. Or to God. They belong to those who created them, to the people of England.'

Sid was jealous. He never knew who she was meeting, and she never spoke about her outings. She bought a new coat and some shoes, a black crêpe-de-Chine dress with crescent moons and stars appliqué'd in gold. Her excursions had to coincide with the hours when the shop was closed and Joe was free. They met only once a week for the first two months; and she thought, not without a pang of vengeful satisfaction, that now it was Sid's turn to be captive in the house, wondering where she had gone, and when, or even whether, she would return. It was a great effort for her to disengage her feelings from Sid: the scars of her commitment still burned, and she was still susceptible to the pain in his eyes; but nothing would now make her risk what she had come to see as her plan for survival.

After a few weeks, Joe asked her to go away with him to a hotel, where they would spend the night together.

SHE TOLD Sid that she would be going to stay with her mother, whose seventy-fifth birthday it was. She didn't elaborate, but the deception was difficult to her, a woman who had always prided herself on her lack of concealment, her principle of speaking the truth and living with the consequences. She was compelled to learn what was, for her, yet another bitter lesson: that principles, no matter how elevated, must sometimes be set aside, in order not to inflict unnecesary pain. Confronted by Sid's air of trapped helplessness, she said, conciliatorily, 'You'll be all right. I shall be back first thing in the morning.'

At that time, any couple who appeared in a hotel were immediately suspect. Only the rich, or commercial travellers, put up in hotels. A man and woman who were not sleeping at home were clearly adulterous. For this reason, on the appointed Saturday, Joe said he thought it better if they avoided the embarrassment of presenting themselves to public scrutiny as man and wife. Since it was a fine day, he drove deep into the countryside. Joe parked the car in a gateway, where the broken-down wooden gate and the hedgerows were overgrown with the green hearts and white bells of convolvulus. He took her by the hand, and they walked round the margin of the field. Then he flattened a space about twenty yards from the edge of the crops. This shocked Glad, who thought it a crime to trample growing crops, or to waste food in any way. He spread a rug on the ripening blue-green wheatstalks; some rabbits ran away, scared, in a flash of white tails. The corn poppies lent their silky red voluptuousness to the afternoon.

There they made love. She was tense; as much from being in the open air and from fear of discovery as from any scruple about what she was doing. For Joe, it was a great release: his wife had wrapped herself in a cocoon of resentment against him, and wouldn't let him touch her. Glad was somewhat taken aback by the vehemence of his lovemaking. She told him nothing about her relationship with Sid; only that they had slept apart for more than two years.

She desperately wanted to conceive. In her eagerness, she responded to Joe with an abandon that he misunderstood. He thought he discerned a passion for himself in an enthusiasm that had other causes. He could easily understand how she might well be seduced by his unusual mixture of charm and radicalism, and was not displeased, although he was uneasy about how difficult it might become later, when he would certainly want to extricate himself from the relationship. He thought he was in control; and, like all the men who knew her, underestimated her depth, her powers of persistence, her intelligence.

She was not thinking about how much she was attracted to him. She had in mind only her own plan, into which he had strayed simply as a random, though providential actor, unaware of his own role. In this way, their whole relationship began as a form of mutual deception; and this certainly undermined the possibility that it might later develop into something more substantial. She had embarked upon a lonely, self-preoccupied project, and Joe was only a shadowy (and as it turned out, minor) figure in it.

He was, if anything, more furtive and anxious than she was about being discovered. For a few weeks, they met frequently. She awaited with interest a change in the weather which would prevent them from visiting cornfields. One Saturday evening, it was raining. They checked into a country hotel, saying that they had come for the wedding of relatives. Although she had dreaded it, nobody challenged them, no one demanded to know the names of the relatives or to see the wedding invitation. It was all very easy. He told her she had read too many stories in the Sunday papers about the policing of marriages, of hired co-respondents and private detectives. Most people are too busy with their own lives to care about the behaviour of strangers. On another occasion, they had made love in his car, parked as far as he could drive it down a sodden muddy path into a beechwood. Afterwards, the wheels had become stuck in the channel they had made, and she had to help him push it onto the road,

She felt it might have been the intensity of her desire that had made her conceive almost immediately. Within less than two months of their first meeting, she was pregnant. Telling her lover was easy; perhaps that was why she relished it less than she would enjoy telling her husband. Joe had wanted to use a contraceptive, but she had always assured him it was unnecessary. Joe was angry, because his view of their future association had been challenged: he had foreseen a continuing relationship with her that would coexist with his marriage, One afternoon, they sat in the garden of a country pub in angry silence. It was late summer. The harvest was finished; the stubble in the fields shone in the late sunshine, and the berries of hawthorn and elder hung in black and red clusters. She said to him, 'You think I've tricked you. Well I haven't. I don't want anything from you. I shan't ask for money.' 'There's no need to have babies these days. I mean, you're not an ignorant shop-girl.' She said, 'You don't seem to have much respect for the people whose lives you're going to raise up. Anyway, I am a shop-girl. Not so ignorant perhaps.' This time, they made no arrangement to meet again.

Yes, she thought, I was trying to trick you, but not in the way you imagine. Did he think she wanted to trap him into divorce and marriage with her? She felt humiliated that he should interpret her actions in this way, and she longed to tell him the truth, that what she had done bore no relationship to him beyond the purely biological function. If she had told him, he would not perhaps have believed her; certainly, he would have been humiliated in his turn. She preferred to let him think of her in terms of the woman scheming to lure him away from his wife. She felt once more the contradiction between his progressive views and his unimaginative perception of their situation.

And by a strange turn which had not entered into her calculations, she felt sad that her purpose was now finished with him. The man she was convinced she was only using had drawn her to him without her being aware of it; like a superficial wound that you scarcely notice at the time, but which wakes you up with its pain in the night. And she came to feel that she was the one who had been trapped – again: she reflected that she was no more capable of being emancipated than he was.

WHEN SHE reached home that Saturday evening, she found Sid sprawled in the armchair in his socks. He had fallen asleep listening to some sports commentary. When she walked in, the radio was playing dance music. She looked at him, and felt pity; tenderness almost. The movement of life within her gave her a sense of connectedness to all living things, and she felt how completely at her mercy Sid was. She was sad to have so much power over him. It was a power she didn't want, because the exercise of it brought her far less satisfaction than she had thought it might. She had looked forward to the moment when she would tell him she was pregnant; she would punish him with it for his own failure to create life with her. Then she thought of the sterile expenditure of his substance with all the women he had known, the deathlike disease that ravaged him, while she was growing with new life; and her moment of tenderness for him gave way to a sense of exhaustion – how wasteful, complicated and full of effort it had been to achieve what happened so naturally to the vast majority of women. Here was distinction indeed; but one that brought her no comfort.

She made tea, and as she set his cup down beside him, he looked up at her, yawned and smiled, stretching his arms. She sat in the chair opposite him. She could not see his face for the late sunlight that came through the curtain, leaving him in shadow. That made it easier. 'Sid my duck,' she began. She had not used the dialect endearment with him for years. He stirred and sat up. 'I've got something to tell you.' He looked at her attentively; the moment had become ceremonious, an annunciation. 'I'm pregnant.'

He looked at her, a look she couldn't see, but could feel. Rage and disbelief. 'You can't be.' But he knew she would scarcely lie about such things. He felt his male pride ought to make him protest, but even this satisfaction was denied him. It would make him look ridiculous. That she had accepted far worse from him was no consolation. He said, 'Who does it belong to?' 'Me,' she said. 'Go on,' he jeered, 'even you couldn't do it all by yourself.'

Calmly, she prepared a meal, which they ate in silence. He would not look at her, but kept his eyes lowered. She felt now that she had only added to their sufferings, and for a moment, entertained a wild idea that she would have an abortion, devote herself to Sid, undo the harm that had been done. All this in the silence broken only by the sound of knife and fork against the willow-pattern plates, the crunch of sliced cucumber. She knew what had happened was irreversible; but she had to prepare herself for what would follow. When they had finished, she broke the tension, pushing her plate aside and said, 'Just listen, Sid, and I'll tell you what I want you to do. You know and I know that we were never going to have children after this' – she gestured towards him, as though his illness were a tangible thing – 'but nobody outside knows that. I want you to say it's yours.'

'Never. You've been carrying on with some bloke, and you expect me to close my eyes to it,' he said with the air of one to whom all deception is abhorrent.

'You should listen to yourself.'

'What if I won't do it?'

'Sid.' Glad spoke softly. 'Who he is is neither here nor there. It really doesn't matter. It wasn't him that I wanted, it was a baby. I'm nearly thirty-five. If we'd had our own... but that can't happen. Not now. And it isn't my fault. But I'm going to have this baby, and you'll say it's yours. No,' she corrected herself, 'you don't even have to do that. All you have to do is not deny it. You'll do it because you have no option. You haven't. You threw choice away a long time ago. I shan't ask anything from you. I won't even ask you to keep it. I don't want money, I can earn. I'll get someone to help in the shop when the baby is born. After that, we'll carry on as we agreed. Then when you are better, we'll separate. It doesn't have to be difficult. Not more difficult than it is already.'

She hated the sound of her voice as she spoke: it was constricted, forced; not herself; so cold and pre-arranged. She had never felt like that at all. She had felt sick with anxiety, had wanted not to go through with it. She was revolted by herself; and it was only the thought of the alternative that drove her on. Sid fell into a moody silence, but in the end told her to do what she thought best. He wouldn't interfere with her plans. It was only when she went to bed that night, passing her body into the cold envelope of the sheets in the big double bed, that she let go and wept. Although everything she had intended was working out, it brought neither satisfaction nor peace. But neither of these experiences was ever vouchsafed her; her temperament and sensibility were so much at odds with the social order, with life itself, that even when she had what she wanted, the manner of its achievement, as well as the context in which it had occurred, robbed her of any sense of victory. She tried to console herself that she was more than a match for both these men whom chance had determined would dominate her life; but it was a sad, savourless triumph.

SHE HAD twins. Sid became the recipient of congratulations by family and strangers alike. He bore it with a stoicism of which he was certainly not capable in any other area of his life. He liked the idea of his surrogate paternity. If people looked at me or my brother and said we looked like him, he was pleased. This did not mean that he had the slightest intention of playing any part in our upbringing, even if this were offered to him. Soon after our birth, he started to go out again in the evenings. She excluded him completely. He must have felt very lonely. He was never allowed to pick us up, to kiss us or touch us, ostensibly because of the infection. But she prolonged his exile. He began to put on weight; his skin assumed the chalky consistency of those who are never touched by loving hands. He resumed his long erotic vagrancy scarcely before he had been declared cured. She did nothing to stop him.

Joe, who was childless, had no access to us either. After a period of sulking over what he regarded as her treachery, he had contacted her again. They had met a few times in town. He had wanted to renew their sexual relationship. She refused; even though she also wanted to. She needed to prove to him that her pregnancy had not been merely a stratagem to trick him into leaving his wife, or for getting maintenance money from him. In any case, she had become so locked into her purposes, and accustomed to the idea that he, too, would abandon her in his way, that she determined to keep him at a distance. As the time to give birth became closer, he changed in his demeanour towards her, taking pride in advance in the paternity which he had originally sought desperately to avoid. When we were born, he protested and wept, and said she had no right to keep him from his boys. But she said, 'You wanted nothing to do with them, and that's what you'll get. Just see whether or not I can manage on my own.'

Twins were a misfortune in more than one way. It was not simply that this added to her burden of labour, although that was also significant; it was that my mother's life had consistently been marked by men in pairs, one good and one evil. A strange dualism had characterised all the males in the family. Her brothers had been judged either 'wrong'uns' or 'good men.' To the former category belonged those who had shown strength of will or character; to the latter those who had been more pliable, more amenable to management by their women. Harry and Joe were wrong'uns. Harry had remained at home with his mother till she died. She waited on him with the last ounce of energy in her body. And Joe, who had lost an arm and a leg in the Great War, was a strange unhappy man, who once had a fight outside a pub with another one-legged man, and tied one of his two sound hands behind his back in order to fight fair; Joe's only son killed himself. In contrast to these was Dick, a self-taught working-class intellectual; a union official, a thoughtful and gentle man. She placed her brothers-in-law in a similar diptych: there was Frank, the responsible, mature invalid husband of Aunt Em, who spent his life gently preparing his wife for the time when he would be gone. He was, said my mother, a saint – a designation which she would never have bestowed on any man who was in robust health; the elevation of his status was directly proportionate to his incapacity to do harm. On the other hand, there was Arthur, consigned, however unfairly, to the wrong'uns, a man whose principal error seems to have been his eccentric views, and his obsessive dislike for Cyps, Wops, Gyps, Wogs, Chinks, Blacks and all others of outlandish origin whom he could dismiss with a contemptuous monosyllable. In this taxonomy of good and evil, good men were those who exhibited characteristics as little associated with working-class males as possible, and those who were bad displayed all the features associated with the stereotype – the boozers and gamblers, those who dominated their women.

Significantly, both Sid and Joe occupied, at one time or another, both categories. In the end, both betrayed her. When my brother and I were born, the temptation to assign us to the received categories was scarcely to be resisted. But her sense of fairness made it impossible for her to damn one of us from birth. I had her restless sensibility and cried endlessly. My brother was obedient and slept all the time. On the other hand, because I was like her, to have made me into a villain would have been to condemn herself. So she hit upon the (for her) happy expedient of telling each that he was the good one, and confiding our badness to the other; so each grew up in the conviction that he was the good twin, and his brother a source of endless pain and suffering to her.

She had been very depressed after giving birth. She had climbed onto the flat roof of the shop, with the intention of jumping from the parapet with us in her arms. We became aware of this story very early on in our lives: its function was to make sure that we would be aware of our redeeming purpose. It was for our sake that she had drawn back from suicide; we had to prove to her that this had been the right decision. There is no more difficult role for human beings to fulfil than that of redeemer, or rescuer; particularly when they are children.

It always seemed to me a great pity to have had two fathers, and to have known neither of them: a bit of a waste really, especially in view of my own fragile sense of male identity. But we grew up to perceive Sid across a vast distance. His emotional remoteness from us was more powerful even than the physical distance he was obliged to keep; so that to be male seemed to me something far off and unattainable, to be aspired to perhaps, but never reached. Sid's prohibited body always appeared to me desirable, hard and strong. Knowing nothing of the source of the taboo on him, I would sometimes creep into the room he occupied and inhale the scent of rancid masculinity, a strange odour of outlawed sexuality. His clothes lay neglected on the floor, his breath had condensed on the window in icy blossoms that seemed to be the physical expression of the forbidden maleness. This abandoned and chaotic quality belonged to men; far from the organised tidiness and reassurance I came to associate with women. It meant neglect, uncultivated growth; a wild mysterious wood that I longed to explore.

My mother worked, an endless penitential labour which suggested that somewhere she still imagined it had all been her fault, a conviction that whatever she articulated about having right and justice on her side, at a deeper level she still felt culpable, a terrible need to expiate and atone for her gender. My earliest memories are of her engaged in a relentless activity of washing, cooking, scrubbing, chopping meat, serving in the shop, yet still never taking her eyes off me and my brother; an endless, exhausting work which, she made us understand, was all for us. But it wasn't a gift. One day, we would have to pay her back; not in monetary form, not even in reciprocating the care that she had given us, but in ways that were not disclosed, so that we would never know whether we had suceeded or not in the work of redemption, whether or not we had, in the end, justified her existence.

TWINS CONFRONTED her with the strangest of dilemmas. Her need for exclusivity and singularity in her relationships underwent a severe test. But she proved equal to it. She constructed our personalities for us, in such ways that all our feelings for each other could be mediated only through her. She made us into strangers to each other. Like a fairy at a christening, she bestowed characteristics upon each of us that would render us mutually incomprehensible.

Of course this attribution of features was not entirely fabricated; it corresponded roughly to some crude division of qualities grounded in reality. My brother was beautiful, well-behaved and tractable. I was clamorous, ugly and clever. He turned out to be practical and capable, while I was imaginative, but clumsy and awkward. Our mother reinforced those features we did not share, and we grew up to deplore each other's all too evident failings. The separation between us was reinforced when she gave each of us to understand that he was the preferred one. In this way, we were rivals for her affection, but rivals who both believed they had won, and who did little to compete, because they could rest in the calm certainty that they were both the favourite. Each of us basked in our superior status, and developed towards one another a profound indifference and lack of curiosity.

She must have dreaded above everything that we might combine against her; but she had done her work well. Twins seemed a curiously appropriate occurrence, since all the men in her life went in pairs. Perhaps her desire to keep us apart reflected her need to keep our two fathers rigorously away from other. Sid and Joe were as remote from each other as my brother and I were to become. Their paths never crossed. She separated them by a variant of the same stratagem that sundered me from my brother. To Joe she represented Sid as a man wild and unpredictable. If Joe ever expressed a desire to see his children, some elaborate casual encounter had to be contrived in a public place – the park or the centre of town – because if he were to visit the house, Glad would not answer for the jealous rage into which Sid might fall. For Sid, Joe was a shadowy figure, never named, so that Sid never discovered the identity of the man who had fathered the children over whom he assumed a hesitant and half dutiful paternity. Sometimes Sid would contemplate us as we sat in our double-hooded pram, seeking traces of a likeness to someone he could identify, so that he would at least know whom she had chosen as the father he might have been. Occasionally, he thought he could find a resemblance to someone he knew: a customer in the shop, the husband of one of her sisters, even her own brother. But she never gave anything away. If Sid ever encountered Joe, it would be in circumstances where no connection would be made. And indeed, he never did know.

Glad herself had, in a way, also had two fathers, albeit in the same individual. While she was a child, and her father remained strong and vigorous, he was a tyrant, heedless and cruel to his wife and children alike. 'He used to knock a kid a year out of her,' they said of him; and the image was strangely apt, as though she were a tree to be shaken for its fruit. It suggested a violence that characterised all his relationships with those weaker than himself. Only in the presence of foremen, bosses or masters did he cringe and make himself small; and resentment as his own powerlessness vented itself on those who depended upon him. But later, he changed. At some point in his fifties, he had a kind of conversion, and became, almost overnight, mild-mannered and loving. His anger seemed to have burned itself out, and he no longer made his strange inturned radical protest at the way things were by beating those weaker than himself, but became quiet and thoughtful.

Her oldest sister's husband, Alec, was the only man towards whom I ever saw my mother express any tenderness. Some twenty years older than my mother, he rode a sit-up-and-beg bicycle. A gentle and much-abused individual, he was a countryman who had started his working life as a policeman. When Glad's oldest sister became pregnant, he was dismissed from the force, it being considered at that time a disgrace not to be tolerated in those whose elevated function it was to enforce the law. After that, he worked in a tannery. His body exhaled the feral odours of the material with which he worked; so that, wherever he went, he left behind him a faint aroma of animal hides. His wife was a spendthrift, an extravagant and selfish woman, a creaking gate from her early thirties, standing perilously close to the grave which nevertheless did not claim her until she was 97. She adored the races, theatrical melodrama, seaside outings and whisky. As such, she was an anomaly in the dour working-class culture of the early twentieth century; she prefigured the consumer society which came later, and of which she was certainly an uncelebrated pioneer. She always maintained that we were 'put here' to enjoy ourselves, which was a terrible heresy to her more serious siblings who thought it was our life's purpose to want and to suffer, which they set about doing with some skill, even though they often denied any divine purpose behind it.

Alec was a sensitive and melancholy man, and as such, found great sympathy with Glad. Once, when I was about fourteen, I came into our kitchen, where I found him looking at her intently and saying, 'Ah Glad, you're the one I should have had.' She did not contradict him, but allowed his hand to rest on hers, while the bunch of dahlias from his allotment shed their petals and disgorged a flow of ants and earwigs onto the table-cloth.

He visited Glad frequently; and always brought her something from the allotment, some crinkly ultramarine savoys decorated with the silvery trails of slugs, some sticks of green and pink rhubarb, a handful of white-heart cherries. I later learned that he had also had a relationship with one of his wife's other sisters, of a far less innocent kind than he had with my mother; had she been aware of it, this would certainly have caused her to revise her opinion of Alec. She always insisted he was a good man, though most of her sisters said he would have been a better one if he had fetched his wife one the side of her face, and put her in her place.

Glad's older brother, Harry, fell into the more general category of men. He never married, but remained at home with his mother until she died. For a long time, he courted a woman called Flo who worked in the same factory and had a tragic history. Her husband and two children had both died within a week during the influenza epidemic of 1919. It was understood that she and Harry were saving up to get married. Trustingly, Flo passed over most of her earnings to Harry each week, so that these could earn interest in a post-office savings account. A sad, placid woman, patient and unhurried, she anticipated the major change of state in her life without urgency. After seven or eight years, however, she thought it was time to assess their financial position. She asked to be shown the savings book. He resisted. At last, he finally admitted there was no such account. Not only had he failed to add a sum each week equal to that which she gave him, but he had also unfailingly withdrawn her contribution for the sake of his addiction to the horses. She was broken-hearted, and the experience was said to have sent her slightly mad.

Harry stayed in the little terraced house with his mother long after all the others had departed. She did everything for him until she died, cooking, washing, waiting on him, just as she had waited on her husband. When she did die, Harry was utterly without resource. He could do nothing by himself. Only when men were stranded by death did they realise the full extent of their dependency, the emptiness of their bluster and dominance. Harry wandered round the silent house, bursting into tears over reminders of his mother, and caressing her old astrakhan hat, her apron, the shoes that had been cut to accommodate her bunion, the birthday cards she had kept in a shoebox. By that time, we had gone to live with Aunt Em after her husband died. She took pity on Harry, and offered to prepare him a midday meal two or three times a week. On the days when he came, she would spread a sheet of newspaper on the table, because he had never learned to eat properly; he ate his food with noisy relish, scattering splashes of gravy and traces of his meal around him. My mother thought he had not been sufficiently punished, and she expressed her disgust at his table habits until Aunt Em was obliged to tell him to stop coming.

So it was that our mother had eight men in pairs around her. The arrival of twins only confirmed this dualism; and we all walked through her life in crocodile formation, in twos, like schoolchildren on an outing.

She had succeeded in tethering Sid to her by a dependency that developed from his illness; and Joe was attached to her by his childlessness and his need – quite deep as he discovered – for paternity. She gave him enough information about us to excite his curiosity, to involve him in our fate, but not enough to allow the growth of any independent relationship. Sometimes, he would park his car along the road, where she took us for walks. Occasionally, he would stop, wind down the window of the car, using the contrived chance encounter as an excuse to look at his children. But she always determined the length of these interviews. She would walk on, leaving him to drive the car slowly beside us, so that he might gain a last glimpse.

But there were consolations, however negative and sterile, in her position. She felt strong. She worked relentlessly, with furious energy, emptying Sid's bucket and cutting up the carcasses of animals as if these had been the bodies of men. Only with May did she sometimes let go, and pour forth her bitterness and disappointment, her anger at the absence of any proper outlet for her energy and intelligence. But she was admired in the neighbourhood. She later became a school governor. Her discretion earned her a reputation for wisdom. Even people from the big detached houses on the main road confided in her, people more avowedly middle class. In fact, she gained a kind of honorary middle-class membership. Nobody ever knew what were her real views or opinions, which remained a mixture of outrageous radicalism and a sad yearning to belong. This latter expressed itself in a desire for conformity in her children; neither of whom was able to gratify her in that respect.

On the night of the blitz over Coventry, we and the neighbours were all on the roof, watching the pyrotechnics thirty miles away. 'See,' Sid was saying, 'it'll be our turn next. Lord Haw-Haw said so on the wireless.' People looked at him and said, 'Anybody'd think you were on their side.' 'Well,' he said, 'he's done wonders for his country, I don't care what you say.' 'Shut up Sid,' his wife said. 'You don't know what you're saying. In any case,' she added, 'if you were in Germany, you'd be one of the first to go.' After that, he said nothing more, any Nazi sympathies sinking into abeyance under his wife's scorn. In the end, she gained from him what she had sought; something too few women received from their men until they were dead: respect.

Four

AUNT EM and my mother lived together for 38 years, far longer than either spent with her husband. The relationship between them was one of intense rivalry, although our aunt was not at all competitive; the terms were laid down by Glad. Aunt Em had a secret denied to her sister. For she had been loved and our not mother had not, or felt she had not. This made her jealous, and out of their temperamental differences she erected a theory of her own moral superiority. Mother had children; Aunt Em was childless. Mother worried and fretted about the world, while her sister was placid and conciliatory. My mother was sharp and quick-witted, Em was slower. Glad foresaw every misfortune that was going to happen, and a great many that never would. Aunt Em always expected the best of people, and although she rarely got it, this did not disturb her serene acceptance of the way of the world. In this calmness was folded the memory of the man who had loved her, inviolable and sure of itself; and this goaded our mother. It remained always beyond reach, beyond contamination.

As soon as we went to live with her, my mother began to complain to me about her sister, as though she feared that some of my emotions might escape the tight vessel in which she had sealed my love for her, and might leak out towards our sweet smiling aunt. For many years, I allowed my own feeings towards her to be colonised by Glad's jealousy. I looked down upon her, thought her petty and snobbish. Only much later I realised I had perceived her, not so much through my mother's eyes, as through the severe filter of one feeling which was certainly not the sum of my mother's complex and companionable relationship with her. In fact, they loved each other dearly, although their temperaments jarred and clashed. If my aunt were late coming home, my mother kept glancing at the clock; went to the front door, came back, saying, 'There's no sign of her'; and the relief of her return was always celebrated each day by a cup of tea, a game of nap, even a glass of sherry.

Later, I made amends to my aunt, and indeed, came to love her more than I loved my mother. In truth, my relationship with my mother had little to do with love: it was inevitable, necessary, an inescapable bonding by sensibility, a kinship of character; desolating, emancipating, crippling and enhancing. It took its course like any other natural phenomenon.

When I was eleven. I had what was referred to at the time as a 'nervous breakdown'. I had passed the 11-plus when I was only nine; and going to the Grammar School was a trauma, in the sense that it showed me for the first time the immense gulf that existed between the sequestered relationship with my mother and the world beyond. But it was Aunt Em who took me into her bed, soothed the long fearful insomnias, told me stories, and stayed awake, sometimes all night, to keep me company, waiting till I slept in the protective chamber of her arms. She offered me the greatest comfort and healing; she reconciled me to the world, her world, which was a place of tenderness and peace, so different from the austere landscapes her sister inhabited. In spite of this, for many years I saw only the shallow and inconsiderate woman of my mother's imagination. For her part my mother preferred her role as martyr; and when people are as determined as she was to be hard done by, nothing can keep them from perpetual self-immolation.

The dramatic and painful circumstances of our conception and birth meant that nothing else that happened to our mother subsequently could ever equal this momentous experience. As a result, the rest of her life was a coda to the most significant incident in it. Something had been used up; an exhaustion set in, so that we never saw her as the robust and vigorous woman she had been, but always in the long decline towards the intense clenched stillness that claimed her in the end.

EVEN IN the nursing home, the rivalry that my mother had one-sidedly entered into with her sister continued. She had had such experience of crafting ambiguities, dualisms and conflicts, that she could not be expected to renounce them simply because she was old; quite the reverse in fact. Old age pared away everything else, so that she was reduced to the emulous, competitive being at her core, the little girl who had had to fight for love and attention in the crowd that was her family.

Eventually, Aunt Em even began to play the game herself. The rivalry at the end, naturally enough, focused upon infirmity and sickness. No one had ever been so ill as my mother; nobody could hope to understand the suffering she had known. Even when Aunt Em had a severe blockage of the bowel – which distended her stomach in a mocking phantom pregnancy with the childen she never had – and was in constant pain, my mother only complained that her sister's restlessness disturbed her sleep, and she asked to be moved to a separate room. But there remained a difference in their final competitive struggle: it became clear that my aunt was willing herself to live for my mother's sake, while my mother was always eager to meet her death, in order to punish her sister; to punish her for being different, for not loving her enough, even though she had devoted the last third of her life to looking after her, just as she had given the previous quarter of a century to her husband.

The nurses offered to take my mother to see her sister in hospital, but by this time, fear even of leaving her room had seized her. They explained to her gently that she might never see Em again; her response was,

'I'm too ill.'

At that time, they were closing the wards of the geriatric hospital. New private nursing-homes were expected to take terminal cases, which were no longer to be accommodated within the health service. Aunt Em lived on, wearily, her smile fainter, but still uncomplaining. It was decided that she should be returned to the nursing-home. 'You'll be better off there,' the nurses told her, although to me they said, 'It's a bloody shame. This is where she ought to stay.'

It was a bitterly cold day in late November. A north-easterly gale shook the silver buds of rain from the black branches of the lime trees. Em was taken by ambulance the three-mile journey across the town. When my mother knew Em was coming back, she would not have her in the room with her, because her presence would keep her awake. Was she much altered, she asked fearfully. Is she thin and wasted? I don't want to see her like that. Aunt Em was given a room to herself. She died during the night.

My aunt was buried on a cold day in early December, as the sun was melting the frost into crystal beads on the grass. Aunt Em had loved children, and she alone in the family had kept track of the ramifying genealogies as her brothers and sisters drifted away from one another, as their children began a family, and their children grew up in their turn. She remembered every birthday, and wrote to them all at Christmas. Although none of them lived far away, few remembered her and none came to the funeral, a bleak functional occasion.

My brother and his wife came. They had not visited for two years. They stood apart; my brother's face crumpled with grief. My mother did not attend, and she never knew that my brother had come to the funeral, for he could not bring himself to visit her. My mother hated the crematorium. The building itself had been given by the owner to his son as a twenty-first birthday present; prescience had told him that burning was the coming thing.

MY MOTHER'S lifelong sickness was only the outcrop of a deeper ill-being. She had always been ill at ease in life. She had suffered a level of estrangement from existence itself that cannot be ascribed simply to one society or another. She and I both knew this; but that does not mean that our apprehension of the forces of social alienation was false. On the contrary, it gave us some insight into where the socially alterable ceased and the irremediable began. From her I understood that we live in a society which promises escape from what is unalterable – selling its corrupt dreams of transcendence through money, insisting that people can have everything, be any-thing they want, avoid suffering and remain perpetually young; while at the same time refusing to do anything about those social wrongs – pov-erty, unemployment – that may be easily remedied; and this profound aberrancy is offered, not only to us, but to the rest of humanity, as the necessary, inescapable condition of our lives.

From her, too, I learned much about myself. She would place her hand over her face like a screen, to shield herself from the world. The fingers of her hand were bent back upon themselves with arthritis. She would close her eyes, and I could feel her withdrawal, her flight from the landscaped refinement of the home in which a desperate, turbulent old age had been planted.

When I sat with her in this withdrawn state, rising now and again only to adjust the cushion against her thinning grey hair, to give her a drink, to lift her for a few moments to provide her with relief from a posture which she could not control, I recognised in her the child I had been. Not in the sense that old age is a second childhood, but in the insistent and urgent demands she made upon me, as I had once made on her. The difference was that she had always answered mine, had responded every time. But there was nothing I could do, even within the time I spent with her. There was no comfort I could give her; I could not reassure her that everything was all right, that things would be better soon. She had not failed me, as I was failing her, in spite of the perfect symmetry of my dependency then and hers now.

Not that guilt doesn't have its place and its value, for without it, we would have no sense of duty or responsibility. Those who imagine they can dispel all guilt and live freely are advocating the freedom of psychopa-thy.

I could anticipate all her feelings, apprehend much of her experi-ence. My mother had always wanted company in her misery; and to this end she made great efforts. She really need not have bothered, at least as far as I was concerned: I was already locked into it through what I had inherited from her; yet even my involuntary companionship failed to con-sole her.

SHE SPOKE again about her childhood. There was, she asserted, a continu-ity between her life in the nursing-home, and life in the shabby brown-painted terraced houses of her childhood; only she couldn't quite see where the connection lay. Then, there were orangeboxes for furniture, sacks at the windows for curtains, bare floorboards, with only a length of scuffed lino. The decor of the nursing-home could not have been more different, with its tepid carpeted corridors and double glazing, its chintzy covers and winged chairs looking out onto the artificially wrought contours of the golf course. One day she said, 'I can see how it's the same. They made money out of us then, and they're making money out of us now. Only the setting has changed.' Here, frailty and helplessness were big business. 'From rags and poverty to a padded cell. No wonder they're happy when we lose our senses; they think we won't notice.'

In her experience was to be read a whole social history: the family that had grown, wild and plentiful as weeds in their youth, had fallen away, become sparse and scattered. In its place there grew an expensive solitude, and with it, a curious inability to care for those we love. Where does it come from, this mysterious mixture of liberation and impotence, of unskilled freedoms, of purposeless emancipations? My mother and aunt joined the sixty or seventy old people who had become the object of other people's labour. Most of these others were young women, some tender young girls who could not bear the contact with old age, querulousness and incontinence, and left within a few weeks. Others resented the inadequate pay, and they looked at old age across the gap of the years as though peering for the first time into another culture, as, indeed, many of them were. Some had never even spoken to an elderly person in their lives, and then found themselves placed in a sub-nurse uniform with a plastic identification tag, offered £3.18 an hour for the most delicate, precious and difficult work it is possible to imagine. There were others, middle-aged women, imaginative, compassionate people, who saw themselves and their own loved ones in the blanched faces and withered skin, and who exhausted themselves in looking after their needs. Yet others were temporary workers from an agency, who came and went by the day, knew nobody's name, didn't know where anything in the building was kept, who slept in the small hours in defiance of their contract, and didn't hear the cries for the commode or for a body to be turned, trapped in the rigours of sleep.

The nursing home was an investment by a company that had envisaged this beautifully tended site as a place for the well-to-do elderly. It was to be a refuge, where sweet old ladies out of Cranford or advertisements for retirement homes would take tea in bone-china cups, where they would knit and read their library books, until one day, they would quietly set aside their needlework, yield a sigh and die with dignity. But old age is rarely like that. Even those with seemingly limitless money became confused or incontinent, undermined by dementia. They cried out in pain and rage, and wept for lost family, relatives who failed to appear, friends who had died before them. The home had to take more and more people supported by the state. The idea of tranquil gentility was set aside.

GLAD WANTED to die, but she also wanted someone to rescue her. Bring me back from this deterioration I have colluded with, she pleaded silently. Hold me back from death or come with me, was the choice she offered me.

I had mourned her in advance. I had worked so hard at grief! Indeed, anticipating this had been my preoccupation for as long as I could remember. It was as though my consciousness of separation from her at birth only foreshadowed the more definitive severance that would come at the end. If I was able to monitor clearly the slightest shift in her condition, every movement in her decline, this was because I had already lived through it beforehand, had expended so much anxiety in foreseeing it.

And of course, I would not go with her, even though I had accompanied her into the impossible places where she lived, into the secret places of her tormented being. I sat with her for days at a time while Em was in hospital. And then, in the long hours of occupationless intimacy, all the other people she had been came back: the gaiety of the young mother who wore lipstick on Tuesdays, which was the day of her meeting with Joe; she left us with Aunt May, confidante and abetter of her plans. We never understood the reason for her lightheartedness, but it affected us too, and we skipped along beside her, while she promised she would bring us, luxury of luxuries, a Bakewell tart for tea. She returned in other guises also: the strong moral presence that brooded over our minor wrongdoings, the compassionate listener in the shop while women bared their wounds to her; the voracious reader of all the books I brought home from school.

Because I knew what she was feeling, I was well aware that the professionals who surrounded her had not the slightest insight into what she endured. I didn't expect them to understand. The doctor-priests who ministered to her relationship with her illness were inept and pallid functionaries, compared to the now redundant expertise I had in the matter.

I still don't know whether I loved her or not. I was certainly drawn into a vortex of dependency and pain. Later, I realised that all through our childhood, it was, above all, my brother's companionship that she wanted. She had no need to waste effort on attaching me to her. His was a foreign sensibility, and she did her utmost to involve him in her distressful experience. She failed; and succeeded only in tying me more closely to her than I already was. My brother was self-possessed, unreachable; he felt her attentions as a violence upon him, an assault upon who he was; and that was why in the end he left her, to noisy remorse and bewilderment. She never knew how she had hurt him, and it seems he never came through the pain in time to reach a reconciliation with her.

PEOPLE TALKED to her in the nursing home. Not only was she in full possession of her faculties, which was rare enough, but something in her still attracted others, her sympathetic ability to draw from them the secret pain they had locked away, the unhappiness they had denied. The whispered confidences that had taken place over the shop counter were heard once more. My mother actually performed the role of counsellor, although it had not yet been systematised in that way. Her own unhappiness, which she could not mitigate, nevertheless gave her an insight that was often useful to others. She had only to listen for them to exclaim in wonder how well she understood them. She was performing the unpaid and unrecognised labour of women into her eighty-seventh year.

She observed that secrets change over time. What had once been matters of shame and concealment later became subjects for the casual gossip of others. It is one thing to protect knowledge that might be hurtful to other people if it were divulged; and quite another to spill out incontinently things which a dignified silence might more fittingly protect. She asked me not to write about her when she was dead; this tribute to her is also a betrayal – part of the inextricable tangle of love, dependency, loss and resentment that binds us to others.

My mother's generation enfolded their secrets. Their lives were often poisoned by what they could not share. Heavy with an unspeakable knowledge, they suffered with an intensity that had no chance to measure itself against the equally silent sorrows of others. In the folklore of our family, pieces of paper fluttered down from behind the clock when a house was cleared, revealing unexpected paternities; battered purses revealed whole lives contained within their worn folds, stories of infidelities and thwarted loves, jealousies and revenge. Those to whom these things were finally – often posthumously – made known were left with a residue of unresolved bitterness and resentment. So much unspoken!

What made it worse was that in such a short space of time the compelling necessity for guarding such secrets decayed. Now, my mother said, it seems that people cannot wait to tell all. There is no longer anything to conceal: no disgrace, no dishonour is too terrible to be offered up for public consumption. Indeed, it sometimes seems, the world is thick with people recounting their lives to the empty air. They have become incontinent. The structuring of the need to keep secrets, and then the promiscuous spillage of them, are socially determined, and as such, serve purposes which the individuals they inhabit can scarcely be aware of; we become the sites of strange changes in custom and habit, of struggles that concern us only obliquely, but for which we must take full responsibility.

When my mother finally told my brother and me what had happened, we were neither shocked nor upset. We were then in our late thirties; and she related it to us with great ceremony and solemnity. Furthermore, true to her need to divide us, she informed us separately; the sameness of our response surprised her. On her seventieth birthday, my partner and I had gone to spend the weekend with her and my aunt; a resplendent weekend in June, when she had wanted us to visit, on the Saturday, the place where Sid had been born, and on Sunday, the place where Joe had lived. We walked slowly through the little town, where the memorial bench to Sid's father had been disfigured by graffiti, and through the hedgerows near Joe's village, where the porcelain dog-roses balanced their shallow cups on their briars and the acrid pollen of cream elderflowers made the nose itch.

She was, if anything, disappointed with our response, which was one of quiet approbation of what she had done. Did she want us to cry and protest and accuse? Perhaps she had expected that we would be overawed, just as she had been, oppressed by the weight of what she had borne for half a lifetime. My reaction was mild and contained; she had to repeat what she had said, thinking, perhaps, that it had been too terrible to be absorbed at a single telling. 'No,' I said to her, 'I can't think of anyone who would have done better.' I kissed her on the cheek and tasted the bitterness of her tears.

Once she had parted with her secret, she began to shake. It was as though the retention of it had been the only thing holding her together. It was this that had informed her sad resolve to endure. It was this that had impelled her to work sixteen, eighteen hours a day, chopping meat, doing the accounts, washing and scrubbing, cooking, anticipating and longing for a future that would only detach her sons from her, take them far from the troubled desertions of her last years. The secret had become both her motivation and her reason for living.

She herself knew that the shaking was a consequence of letting go.

She was told she had Parkinson's disease. She said contemptuously, 'What do they know about it?' It was as though she had been emptied of her substance; the effort of containing it as monstrous as a 35-year pregnancy, a sort of cancer of the emotions. It was, perhaps, not so much the gravity of the secret as the importance of its function in her life that was revealed by the telling of it.

During those years, she had seen so much stripped away: the family broken and dispersed, the great reservoir of humanity in which she had grown, depleted and gone. The twelve children of her generation, whose lives had been so profoundly intertwined, themselves produced only twelve between them, almost all strangers to each other. The neighbourhood had been demolished, the community become a mass of dissociated individuals. The reason for existence of the town itself – the leather and shoe industry – had been abolished. To have lived through this confusion, the destruction of a whole way of life, is an experience difficult to understand; and yet it has affected so many groups of people in the world in this century. A relativising of the core belief is one of the most wounding things that can happen to human beings; and all this accompanied my mother's sense of personal dereliction. No wonder she wanted company in the lonely wanderings of her spirit. Perhaps this was why she sought all her life to be still – the distances she had covered were immense, the migrations and upheavals of the spirit an intolerable imposition; even though she never went anywhere.

She had been brought up in poverty, yet her life was to be an experience of continuous loss. Even when it seemed there was nothing else that could be taken away from her, she was nevertheless exposed to further dispossessings. Without disputing that the ragged and hungry insufficiency with which she had grown up was itself an appalling visitation, the forms of insecurity, exposure and suffering that accompanied the material improvements she knew, meant that her sense of what was forfeit prevailed over the advantages she saw. Those who have sought to measure human satisfactions in terms of a precise monetary sum, one limited measure of wealth, miss the point. If an absolute deficiency of subsistence is the worst thing that can happen to human beings, this does not mean that happiness may therefore be read in continuously enhanced purchasing power. A deep truth is here being used to serve an even deeper lie. This was her experience, and the transmission of its truth, one of her many great gifts to me.

SID AND GLAD were indeed divorced, but not until long after he had recovered; although he returned to the compulsions of sex as soon as he could persuade the doctor to tell him he was no longer at risk of spreading infection. He revved up the lorry again, set up clouds of ochre dust, and the vehicle would rattle away down the road, leaving the hedgerows dancing in the wind behind it. We would not see him for days, even weeks at a time. Occasionally, Joe would come to the house. Whenever we went into the living room and he was there, I was aware of a strange tension, and he exhibited what I resented as an intrusive interest in my brother and me. He was present, moist-eyed, when my brother got his apprenticeship, when I went to university. He loked at us with what I now see was a proprietorial tenderness, although at the time, it felt like the irksome, almost indecent, meddling of strangers.

She divorced Sid on grounds of cruelty. The true story could not, of course, be told. When the news appeared in the local newspaper, some of the sisters came and shook their heads. Knots tied with the tongue can't be untied with the teeth, they said. 'Ah,' said Glad, 'if you can only knew.' This was a frequent saying of hers throughout our childhood. We saw in it her claim to distinction in her unequalled capacity for suffering and endurance; we could not know with what force she felt it. Some of her sisters who had tolerated what they considered marriages no less oppressive than hers, took a fierce pride in the fact that they had not had recourse to such extreme solutions. 'If I had to choose between marriage to him and a noose round my neck, I wouldn't hesitate,' said an older sister, referring to her own experience. The implication that death would be preferable to divorce struck Glad almost as an invitation to suicide; but she was long past any such idea.

They agreed that the worst marriage they had known was that of their own parents. They spoke of our Gran on Christmas Eve, while her husband lay dead drunk in the gutter, holding in his hand the rabbits they were to have eaten for Christmas dinner; a passer-by thoughtfully dragged him out of the way of the traffic, and for his pains, took the rabbits. No. Divorce was the option of the rich. A despised easy way out. And easy ways out were despised by those stoical, self-punishing, heroic, hopeless women of the working class. Divorce was not only a sign of weakness: it also had distinct overtones of social aspirations that could not be countenanced.

This was in the late 1940s. Some of her customers, indignant that our mother should have taken her marriage vows so lightly, came, ostentatiously self-righteous, to retrieve their ration-books, and went to claim their tenpence-worth of meat from tradespeople whose morals were more trustworthy. Others, not so sophisticated, refused to deal with her any longer, because now there was no longer a man in the shop, they remembered that menstruous women handling meat cause it to go bad. Some men, whose idea of a divorcee was created by the popular press and the cinema, came to proposition her over the chipped enamel trays of liver and faggots. One Tuesday, we were setting off for town and walking towards the bus stop, when a man in a car hooted. 'Come on,' she said to me and my brother, 'we've got a lift.' We ran to where the car had halted at the junction. He wound down the window and said, 'Oh no, I was just saying hello. My wife wouldn't like it if I let you in the car.' I could feel her humiliation, and I wanted to kill the man, as he wound up his window and drove off.

Sid married again, at least twice. I met his first wife at the golden wedding party of his parents (our false grandparents, who never learned that we were unrelated to them). I was then about eighteen, and had entertained melodramtic fantasies over how I should behave in the presence of this woman who, I indignantly imagined, had stolen our father and ruined our family. Should I treat her with scorn, with cold disdain, or with sorrowing magnanimity? In the event, she was a homely woman, with a forced brightness that seemed to conceal a premature disillusion with the match she had made, and the blistering remarks I had rehearsed went unsaid. When mother asked what she was like, I said, 'It won't last five minutes.' As indeed it didn't.

His final marriage must have taken place when he was about sixty. He married a woman with several children, who lived in a council house. Later, when he had cancer, he spent nights in his van parked outside the house, because he could not bear to feel shut in, and his coughing disturbed the family.

I saw him once more. He was working for the council, cleaning roads. Thin and old, his crinkled hair grey, a cigarette burned close to his lips, while he creased his eyes against the sun and the smoke. He was pushing a handcart into which he tipped the sweet-wrappers and dogshit which he shovelled up with a broom and metal pan. He said to me, 'You doing all right at school?' I was twenty-seven.

When I learned he was dead, it didn't occur to me to go to the funeral. I tried to feel sad, but all I could do was take refuge in a generalised sentiment of sorrow at human mortality. I could find no point of contact with him, neither with the man who had shared our house, nor with the father I still believed him to be. Nothing. An absence of feeling. It made me think I was cold and hard; but my mother had so effectively absorbed all my feelings, and enclosed them so tightly within her, there was nothing left to spare for him, or indeed, at that time, for anyone else.

Some years after he died, I spent a summer with my partner in the country, at a village near Olney. In the pub one evening, the young woman serving behind the bar said, 'Are you Jeremy Seabrook?' 'Yes.' She said, 'I'm your sister.' I wanted to say, 'No you're not'; but I smiled and said, 'I always wanted a sister.' I never saw her again.

MY MOTHER was an angry woman, and with good cause. To a limited extent she was able to direct her anger at the disabling social influences that had determined her life; but much of it went underground, in that long guerrilla offensive which women traditionally waged against men by taking a powerful emotional control over the children, especially sons. To my brother and me she whispered without saying it, Grow up to be anything you like, but not men.

My mother's sensibility had also been influenced by the shoemaking culture of the town where she was born, and it is impossible to understand her fully outside that context; a distinctive regional character, rooted in the original semi-domestic occupation of the leather workers. It may have been the rural origins of their work, cattle, tanning and skins, that preserved something almost peasant-like in the people. They were stubborn and parsimonious, superstitious; parochial, sceptical, unwilling to express feelings, compelled to disagree with received wisdom, reluctant to believe anything they were told by their betters. They dissented, even from what were quite obvious truths, and they never went with the grain if they could go against it.

The shoe people were puritanical, unimpressed by money or station, sour, self-righteous, unforgiving, but incorruptible. And my mother was all these things. That she remained with her husband until he recovered was characteristic; but that she should continue to punish him until the end equally so.

The lives of her generation seemed to me, as I grew up, to be not lives at all, but only an austere sketch of living. I hated the frugality of their unadorned houses, wooden chairs, cold lino and rag rugs, enamel bowls in fire-clay sinks, coco matting, the women rattling their zinc pails and scrubbing immaculate floors with coarse brushes. Their lives seemed an endless penance, and their pleasures – drinking bitter beer and growing sour apples on their allotments, playing darts and dour philosophy – seemed no less grim and melancholy. Their view of the world was a compound of double negatives. There was nothing done without trouble in this world. They wouldn't be surprised to see things get worse before they got better. They didn't believe in being beholden to anybody.

Perhaps it was because they expected so little that they put up with what ought not to have been tolerated. It was doubly unfortunate that my mother was condemned to live out her bleak beliefs in altered circumstances, so that, no longer upheld by the values of community, she was alone with her unhappiness. Her stoicism was no longer that of a collective culture, but of an isolated individual. No wonder that keeping the pain to herself took such a heavy toll of her emotions and spirit; and it was bound to distort the relationship with her sons.

Even so, I well know that, even if our past had been all simplicity and straightforwardness, I would still have inherited the same fretful and restless disposition; just as I would have inherited the scepticism, an instinct to reject the unexamined wisdom and the ignoble orthodoxies of the society that sheltered me.

SHE HAD summoned me to her deathbed so many times over the twenty years before she died that it seemed inconceivable that I would be absent when death came. I was in Uttarkhand in northern India when she died. As she got older, it was as though I had concluded the grieving for her which had begun before I could even articulate it. I became more free of her power over me, and I went away as I had never been able to do when I was young. Partly, also, I too felt the tug of a desire to stay at home, the security of being safe, the attractions of immobilism, and in order to avoid these I had to do violence to my instincts, and wrench myself away from the familiar, oppressive comforts of home.

But the feeling that I had deserted her was strengthened by what I heard from the women of the Himalayan foothills. For they said it is always the men who leave. The men go from the marginal farm, the forest, the hillside village, into the city. What is usually seen as male enterprise and intrepidity looks differently to women. Men are more easily defeated, that is why they depart. It is the women who stand and fight the daily war that is waged against the poor at the level of the resource-base, in the homeplace.

In a quite different context, my mother had been like the women of

Uttarakhand. She had remained. She had endured, and to some extent, overcome the devastation of her life, its ruined landscape, and had salvaged from the degraded emotional environment some dignity, even a quiet heroism,

A strange thing. I returned to Delhi that night. Towards eleven o'clock, as I sat in the dusty hotel room, the door opened, and an old, old woman walked across the floor. Without speaking, she went to the window, and then turned round and walked back, without a word. She had, I assumed, mistaken my room for hers. Yet there was no old woman staying in that corridor. This was about eight or ten hours after my mother's death. I've never had any experience of the paranormal; but she had always said to me, as she had of Aunt May, 'If anybody ever comes back, it'll be me and your Aunt May.'

One of the reasons I had distanced myself from my mother as she approached death was that I feared she would want to take me with her; that she would want my company, as she had sought it in life. I thought she would die in the way she had lived, turbulently, angrily, protesting.

But it wasn't so. She had a chest infection that failed to respond to antibiotics. The day before she died, she said to the workers in the nursing home, 'Have you sent for my son?' They said yes, but had not thought it necessary. The following afternoon, they were giving her a cup of tea. She sighed and closed her eyes; then opened them again, raised her head to take her last breath. An easy death, everybody said. A lovely way to go. Silent pneumonia. The friend of the old.

When I got home, I needed to see her. Her body was in the undertaker's chapel of rest. The undertaker made me wait a few minutes, and then he said, 'Mother's ready for you now', as though she were his mother too, and she had made an appointment which she would keep on her own terms. They had dressed her in a white gown, with silver embroidery and lacy cuffs; raiment really, going-to-heaven-wear, the robes of her childhood Sunday-school hymns. I was not overwhelmed by her death, as I feared I would be. I thought of the women of the foothills of the Himalayas, who had stayed to fight the destruction of their environment; and I could understand the kinship with them of her, my mother, who had remained to fight the inner desolation of her life. I am profoundly grateful to her for the insight she gave me into the endurance of women, across societies and cultures; women who remain and remember, while men run away and forget.

* * *

Send for our free catalogue to GMP Publishers Ltd,
P O Box 247, Swaffham, Norfolk PE37 8PA, England

Gay Men's Press books can be ordered from any bookshop in the
UK, North America and Australia, and from
specialised bookshops elsewhere.

Our distributors whose addresses are given in the front pages of
this book can also supply individual customers by mail order. Send
retail price as given plus 10% for postage and packing.

*For payment by Mastercard/American Express/Visa, please give
number, expiry date and signature.*

_____

_____

Name and address in block letters please:

Name
_____

Address
_____

_____

_____